The Speculative Teachers' Lounge

Also from Metaphorosis

<u>Metaphorosis Magazine</u>
Metaphorosis: Best of 20xx
Metaphorosis 20xx: The Complete Stories
annual issues, from 2016
Monthly / Quarterly issues
Library Collection series

<u>Plant Based Press</u>
Best Vegan Science Fiction & Fantasy
annual issues, 2016-2020

from B. Morris Allen:
Chambers of the Heart: speculative stories
Susurrus
Allenthology: Volume I
Tocsin: and other stories
Start with Stones: collected stories
Metaphorosis: a collection of stories

<u>Verdage</u>
Reading 5X5 x3: Changes
Reading 5X5 x2: Duets
Score — an SFF symphony
Reading 5X5: Readers' Edition
Reading 5X5: Writers' Edition

<u>Vestige</u>
The Nocturnals, by Mariah Montoya

<u>Joyful Heave</u>
Museum Piece: an unusual collection

The Speculative Teachers' Lounge

*speculative stories
by educators*

METAPHOROSIS LIBRARY COLLECTION

edited by
B. Morris Allen

ISSN: 2573-136X (online)
ISBN: 978-1-64076-298-5 (e-book)
ISBN: 978-1-64076-299-2 (paperback)
ISBN: 978-1-64076-300-5 (hardcover)

from
Metaphorosis Publishing

Neskowin

Contents

From the Editor

The *Metaphorosis Library Collection* arose from a conversation with a Metaphorosis author who is also a librarian, and is initially intended to suit library needs. When a reader comes in and says, "Hey, do you have any SFF stories by this type of author?" here they are! But of course, the books are available to any reader.

Educators, by their nature, are constantly engaged in creative endeavours — how to bring excitement and anticipation to subjects that may seem dry or dull, but aren't if seen from the right perspective. Much (but not all) of that effort is focused on children or young adults — people whose view of the world is fresh and who look at things from new and unexpected angles. The work of teachers, in other words, keeps them on their toes in explaining the world around us.

This volume focuses on stories by **educators**. It's one of the largest volumes in the series, and while perhaps unsurprising, it's a great sign — we *want* the people teaching us to be thinking deeply, to have their minds open to new ideas, concepts, and approaches. Here's a fascinating selection of what comes into those minds when they take a break from teaching.

B. Morris Allen
1 July 2024

The Wife of Fabian Vitalik

Mariah Montoya

The day that Fabian Vitalik's wife left, rain masked the roar of the sea just beyond their rock garden. Fabian ended fishing early because of the storm, and came home to find his wife dozing on the sofa by the window, unfazed by the sharp *pat pat pat* of rain fingers on glass.

He found her enthralling when she was still and senseless like this, so he sat down and watched her breathe, the pearl necklace that rested on her chest rising and falling like waves. Their handmade string of seashells hanging from the ceiling tinkled above her head.

"I love you," Fabian whispered to her sleeping figure, rubbing fish grease on his pants. He thought his wife was most beautiful when she was human.

Of course, she was famous for her shape-shifting. When he'd first seen her high up on the stage, twirling and morphing into other things, the audience had gone wild for the black sleekness of her cat's fur, the shine of her teapot porcelain surface, the perfume that wafted from her petals when she mutated into a lilac bush. Oh yes, he remembered the hoots and howls of men when she danced her way across the stage as only a dress, the movement of shimmering fabric emphasizing the curves of the woman that would be underneath.

He had stared up at her in that crowd, marking the flashes of skin when she would have to, for a moment, be herself again before transforming into something she was not.

Now her overalls were fraying, her hair graying at the roots, the creases of fake smiles ebbing over her face. But so beautiful. Perhaps that was why she had married him, a simple fisherman living in Camber who'd tracked her down when the rain started pouring and the audience dispersed with newspapers over their heads. Nobody had glanced her way after she converted back into a woman, rain-soaked and delicate and normal. Nobody but him. And thirty years later, Fabian could not stop staring.

It was only when the rain stopped that she tensed and shifted her body on the sofa, as if the lack of pattering on the window was an alarm. The seashells clinked to a still. Her eyelids fluttered open.

"How did you sleep, love?" Fabian asked from his armchair, drinking in her presence.

She blinked at him, flexed her fingers as if amazed that she had fingers at all. Far off, they could finally hear the ocean again, roaring and crashing onto the beach. She looked back up at him. "What have you been doing this whole time?"

"Reading," Fabian said, although his book lay unopened on the other end of the coffee table.

"How'd fishing go? I assume the rain ruined things."

"Caught some, but not much. Had to come back early."

"Hmm." His wife glanced out the windowpane, where the rainstorm had leaked into a gray drizzle. The stones in their garden glistened with the residue of the storm. "You know," she said, "I have always wanted to shift into wind. Or fire. An element of some sort, but I don't know how. Which muscle do I reach for? Which thought do I think? Which color do I let fill me up?"

Fabian did not answer, only stared at the curve of her mouth, thinking about love and fishing and the sea. How many times had he woken from a night of lovemaking to find something else on his wife's pillow — a dusty book, a glass doll, a starfish? When she was transforming, she was so much like the sea, wild and unpredictable. But when she was human, she moved like a butterfly, gently, gracefully...

" — simply rise and plummet where I please."

Fabian nodded, not knowing what she had just said. He remembered his wife giving birth to their three children, who were all grown and traveling now — Josiah had come out covered in fur, his shape-shifting abilities stuck between some kind of animal and the baby he was. The doctors had panicked until the little guy had given a sharp, sputtering cry and shifted back into baby skin.

None of their other children could shape-shift, and Josiah never did again. The curse, the blessing, of having an ordinary father.

" — hear me, Fabian? Does it not faze you, what I just said?"

"What?" Fabian jolted out of his visions, refocusing on the woman before him.

"I don't want to stay here anymore. With you, with this dratted, God-forsaken house." His wife stared at him with the haltingness of a sand crab caught by a seagull eye. "I want to simply rise and plummet where I please. You, Fabian, do not appreciate my needs to escape confinement, and —"

The crash of the ocean. Fabian's ears roared with the sound. He did not know whether his wife meant confinement in his house, or in her body, or both. She was touching the pearls on her neck, the pearls he had plucked from shored oysters himself.

" — and my love has crumpled inside me, Fabian. I feel like a rock when I am with you. You never admire me when I'm a cricket singing you songs at night, or when I'm a vase of flowers in our kitchen, or when I'm a wardrobe holding our clothes." Angry blotches were rising on her cheekbones now. "I feel like a rock," she said again. "I have since I met you. I want to feel like — I don't know, *something* lighter, something more free and beautiful and untamed than I am now."

Fabian stared at her. He wanted to say he didn't *need* a cricket to sing him songs, her human heartbeat was enough at night. He didn't *want* a vase of flowers to make their kitchen pretty, his wife cooking was enough. He didn't need another wardrobe to hold his clothes. He wanted to hold *her.* That was all he'd ever wanted. Why couldn't she appreciate it, the boundless depth of his love?

But the words curled inside him, drowned by hers. *I want to feel like* — *something lighter, something more free and beautiful and untamed than I am now*. Flashes of soft butterfly wings fluttered behind his eyelids.

"Do you understand, Fabian?"

He blinked. Those seashells above her head turned on their strings, but did not touch each other, and so were silent. "I understand," he said. "I want you to feel like a b- to feel beautiful too, darling."

She did not reply, only rose from her seat and wafted toward the kitchen, wispy like wind. He could hear her clanging in their cupboards and fridge, bringing out wrapped tuna and a knife. He could hear the metal of the knife slicing through scales and skin, the smell of innards floating into the living room. Fabian only stared down at his fishing calluses.

I feel like a rock. Did she really think all his fishing and hard work and love only amounted to rocks? Was she really so cold to his efforts?

Long after the knives quit chopping, he heard the sudden disappearance of his wife and the padded prowling of some creature that took her place. But for all his curiosity, he did not look back to see what his wife, in her disguised grief, had transformed into this time. He only knew that no butterfly was about to flutter over to him and rest gently, silently on his shoulder.

●

Fabian lugged his empty fishing bag through Camber, past the barber shop and post office and butcher's, all vacant in the grayish night. His footsteps splashed in cobblestone mud. He didn't know why he was making his usual daytime trek through town in the dead of night, especially when he'd spent the last few weeks simply staring at the sea, not brave enough to face fishing with his wife disappeared. But he'd heard the fishermen talk of her performing again and wanted to know, wanted to *see* her one more time....

Up ahead, lights and shouts from Patty's Tavern grew with every step. Music, clapping, hollering, a man stumbling onto cobble with his boots on his hands. Fabian slunk to the open front door and peered inside, where an audience was roaring and hooting, circled around a spectacle in the center of the bar.

She danced and twirled and morphed. She was a spinning wheel, polished, rotating, churning out strands that a few men reached forward to touch... Fabian felt a sharp prick of jealousy... and then the thread was gone. The men staggered forward, fell on their knees to the roar of audience laughter, and there was a split moment when Fabian saw his wife again, her glowing face and upturned smile and brief mien of concentration, the pearl necklace he'd made for her still dangling around her neck.

Then she was a violin playing itself, a bluebird that screeched and spiraled into a waterfall of buttons, which exploded and clattered to the rotted floorboards. A single button rolled to the doorway. Fabian bent to pick it up, but just as he touched the button's smooth, rounded edge, it disappeared between his fingers, and in the center of the bar there was suddenly a fishing boat, rocking as if on a boiling sea.

She knew he was there. Knew his touch.

The empty fishing sack slipped through Fabian's fingers. He left it there, left it at the open doorway where his wife was performing, and staggered around like a drunk, away from the tavern, back toward his home. The world spun around him. Shapes bloomed in the darkness — buttons, birds, spinning wheels, flowers, teapots. Even the eyes of some nighttime cat seemed to glow green in the darkness between two run-down houses. Fabian yelled at them. The eyes blinked and vanished, but other shapes continued to blossom in the darkness, haunting Fabian until he made it to his doorway. He reeled inside and ran to his bed, where, for a moment, he thought he saw his wife's sleeping figure breathing on the bedsheets.

But no, she was long gone, entertaining other men, transmuting into other things.

Fabian stumbled to their closet and rummaged through shoes, coats, dresses, anything that his wife might like to turn into, anything that he could pretend was her until morning. He knew she would never morph into anything simple; his fingers clasped something cold, and he pulled out an old candlestick she had used to hold candles during winter storms. With its twisted, ornate silver twining around the hilt, the candlestick was intricate enough that it would do. Fabian brought it to his bedside and gently placed it on his wife's pillow.

Then he crawled into bed. The coldness pressed in all around him, but he looked at the candlestick where his wife should be, and its shape comforted him.

"Goodnight, my love," he said to the candlestick. It did not reply, but he placed his fingers on its silver and soon found himself sinking into dreams, dreams where his wife was not betraying him in the tavern; instead, she drifted back home to lie by his side once more.

●

He awoke to her meow.

He mumbled, reached out across his pillow, found the cold hilt of the candlestick. Something wet touched his hand. He opened his eyes to see a cat staring at him on its haunches — his wife, *his wife was finally back.* Fabian's chest leapt with a burst of adrenaline. He wiped his eyes and sat up to look at the cat better.

But his wife was always a sleek, black cat when she morphed, not this dirty tabby nudging his hand, its ears crooked and nose scarred.

"What...?" Fabian asked. The cat jumped off his bed, knocking the candlestick to the floor.

Perhaps she had aged so much that her cat form had aged too. Fabian tried to think back to the last time his wife had become a cat and couldn't recall. Suddenly he wished very much that he had turned around to see what she had become in the kitchen the day she'd left.

The cat yowled, racing into the living room and out his front door, which Fabian must have left wide open last night. He staggered after it, every step making his stomach plummet as he realized that the cat was not his wife, and the candlestick was not his wife, and all the chairs and windows and outside trees were not his wife. When he saw the tabby waiting for him in his rock garden, he could have kicked it away.

But then he noticed what was resting at the tabby's feet in the rocks, like a mouse that the cat had dragged to his doorstep as a prize: his wife's pearl necklace.

"What did you do to her?" Fabian said slowly, bending to pick up the necklace. The cat meowed again. Fury tumbled inside him. "*Where is she?*" he said. "*Where the hell is my wife?*"

The cat turned and streaked down his yard toward Camber.

Fabian ran after it, past all his neighbors' houses and onto the main street of the town, through the daytime vendors who shoved flower seeds and shish kebabs and painted seashells in his face.

The cat weaved through the crowd, past the dry and emptied Patty's Tavern, shooting down a shabbier, muddier avenue, where hedges lined the yards of run-down hovels. Fabian followed it to the furthest hut, where the cat slipped inside the open doorway and meowed a greeting to whoever was stirring inside.

"Fabian Vitalik?" somebody called.

"Who...?"

A man from beyond the open doorway shifted, then emerged onto his front steps with a wan smile. Fabian recognized, with a jolt, the town herbalist, whom he'd only ever met once at a neighborhood funeral.

"Come in, Fabian Vitalik," the herbalist said with a beckoning hand. "Your wife — she is here."

Fabian did not hesitate as he ran into the depths of the house after the man. Soil caked the floor, moss was growing on the molding, and sunlight surged through a vast open window toward the back of the house. Sitting on an earthy rug below this window, surrounded by an array of plants in clay pots, was his wife. She was human.

She was also swaying, as if to music that Fabian couldn't hear.

"Darling," Fabian said, but the herbalist put a hand on his shoulder. The cat was twisting itself around his wife's rocking body, meowing.

"We found her in an alleyway last night, Fabian Vitalik, soaking wet and unable to speak. My little helper here —" He nodded at the cat. " — is adept at sniffing out illnesses, and brought me to her. I believe she has suffered some kind of stroke from excessive shifting."

Fabian clutched the pearl necklace tighter. The herbalist moved toward a rounded table, where he swept a hand across bowls of powder and jars of dark green liquid. "I have given her turmeric stewed at midnight, but she still won't speak. Ashwaganda ground in halibut. Thyme and flax seeds. Her condition has not changed. She has the mind of a three-year-old, and I fear —"

" — Darling," Fabian said again, crouching low, not wishing to hear the rest of the herbalist's prediction. His wife looked up at him. Docile eyes. A sweet expression that softened her wrinkles. She would not stop swaying.

"She needs someone to take care of her, Fabian Vitalik. I fear she will not get better." The herbalist crouched beside him and peered into her face. "She certainly cannot shift anymore, and if she attempted to it would be catastrophic. She needs fed, bathed, dressed, put to bed —"

"She's not my wife anymore," Fabian said for the first time. "She left me. Somebody else has to take care of her." He felt the coldness rush up his spine at these words, desire and anger clashing like crests against a boat. His wife smiled sweetly at him, and he felt bile in his throat. If he had just stayed at Patty's Tavern last night and stopped her from continuing to perform... of course she would have hated him for it, but she *already* hated him.

The herbalist was watching him steadily. His wife swayed like waves.

"There is no one else to take care of her, Fabian. No one else that cares for her when she is stuck in this form."

"She left me," Fabian said again, the pearl necklace in his hand slipping in sweat. He did not want this to be so valid an excuse that she couldn't stay with him, but he wanted an apology, a sad sheen of understanding in her eyes, some subtle sign that she was sorry, and that even if she had not gotten sick, she would be returning to him.

But vacancy stayed spewed across her face.

"She is the mother of your children," the herbalist said gently.

And at this, Fabian felt himself break down. Of course. Of course he would take her in. He would slave over her until she got better, because she *had* to get better. And then he would let her go, for surely, even if she couldn't shift, she would want to leave him again when she healed.

"Fabian," the herbalist said, as if in reply to his thoughts. The tabby meowed. "She *mustn't* try to shift. I doubt she would be able to, but if she *did* manage it... she would be stuck. Stuck in another form forever."

"There'd be no way of bringing her back?" Fabian asked, finally standing up. He tried to imagine his wife stuck in her cat form, or worse — some kind of inanimate object. A decoration, or a candlestick.

The herbalist bowed his head. "If she shifted, there would be no way of bringing her back, no."

A cloud must have passed over the sun, because in that moment, the room was cloaked in eerie, greenish shadows. Fabian bent, strung the pearl necklace around his wife's neck once more, and heaved her into his arms. She allowed this as if she were little more than a rag doll. Fabian started toward the door, then hesitated.

"Isn't there anything that can be *done*? She — she hates her human body." His wife seemed to feel the tremor that ran through him, because although she did not stop smiling, a flicker of unease ran across that strangely vacant face.

"As far as concoctions go, none that I know of. Just love her, Fabian Vitalik."

Fabian nodded, turned away from the herbalist and the cat, and stepped back into broad daylight. His wife's dead weight threatened to bring him to his knees, but he did not stop carrying her, not when he made it to Camber's main street again, not when pedestrians stopped their market trading to stare. He hauled his wife all the way to their house at the shore, sweat beading on his forehead. When he finally made it through their rock garden and set her down underneath their string of seashells, she began swaying again.

His wife was back.

Yet Fabian wanted her to be capable of talking. Of shifting. Of leaving him again. Because only if she was capable of leaving would her staying mean she loved him back.

Shouts, music, and the clanking of glasses washed over him in a buzzing void, but Fabian, sitting at the bar in Patty's Tavern, concentrated on one sound. A pepper-haired man was giggling as he and some comrades danced around an empty plastic pail by the smoke pit, chanting, "Shape-shifter, shape-shifter, alter faster! Quicker! Swifter!" They hooted, hollered, whistled like they had that first night Fabian had peeked into the bar, and eventually a guitarist began strumming his instrument in tune to the mantra. Soon, so many men turned on their stools that half the bar was singing to the plastic pail, slopping beer down their shirts, believing the pail to be Fabian's wife.

"You know what I think?"

A woman slid onto the stool next to him. Tall, long legs. Her jacket swelled where it buttoned up over her breasts, and oh, she smelled good, like lilacs and shellfish and wine. His wife used to smell like that, whenever Fabian would come home exhausted and lay his head down on her lap and listen to her hum songs.

"Well, if you're not going to answer," the woman said, fingering her shot glass, and now, at last, Fabian was zeroed in on something other than those wretched men fawning over a plastic pail. "The name's Zoey. And that bucket was being used to catch a leak in the roof long before those assholes came in. If you ask me, the shape-shifter's anywhere but here. After that one fiasco last month? I'd say she's out of the continent."

Fabian grunted, took a swill out of his mug as he pictured the shape-shifter lying on his bed half a mile away, taking her daytime nap, very much in the continent. A word surfaced to his brain.

"Fiasco?" he repeated.

"Yeah, I was there." The woman brought her glass to her lips and drained it in one gulp. She wiped her lips. "The girl — well, she's more an old lady now — she was performing, you know? And she was turning into all kinds of things, vines and animals and all that drat. She said to get ready for her grand finale, that she was going to turn into wind — and then she just... exploded. Into all these butterflies"

"Exploded into butterflies," Fabian said. In his mind, he heard, *I want to feel like a butterfly again,* although he wasn't sure if his wife had actually said it or if he had simply fabricated those words in his mind.

"Yes, and the butterflies began twirling like a tornado. Almost wind, but not quite. Only, the tornado was screaming. God, it hurt my ears. Then the whole thing just disappear — hey! Where are you going?"

Fabian had fished into his pocket, smacked some coins on the counter, and started toward the door, leaving the woman and her long legs behind. Once out on the street, he targeted the peddler's cart that sold flower seeds, and asked the vendor which flowers attracted butterflies.

For the past few weeks, he had been trying to get his wife to talk. Shifting would be, as the herbalist put it, catastrophic, but *talking?* Fabian had thought she'd find her voice again if he read to her, but maybe she needed a reminder of what was beautiful before she found herself again. Maybe she needed butterflies in their garden instead of rocks.

Once the vendor had sold him a packet of daylily seeds, Fabian hurried to the house, where his wife would be waking up from her nap. He left the seeds on the kitchen table and rushed into the bedroom, where his wife was sitting up in bed, swaying, smiling pleasantly.

"Hello, beautiful," Fabian said, opening the window blinds to let sunlight through. "Are you hungry? I've finally gone fishing again, and I found some mussels with nice, hearty meat in them. You love mussels, remember? And I have a surprise for you, too. It might take a while — they need to grow first, but you're going to love it."

His wife just smiled.

Fabian began his usual routine of setting his wife near the sofa where he slept at night, cooking, cleaning, talking to her as if he expected a reply. Occasionally, when he had the spare money, he would buy some paper and finger paints and place them on the floor in front of her. These were the only times she would finally quit swaying, dip her fingers into the paints, and create.

The pictures were crude, to say the least, as if a toddler had painted them. But Fabian had still been able to decipher wind, fire, earth. Today, as he popped open the mussels and set them over a small kitchen fire to sizzle, she was drawing a distorted ocean. Sun glaring down on miniature whitecaps, seashells as big as ships, curling, spiraling waves.

It happened after feeding her supper and taking the trash out. Fabian came back inside to find his wife's pictures abandoned on the floor. For one jolting moment, he thought she was gone.

Then he saw her swaying in the kitchen. She was sitting neatly in their tarnished tin tub that he bathed her in at nights. Her clothes were in a pile on the floor, so that only her pearl necklace gleamed on her bare chest.

"It's not bath time yet, darling," Fabian said, shaken. He started forward to pick up her clothes and dress her when a change flashed over her face. A frown. Then that soft, sweet smile again. But for a brief moment, he had seen the crunch of her eyebrows, that concentration she wore when she was trying to shift.

"How about we just have bath time now, then?" Fabian said slowly. But even as he walked toward the faucet, he saw that flash of concentration again, heard the small whimper escape her mouth. They stared at each other. His wife's smile was still etched on her face, but the corners of her mouth were quivering. And suddenly, Fabian knew that he needed to plant those seeds *now*.

"I'll be right back," he whispered, backing away. "*Right* back. Please don't go anywhere."

He grabbed the packet of seeds from the table and in a flash, leaving his wife in the tub, was on his knees in the rock garden. The sky overhead was churning and the sea's high tide was a sharp crash in his ears, but Fabian dug rock after rock out of the dirt and threw them to the side. He felt the sharp plop of water on the back of his neck, but he welcomed the rain that splashed onto the soil beneath his fingers.

"Butterflies," he murmured, ripping open the packet and pouring beetle-black seeds onto his palm. He dug into the dirt, feeling the prickle of time pepper his head, as if he could only save his wife by planting fast enough. He dropped the seeds into those little cavities in the earth, covered them back up, and stood, panting.

His front door was still ajar.

Fabian crept back into the doorway and peered inside, where the shadowed sky cloaked their living room and kitchen in dim shades. His wife's picture was flapping in a sudden wind that swooped past Fabian, into the house. Her clothes still lay discarded on the floor.

But the tarnished tub was empty.

"Hello? Where — where are you, darling?" Fabian called. The paper flapped, moving across the floor. The sea still sounded in his ears, but otherwise there was no sound.

Fabian moved further inside and called his wife's name. He went into the bedroom, but she was not there either. And now his heart was crashing in his chest, and he began racing to every corner of the house, calling for her, trying to find her again, and the sound of the sea was slapping against the shore, slapping against tin...

Against tin?

Fabian halted. He turned, looked at the tub still sitting in the kitchen. The slapping sound was coming from the tub's direction, so Fabian took a step toward it, then another. When he was finally hovering over it, he looked down and saw that the tub was not, as he had thought, empty.

Water was sloshing inside, sloshing as if desperate to free itself. His wife's pearl necklace bobbed on the uneasy surface, tossed back and forth by miniature waves.

Fabian fell with a thud to his knees. He clutched the edge of the tub and moaned into it. The water shuddered, rippled, whirled like the sky and sea outside.

If she shifted, there would be no way of bringing her back, the herbalist had said. When Fabian had thought of all the things she might turn into, he had pictured animals, objects... things he could continue to protect and serve if need be. He had never imagined *water,* wild and ancient, something he could not contain even if he wanted to.

But deep within himself, he had known she would never be satisfied in her human form. Not when the whole world waited for her.

Love her, the herbalist had said.

So Fabian grabbed hold of the edge of the tub, dragging it across his living room and over the threshold of his front door. The cleared circle of soil in their garden was soaking up the rain, but his wife would never see it. Never see it, unless —

The tub flinched forward in his hands, her water centimeters from slopping over the edge and splashing onto the soil.

He could water the flowers with her, and when the first buds poked through the earth, when the first petals uncurled themselves, stretching toward the sun, they would *be* her. The butterflies that came to rest gently, silently among the flowers would be her, too, and when he drank coffee on his morning porch he might feel their weightless presence rest upon his shoulder, as if his wife was touching a delicate hand on him once more...

Love her, the herbalist had said.

He just wanted to *be* with her, but she wanted to be a butterfly, or something like a butterfly, free, beautiful, untamed, always stationed in his garden, always with him...

The realization bubbled up inside Fabian just as he was tipping the tub to pour it over his seeds. She did not want to be a butterfly captive in a garden. She never had. She had morphed into an element for a reason.

Love her, love her, love her.

Fabian looked down into the contents of the tub, saw her water drinking up the rain. He had always loved her how he wanted to love her, not how she wished to be loved.

With a sudden surge of will, he put both hands on either side of the tub and lifted the whole thing. It was heavier than his wife's human weight, but he blundered toward the roiling shore, the tub pressed up against his chest, the sound of her waves mingling with the sea's. Pebbles turned to sand. Water lapped up to his boots. Sea foam sprayed his cheeks like tears.

Fabian collapsed. The tub overturned on its side, and he watched as the water within gushed out, joining with the sea he loved. The pearl necklace caught on the tub's handle, and for a moment, Fabian had an urge to snatch it, to keep that last remnant of his wife.

But he found his fingers untangling it, feeding it to the sea. The waves dragged it underwater and out of sight, and then she was truly gone, freed as she had always desired. He exhaled, touched his lips to the surface of the water to give her a last kiss.

Then he retreated, leaving the tub lying by the shoreline, using the last of his strength to get to his feet and limp back to the house alone. Once inside, he eased the door shut and looked past the string of seashells out the window. In that garden, flowers would still grow. Butterflies would come to rest among them, although they would only be fluttering reminders of what he had wanted his wife to be.

But past the garden, Fabian would always be able to see his wife in her true form: a dazzling ocean, swaying, untamed, free — constantly ebbing to kiss the shoreline where he'd stand.

Mariah Montoya's story "The Wife of Fabian Vitalik" was originally published in Metaphorosis on Friday, 24 November 2017. See magazine.metaphorosis.com

About the author

Mariah Montoya is a writer and mother from Idaho who has also worked as a preschool teacher in the past. She currently runs a local toddler program during the day and continues to write fantasy novels at night. Her newest book, *By the Orchid and the Owl*, features her favorite thing to write about: magic academia. You can follow her journey on Instagram @mariah_author.

Packing List for Oblivion

Cameron Bertron

The statue was nothing like Enefai remembered. Before, it had been buried to its stomach, with both hands reaching forward to rest almost perfectly, palms up, on the hungry earth. Age had softened the statue's face, which crawled with orange lichen, to a shroud. Its open mouth was turned up to the sky and overflowing with dust. Enefai had watched, for a long time, as the wind spilled grit from the corner of its lips like an hourglass. Now, suspended in holographic color in the center of the council chamber, it looked sanitized and frail. Enefai appraised it for the last time, knowing the outcome before the first votes flickered in. The piece was not particularly innovative; it was not of historic value. It was not vital, it was only beautiful. It would be left behind.

Enefai fixed her eyes on the statue as she cast her vote against it. No councilor volunteered to speak on the piece, so the judgement was swift. The holograph blinked and was replaced by a new sculpture, but the previous image stayed on in Enefai's mind. The decisions were getting harder. At its start, the council had been a mess of overdrawn debates and personal attacks. But Enefai would rather deal with the chaos of those early days than the current, brutal pace of their decisions. It had taken several years, but time had run out for ego and guilt. Enefai was reminded every moment, by the defeated silence of the council and the packing crates in her own home, that the world was ending this year.

The news had broken slowly, then all at once. Before the first dispatch shuddered their calm, Enefai's partner Moore had read the signs in the planet around her. For months, she had come home from the fields with her mouth twisted to one side, calloused fingers thrumming against her leg. She had tried to explain to Enefai about the sourness in the soil and the odd patterns of the rain. Enefai understood little beyond the alarm in her voice, but they both dared to hope that the change was peculiar to their region. It was not. The planet Kenlanli's terraformation was reversing. It had happened on a string of other planets. Now the societies of Kenlanli, so recently settled, were packing back up into the finite space of stations to await the terraformation of a new home planet.

Moore had volunteered immediately to work in the countryside, spending long months collecting soil samples to assess the rate of decay and assisting frontier families in their preparations to leave. The crisis had unwrapped something in her. She swung into action as though she had been preparing for it her whole life. Enefai had done her duty as well, accepting the summons to serve on the council for cultural preservation. She had also received requests for consent to send in her own collection for consideration. She left the requests to collect dust, with everything else in her studio.

Another sculpture was on display. Its superb craftsmanship was doomed by the choice of material. Marble was shipped in from off planet, and the piece would be judged insufficiently Kenlanliin. Enefai hoped that it would be taken in by another planet or station. In the far future, perhaps it could find its way back to Kenlanli's people wherever they might be. It was one of the few thoughts that still offered consolation.

The marble statue was the last of the day. When the session closed, Enefai brushed her way out of the chamber and through the honeycomb halls, exchanging a few nods and sympathetic words with her fellow councilors. Everyone's voice was low, their exchanges quick but sincere. They also had homes to pack. Enefai stepped outside to a sky bruised with evening and stretched her legs as she waded through the city's shallow outskirts into the countryside. The long path home took her past one of her own sculptures. She did not slow as she passed.

She had carved it the same year that she met Moore. As they rattled through the countryside in the back of a transport vehicle, Enefai had felt something tipping over inside her the longer she spoke with this sprawling woman in muddied boots. Probably it was the apocalypse playing tricks on her, but all the memories from that time felt warm. Enefai missed the weightless quiet between them. She missed the long evenings in her studio they spent tinkering at her worktable, Enefai with her designs and Moore with her tools or sketches. These days, the ice cracked beneath their every conversation. When Moore was not working in the countryside, she was brimming with hard choices. Enefai dodged conversations about the space station. She wanted to preserve at least the bubble of their home from the world outside as it ransacked itself. But Moore kept opening the door.

In her head, Moore was already living on the station. Sometimes, it even seemed to Enefai that she was excited about it. Moore planned ceaselessly, scrambling to assure Enefai that they would have everything they needed. But it wasn't their future that weighed heaviest on Enefai, even as it seemed to consume Moore, it was their life on Kenlanli. It was the slide of sand under her boots and the way that sunrise tangled in Moore's hair. In her birth province, at midday the desert's horizon disappeared with a shiver into the pale sky. How to forget that? How to remember?

Her back was slick with sweat when she saw the welcoming round roof of their home. As she stepped inside, the peace earned from her evening walk was dissipated by the boxes crowding the floor. Moore was out for the week, but due back any day. She had left Enefai a list of requests to help with the packing process. Enefai did not need to look at it. Everything was done except one item. She needed to pack her studio.

She quickly ate dinner and prepared a cup of tea. She kept herself moving, knowing that if she paused in her momentum, she would not do any packing tonight. Mechanically, she entered the studio and evaluated the single crate reserved for her belongings against the gentle mess of her studio. The floor and work benches were cluttered with models, sketches, and photos. Only her tools stood in perfect order, hanging on the walls and from the ceiling. The darkness outside converted the studio's large windows to mirrors and Enefai kept catching sight of her own movement as she worked. She tried to summon nostalgia as she packed, but her memories felt glossy and distant. Each tool slid into the crate only left her feeling heavier.

By the time she stopped for a break, her studio was decimated and her tea was cold. Enefai sat down heavily on the floor, her legs splayed in front of her and her back against a slab. Its porous rasp felt reassuring on the back of her arms. Years ago, she had brought the stone from her home province for a design she planned. The rock was unique to her home, stark white and ribboned with pale orange and crimson. As a kid, she used to find patterns in the traces of color, pulling shapes out of the cliffsides. She wondered bitterly what abstractions she would be able to find in the expressionless plaster they would use on station.

She slid away from the stone and regarded it from her place on the floor. She had seen more statues in the last few years than in all her life. She imagined their shapes in the slab and marveled at what had been accomplished with a piece of rock, a set of tools. But it hadn't saved them, extinguished in a flash of holographic light. With time, their craftsmanship, her craftsmanship, would be weathered back to featureless slabs like the one which stood before her. She felt powerless against that future, against her unreasoning anger at Moore's resilience, against her love for Kenlanli. She felt small beneath the slab that stretched above her. Hardening her gaze, she stared into the stone to calm her mind and began to slowly trace the fiery streaks in the rock from top to bottom.

She remembered the design she had planned for this slab when she picked it all those years ago. She could see now that it was all wrong. The arch of a spine was already in the slab's contour, thinly submerged. Veins of color netted together in the side. They would run over an open palm like sunlight. She could only catch the shape in pieces, barely coherent, but it was enough. The night hours were re-aligning. The studio's gravity bent around the work. Moore's expression when she inspected her crops, when she lifted a long shoot with the tip of her thumb, was already in the stone. Enefai reached for it. She smoothed the memorized lips and rounded the jaw. She crinkled the eyes that would watch, unflinching, as their planet's atmosphere slumped to reclaim the horizon. She followed only that instinct which had first searched out shapes in the mountainsides. She followed it until the sunrise dripped dirty pink into her studio.

When it was done, she would face it towards the window, pack her tools away, and leave this room forever. But for now, she closed her grainy eyes and pressed her forehead against the statue's unhewn base. Through her headphones she could not hear Moore's clattering entrance. The world was quiet as arms encircled her. Quiet as a kiss was buried on her neck. She would take it to the stars.

Cameron Bertron's story "Packing List for Oblivion" was originally published in Metaphorosis on Friday, 6 January 2023. See magazine.metaphorosis.com

About the author

Cameron Bertron currently lives in Erdenet, Mongolia where she works as an English teacher. She has been a volunteer firefighter and a student of Slavic literature, but her most memorable work was as an almond milkman in her hometown Tampa, Florida.

Useful and Beautiful Things

E. Saxey

This suburb has rows and rows of identical 19th century houses, but when any single home is opened, it can contain wonders.

It's late in the hot afternoon when I report to the address the Guvnor sent me. A mahogany behemoth is escaping through the ground floor sash window: a George III wardrobe with claw feet. A remarkable piece of furniture, requiring a gang of four sweaty men to wrestle it through the window.

"Frankie!" I recognise one of the men as the Guvnor, the gang's coordinator. He's hauling at a claw foot, struggling with the weight. "Give us a hand, girl?" I step in and take some of his burden, protecting the wardrobe from damage as we bring it down to the ground. The men are thankful, if confused. I'm stronger than I look. The Guvnor slaps me on the back. "Ta, Frankie. This is a hell of a house. There's so much bloody junk, we've only got half of it out."

I follow him up the garden path. The back of his T-shirt reads 'St Lucian 'till I die', providing his own provenance. Alongside the path, I see marvels: a Chinese *famille-verte* floor vase, which shouldn't be standing up on the uneven lawn like that. I lay it gently on the grass. Sheltering under the hedge is a herd of six dining chairs, Queen Anne style, two of them stacked awkwardly, like animals mating.

"Sorry about your Ma, Frankie," calls the Guvnor. "You doing alright?"

I catch his anxiety and reassure us both: "I can work solo."

The Guvnor beckons me indoors, and upstairs to a sunlit study. "This place is a total hodgepodge, Frankie." He flaps his hand at walls, which are lined with shelves. Most are packed with books, but one shelf holds statuettes of gods, a dozen of them, an international pantheon. "It's a bad scene."

I wonder why he sounds dejected. There's death, here, certainly, I know the signs. This house was a man's home, he was the gravity which kept these objects together. Without him, they spin off and spill into the garden, and get damp and chipped. But estate sales are bread and butter to the Guvnor; he's a genius at house clearance, he can strip a place in a day. He helps to mitigate the tragedy of death by finding every item a new home.

"What have you found?" I ask him.

"We put it over the back, there. For safety."

Pushed to one corner of the study is a small low table. My discernment stirs: the table is circular and wooden, satinwood, 19th century — yes, 1860s — with a *pietra dura* marble chess board in the centre. My skills still function, thank goodness. Despite the worries of the last few months, I can do my job.

A chess set made of stone is laid out, ready to play.

I stop dead in the middle of the room. I can't intuit anything about the chess set.

I recognise the shape of the pieces — the nobs and planes of the ultra-traditional Staunton design — but little else. I suppose the translucent pieces could be rock crystal from South Asia. Too vague, much too vague! I try to keep my heart from tick-tick-ticking in panic. The set is slightly uneven, the pieces not symmetrical. Handmade, perhaps by an amateur; such objects are always hard to identify. The dark pieces are carved from malachite, dark green with vivid spots like moss or mould.

"What's wrong with it?" I ask.

"Three of my boys couldn't put this bloody thing away," the Guvnor informs me. "I'll show you what it does." He plucks the dark green queen from the table, blinks, puts her back, nods. "Here, I'll show you." Picks up the queen again and replaces her. He remembers nothing, resetting before my eyes. "Wait a mo, I'll show —"

"You showed me."

"Damn! Did it mess me around, again? Well, you get the idea."

"What do the other pieces do?"

"Not a clue. But one lad who touched them was acting so funny, I had to send him home. It's all yours, if you want it. Usual terms? You take it away, fifty-fifty if you sell it on?"

That's fair, so we shake on it. The Guvnor leaves me to my work. I slough off my backpack, tie back my hair. I don't go back to the chess set, at first, but poke through the bookshelves in case there's a box for the set, or any provenance or context.

"Hey! You can't take any of those."

I jump back. I overlooked the person frowning at me from the far corner of the study, because she wasn't part of my jurisdiction. I take her in: rounded, wearing dusty dungarees, about three decades old, but people are hard to date. Her dark brown hair, in a shaggy bob, is a couple of inches longer than when we last met, and her expression is more combative.

"My employer has an agreement for the books," she says. "I work for Sotherans. I'm Tamsin Zhang."

"I know. I mean, we both worked on the Griffiths estate, in Portslade. I'm Frankie Cornish."

"That was woman with you, an older woman. She got the *Mabinogion*."

"My colleague." My mother. Yes, she took the *Mabinogion*, an 1880 edition, lavishly illustrated, cloth-covered in green. What a memory for an object Ms Zhang has. I recognise a kindred spirit. I need to reassure her. "I'm only taking the chess set."

She walks closer. Her spectacles are round, with faux tortoiseshell and strong lenses, and I think I come into focus for her because her frown relaxes.

"Oh, yes! I remember you. Why are you in my books, then?"

"Looking for anything related."

"The dead guy had a secretary, who took all his papers."

I sigh at the news. She could go back to her work, but she lingers, perhaps regretting her initial hostility. "What's so important about the chess set?" she asks, peering down at the pieces. She is 5'3", not as high as my chin. "They carried it in here like it might explode."

"I'm disposing of it."

"You're throwing it out? Can I have it?"

"No! Sorry. I mean, I'm taking it away with me. To evaluate."

"Are you taking any of this other stuff? This house is ridiculous. What was he doing with all these?" She points at the shelf of gods, where a fist-sized blue baboon (sixth century BC) hides in his newspaper wrapping from a bronze leopard (17th century, probably stolen in the sack of Benin City). Some of the gods are genuine and some are replicas, and nobody will want the whole mismatched collection, but the Guvnor will find each god a new owner.

In the second during which the gods distract me, Tamsin reaches for a chess piece.

"Don't!"

"I can be careful. I handle fragile books, that's my job." Tamsin is so sure of herself, so indignant, that I pause. She plucks up the green queen, places her down again, blinks and resets. "I'll be careful." She picks the queen up again, puts it down. The possibility of danger overrides my manners, and my hand shoots out to grab her wrist, to stop her third attempt. But Tamsin is already drawing back, and my hand closes on empty air. "Ooh, that's weird. That's *clever...*" She touches the head of the green queen, blinks a few times and laughs in astonishment. "Bloody hell."

"You have to stop. It might not be safe." I sound priggish. She doesn't seem to take offence, but does give me a hard stare, eyes huge through her distorting spectacles.

"Did you know it would do that?"

There's no chance of bluffing, she's felt the weird effect herself. "I knew it would do *something*. That's why the Guvnor called me in."

"Does this kind of thing happen often?"

"To me, yes." She looks at me with avid interest.

"So how does it work?"

"I don't know." I have a handful of hypotheses. "I have to take it away and test it."

Her frown returns, similar to when she mentioned the *Mabinogion*: unwilling to let go. "Wait! I have something that might be connected. We can investigate!"

I am so used to working with my mother that the offer of collaboration is a comfort.

●

The owner's name is Magnus Owens. Earlier that day, Tamsin found his diaries, which were shelved with his books and thus escaped the notice of his secretary.

"Check these out," Tamsin says. They're half-bound in Moroccan with blind tooling. "Bit creepy, other people's diaries. Not my area."

She passes me a volume. Diaries are the most personal, the least transferrable objects. I know these ones may not find a buyer, despite their fine bindings. "Are there family members who might be interested?"

Tamsin shrugs, indifferent. "Dunno. Owens doesn't mention having a wife or kids, in the parts I read. He was mining graphite in Sri Lanka, obsessed with his collections. He lists all the things he buys, there are cross-references to a stack of auction catalogues, I showed them to the Guvnor." I'm glad. That will help him re-home the objects. "But look at this." Tamsin stands close to me, turns the pages of the volume I hold, and points to the notes and number at the foot of each page: *Won in 22, Sicilian Defence, Smith-Morra Gambit. Lost in 10, Dutch Defence.* "This is the main thing, apart from collecting, that he bothers to write down. It's a record of chess games." She flips forwards, backwards. Numbers on every page.

"He played every night?"

"Yeah, almost. So, do you think he made this freaky chess set to confuse his friends? To win more games. Maybe to win money?" I admire the leaps of her logic. But there's no money mentioned here, only a tally. I flick the pages, find a month when things improve for Owen: *Won in 12. Won in 10.* Only a week before, I find a description of his chess set arriving from Rajasthan.

As soon as I read the place-name, I am flooded by images of Rajasthani stone-carving: Jali screens framing the sky in a lattice of stars. A provenance! I feel it like a delicious cool wave. My heart calms. And the diaries have proved useful, after all.

Tamsin quizzes me, as I take photos of the relevant diary pages

"So do you ever get called in to deal with books? Books which do weird things?"

"Sometimes."

"Magic books?"

"Not magic."

"Alright, *freaky* books. Do you have any? Could I see them?"

"Thank you, but I'm not planning to sell any. You're with Sotherans? I'll think of them, the next time I have one." She looks a little annoyed. I suppose it would have been a professional coup, for her to bring in an unusual tome. I pick up the green queen and stow her in my backpack.

"Hey. Frankie!" She touches my arm, suddenly agitated. "How can you touch the pieces, like that?"

I've made a foolish mistake. Normally I'd wear gloves, to keep up appearances. "I have a high tolerance."

"For freaky stuff." Tamsin's eyes shine. "It doesn't do anything to you?"

"I'm not very sensitive." The room is too hot. If I were staying, I'd throw up the sash windows, invite a breeze in to ruffle the packing paper. But I'm leaving.

Tamsin asks: "If you're not *sensitive*, how will you find out if the other pieces do the same thing?"

She notices too much, and she thinks too fast. I look at the ranks of chess nobility, slightly askew as if drunk, gazing over their pawn army. Each piece could be hazardous. Normally, my mother would test the pieces, at her workbench back home, with great interest and care.

"I'll help you," Tamsin offers.

"You can't."

"I can. They won't do me any real harm, will they?"

"One of the Guvnor's boys went home, sick."

"He might have skived off to enjoy the weather. I'll help you find out."

I have a book of contacts, from my mother, listing trustworthy people who buy strange things. I have storage facilities, and a network of folk (including the Guvnor) who put interesting artefacts my way. What I don't have is someone to do what my mother did: interact with objects, and let them work on her, demonstrating their properties. The nervous ticking fills my chest again.

"I won't *steal* them," she protests. "I'm a *book* person!" I think she's teasing me. I find her hard to read.

"Maybe, thank you. Yes." I make one stipulation for safety: "But not until the house is empty."

●

For the next few hours, Tamsin works at the far end of the study, chatting with me between periods of intense concentration. She asks me again about unusual books, and I describe a handful that I've seen, and their hazards. I tell her in the hopes she will respect my expertise, as I respect hers, but she seems unsatisfied.

At six in the evening, the shouts and crashes downstairs die away. The Guvnor hands me the keys, and the house is silent.

"So I pick the pieces up," asks Tamsin, "One at a time?"

I hold my notebook and pencil ready. "And tell me the effect."

"Just the greens, or do you think the whites do anything?"

I try to think like Magnus Owens. "He wouldn't want to disadvantage himself."

"Yeah, but could the white pieces do *positive* things?" She puts herself in the shoes of the dead man, so easily.

"Perhaps. Let's try them first." I sit on the floorboards, cross-legged by the chess table. In my experience, it's better not to have too far to fall. Tamsin sits down, not across the board where an opponent would be, but on the adjoining edge to me, our knees almost touching.

I can see how deftly Tamsin must handle delicate books. She walks her index fingers with care along the heads of the pawns. King's pawn: "Nothing." Knight's pawn: "Nothing." I write, for both: *No effect.*

Bishop's pawn: Tamsin sneezes violently. Her bobbed hair falls forwards. "It wasn't the pawn! It's dust." *No effect/allergenic?*

Rook's pawn: "I feel calm. Really chill." *Relaxing?* Then she looks about the room and sighs. From up on the shelf of gods, the small blue baboon watches us. "This damn house. Why don't I have a house like this, a collection like this? Oh, hang on." She throws the pawn from hand to hand. "It's this piece. It makes me feel like I deserve everything."

"Confidence?"

"Entitlement. Resentment."

Queen's pawn: "Oooh. This one feels *nice.*" Tamsin clutches it to her chest. "Satisfying. Like dumplings. Maybe I'm just hungry." She lifts her arms over her head, savouring the stretch, and regards me with a catlike smile. *Sense of wellbeing?* "What do you want?"

"Sorry?"

She's taken out her phone. "Wonton soup?"

"Dim sum," I say, for the sake of appearances.

"It'll be here in half an hour, you owe me a tenner." Her fingers take three last steps along the front rank of pieces: rook's pawn, bishop's pawn, knight's pawn. "And these are all duds. You could let me have one as a souvenir."

"I have to keep the set together." But perhaps I should pay her half of what I make from the set, because her evaluation will inform me about how to sell it. Not on the open market, of course, but using my mother's list of trustworthy collectors. I would have to stay in contact with Tamsin, to arrange payment. The prospect cheers me.

Tamsin plucks up the white bishop and squints at a bookcase, more than three metres away. "I can read all the titles." She takes off her glasses. "Hey, my eyesight's fine. Holy crap! Has this thing fixed my eyes?"

"It may have optimised how your brain works with your eyes." *Positive minor visual effects,* I write.

"Wow. Can I buy it, seriously?" Her glasses have left a pink dent on each side of her nose. "My eyes are so rubbish, this would be a life-changer."

"We don't know how it works. It could be doing terrible damage to your brain."

White bishop is grudgingly replaced, as are Tamsin's glasses, and she scoops up the white knight. "I feel confident." She chuckles. "No, I feel *lucky.*"

"Shall we test it?" In my pocket, I find two dice and hand them over.

Her expression is sceptical, but she sends the dice rattling across the floorboards. Two sixes. I retrieve them, and Tamsin rolls them again. Double sixes. I write *positive effect, good fortune* while she glares at the white bishop, its eyeless face and aghast mouth.

"So this little blobby boy is actually affecting the world," says Tamsin. "But double sixes are a completely arbitrary symbol. How does it know that they're lucky? Wait, are those dice loaded?"

"I can give you a coin to toss, if you'd rather."

She stands and paces back over to the bookshelves. Impossible questions are grinding together in her mind. She's probably going to leave, now. I may not see her again, except at contentious estate sales, at intervals of years. That's alright. People are allowed to relocate themselves.

Tamsin uses both hands to unshelve a large dictionary, Bosworth and Toller's Old English, cloth-bound in burgundy, and carries it back to me. She opens the cover carefully. Inside, the pages have been hollowed out to hide a flat bottle of Talisker 25 year single malt whisky. "I found it this morning. Isn't it tacky?" She upends the bottle into her mouth and there's an audible glug. She hands it over to me.

"I don't know if we should combine alcohol with..."

"We totally should, because people are going to play with these pieces when they're drinking sherry, or what-have-you, and you need to know how bad that would be." She folds her legs up and re-joins me on the floor. She's misjudged our proximity, and now her knee presses mine. "I bet Owens got his friends drunk, the filthy cheat. Why do you have dice in your pocket? Does this kind of thing happen to you a lot, eh?"

"I have some cufflinks which work the other way. Gold with blue enamel." Translucent lapis blue over hatched engine-turning. They're in my mother's permanent collection, never to be sold. "Fabergé."

"Unlucky cufflinks?"

"Three owners found them... difficult." I realise I'm showing off. I shouldn't. It's dangerous to invite her to look closely at my life.

"Wow. *Terminally* difficult? And you kept them? William Morris wouldn't like that." She prods my shoulder and takes back the whisky bottle from my hands. I want to share her joke but I can only think of William Morris' floral patterns, looping across mid-C19th sofas.

"Why would he care about my cufflinks?"

"He said you shouldn't have anything in your house that you don't know to be useful, or believe to be beautiful. But your house is full of *awful* stuff, by the sound of it. Am I right?"

I think of my mother's workbench, and all the artefacts my mother restored and rehomed. Then the wall of strongboxes, one of which will hold the chess set. I picture the peace that will fill me when I close the lid. "It's a very useful place, overall."

"Oh, Frankie, you should have a beautiful house!" This time it sounds less like a scolding than a wish: Tamsin thinks I deserve a beautiful house. Before I can ask her, she adds: "What's your favourite thing that you own? Is it a book?"

I've never thought of that. I don't truly consider the objects in my collection to be mine. They're only resting with me because nobody else can own them, at present. "I don't have a favourite."

"Not even that *Mabinogion* you snatched?" Another nudge on my shoulder. "Was it freaky? What did it do?" It could be a joke, but perhaps her excellent memory for books is supported by a great capacity for grudges. I shake my head.

White rook: "Nothing. No, wait." She holds out her wrist. Should I admire her bracelet of 1970s cloisonné beads, patterned with bats? "My pulse. Feel it."

I touch her warm soft wrist, and the flicker I find there slows and slows. "You should put the rook down."

"But I feel really calm. Really on top of things..." I pluck the rook from her hand. *Induces catatonia?* "Spoil-sport," she accuses, rubbing her wrist where I touched it. "The queen's got to be the most powerful one, right?" She lowers her fingertip onto the milky crown of the white queen. "Oh. I'm the most important person in the world. Anything I do for my own benefit is just fine. Cool." *Solipsism?*

White king: "Wow. The board just lit up." Tamsin sits bolt upright. "I can see all the moves. I haven't played chess since I was ten, but I can see every way it could possibly go..."

She turns her gaze on me, and lapses into silence.

I write down *strategic foresight*.

"How do you get into a job like yours?" she asks, still staring.

I write *overly curious*, because I know she's reading it.

"No, but seriously. It can't just be because you're *insensitive*."

Persistent intrusive questioning. I shouldn't have shown off about my cufflinks. I need to turn her attention aside. "Is there more whisky?"

Tamsin reluctantly relinquishes the white king. "I can't keep it?"

"It might give you something like concussion."

"But you're still going to sell the set?"

The list of people I would trust with them has dwindled with each piece, each power. "I'll see."

"Or get rid of them. Throw them away."

"No! Don't say that!"

"Why not? God, you sound like those people who get sentimental over books being chucked out. Do you know how many terrible, waste-of-space books there are? You can't hang on to *everything*, you can just bung stuff in the bin..."

I shake my head, over and over. I worry I might scream.

A chime rings round the room. Tamsin springs to her feet. "Food's here!"

●

Tamsin thunders down the stairs, and the vibrations set one of the shelf-gods wobbling. I nudge it further back, to safety. I would love to have a day to hold each of the small statues in my hands and know who they are, where they come from. But they're not dangerous, so they're not my business.

I should be wary of Tamsin. She lulled me into thinking of her as my work partner, but I didn't choose her. She keeps teasing me and touching me, but I should keep a level head. I hear her chatting with the delivery man, which gives me time to pluck up all the pieces we've tested and stash them in my bag, away from temptation.

When Tamsin returns, her face is somewhat pallid. "The delivery guy told me that Owens *died* here. In the house."

I remember the Guvnor saying this was a *bad scene*, and wonder if he meant the manner of Owen's death. "It's understandable." People die. Things endure.

"It's grim." Tamsin lays the pots of food out on the floor. "Hey, where did the white pieces go?"

"They're safe. What do you think Owens was like?" I ask, to distract her from my tidying, and from the fact that I won't eat the dim sum. And because I want to know her opinion.

"An English man collecting colonial curiosities to make his Englishness more interesting." She puts herself in Owen's place, then puts him in his place, too.

"Did you get that from his diaries?"

"I got that from his book collection — lots of international publications, lots of uncracked spines. Don't be sad! All the better for my bosses, to have pristine Bengali poetry. *Gitanjali* will end up with someone who appreciates it."

I wait until Tamsin wrangles a steamed dumpling into her mouth. "The green pieces," I say. "I shouldn't let you test them."

"*Let* me, hah." She can still argue with her mouth full.

"The green ones may be terrible."

"No, because look..." She swigs her coke. I've hidden the whisky under my backpack. "They can't be that godawful, or nobody would ever play chess with him twice.

They're not going to make you cough up your lungs, are they?" She's three moves ahead of me. "And *you* need to know how they work. Don't you? To be a good caretaker."

I need to know the full extent, to judge what to do with the set: who might safely buy it, or more likely, how I can store it. Whether to seal it in clay or submerge it in running water. But must I rely on Tamsin?

"Let's just do the pawns," she offers, as a compromise. "They're only small."

The pawns will perplex us both.

●

King's pawn: "Nothing." No effect. "It's not doing anything at all." She chuckles slyly.

"Tamsin, are you lying?"

"Nooo, heh-heh." I write *Induces duplicity/hysteria?* Tamsin shivers. "Holy hell, that was stranger than the eyesight thing."

"And it made you lie?"

"It didn't do anything! I was fine. Heh-heh."

I reach to take back the pawn, and she makes a fist, twists and turns, play-wrestles my fingers with her own. I don't like to look strong, and she's wily and enjoying herself, so the fight goes on for longer than it needs to. When the pawn is out of her hand, she asks: "Why would that help Owens win? I suppose it would encourage his opponent to cheat."

Bishop's pawn: Tamsin sighs. "I'm rubbish at this, anyway."

"At chess?"

"At everything." *Hopelessness.*

Knight's pawn: "I want to bet you a lot of money that I'm going to win." *Risk seeking? Over-confidence?* "What happens if —" Before I can stop her, she's palmed two pawns simultaneously. "Ha! I think I'm going to lose and I don't care, I still want to bet on it! I wish you could feel this!" Her grin is contagious, her eyes are alight. This is all irresponsible, reprehensible. I should be working alone.

"Stop. Please." Thankfully, she does.

Queen's pawn: "It's telling me just do anything, move wherever, don't overthink it."

Hazardous rashness. "Does it have a voice?"

"No, it's just a feeling. Do some things have voices?"

I think of the rooms in my mother's house — my house — filled with items that charmed and berated her, to which I am blessedly oblivious. We were perfect colleagues. "Sometimes."

She leans in closer to me. Does she want to be hugged? I could do that. She swipes the whisky from under my bag. "Queen's pawn makes you thirsty."

Rook's pawn makes Tamsin jump to her feet, knocking over the remnants of her takeaway. "Sorry! I can't sit still." *Restless.* "Why does he get all this stuff? How can anyone deserve..." *Psychologically restless?* "I feel small. Do I seem small?"

"Not more than you — no."

"You're not taking me seriously!"

I should have said something kinder, more respectful. "I'm sorry. Put the pawn down?"

Instead, she sweeps up more pieces, handfuls of them, stuffing them into the pockets of her dungarees, and runs.

I lunge at her but she's quicker. She's off down the stairs, almost flying, bursting out of the back door and vanishing into the overgrown garden.

I have to follow. It's dusk, and the trees cast deep shadows. There's a pale path, but as I run down it, chasing her, I feel thorns catch at my clothes. I hear Tamsin, rather than see her, ahead of me. Please let her not be hurt. Let her not drop anything, either. Let me not have to hunt for the dark green chess pieces amid brambles in the dark.

My eyes adjust and a movement draws my gaze to Tamsin standing in an old wooden gazebo. I should jump at her, pin her arms, make her release the rook's pawn. But I can't imagine hurting her.

"Come on! Take them off me." She raises her fist and waves it from side to side. "This is most the important thing, right?"

It is an accusation, but it is true. People pass, things endure; my responsibility is to things. While I hesitate, I see a quick arc in the dark, her arm as she flings the pawn of low self-esteem far into the garden.

Her penitence is instant. "Oh, God, sorry! Shit! I'll find it!" Her face glows in the light of her phone. "It went in that direction..."

I have a keyring torch, and I spot the pawn before she does, resting in a patch of dandelions. I turn my back to Tamsin before I stoop to pick it up. I need to keep it secure. I dust off the dirt and place it on my tongue, force myself to swallow, feel the nobbles as it slides down my throat.

"Found it," I call.

"I've found something else." Tamsin has her phone light trained on a flickering tail of plastic tape in the bushes, with lettering: POLICE LINE DO NOT CROSS. "I think he died in the garden. Owens." Tamsin stares up at the house, the sash window glowing with light. "Maybe he jumped out of the window of his study. Do you think the chess set killed him?"

I thought not: he should have known its properties. But what pieces might he have touched by accident, in what combination? Did he grab recklessness, self-doubt, and foresight all in one hand, and throw himself away? And now all his possessions have followed him, flung outwards, dispersing.

Tamsin, standing beside me, says: "You'll get rid of it, won't you?"

"Don't worry. I won't pass it on to another owner."

"No, I mean you should trash it. Smash it up and bury it."

I dislike this line of thought. I dislike it very much. Inside me, things tick painfully fast.

The horrible plastic police tape dances about in the wind. I am seized by a pang of fear. I'm not mourning Owen, or thinking of the ways he might have died; I'm empathising with the objects he's left behind. I never want to be wrapped in a rug, left on a lawn. I don't want to be forced to seek someone new, someone who appreciates me enough to keep me.

My internal mechanisms are spinning wildly. I need to be calm. I remind myself: I may not have an owner, but I have a place in the world. I have earned it.

I duck into the gazebo and sit on the bench I find inside. "You can't throw an artefact away," I say. "Just because you don't have a use for it at the moment." I'm speaking to myself more than to Tamsin.

She hears me, though, and shouts back: "But you can't hang onto it indefinitely, either. Not if it's toxic!"

"I'll keep it safe."

"But you won't live forever, will you?"

I don't know the answer to that.

Tamsin stumbles into the gazebo and joins me on my bench, pulling out her bottle of coke (into which, it occurs to me, she has poured a lot of the whisky) and drinking deeply.

"Let's do the rest of them quickly," she offers.

I shake my head.

"But we're almost done." She points to her dungaree pocket. I see the bumps of the stolen pieces through the denim. "You get them out."

I work my hand into her pocket, ignoring the warmth of her body, and retrieve them. I line them up on the bench, within arm's reach, and lay my torch alongside, to light them. I take out my small notebook and pen. I can complete this quickly and depart.

Green rook: "I shouldn't be here," says Tamsin.

"The same as the rook's pawn?"

"No, that was just twitchy legs. This is: I need to get away, right now! Shit, do you think this is the one that killed Owens? Sit on my feet. Come on, it'll slow me down if I try to run off." She's tucking a foot under the bend of my knee, wriggling it until it's wedged. "There, like that."

Need to be elsewhere? Self-destruction? My handwriting is not neat.

Green bishop: "Do you ever wonder what you're for?"

I did. I do. Has the bishop given her telepathy? If so, does she know how conscious I am of her wriggling foot?

"Go on, write down *existential doubt.* Or *moody cow.*"

Green knight: "I want to fight you. I hate you!" She wrenches her foot free from under my leg, but falls backwards to the floor. I spring up, hit a gazebo pillar and shake down cobwebs and dust onto both of us. I want to help Tamsin stand, but her arms are flailing, she is still furious at me. She takes a wild swing. The chess piece flies from her hand. "Gah! Vicious little horse bastard!" she cries.

I crouch down to pick up the knight, and quickly swallow it, to join the pawn. I am the safest temporary store for small, wicked objects.

Before I can stand, a hot hand lands on my back. I hear Tamsin's breath. Her hand slides up, she slips her fingers into my hair, to stir deliciously against my scalp.

"You're a very attractive — whatever you are. A very cute curator."

Her voice is low and tender, all her rage boiled away, and her heat warms me. But only one of her hands is in my hair.

She's holding the green king in the other.

It's not fair to let this go on. I twist around and prise her fingers open as gently as I can.

I know it's worked when I hear her swear, and she pulls away from me and stomps to the other side of the hut.

I eat the green king. I focus on finding my notebook. I write: *Emotional connection?* A euphemism. The lust-inducing king is even less explicable than the rage-knight. Would desire distract your opponent? It's distracted Tamsin, who is holding her head in her hands.

"Is that the last one?" she asks, flatly.

"There's only one piece left, and we know what she does. The green queen. Amnesia, or confusion."

We are confused enough. "Yes."

Tamsin raises her head, sucks in the night air. The aphrodisiac effects of the green king have disgusted her. And I'm to blame, I wanted to impress her by my association with wonderful things. My back feels chilly, now, where her hand had rested.

Tamsin raises her head, sucks in the night air. "Is that the last one?" she asks, faintly.

"There's only one piece left, and we know what she does. The green queen."

"Oh! Her." The monarch of forgetting and re-setting. Maybe Tamsin would appreciate some amnesia.

I look back to the house, and through the back door glimpse floorboards of rich golden oak. Carpets fade and moths consume them, but wood goes on for centuries. Until you burn it. Even then, it's useful.

"You have to get rid of them all," Tamsin instructs me. "Apart from the one which fixed my eyesight…"

"White bishop."

"You could give that one to a doctor. All the others, though, they need to go! You can't let people use them to start fights, or win elections. Or as a bloody truth drug."

I can't read my notebook, so I double-check my mental list of the pieces; none of them worked as a truth drug. Her anger's making her exaggerate. "I'll keep them away from anyone," I promise her, as I pick up my backpack. "I'll use my best strong-room."

"But you could fall under a bus tomorrow. They'll get out into the world again. Why not destroy them?"

Tick-tick-tick, my heart stutters, faster than I've ever felt it. I can't speak my objection.

"They're lethal!" she insists. "They might have killed their last owner!" I know the fuel for her hate isn't the self-destructive bishop, or the aggressive knight. It's the green king, the piece that made her want me. "*And* they're ugly! They're failing the William Morris test on both fronts."

"I do believe that almost everything can find a new owner."

"Really? How long have you been hoarding those murderous cufflinks? Objects have to earn the space they take up in the world! Things have to be useful…"

And to my surprise, tears well up in my eyes and drip onto the golden oak floorboards.

"Not you! I didn't mean you! Oh, damn…" She scrambles across the bench to wrap her arms around me. "You're remarkable."

"Am I?" My mother did a lot of work to make me appear ordinary. "Is it obvious?"

Tamsin continues her clumsy hug and clumsy reassurance. "No, no, not unless you look really closely." People don't usually look at me closely. "I'd never have noticed, except the white king made me understand how things worked. Oh, and then you ate those chess pieces."

I clear my throat. "I've lost my mother." My co-worker, the one who restored me. Almost all my memories are from after she mended me. "She died, two months ago, she died."

"I'm sorry."

"This is the first job I've been on, without her. I need to know I can still do the work, that I'm useful."

Tamsin loosens her grip and I think she'll let me go but she settles into a more sustainable embrace. "I understand. Everyone wants to be useful."

"But every thing *needs* to be useful."

Tamsin shakes her head very hard, brushing her face against mine. "No, no, no. You don't need to be useful."

"I do."

She is trying to think of arguments against all her earlier pronouncements. "Beautiful! You could be beautiful, instead."

I want to correct her: no, someone else must *believe* I'm beautiful.

I want to ask: does she believe I'm beautiful?

Instead, I ask: "Which chess piece makes you tell the truth?"

Tamsin buries her face in my shoulder without answering. It is the green king, then. I study her cloisonné bracelet in the dimness and listen to the tick-tick-ticking of my heart.

E. Saxey's story "Useful and Beautiful Things" was originally published in Metaphorosis on Friday, 22 December 2023. See magazine.metaphorosis.com

About the author

E. Saxey is a queer Londoner who works in Universities and volunteers in libraries. Their current writing desk used to belong to the Ancient Order of Druids.

thelightningbook.co.uk, @esaxey

Tree and Flame

Rob Francis

These last few days beneath the reaching boughs of the amberfires had been among the happiest of Thya's life. She had never seen forest like this; the blazing foliage and crimson branches shining even through the morning fog that lay heavy on the mountainside. Each day she had enjoyed scaling the faces of rock outcrops nearby, finding strange new tubers and fungi in the wet earth. And at night she had slept deep and untroubled amongst the trees.

The peace of the forest was wondrous. The only thing better was the moment Father returned from Quiet Castle, striding into the clearing through a drift of orange leaves, a smile on his face as wide and open as the sky.

"You waited."

"Of course." She rose, folding her new collection of leaves and flowers into the roughspun cloth they had been spread upon. A few steps and she stood before Father, eyes narrowed in appraisal. His old clothes were gone, replaced by a hempen robe the colour of earth, and unadorned. The sandals cushioning his feet were woven from grass, a type she had not seen before, while his hair, which a short time ago had been matted horsetails of grey, had been shorn almost to the scalp. Yet it was the smile that was most unusual. She couldn't recall Father smiling since she had been a little girl. But it fit this strange new man, who stood tall and unbent, looking straight at her, no longer turning his face to hide his empty eye socket.

The long shadow was gone.

Thya folded him in her arms and kissed his forehead.

"Are you recovered, Father?"

"Yes, lamb. The Sylvati took it away, all of it. The world burns as bright as when I was a boy, I'm pleased to say." He plucked an amberfire leaf from the ground and stroked his fingers over it wonderingly.

"Thank the gods." She jogged to the base of the greatest amberfire, the one she had chosen to camp beneath. She had been preparing for this moment. Her pack was full of roots she had foraged from the mountainside, along with a small portion of ripe slipperberries. The waterskins were full of sweet stream water. Father's axe stood against the tree, its edge clean and sharpened; no weapons were permitted amongst the Sylvati. Thya slipped on her knife belt, then hoisted the axe onto her shoulder, its weight unbalancing her.

"We'd better hurry, Father. The highfolk will be waiting for you, though I'm sure Sylk and Crux will be doing their best to persuade them you're dead. Well. Sylk, anyway." Her little sister had always been trouble. Crux wasn't perfect by a long mark, but Thya's big brother had always looked out for her, and he loved their father.

Thya sucked in a breath and exhaled loudly. It felt good. "Now we have you back, all will be well." She held the great axe out to him, its bearded blade shining in the afternoon sun.

Father smiled but made no move to take it. Instead, he crossed the clearing to the tree and lifted the pack and skins, shouldering them easily.

"Carry the axe for me, lamb. Its weight would be unwelcome right now."

They followed a slender stream down the mountainside, leaving the stand of amberfires behind and passing through ranks of twisted windling trees, their grey bark smothered with moss and creepers. Treeskippers leapt from branch to branch or flitted between the crowns, calling to each other in high trills. After a short time, the soil deepened and the forest thickened, straight and imposing bluethorns standing tall around them. Pygmoles burrowed beneath the trunks, kicking out dirt as they made their homes. Thya was glad to see it all.

She led the way, trying to push them both along. The sooner they returned, the more chance they had of countering the invasion. The gravel-eaters were coming.

Father didn't hurry. He walked carefully, looking around at all the mountain had to show. Thya would have liked to do the same, but she was fired now, keen to show everyone at home that Father was well.

Father was well. Sylk and Crux could do what they liked; try to lead the highfolk where they might. Father was well, and when they returned, everything that had come before wouldn't matter. The gravel-eaters would be dealt with, and her people would be safe. Father always had the answers.

They came to a bluff, the rock outcrop overlooking a small valley where the river gathered pace and width. To the north stood Quiet Castle atop its narrow peak, the odd lightning-blue stone of its walls almost lost now against the darkening sky.

Father stopped at the lip of the cliff and turned to the castle, regarding it silently for a long moment. His face creased happily, as if at some treasured memory.

Thya placed a hand on his arm. "What did they do, Father? The Sylvati. It must have been some magnificent sorcery."

He smiled and kissed her forehead as she had his.

"They cured me. And you are right, lamb. It was magnificent."

Thya stared out at the treetops. Leagues away, the people of High Crag would be asking each other, *What now? If Lord Brent doesn't return? If he is lost forever?* And the gravel-eaters would be creeping closer, while some of the highfolk sharpened their knives, and others turned their faces away and stared only at each other.

"Do you remember? Any of it?" It hurt to ask, and she was wary of upsetting Father, but she had to know. A lot might depend on it.

"The bloodshed? All the times I took the highfolk down into the valleys to raid? The scores I killed? Losing my eye? Losing your mother? Yes, lamb. I remember. But it's like a song, a tale, something that happened to someone else. Now I see only the wonder in things, not the pain."

He bent to pick a fist-sized rock from the ground, holding it out for her to see.

"This stone has been through a lot. The gods forged it as a mountain, raising it high above the world. The rains and the trees worked at it, breaking it, tearing it from the mountainside where it belonged. Smashed and scarred it. Now here it sits, on its long journey to the river, the sea, and to dust. Yet it is peaceful. Here and now, the rock only dreams. It knows its fate, and accepts it. Fate pulls us in its current. We must learn to flow with it, not struggle against it. That way leads only to sorrow."

Father gently returned the stone to the ground.

"Now come. The sun will set soon, and I have lately grown very fond of an evening fire. I want to watch the flames before I sleep."

"Father, what about the gravel-eaters? They are coming, and Sylk — ."

"We will discuss that when I have looked again at the flames, lamb. They have much to say, and will send us an answer."

He maundered along the bluff, still smiling at everything and nothing.

"Right. Well. I hope so, Father." Thya adjusted the axe on her shoulder, and followed.

●

They camped beneath the bluethorns. Thya made a fire and boiled water in a small iron pot from her pack, adding roots and a few mushrooms to make forage stew. Father ate sparingly but with every sign of enjoyment, gazing up at the stars as if he'd never seen them before.

Thya watched a whisper of moths weave through the flames, one moment close to burning, the next safe. They had no choice. Determination and faith kept them going. Determination to brave the heat, faith in the light of the flames. She swallowed a mouthful of stew.

The gravel-eaters were coming.

But Father was well again.

Father turned his face towards her. The firelight cast it in shadow, the cave of his missing eye impossibly deep.

"We shouldn't call them gravel-eaters."

"Father?"

"They call themselves Kuhns, or Kuhnish, and they are from the Hinterlands, far to the west. They live on the shores of the great lakes there, and that's why some call them gravel-eaters, from the vast shingle beaches of that place." Father threw another branch on the fire, so that sparks swirled into the night and the moths changed their dance in response. "The Sylvati told me."

"So why do they come? The horsemen of the plains fought them, and were overwhelmed. The valley folk fight them, and still they come. We'll be next. What do they want?"

Father smiled. "That, the Sylvati didn't know. But the flames tell me they must be looking for something."

"Looking for what?"

"Something that would justify their desperate conquest. They do not settle, as we would, but push on, keep moving. And they suffer. They are superior soldiers, but that doesn't stop them dying in droves. No, they are moving fast, and with purpose. Searching. Perhaps they will find what they need soon and all will be well. And if they don't..."

"Then?"

"It won't be so bad, lamb. You'll see."

Father closed his eyes and breathed deep, relishing the night air.

Thya scented the rich sweetness of woodsmoke and dark earth. She lay on the grass and stretched her limbs until she felt comfortable. She wanted to find a trace of the peace she had felt beneath the amberfires, take it to sleep. Father's words had somehow been both unsettling and reassuring. Above her, tree rats scurried in the branches, tails swinging. She watched them run.

Someone was looking down at her.

Thya yelled at the same time as the figure in the branches, then she was rolling to grab her knives and on her feet, a blade in each hand. There was a snap above, and moments later a body struck the ground, the impact eliciting a heartfelt groan. Thya stepped forward, knife ready to thrust, but hesitated when the figure turned over and started to suck in a breath with great effort.

It was... a man, she thought. Tall for a man, with skin pale as mountain snow, except for the fierce red lines that marbled it, and his hair was as purple as the slipperberries in her pack. His clothes were made from patches of dark cloth stitched together, different hues of grey and black that were hard to focus on. But the shape was right. Almost certainly a man. Of sorts.

"Father?" she hissed, knife still held high. "Have you seen one of these before?"

Father hadn't moved. His attention remained focused on the fire and its attendant moths even now. His eyes flicked briefly across to the gasping stranger, then back to the flames.

"If I were to guess, I would say it's one of your Kuhnish gravel-eaters, lamb. From the paintings in Quiet Castle, they have such skin and hair."

"Brraw!" The man sat up, coughed, and then lay down again with his eyes closed. He was muttering something under his breath that Thya was certain must be some foreign curse.

She lunged, slamming the knife down in the soil next to his head. His eyes jerked open, then he was bolt upright, pale hands spread in front of him placatingly. His face was slender and odd, the nose tall and pointed, ears small, lips startlingly red, even against the scarlet veins that ran across his skin.

Thya couldn't stop looking at him.

He barked a few guttural words that she couldn't understand, then seemed to calm himself. "Wait." He spoke the high tongue deeply, like he was talking from the back of his throat. Then he was on his knees, patting the grass, searching.

Thya waved her blades. "If you're looking for a weapon, it won't help you. I'm certainly faster than you."

He lifted a small tangle of thin twisted metal from the ground, and to her astonishment hung it on his face. Two stems rested on his ears and another across his nose. The metal held two discs of clear ice in front of his eyes, which somehow seemed larger behind them. The flame-yellow pupils burned like two tiny suns.

The man smiled.

"You. You are... high-folk?" He touched his hair. "Black." His face. "Brown." He held his hand level with his chest, palm towards the ground. "Short."

She snarled. "Yeah! And what about it, ratface?"

He looked confused. "What is 'ratface'?"

Thya hesitated. "Never mind."

Father stood and stepped to the stranger, clapping one of his broad hands on the man's shoulder. He pointed to Thya.

"This is Thya. I am Brant." He placed his hand on the man's chest. "You?"

The man stood a little straighter. "I am Lammash." He put his hand above his eyes as if to shield it from the nonexistent sun while he gazed into the far distance. "Seeker."

"Kuhnish?"

The stranger grinned. "Yes!"

Thya swore. "What are you doing here?"

"Seeking."

"Seeking what?"

He pointed above him. "Trees."

"What about them?"

He walked to the nearest bluethorn and pretended to screw a finger into the bark. He looked at Thya expectantly.

"You want to kill the trees?" She frowned. "Or...."

"Sap," said Father. "He's searching for tree sap. But the bluethorns don't have much sap; not that can be drawn forth, anyway."

Lammash took a bluethorn leaf from the ground and offered it to Father. "Flame," he said.

"Bluethorn leaves don't burn so well, my friend. Just the branches."

"Not this. Not this. Flame. Flame tree." Lammash made his seeking face again, peering at the forest around him like he was acting out a fireside saga for children.

Thya felt a little shiver through her bones.

"This?" She pulled the cloth from her cloak and unfolded it on the ground. Teasing out an amberfire leaf she had collected the day before, she held it out triumphantly. "Flame tree?"

Lammash's eyes flared, and Thya felt a tiny tickle of delight. He reached out a trembling hand and took the leaf from her, holding it in the firelight to see it clearly.

He whispered something in his own language. Then, "Flame tree." He lifted his eye shields and wiped at the tears running down his face.

"He's crying," Thya whispered to Father. "I thought the gravel-eaters were great soldiers?"

"The man who's never shed a tear doesn't exist, lamb." Father looked at her carefully. "You camped among the amberfires. Did you try to tap them? Or notice anything special about them?"

"It never occurred to me. They aren't all that common, except up here. Even then."

"The Sylvati grow them in the Castle grounds. Great orchards of them."

"Why? Fruit? Timber?"

"No. The fruit is inedible, the wood too soft for building and too wet to burn."

"Sap, then."

"Must be. But why?"

They turned to look again at Lammash.

The stranger must have read the confusion in their faces, because he held out his hands once more, then began to scrabble around in the detritus of the forest floor, collecting twigs, branches, leaves and stems. Then he sat by the fire and took some string from his tunic pocket. In silence, without looking at them, he started tying the debris together.

"What's he doing?" whispered Thya. "Do you think he's..." she tapped her head, "...missing something?"

"No. He can't tell us, so he's showing us." Father sat down again, and she did the same. Thya studied the man while he worked. His hands moved quietly, long fingers plucking at the leaves and twigs. The firelight glazed his marbled skin and made him look even more otherworldly than he must in daylight. Thya could tell he wasn't a soldier — not enough muscle, by far — but his eyes behind those strange discs of unmelting ice were deep and thoughtful.

She wondered what that purple hair would feel like under her fingers.

Finally, Lammash held up the fruit of his labours. It was a doll of sorts, almost like the kind children would burn to ward off sprites. A person made of bark and twigs, long and thin. A long body with spindly arms and legs, the hands exaggerated and claw-like. The head was a triangular chip of bark, and Lammash had used the end of a firebrand to mark two large dark eyes on its face, and an angry slash of a mouth. A plait of twisted grass poked out at the bottom, a crude representation of a tail.

"A'grak," he said. Then he took a small wooden box from his pocket, and from the box a small needle and a tube of the clear ice. He carefully folded the amberleaf, slipped it into the tube, and then fastened the needle on the end to make some kind of weapon. He looked at them both, then grimly pushed the needle into the chest of the doll.

"A'grak," he repeated.

Thya looked at Father. He wasn't smiling anymore.

●

She walked the pathways of High Crag, past houses of cut stone covered with moss and plants so that they seemed little more than small hillocks. All was silent. No-one looked from the doorways to wonder at her return. No-one waved to her from the wooden platforms above. The settlement was deserted.

A faint roar turned her around. She slipped between two houses and followed the path down, to where it opened onto a small plateau. From behind an ironbark tree she peered at High Hall, her Father's home and the only wooden building in the town. Two guards stood at the doors, swords in hand, but even from a distance Thya could tell that they were not very interested in guarding, but instead trying to listen to what was happening inside.

A convocation.

Sylk. Or Crux. It had to be.

She considered going back to fetch Father and the grav — *Lammash* — right away, but decided against it. First she would need to know what was happening.

Thya strode towards the Hall. The guards would know her. She recognised them as Toln and Telm, twin brothers and distant cousins of hers. When they saw her they raised their swords, then lowered them awkwardly.

"Lady Thya!" They rapped their hands against their chests in deference.

"What's going on?"

Both of them stared into the middle distance, until Telm nudged Toln meaningfully. "Leadership contest, Lady Thya." Toln swallowed. "What with Lord Brant being... gone."

Thya patted her knife belt thoughtfully. "I see. Open the door. Quietly."

"Yes, Lady Thya," he whispered, then dragged one of the doors open just enough for her to slip through.

It seemed almost the entire population of High Crag had managed to squeeze into the Hall. No-one registered her presence as she sidled in and pressed herself against the wall. All eyes were on the raised dais and the empty stone chair that stood atop it. And the two siblings circling it, and each other. Sylk and Crux.

As ever, Sylk was the more animated of the two. She stalked the stage angrily, hair mussed, eyes narrowed, the rapiers on her belt slapping against her thighs. Crux plodded heavily, a benign smile on his face, his iron maul propped against Father's chair.

"*Of course* they will come!" Sylk cried, to much murmured support from the crowd. "They want to take the world for themselves. The valley-folk are weak. They will fail. But if we strike these gravel-eating bastards before they turn to the mountains, we can make sure they don't ever dare to come here. If we move first, the other highfolk will follow! They will look to us for leadership! We will show them what strength is."

Cheers, howls from the people. A few shaken heads and jeers.

"Sister, sister!" Crux raised his hands as if calming a child. "The gravel-eaters are not coming here. What do the mountains have that they would want? Stones? Trees? There are no gems, no gold buried under our hills. No good land to farm. We are few and far between. Why would they bother with us? It's a long way to come, and if they do, we will fight them here and they will lose ten soldiers for every one of us. They would try, and then they would go back to the valleys. We need do *nothing*. Don't excite yourself needlessly."

A large group of men in the crowd roared their approval. Crux was less popular than Sylk, but he had his share of support, and those who favoured him were influential amongst the highfolk. If this was a leadership contest, it could still turn ugly.

Thya began to move forward, threading her way through the crowd. Those who complained quickly held their tongues when they saw her. Slowly she approached the stage, and the hushed whispering she brought with her made her brother and sister falter in their arguing.

Crux grinned, pleased as ever to see her. Sylk scowled, contempt for her older, more timid sister plain on her face.

Thya raised her chin and stepped onto the dais, as boldly as she could. "Who called this contest?"

Crux reddened and turned away, but Sylk bared her teeth.

"It's time, sister. I see you return alone. Father is gone, and so it is time." She sneered. "Or do you think to stand yourself? Will you bring in the trees you love so much to vote for you?" Sylk loosened one of her swords from its sheath meaningfully. "Or did you have other challenges in mind?"

Thya opened her mouth but before she could speak there was a cry from the back of the Hall.

"I am not yet gone."

Father strolled into the room, Lammash at his side.

Some of the highfolk knelt or moved aside, others gaped or swore or grabbed each other.

"What in the hells is *that*?" shrieked Sylk, her finger stabbing at Lammash as if she could skewer him from across the Hall.

"His name is Lammash!" A hundred faces turned towards Thya. "He's Kuhnish. That is... a gravel-eater."

More shouting and jostling. An empty flagon sailed out of the crowd and bounced off Lammash's head.

"Cease this!" bellowed Father. "This man is not a soldier, he's a sage! Let him alone."

"Why have you brought a gravel-eater here, sister?" hissed Sylk. "You bring the enemy right to us!"

Father shook his head. "They are not our enemy, Sylk. The Kuhnish flee a great evil. Far to the west a threat has emerged, something terrible, and it has decimated their people. They fight back, to counter the threat and stop its spread. They have, in their way, defended us all. For a time. But they are losing. The Kuhnish have weapons that we can't imagine, and sorcerous abilities that have been forgotten across much of the world. But they need more. This man," and he placed a hand on Lammash's arm, "is a seeker, an explorer. He was sent by his masters to find trees of flame in the mountains, so that their sap could be collected. It is important for their fight, it seems. Those trees are amberfires, which grow high in the mountain passes. The Sylvati cultivate them, around the Castle. Thya and I have seen this."

Sylk sneered. "So they need it to build a weapon, or cast a spell. And then what? They will turn it on us, and complete their conquest. Why else would they attack the grasslanders, the valley folk? You are a fool, Father."

"They advance, yes. They fight. Some of them remained in their homeland, to stop the spread as long as they can. Others moved east, to find safe lands, to warn. But they were attacked. Persecuted. So they fought. Everywhere they met with resistance, they struck back hard. And so the situation worsened, as it always does with war."

"So what is your instruction, Father?" Crux looked uncomfortable. "Invite them here, to take the sap from the amberfires?" He frowned at Lammash. "How can we trust them?"

Thya spoke up. "We don't bring them here. There is no need. Taking this land would be hard for them, and us. Many would die, and they would be unable to hold it. And they can't set up a supply chain without doing that. Unless we do it for them."

Crux frowned. "Trade?"

"Yes. The Sylvati have amberfire plantations. The sap means little to us, but much to the Kuhnish. And in return the Kuhnish have knowledge that they hold lightly, but could change our lives for the better. These are the little imbalances that keep the world turning."

Father nodded. "I will return to the Sylvati to discuss tapping the trees. They will be happy to do so, I am sure."

"You would bargain and deal before we even attempt to fight? Before a blow is even struck? Where is the Father I respected? Where is the bloodthirsty bastard who led us with strength!" Sylk spat on the floor.

"You are not Father, Sylk," said Thya. "And you never will be."

Sylk drew her rapiers and sprang towards Thya in one smooth movement. Thya turned from the blow and slipped a knife from her belt as the sword point skewered the air by her face. She moved, circling round to where Crux stood, mouth open as he stared at his sisters. She balanced the knife in her hand, judged the distance between her and Sylk.

"Sylk! What are you doing? Thya is no part of this!" Crux stepped to his maul.

Thya moved, darting forward to get a better position, even as Sylk began to run, closing the distance fast. She threw the knife low, aiming for Sylk's leg, to slow her down before she got one of them killed. But Sylk was too skilful. With a flick of her rapier, she sent the blade spinning into the crowd.

Thya pulled another knife from her belt, but Sylk was there, one rapier blade sweeping so that Thya had to twist to block it, the other jabbing at her shoulder. The point sank deep to send lightning whipping down her arm. She cried out, stumbled back to fall into the great stone chair. Blood began to soak into her tunic.

Crux turned to Sylk, his maul raised. Then stopped.

There was silence in the Hall. Even Sylk was still, rapiers dipped, staring into the crowd.

Father stood with Thya's knife through his throat, the haft tight against his neck and the point peeking from the other side. His expression was placid, as if he hadn't even noticed.

Lammash looked from Thya to Father and back again, mouth slack.

"No," whispered Thya. "Please, no."

Father lifted a hand to the handle and gripped it tight, then slowly pulled it free. The blade was bloodless. Father cleared his throat quietly and smiled.

"Of all my children, Sylk, you are the one made most in my image."

The world erupted with people shouting in confusion and anger. Some reached for Father, others for Lammash. Some moved towards the dais. At the rear of the crowd a scuffle broke out. Thya felt faint.

Then Crux was above her, a foot on each arm of the chair, maul raised. "Guard!" he roared, and the men who had shouted their support for him during the debate moved as one, pushing through the throng to the stage, lifting Father and Lammash and placing the family together, then forming a circle around them.

Lammash hurried to Thya and pulled a small roll of silver cloth from somewhere in his tunic. Face grim, he began looping it around her shoulder to staunch the wound.

"Quiet!" Her brother's face was flushed, his eyes narrowed in anger.

Gradually the noise subsided. The Hall doors were opened and the few who had been injured in the confusion were dragged outside to be treated. Crux waited, to be sure that everyone was listening.

"Father. You live, but don't bleed. Why?"

"I owe you all an apology," he said to the gathering. "When I left here, my life was tainted. Those decades I led you were full of dark years. Needless death and bloodshed. Raids on the valley folk. Murder and rape, and worse. All for vanity. All for nothing. Some of you liked it. Too many, I realise now.

"I was a terrible man. The shadow fell on me, and I deserved it. Thya took me to the Sylvati to be cured, so I could lead again. But my life was rotted through. The Sylvati cured me by taking it away. I have not come back to lead. I have come to counsel."

He climbed the steps to the dais, walked across to the stone chair where Thya sat, still bleeding but not so much now, Lammash's hands busily binding her shoulder.

"And my counsel is this: trade will ensure the survival of us both. Fate has sent us an envoy, in the seeker Lammash. Not a warrior, but a scholar. A man of peace. And it has sent us Thya. Thya, who has no desire no lead, no love for glory. Just love for us all. Fate has brought us here. We must accept it."

Lammash finished wrapping the cloth and looked at her with a smile, oblivious to what Father was saying. "You will not die."

"Good," she said, before the world slipped away from her.

●

A fine rain fell, and Thya tilted her face to it. From atop the sentry stone she watched Lammash cross the scrubland to where the small party of Kuhnish waited. They were tall and pale, like him, formidable in their red lizardskin armour and iron helmets. But they didn't move with his grace. They did not glow with curiosity and compassion, like he did.

She shifted her weight, leaning on the bearded axe she had carried from Quiet Castle. Father's axe. She couldn't use it, but it looked impressive. In a rare moment of insight, Crux had noted that negotiations tended to go more smoothly if you were holding a big axe.

Father stepped to her side. "They will see the sense of trade, lamb. And when the deals are made, I will return to the Sylvati. We will give you a steady supply of amberfire sap. But I will not return. This world holds no place for me now."

"I'll miss you, Father."

"And I you." He touched her elbow gently. "You like him, lamb. I do too. He carries a peace within him that I never did."

Thya glanced at Father. "How can you tell?"

"I've only lost the one eye, lamb. The other works well enough."

"Sylk and Crux would disapprove."

"True. Sylk needs a distraction. You should send her west, to find out more about these... A'grak."

"And Crux?"

"Crux lacks imagination, but his heart is strong. Put him in charge of the supply chain. He would excel there. And I would be pleased to see him at Quiet Castle sometimes."

"I will."

"And if either of them objects, claim that such a partnership is strategic. To strengthen the bond between two cultures. The truth of it is for you and Lammash to forge."

She smiled. "Thank you, Father."

He shook his head. "I've done nothing. Your actions offer hope, lamb." He pointed to Lammash, deep in conversation with what must have been the most senior Kuhnish. "And his. For everybody."

Lammash turned and waved, beckoning for her to approach. It was time.

Thya embraced her father, then stepped from the stone. She left the axe where it was. Whatever fate held for her, she was sure she wouldn't be needing it.

Rob Francis's story "Tree and Flame" was originally published in the anthology Score: an SFF symphony *on Sunday, 24 February 2019. See books.metaphorosis.com*

About the author

Rob Francis (he/him) is a professor and writer based in Bedfordshire, England. By day he teaches university students ecology and environmental science, or researches the biodiversity of cities. In the evening and early hours of the morning he writes short fantasy and horror.

Rob's stories have appeared in magazines such as *The Arcanist, Apparition Lit, Metaphorosis, Cosmic Horror Monthly,* and *Weird Horror.* Rob has also contributed stories to several anthologies, including *DeadSteam* and *DeadSteam II* by Grimmer & Grimmer books, *Under the Full Moon's Light* by Owl Hollow Press, *Alternative War* by B Cubed Press, and *The Old Ways: Anthology of Ritual and Lore* by Eerie River Publishing. Rob lurks on Twitter @RAFurbaneco

Midnight's Second Station

Chloe Smith

Errant had studied the reports, had marveled, had thought he'd understood as much as anyone did — but his eyes still rejected their first sight of Midnight's trees.

He squinted down through the shuttle's window. A few hours before sunset, the passing terrain was a crumpled expanse of ashy browns and pinks, covered by the pale, irregular blooms of fungal webs and the fine, regular lines of insulated pipes. Interspersed among both of these patterns, though, was another: an array of shapes cut out of absolute darkness. As much as Errant tried to make out gradations of color or get a sense of form, he saw only absence, shapes like holes gnawed through to the realm of antimatter, even as the pilot angled their craft downward and the ground rose to meet them.

They landed beside a pipeline that had looked threadlike from the air but turned out to be at least half Errant's height. It stretched away behind them, over the horizon and towards the power station's reservoir, half a hemisphere away. Just ahead, it crossed a stripe of white paint and disappeared behind the matte silhouette. Errant leaned forward, trying to see where the human creation and alien thing met, and asked the shuttle's other passenger, "What does the line signify?"

Supervisor Heren, Positive Delta Energy's ranking onsite employee and one of the only survivors of the explosion, snorted. "Safety. Rules say we need a 10-meter perimeter. Of course, they also say to monitor trunk surface temperatures."

"And you can't do both?" Cygni Authority had hired Errant as a safety inspector because he could analyze complex systems, trace the impacts and risks of human interactions with strange new biomes. In practice, a lot of that meant pinpointing profit-driven cheats and paradoxes in corporate policies.

Heren's tone was all vinegar. "We can't do the work from a distance. The perimeter rule's just a way for PD to cover their —" She cut off, and her eyes, framed within the narrow opening of her lifted viewplate, flickered towards the pilot.

Her crewmate just leaned back from her controls with a sigh. Errant didn't think he'd heard her say more than five words together in the two days he'd been down this gravity well.

Heren shook herself. "It's fine. Like I said, we have to do it regularly. Those reports I *assume* you read through don't show any correlation between the explosions and us touching the trees."

"I remember." Errant heard the defensive note in his own voice and wanted to cringe. He should be used to wiping metaphorical spit off his face. Cygni was the only interplanetary body with enough leverage to force inspections, and maybe even change, on companies like Positive Delta Energy. When he'd started visiting sites, he'd thought workers would understand he was there to help, but experience had taught him that most assumed him to be an enemy, looking for "gotcha" moments. From their perspective, his report would most likely be toothless or, at worst, an excuse for Positive Delta to fire them all.

That won't happen. That's not what I'm here for! I'm going to help keep you safe, so no one else dies. He recognized the impulse to babble assurances, ignored it.

You always care too much, Stephen said, in his head. He forced the memory down, along with the messy emotions it unleashed. This was work. He could only do his best to understand what was really happening here on Midnight. He lowered his own viewplate and turned on his comm. "I'd like to get closer, then."

But he hesitated once his boots hit soil, staring up at the void-shape before them. Its edges shifted in the wind of Midnight's thin atmosphere, ragged bits of shadow lifting and settling back.

"Don't forget to change your settings to infrared." Heren's words were still clipped, but there was none of the animus he'd heard before. It made him wonder. Maybe she *didn't* hate him on principle.

Then he switched his settings and stopped thinking about anything else.

The landscape around them faded to crepuscular greys, but the tree's utter blackness resolved a fraction. Errant squinted. He could just make out the suggestion of features — leaves moving against each other and the curve of the trunk beneath them even clearer. He took a cautious step forward, boots over the perimeter line, and another step, and another, until he could put one hand on the trunk. He felt the barest suggestion of heat, transmitted through the fierce insulation of the tree's surface and the protection of his gloves.

"It's hard to makes sense of, isn't it?" Heren's question surprised him again.

"Yes." He still felt the need to defend himself. "I did my research, you know. I don't make it a habit to charge blindly into projects involving unique xenobiology, especially when the organisms generate this much power."

There was nothing like Midnight's trees anywhere else. A plant-analog that absorbed such a complete spectrum of light shouldn't be able to exist. And yet here were the trees, with their blacker-than-black leaves and inscrutable trunks, insulating and protecting the explosively charged cores within them.

"Everyone's overawed at the start," Heren said. "The first tappers who went in to drill the siphons and lay pipe, they couldn't get over how uncanny it all was. Soren said —" She stopped again. Soren was the name of the first station's supervisor. One of the dead.

Errant pulled back, torn between two investigatory desires. On his long transport ride to Midnight, he'd studied two documents to the point of near memorization. One was the anonymous message to Cygni's Planetary Resource

Operations department that had launched this inquiry. The other was Heren's post-accident debrief, a series of monosyllabic responses to the company rep's leading questions. He knew he'd have to re-interview her about what happened, to get more than the pain-filled silences between her answers. He'd been dreading it. And here she was giving him an opening — at the moment when he really needed to focus on the facts of the physical environment. He tried to approach both topics at once, and bungled it.

"There's no explanation of how they manage not to overheat, right? There weren't any clear indicators, before, when the heat control failed?"

Even faceless inside her helmet, he still *felt* the look she gave him. "No, Inspector. We don't have any certain way to predict the explosions. Don't you think, if we could have anticipated a blast —" Her gloves fisted at her sides.

Elda the pilot spoke up on the channel. "Time to inspect, Inspector."

Errant hesitated, tried to think of a way to walk back his words, and gave it up. "Right."

He returned to the tree, circled it with fingers trailing against the not-bark. The siphon jutted out at waist height on its far side, half-hidden in the artificial dimness. Once he remembered to toggle the infrared off, it seemed to float, a crisp shape even in the afternoon light, against the matte blackness. The tap line that stretched down the trunk from the spigot was just as distinct. It ran over the few meters of uneven ground between tree and pipe, a vein in the larger network.

"This tree's fallow right now." Heren had moved up beside him, and tapped the meter-transmitter on the spigot's crest. "PD rule is to give each tree a local-year off. The idea is to prevent the power gradient from becoming unsustainable."

"Do you know how they settled on these safety guidelines?" Errant asked.

"Do you?" her voice had returned to its low-grade caustic register. Errant wanted to follow up, to push her for thoughts on the soundness of company safety policies, but he was wary of another misstep. *Focus on the physical inspection, for now.*

He dropped to one knee and began digging his bots out of his pack. Humans were complicated messes of conflicting ideas, intentions, and understandings. Bots, by comparison, were much easier. And these bots were very straightforward. They just wanted to take readings and broadcast them to his terminal back at the power station. He set them in a row on the ground, where they unfolded jointed legs and began scurrying around.

"Those little guys might not make it long enough to give you your data," Heren said. "The fauna on this planet aren't very large, but they're tough and very fast. Their biome's got plenty of power, after all. They avoid anything our size, but they could destroy that little thing without even trying. Then there's the fungi. Spores grow on *everything.*"

"Fortunately, I've plenty of bots. We'll drop this many at every tree we visit," Errant told her.

Some of the bots went up the trunk, where their surfaces glittered against the abyssal black, and some began burrowing into the bare ground. Besides the dark trees, Midnight was shockingly short on anything that looked like plant life: no dark shrubs or grasses, no competing species that used the same light-absorbing technique to feed itself. The terrain's varied color came instead from the fungi. The report from the planet's initial survey team, before PD had staked a claim on Midnight, suggested that not just the giant webs, but an uncounted array of other spores infested the planet's soil.

Errant looked across the landscape, from one distant trunk to another. PD's pipe map showed even spokes stretched across half the small planet's surface, meeting in a point at the heartwood reservoir. He'd assumed that they'd chosen to tap only those trees that happened to stand isolated — but it looked as if the pipes' spacing followed the trees'. It was like they'd been laid out by some vanished park architect or farmer.

He was about to turn away, when sudden movement caught his eye. "What was that?"

"Elda?" Heren was staring at the point where the horizon had *shifted*, where the curve of a hillock humped up instead of sloping down. "Query Second Station. David's monitoring the pipeline grid right now. Anything go out of alignment?"

Fear rinsed through Errant's gut as he trailed Heren's hurried steps back to the shuttle, listened to Elda relaying the question.

Then there was quiet as they climbed back through the airlock — as Elda presumably listened to the response from the power station. Errant tried to lengthen his breaths and not think about the footage he'd seen in his research, images of the first station's wreckage, of the scorched remains of its inhabitants. *It just went*, Heren had said in her debrief. He wondered what Stephen would do if he died here, at the foot of an exploding tree on planet Midnight. *Probably cry into the shoulder of the next sucker.*

Elda said, "Right." She looked up as they reemerged into the shuttle's cockpit, nodded at Heren, who already had her faceplate open. Errant hurried to do the same and caught the tail end of a report.

" — a few centimeters' shift on Foxtrot 7 line, but it doesn't look like anything the struts can't adjust to." Errant recognized the voice of Heren's second-in-command David, tinny over the ship's cheap speakers. "We can move that line up in the check rotation, but I don't think it'll be a problem. Looks like that hill migration mostly missed the grid."

Heren sighed. "Copy. We'll move to the next tree." She had lost the urgency that propelled her towards the ship, and Elda looked as phlegmatic as ever. Errant imagined they could hear his heart trying to pound its way out through his breastbone. He tried his question again.

"What was that?" He hoped it wasn't something he'd read about and forgotten.

Heren gave him a look he couldn't read, all tight eyebrows and narrow eyes. Then she said, "The ground shifts here. Maybe better to say it swells and sinks. We have to keep a tight inspection and maintenance schedule all along the pipelines, to make sure there aren't interruptions to the flow."

That definitely hadn't been in the reports. Errant tried to fit this new and disturbing piece of information into what he knew. "It's not the tapping activity that causes the groundswells?"

Heren shrugged. "It happens near tapped trees, and near untapped ones. It's like everything else. There's no clear correlation. That's why..." She shrugged her next words away. "That's everything PD's tame scientists bothered to figure out."

Errant couldn't tell if she was challenging him to do better, or finding another way to tell him his efforts were useless. He looked away and out the window as the planet's surface fell away again. "This is a strange place."

"I'm not used to it," Heren said, "and I've been here longer than anyone still alive."

●

It took hours to drop the rest of the bots. At least there were no more sudden groundswells, although Errant turned a new, sharper eye to the folds and humps of earth around the trees they visited. Night had overtaken them and masked the trees' impenetrable shadows by the time they got back to the station, a warren of prefabbed bubbles half dug into the planet's surface. It was farther than the ruins of the first station from the reservoir full of molten heartwood. Whether that was a safe distance or not — well, he was supposed to find out, wasn't he? Errant shivered as he crowded into the airlock-shower with Heren and Elda.

The rinse in the airlock, Heren had told him when he first arrived, was because of the fungi. Even with it, interior walls and air filters clogged with wayward spores and required regular scrub-downs, no matter how tight they kept the seals. "It's a whole pain to delegate half my on-duty people to housework each shift," she'd said with a shrug. Errant had noticed the yeasty-metallic tang in the air when he'd first landed, but that same early survey had established with certainty that the biome's fungal inhabitants were nontoxic. Cygni would never have designated the planet open for companies to claim, if they hadn't.

Inside, Heren went to confer with her on-duty crew and Elda turned her back on him. Errant retreated to the bunk-sized closet that counted as visitor's quarters.

He tried not to take it personally. He was an outsider, a tenderfoot who couldn't really understand tapper life, even if he hadn't been from Cygni. Still, it was lonely.

It was too early to check the data streams from the bots. Without fully meaning to, he opened his terminal and pulled up Stephen's most recent message one more time. Familiarity, guilt, his better judgement, none of it stopped the toxic mixture of warmth and dread, longing and resentment, that flooded him at the sight of Stephen's hollow-cheeked, handsome face. He listened again to the latest earnest, full-hearted, meaningless apology.

I know I keep doing this. I know you have no reason to forgive me or want to see me again. I'm broken. I know it. The times when I'm with you are the only —

The door alert pinged. Errant snapped the file closed, feeling like he'd been caught indecent. He scrubbed at his cheeks, as if he could smooth some of their heat away, and then released the hatch. It was Heren.

She hesitated, as guilty-looking as he felt. It took a moment to unsnarl himself from his irrelevant emotions, to remind himself about exploding trees, and hazardous work conditions, and Heren's ambiguous responses. "Hello, Supervisor. Can I help you with anything?"

"Can I come in?" She actually glanced over her shoulder. Errant wondered if this was a proposition, thought about trying to head her off... *I'm sorry, ma'am, I'm currently in a decaying orbit around a relationship black hole named Stephen...* Then she looked back at him and killed that notion with her next words. "I'd like to make sure of your report."

She wasn't a big woman, out of her environment suit, but her intensity took up its own space between them. He hadn't pegged Heren for a company stooge, but she was in charge here, on an empty planet...

"Of course," he said slowly, and let her inside.

Heren didn't make him feel any better once the door was closed. She kept standing, arms stiff and fists clenched at her sides, the way they'd been out by the tree. There wasn't enough room to back away from her.

Finally, she said, "I sent the message to Cygni."

"Wha —" The implications of her razor-wire tension and furtive aspect grew evolved into new patterns. "Oh — that's — okay." Errant took a deep breath, bottled up the urge to begin bombarding her with questions. "Is there — is there anything you'd like to add to that initial report?"

The anonymous alert had been a simple text file, without much more than the bare outlines of PD's Midnight operation: The company had to build a second power station because the first had been destroyed in an accident; the operation had a shocking mortality rate, even for a frontier project.

Heren closed her eyes, then opened them. He *saw* her walls buckle, her expression melt into grief and pain. "You have to make them pay. Your report, whatever those little bots dig up from the fungi-soil and the trees, that work needs to damn Positive Delta. Burn them to ashes."

Errant swallowed against the urge to make some promise, to make her feel better. Meaningless words wouldn't wipe away her suffering. "If you believe the company is at fault, why did you send your tip anonymously? Testimony from an employee, especially one who," he hesitated, "who has direct experience of the dangers, would be the strongest voice in an argument for reckless endangerment."

"And give them an easy target?" Heren demanded. "They could have sent me on my way before you even got here. And how could I know they wouldn't buy whoever Cygni sent out? I had to see that you actually wanted to know what happened — and I'm still taking a risk. It's always easier to fault the workers. We must have made mistakes. We can't have followed all their oh-so-carefully-researched guidelines." She took a breath, settling herself. "PD could use whatever you write to axe me *and* my people. Then they'll say they've fixed the problem on the ground, and carry on making money with a new crop of desperate hires. There are *always* more desperate hires."

She wasn't wrong. Even Cygni's reach was limited. The report would need a convincing argument about the causes of the explosions here on Midnight, to have a hope of making the Positive Delta admit wrongdoing or change their policies.

"Alright," Errant said. "Let's start by going back over what happened before. I'm sorry; I know this will be painful, remembering —"

"Oh, don't worry." Heren's lips stretched in a not-smile. "I'm always remembering. You don't forget coming back from patrol to find a crater where your people should be."

●

At least Heren's testimony drove Stephen and his messages out of Errant's head. Over the next few days, as he watched the data streams from his bots and began playing with different analysis programs, he kept hearing her words again.

The explosion traveled down the line from the reservoir... They made me sift my people's bones from the 'valuable' wreckage so that they could start over.... Some of them we never found. The ground shifted and they were gone.

It wasn't just the horror of it though, the way her face went from pain to rage to uncanny stiffness and back again as she talked. He also kept thinking about the groundswells and earth movements. It was weird. The planetary survey hadn't found tectonic activity, and this movement was smaller-scale anyway — more like something caused by burrowing animals or the shifts of defrosting soil.

His feelings about the strangeness of the data set grew, the more bots he placed in the field, and the longer he looked at what they gathered. There was *a lot* of information: vast and complex chemical mixtures, spikes of electrical activity. He sat for hours in Second Station's mess, out of the way of most of the tappers, trying and failing to make sense of it.

He had closed his eyes in the face of the ever-growing bulk of information, and was rubbing the heels of his hands against his forehead, when his terminal bleated: the alert for an incoming message, coded personal. Errant swore.

"That bad?" Elda stood in the doorway. He blinked at her. He'd gotten so used to the tappers' stonewalling that he barely noticed when they skirted him. But it seemed silent Elda, of all people, softened at the sight of his self-pity.

"Not how I treat mail from home," she said with a shrug.

"Oh — no." He shook his head, reminded again how isolated they were here. "It's just — I can guess who it's from." No one else would ignore his out-of-system auto-response, would pretend he wasn't busy and working and just completely fed up....

Elda raised an eyebrow. His own words slipped over each other into her silence. "I don't — I don't know what to do. He's toxic, but he needs me, or he needs *somebody*, and every time I see him, it's like the reasonable part of my brain just fades away..." He forced himself to stop, mortified. "Sorry."

She just nodded. "Pheromones, probably."

"Huh?"

"There's no logic to it, but there's a feeling. Something you get from him. Or something he gets from you." She served herself a bowl of vat-protein and rehydrated starches, dug a spoon in, licked it. "I've been there. Sorry to hear it." She sat down with her back to him; conversation concluded.

Elda's presence gave him the discipline not to immediately open Stephen's message. Instead, he went back to staring at the data. Something she'd said niggled. *Pheromones....*

He added another factor to the program he'd been running, watched the patterns of analysis reshape themselves.

The idea was far-fetched, improbable. If he'd been working with a team, he would have been embarrassed to even suggest it — but once it had occurred to him, he couldn't let it go. Instead, the notion gained weight and substance as the bots' output kept accumulating.

●

He was almost ready to risk his theory to a recording when another tree blew up.

The shockwave ripped through the earth and shook the station habitat. Errant scrambled to his feet as people who'd been off-shift flooded into the common area, wide-eyed and still in pajamas. The four tappers monitoring the grid were still cupped within their screens, hands flying as they tried to assess the damage.

Heren pushed herself through the press of people and turned to the nearest monitor. "Which one?"

Her eyes didn't leave her screen. "Zed 12."

Everyone started speaking at once. "What —" "No —" "That can't be possi —"

"Alright, then!" Heren shouted them all down. "Cyn, are you sure?"

The monitor nodded. Errant's gut clenched. He didn't remember all the designations, but Zed was the spoke of the pipeline starburst that ran closest to the station.

Someone else was asking questions now. "Any fluctuations beforehand? No warnings?"

He needed to see what his own data showed. He pulled out his handheld, skimmed the feeds. Most bots were still transmitting. The feed from Zed 12 was gone, of course, but what the history of the last few minutes showed — it made his breath go tight. "Wait, Heren!"

Heren glared at him. "What is it? What's causing this?"

"I don't want to jump...." His voice faltered.

"You don't want to jump to conclusions, and what, maybe prevent anyone else from dying?" Heren scoffed. "I don't know why I tried so hard to get you here, if you are going to sit back and take *notes* while trees go up around us —"

"Wait." That was Heren's second, David, bristling and stepping into her space. "Heren, *you* called in Cygni? You risked all our jobs for some data-jockey's writeup?"

"I'd rather that than keep risking your lives!" Emotion broke in Heren's voice, and everyone started talking again.

She was right. He had to choose the clearest path towards safety, too, whatever everyone else thought. "Supervisor?"

Somehow, she heard him amid the hubbub. "Quiet, everyone! I said, quiet!"

Errant spoke into the grudging silence. "I'm not certain, but If I'm right — we should evacuate now."

"You can't wait until you file your report to get us fired —" someone began.

"No." He took a deep breath. "The reports PD sent me. They mentioned the way, when the first power station went up, that there was a series of earlier explosions."

Heren nodded, but David waved that point away, "Yes, but it wasn't like they triggered each other. We don't know why that is. The tap lines between the trees run in parallel. The blasts were isolated by both time and space.

"Yes, but the connection isn't about what happened; it's about what *didn't* happen." Errant looked around at the confused faces, and forged ahead. "All my monitoring points to a lot of activity throughout planet's soil, and I mean *a lot* — electrical and chemical movement in patterns I can barely see the edges of. It's at a level of complexity that suggests advanced processes, things like awareness, communicative movement.

"One thing I did see is that all that faded away from Zed 12, starting a few hours ago, and then dropped down to nothing just before it went up. There are a lot more fading spots right now, around a lot more trees."

A hailstorm of sharp-edged words. "Communications? How could you possibly —"

" — So your little bug bots just set it off —"

"Things were fine until —"

Errant held up his hands. "Please! Cygni sent me because of the explosions, but the problem is really something bigger: *They don't understand how this biome works*. Neither do I, fully, but it looks like there's something here, and it has decided that it's tired of firing warning shots."

There was silence as they all tried to make sense of that.

"You think," Heren said at last. "The trees are *sentient?*"

He knew how it sounded. "It's one possible explanation. There has to be some calculus at work, something driving that level of complex interaction."

"Why would they blow themselves up, then?"

"I don't *know!*" He hefted his handheld, trying to suggest the scope of what it held. "I could walk you through the pointers in my data, explain my bots' readings, but the patterns I'm seeing tell me we don't have time. We need to get out of here. It's not safe."

The pause after his words was full of shifting glances, until Heren asked another question.

"Can you prove it? I mean, really prove it, with hard evidence besides your voice and maybe ours —"

"If we believe you," David muttered.

" — And maybe ours?" she repeated. "Positive Delta's not going to let go of this place, this much energy, if they get any choice in the matter. Say we evacuate now; if PD doesn't accept your report, they'll be back with a new crew soon enough."

She was right. He didn't want her to be; he wanted her to get them all offworld right now. He admitted, "The strongest evidence would be to have some of my mobile collectors with their samples. Physical evidence is much harder to deny — but it's all out in the field. It's too much of a risk to re-collect all the bots."

Heren gave him that same folded-brow look, long and piercing.

Then she lifted her chin, turned to Elda, "You're going to pilot the big shuttle." To her second: "David, you're in charge on the flight out." Other questions started to fill the air, but she kept talking. "Inspector Errant. I'll ride with you, and before we leave, we're going to retrieve at least some of your little bots."

●

The flurry of evacuation passed Errant by. He didn't want to think about what was coming next, so he stared at the data feeds. Energy signatures kept fluctuating and spiking among the roots of every tree he had monitored. It could well be the cadence of a language he had no tools to translate — but even if that was true, there was much he still didn't understand, much that still didn't make sense.

He and Heren sat in the shuttle as the station's emergency evacuation craft lifted off. Heren spoke up on the common channel. "Good speed, people."

There was no response from the bigger ship. It rose and dwindled in the purple-grey sky, and Heren woke the shuttle's engines.

"Where to?"

He checked his handheld one more time. "Go west-southwest, along pipeline Bravo. It looks the most stable right now."

Even with the shuttle at its maximum velocity, the nearest tree was long minutes away. Heren, bent over the controls, spoke without looking at him. "So, will Positive Delta face sanctions for reckless endangerment after all this?"

Errant tried to visualize the shape of his completed report. "Probably not. If it's a new sentient species, Cygni will start assessing Midnight's planetary sovereignty before they rule on how PD was running this harvesting operation. Findings about worker treatment may get lost in the shuffle."

"The fuck you say." The yoke twitched under Heren's hands, and the entire shuttle shuddered. "PD kept us here when the trees started *exploding*. An *entire station* was destroyed. They don't get to treat that like nothing."

Errant cringed at the swooping flight, at his own helplessness. Memories of Stephen intruded suddenly — this trapped feeling was the same as the worst of their fights. He tried, as he had then, to find the words that would move the other person. "I know it's not what you want, but it does stymie them. What's at stake here, now, what we could prove, is bigger than showing what went wrong before. An intelligent species — that's a discovery that changes things. There'll be more research, different regulations on the planet, xenolinguists and biologists coming in to try to understand them — if we ever figure out how to approach them without triggering more tree explosions. Positive Delta certainly won't be able to harvest energy here any time soon; maybe not ever again."

Heren's hands steadied on the controls, but her voice didn't. "You know my crew all hate me now? I just put them out of a job. You've got to be desperate to take one like this, and they were good at it. They're just as good as Soren and Ida and the rest of my first crew. Just as disposable."

She paused, and Errant saw her throat work. "I could have taken the company's hush money. They offered a ride out of here, early retirement after the accident — but they shouldn't get to just keep going."

"They won't —" Errant tried to say, but his terminal interrupted him with a shrilled warning and, while the tone still jangled the air of the cockpit, an explosion bloomed, blue-white and closer than the horizon's line.

Errant clung to his seat. "Do you think we should —"

Heren angled the skimmer's nose down. "We're coming up on Bravo 1. Do your readings say we can land?"

●

They bounced down by a tree that looked just like the first he'd visited. Errant forced muscles knotted in anticipation of another eruption to unclench. Out of the shuttle, across the meaningless line, he dropped down at the foot of the tree. His fingers were clumsy in their gloves, but they managed to scoop up three of the bots, which had responded to his recall command and swum up out of the earth.

He hesitated, scanning the data feeds. There were a handful more bots converging on this point. He looked out across Midnight's lonely terrain. It looked like there were more of the pale fungal webs now, more uneven swells across the landscape. The sight shifted something in his mind, in the way his thoughts worried over the data.

Something you need, Elda had said. What did the trees need? What did they have? What — or who — had the agency here?

"Errant." Heren hadn't left the shuttle. "Can this tree *see* or feel us here?"

"It's not the trees," Errant said. The nearest bot was seconds away. "It's the mycelial network."

"What?"

"The mycelial network," he repeated, "the fungus system that connects the trees underground. It must somehow draw off the excess energy the trees absorb — that's how they don't overheat — and it diverts minerals from the soil to them. How else could those trees get enough nutrition, without other plant-equivalent growth around?" He shivered, thinking of the network beneath them, a mass of impulses, awareness, and intentions woven into the earth and through the roots of the dark tree, wicking away its overburden of energy and subtly directing its growth.

"How does that even —" Heren began.

Then the data feed from the incoming bot — from all his bots — disappeared. The earth beneath his feet shivered, even as he pushed himself up and into motion.

"Come on!" Heren shouted as he stumbled forward. The ground bucked and white filaments spread around him like starbursts.

He threw himself into the shuttle's airlock. The engine raced, but he felt no lift.

Heren swore. "Something's caught —"

Errant made it to his seat in the cockpit as she fought with the controls, finally rotating the thrusters and gunning them to rip free of the filaments that had seized the landing feet. The shuttle leapt from the ground.

The air around the ship turned to fire as the tree went up beneath them and the shockwave threatened to knock them out of the sky. Heren stayed glued to the controls, leaning forward as if she could will the ship faster. Gravity dug its claws into Errant's bones and flesh as the shuttle shot upwards on a steep trajectory.

"The whole grid is going," Errant didn't have the bot data anymore, but he could watch the feeds from Midnight's human-made structures disappear one by one. "That's the reservoir. That's the station." He imagined the web of explosions spreading across the planet's surface beneath, all that pent-up energy released in a great, cleansing rush.

The shuttle's engine strained, and then the cockpit's viewscreen turned black and bloomed with stars. Another few moments of pressure, and the gee forces of acceleration fell away, leaving them in the calm of freefall.

Errant had a new, uncomfortable thought.

"Can this ship do interplanetary distances?" His Cygni transport wouldn't be back in system for another five standard days.

Heren made a noncommittal noise. "Not officially. We'll make it to the relay station, though. That's where the escape craft was headed."

"Oh. Will you meet your crew there?" He saw her expression change, and regretted the words.

"Former crew." The bitterness was back in her tone. "They won't want to see me. Besides, I think I should stick with you for now. Go on record about everything I saw and did at Midnight's stations, the first one and the second." She gave him a smile that was almost convincing. "That has to count for something, right?"

"We'll make PD feel it," Errant promised her. "And your people will come around."

Heren shrugged. "Maybe. I did betray them."

"I'd hope they see that losing a job is the smaller evil in all this. Hell, if an alien fungus can blow up half its own planet to get rid of its human parasites —" He stopped, afraid that he might have been too flippant in the face of everything she'd been through, but she nodded.

"You have to excise the rotten bits, so they don't kill you."

"Huh." Errant let that idea settle into him for a long moment as they pushed farther into space. "Yes, you really do." Then, because they had some time before they reached the relay station, he pulled up his personal correspondence files on his handheld and deleted some messages that he didn't need respond to.

Chloe Smith's story "Midnight's Second Station" was originally published in Metaphorosis on Friday, 27 May 2022. See magazine.metaphorosis.com

About the author

Chloe Smith was born and raised in the San Francisco Bay Area, and she lived in Texas and Washington states, New York City, and rural France before coming back to California, where she has been a teacher for 12 years. All of that time has been spent in middle schools, which would have sounded like cruel and unusual punishment to her when she *was* a middle-schooler. It turns out, though, that teaching English and history to 14-year-olds is a strange and satisfying challenge. Chloe also has a masters' degree in library science, and may at some point retreat to the sanctum of the school library—if only so that she can kick its doors wider, to bring in more readers and help more students find themselves in fantastic worlds. Despite having a job that takes all the energy she can give it, she also writes science fiction and fantasy stories whenever she can make the time. Her short fiction has appeared in *Three-Lobed Burning Eye, Daily Science Fiction, Bourbon Penn*, and elsewhere. Her debut novella, *Virgin Land*, came out from Luna Press Publishing in 2023. You can find more about her work on her website, imaginaryresearch.wordpress.com, or follow her on Bluesky @chloehsmith

Pages Missing From the Diary of
Samuel Pepys, Esq.
David Berger

It is well-known that there are several pages missing from Samuel Pepys' famous diary: pages, moreover, that he himself seems to have removed before the various volumes were bound under his direction. Two years ago, the following excerpt was found at Christ's College Library inside a bible that was known to have been owned by Pepys. By a happy coincidence, the discoverer of the pages is Mr. John Rawlinson, a fellow of Cambridge College and a collateral descendant of the Rawlinson mentioned in this excerpt.

Two years have been taken up by exhaustive tests by paper experts, specialists in Pepys' handwriting and in the shorthand code Pepys used for his diary. After all this, the pages have been pronounced genuine!

Because St. Cuthbert's Church, Bedlington, has undergone extensive renovation since the time of Samuel Pepys, no trace of the carving mentioned has survived. There are no known tellings of the story in records of local folklore.

As to the subject matter, it is extremely curious. Pepys, while certainly a collector of anecdotes, some of which were spurious, was never known to be either gullible or to have written any fiction. And these facts lead us to the obvious question: Why were the pages removed? Perhaps we will never know, but a reasonable surmise is that publication of this material might have held Pepys open to a charge of falling for a well-told tale. However, the second portion of the manuscript, dealing with Pepys's own excursion to Bedlington, is even more remarkable.

There are, incidentally, in all the records of the Lost Colony of Roanoke, no records of a family named either Rawlinson or Kent or of a group of Lollard families.

We, the Fellows of Cambridge University, are publishing these missing pages for the first time, and have taken the liberty of naming them the Pepys-Rawlinson Fragment.

●

29th. In the morning to Westminster-hall to see to some business for my Lord. Afterwards to the house of Wm. Joyce for some coffee, this drink being newly popular in London. It was most excellent and refreshing. Back again to White-hall. At noon my father dined with me upon a good capon with beans and bacon. Afterwards I to Mrs. Alders. She being gone from the house, her maid Miss Clayon and I had a very nice bout, wherein I rattled her up somewhat in her bed. And so home to my own bed.

30th. Up by seven o'clock, and so to work. But before I went out, calling, as I have of late done, for my new boy's copybook, I found that he had not done his work. So I beat him, and then went to fetch my tarred starting rope to beat him further. This article I learned to use for punishments from visits to Navy vessels. But before I got it the boy was fled. I searched the cellars with a lantern. Could not find him. So by water to the Temple, to my cozen Roger; who, I perceive, is a deadly high man in the Parliament against the Court. He shewed me how they have computed that the King hath spended, or at least hath received, about four millions of money since he came in. This is most shocking.

This evening dined at The Crab with a gentleman, a Mr. Coombs, who has business with the Admiralty. Along came his daughter, a perfectly pretty, but quite short and somewhat stout, young lady that lately came up out of the country, particularly Berks. So all by coach to my house, where I found my wife, and we all drank, and then they went away. After, with my wife, to the King's house to see "The Queene at Rest," a new play of Mr. Codgehill, a new playwright. This is a comedy with a goodly part done by that pretty, witty Nel Gwyn. I have never seen such good performing. The Queen and Duchess of York were at the play and seemed to enjoy it with some degree of pleasure. Then we home, and to bed.

31ˢᵗ. Up betimes and at the office all that day, with scarcely a moment to dine. My work being done, that it can ever be done, I walked in the garden of White-h with Captn. Shrewton, where he began to tell me a strange story, which he got on a recent trip to Newcastle. Then there comes into the garden to me Mr. Sleak, that I once knew at Cambridge, and I took him in. Over at the Cheshire Cheese, I called for a surloyne of rost beefe, which we had for dinner. I must note that the Cheese, rebuilt since the Restoration and the Fire, has service as fine as in earlier years. Then we three to the Dolphin, and therewith a quart or two of sacke. Then Captn. Shrewton began us this discourse, which did please us much.

Dining one eve at the Nevyll Inne in Newcastle, a year ago, the Captn. met a prosperous farmer and Justice of the Peace, a Mr. Pepper, who was down in town to deliver a load of hay for the victualling y'rds. And after a shared bottle of Sack, Mr. Pepper told this amazing story, scarce to be believed, but well-known in the country 'round Bedlington, where Mr. Pepper hailed from. Mr. Pepper said these happenings ran their course during the time of his great-grandfather, who delighted in telling this story to whomever would have their ear bent.

According to Mr. Pepper, some eighty years or so before, during the reign of Her Majesty Elizabeth I, a great stone fell from the sky on a farm owned by a Mr. Bowey. The landing of the stone was accompanied by loud claps of thunder and a shaking of the earth around Bedlington. (An account of this stone falling, so says Mr. Pepper, was at one time in the Parish Record for Bedlington.) And when Mr. Bowey and one of his sonnes came out to the fields, they found a great pit in the earth several yards deep. And in the pit was a great hot stone, the size of two large ale butts.

At this time, it being late, after some more ale, and promises to meet next eve to continue this tale, went we home. My wife being still up, I played for her on my flageolette. She did sing finely. And thence to bed.

1st. Early to wait on my Lord. A day of much urgency. The Commissioners of Parliament met this day to make policy over the Fleet. There is some fear of the power of the seamen, who are highly incensed against them because of past wages due. By and by comes in my Lord. We went by water to the Tower. There we dined on a good chine of beef. And he and I did talke of many things in the Navy, one from another, in general, to see how many great things are committed to very ordinary men, as to parts and experience, to do. This doth not please us.

In the evening, to The Dolphin with much anticipation, to hear the story of the events at Bedlington from Mr. Pepper per Captn. Shrewton. We first had a peck of oysters, and then cuts from the tender part of a baron of Scots beef. And after some ale, the Captn. began, to our delight.

So after approaching the pit, Mr. Bowey and his sonne poked the great stone with shovels, and they were amazed. The stone easily broke apart into two halves. And even more dramatick there was within an object very like a brass church bell, but rounded on both ends, like what is called in geometrie a rounded cylinder. This was a thing of beauty and delight. But so hot that Mr. Rawlinson and his sonne could not touch it.

Mr. Bowey spread word by his sonne, and the next day came many townsfolk to stare at the thing. It was agreed by the local folk, by the suggestion of Rev. Rawlinson, the Vicar of St. Cuthbert's in Bedlington, that it should be took over to the churchyard. So, as the stone and the cylinder had cool'd, some local miners made a rigging. The two halves of the stone still warm to the touch was raised. They was placed on a dray, along with the cylinder, and pulled by four mighty horses to the yard. There the parts of the stone and the cylinder lay until nearly the whole parish was gathered to see this wonder. Even the Bishop came rushing over from Newcastle to see it. And there was talk of perhaps bringing the things, by stages, to London, perhaps by barge.

I remarked that should this have happened in our day, the Royal Society, which I have recently had the honour of being elected to, would have sought this thing out. But the Society had not yet been born at the time.

We then spoke briefly of some of the newest
revelations from the Royal Society. Including Robert Hooke's
Book of the Microscope. None of which seemed pertinent to
the business of Mr. Rawlinson's cylinder. I proposed a toast
to the Royal Society. Whereupon Captn. Shrewton
continued Mr. Pepper's tale.

With the arrival of the Bishop, whose name Mr. Pepper
could not recall, the news of the stones and the cylinder
was spread even wider. The Bishop sprinkled the cylinder
with holy water, and then departed. That evening, the
Parish Council decided to employ several miners to break
open the cylinder. The effort to begin the next day.

All the next morning, three miners from one of the
collieries bashed at the cylinder, that was hanging from a
set of blocks. Suddenly, there came a great cracking sound.
The watching crowd gave a great exclamation as the
cylinder broke open. Mr. Rawlinson led the townspeople in a
rousing cheer. Looking inside the lower part of the cylinder,
the miners saw a strange box. One of them reached in and
brought it out. He having no difficulty lifting it. The box was
a gleaming black. And it measured about a yard by eighteen
inch, by eighteen inch.

Having listened to this tale, herein shortened
considerably, for several hours, and having enlivened
ourselves with some good porter, I suddenly began to feel
sleepy. And so I gave my excuses to the company and
invited them to meet on to-morrow at Ye Olde Cheshire
Cheese at Fleet Street. Then Captn. Shrewton and I walked
into the City. We parted, he to go to the inne where he is
lodging, and I home to Seething Lane and to bed.

2nd. Early with a Mr. Heatherton about Sir Wm.
Penn's concerns in reference to Fleet victualing. The details
are many and will involve much time. Dined with Mr. H at
Mr. Crew's, on my favourite venison pasty. After dinner I
went to the Cheese, where I found Captn. Shrewton and Mr.
Sleak waiting for me, they having supped. The Cheese held
but few people, which I thought strange, wondering if there
was some event that night at Court.

And so, after a glass or two of a good sack, Captn. S
continued the story of the events at Bedlington. So, said

Captn. Shrewton, whose Christian name is Wm., like my Lord, the miners shewed the box, which was of black metal, to the Vicar, Mr. Rawlinson. The box seemed all of one piece. And no way was there to open it. One of the miners suggested that he try to breake open the box with his sledgehammer, but this was objected to by Mr. Bowey. He asserted that the box, being found on his land, was his property. Some words were said about this and some small monies were exchanged. A message was sent out, instead, to reach a certain Thom Woodcoke, from a nearby hamlet, which was a smithe of great skill. It took near an hour to fetch this Woodcoke with his tooles, who came only on a promise of a good payment.

Woodcoke used his smallest hammer and chisel to tap about, just below the rim of the box. And, suddenly, with the tiniest hissing sound, a split appeared, and it became apparent that the box had a lid. Gingerly, Woodcoke lifted the lid, and a great wonder was seen by those standing around him. Inside the box was a Babe! An ordinary Babe, naked, but wrapped in blankets. It appeared to be asleep, but after a moment the Child opened its eyes and gave out a lusty cry.

Mrs. Rawlinson, she the Vicar's wife, took up the little one in its blanket and cooed and cuddled it. Whereupon, the Child reached up and poked at the good woman's nose and broke it! This causing a flow of blood onto her face Mrs. Rawlinson shrieked, and her husband took the Child from her. He held it at arm's length and shook it angrily.

The Babe gave another cry and shrugged the Vicar's hands away with a strong shake of its shoulders. This caused Mr. Rawlinson to let go. But instead of falling to the ground and hurting itself, the Child, wonder of wonders, floated in the middle of the air. It slowly rotated itself around, and flew into the air: first up perhaps thirty feet. And then it flew away to the steps of the church ab't one hundred feet away.

The Vicar and his wife, followed by the parishioners, ran over to where the Babe had come down. Mrs. Rawlinson, goodwife if there ever be such, lifted it up again. The Babe then began first to cry and then to coo. She wrapped it up again in its blanket and held it against her breast. And declared that she would raise the Child as her own. At the time, all could see that around the Babe's neck on a wire was a large and intricate amulet, covering almost half its chest.

There is a carving on the church wall that shows the Child leaping into the air, but some say this is an old carving of an angel in flight. Some say it is a demon.

Afterwards, the great rock was pounded up by the miners and the residuum dumped in a pit. The cylinder was brought into the church, but it was melted down for cannon during the Civil War. And the box and robes of the Babe were kept for many years in St. Cuthbert's. Until one night thieves broke in the Church and stole the box along with a pair of silver candlesticks. (These were candlesticks that the Vicar, not Mr. Rawlinson but one of his successors, had saved from looting by some troopers calling themselves Soldiers of His Majesty but 'twere mere looters.) The thieves had also started a fire to burn down the Church. But it had been put out. But not before the Parish Record and many old documents of the Parish and the Church had been consumed as well as the vestry.

"And that's the end of this tale," said Mr. Captn. Shrewton loudly. He had become red in his face with the ale he had drunk. Mr. Sleak and I questioned him closely about this marvelous event. What color was the great stone? How heavy the cylinder, &c. But the Captn. recalled to us that this was a story he had got from Mr. Pepper, who had got it from his grandsire, who had got it from his father. Who it was by no means clear had been a witness. And anyway it was a tale of Mr. Rawlinson and his wife, not of Mr. Pepper's family. I thought this remark to be a naif one. And one which, with the missing rock, and the cylinder, and the Parish Record also missing, cast a pale light on the tale. This might have been a fanciful story gotten up to explain the carving on the church like many monsters on our old cathedrals from which many olde tales have arisen.

So home by carriage, and I with my head full of thoughts of Mr. Rawlinson's great stone, and the cylinder, the box and the Babe. I ate a bit of bread and cheese. And so to bed.

3rd. Up early but then lay pretty long in bed gaining pleasure with my wife, and then to Westminster, where the Commons is sitting. Here I met with various mediocre folk, who did give me petitions for preferment. Thence to ye Cheshire Cheese, but I found myself not willing to speak to any of my friends there. Having Capn. Shrewton's tale much on my mind. Then to finish my letter for Sir W. Batten, himself Surveyor of the Navy, on errors in the methode of procurement of stores for the Navy and rumors of peculation.

It being three o'clock ere I had done, when I come to Sir W. Batten, he was already in a huffe, which I made light of. To my distress, he found displeasure with my letter. But he signed it, though he would not go to my Lord Chancellor's. So I, myself, presented it to My Lord's Secretary. The rest of the day, at White Hall, I hoped to hear further news about the letter, but nothing, and then home to supper, and they we sat together very lovingly, and then we to bed. Even so, I was much disturbed in my sleepe.

4th. Up early and by carriage to White Hall, and there I worked again my letter criticizing the whole business of Navie procurement. That eve, I came to Sir W. Batten to further discuss the letter, though he now liked the letter well. I down to the Tower Wharf, and there got a sculler, and to White Hall, and so I delivered it to Sir W. Coventry, in the cabinet, where I leave it to its fortune. And I by water home again, and to my chamber, to even my Journall. And then comes Captain Cocke to me, and he and I drink a measure of sack and have a great deal of melancholy discourse of the times, giving all over for gone, though now the Parliament will soon finish the Navy Bill for money. He being gone, I again to my Journall and finished it, and so to supper and to bed.

4th. Up and to the W-Hall and amazed to discover preparation of a coach and four to be put at my disposal. Because of my letter, I am dispatched to Newcastle there to uncover the state of the Navy procurement. It is now being said that peculation and theft have wrecked the condition of foodstuffs and shipbuilding there. At noon to the Three Tuns, where D. Gawden did feast us all with a chine of beef and other good things, and an infinite dish of fowl. Thence to W-H. The coach being ready, it took me home for my kit, whereupon I am off to Newcastle for the inspection. The coach departed from my home at 6 in the evening with the weather being on a sudden set in to be very cold.

7th. Arrived at New Castle this morning at 8. We arrived there just as it commenced to rain hard, and the horses to fail, which was our great care to prevent. Thus ending a cold, hard journey. To sum, nothing but cold and wet and some of the most miserable innes I haf ever slept in. As we proceeded north, the food became worse and the wenches uglier, with the weather. Entering the Yard, the coach brought me to the offices of Sir Donald Dulking, Adm. of the Yard. I then dismissed the coach and instructed the driver to return to L, expecting to journey home by packet boat.

I was soon informed that the Adm. was onboard one of the ships, inspecting a cargo consignment. (Strange actions for an Admiral, I think.) I was exhausted and was urged by the Adm's adjutant to partake of the regular Navy (not Naval officers') mess. I found the provender to be disgusting, but I was assured by my escort, a young Midshipman named Davis, that the Admiral himself regularly partakes of the regular mess. I left the table wholly unsatisfied. A half-bottle of inferior claret did not mollify me.

After a long wait, I finally met with Sir Don'ld Dulking, Rear Adm. We discussed the issue and he agreed there may be some corruption present, but it is of a trivial nature. He invited me to tour the Yard and even board some of the ships, which apparently is his wont. But I preferred to review the accountables. After some hesitation, I made the acquaintance of three of the Yard's bockkeepers, non-Naval men. These three affected a very casual demeanor which, in ordinary, would have offended me greatly. But in their stances, along with the behavior of the Adm., I have become suspicious.

That eve, after finishing the first few hours' work with the bookkeepers, I expected to be formally received by Admiral Dulking or one of his senior staff. But no such event took place, which, again, I took ill. Young Midshipman Davis approached me rather timidly and said that he had been instructed that I was to be housed at the Senior Officer's Quarters. I asked if there were a good inn nearby. And the lad said there was, just outside the Yard gate. It was called the Old Charles. We walked over there just as it began to rain hard. We sat and talked about the Yard. Then there came to us an aged sea captain, a summat foolish man named Captain Seabright. And he and I entered into a great but humourous dispute concerning whether the Navy were better now than during the Protectorate. This discourse took us much time, till it was time to go to bed, but we being merry, we bade the Midshipman goodnight, and continued to drink.

As a stab in the dark, I asked Cap'n Seabright if he had ever heard of Captain Shrewton. He said he had, but had not seen him for several years. I then asked of him if he knew of a Mr. Pepper, a farmer from the vicinitee of Bedlington. To my surprise, he told me that Mr. Pepper is a cozen of his on his mother's side. And he had just come in to New Castle. After a quart or two of wine, the good Cap'n agreed to bring Mr Pepper for breakfast in the morning so I might speak to him, and I to bed.

8th. I had a strange dream and having kicked my night clothes off, I got very cold, and in the morning had a good deal of pain. This and the rain made me very melancholy. But when I went down for breakfast, I found Cn Seabright at table with the gentleman Mr. Pepper. This was the manne who first recounted the tale of the Babe to Cn Shrewton (who repeated the tale to me and my friends); he being exactly the manner of stout and redd-faced farmer you might think of. The pain that I had got last night by cold had not yet gone, and troubled me at the time. Captain S, Mr. Pepper and I enjoyed a breakfast of a fresh halibut and small beere.

In short, Mr. Pepper confirmed to me the main of the story of the Babe of Bedlington, as he had heard it from his grandsire. There were still, he said, some remnants of the storie, including the pitt when the Greate Stone had been broken up. He told me that he would be returning to Bedlington on the morrow, and if I cared to join him, the journey would be but 16 mile. I could rest over at his farme which, he swore was large and cozy. I agreed and we will depart from this inne tomorrow afternoon, after I hope to have concluded the Navy business here in Newc'le.

So up and to the Navy Yarde and about business. I examined people as to what they could swear concerning the vittles, cordage, Etc., that is being supplied. And I can only, when joined with the worke of the Acc'ts, conclude that the whole is become the business of cheating rogues and peculating knaves. For part of my examinations, Admiral Dulking sat with me. I conceive that he was uncomfortable as some of the blame for this criminal behavior must fall towards him for which we hope he can give explanation. Thence after the examination, it being too soon to go to dinner, I walked up and down the Yarde, not helping but to notice what I felt to be an overall melancholie.

At last got back to the inne and dined well on another halibut, which was very welle prepared with a mustard sauce. I being cold to my bones, to bed presently, and had a very bad night of it.

9th Sabbath. I slept till 7 o'clock, it raining mighty hard. I know not what will become of the corn harvest this year, as we have had but four fair days this month.

After breakfasting alone on some cold oysters, soup and a half of claret, I was hailed from my table by a voice from the inne y'rd, it being Mr. Pepper. I joined him on his handsome hay cart and greatly enjoyed the trip to Bedlington, as the rain stopped almost as we set out.

Arriving in Bedlington, Mr. Pepper invited me to his home where we sat and talked, and drank, and ate an hour or so. He gave me directions away to the Church of St. Cuthbert's and lent me a horse. He begged me to ride it to Newcastle and leave it at the stables in the Navy Yarde whence he would retrieve it the next week. I replied that I would and parted with Mr. Pepper, resolving to myself that I would do him some preferment when I returned to Newcastle. It took but a half hour to reach the Church, whereupon I searched about for the vicar. And finally, having encountered some ancient natural, I was led to a small building, barely more than a shadde, behind the Church proper.

This lowly place was the vicarage, and to my delight, the current holder of the parsonage, Rev. Mr. Johnson, was at home. He received me cordially and delighted me with a second breakfast. It so turned out that Mr. Johnson is a close friend of my cozen, Angier, at Cambridge and knew, slightly, my brother John. Mr. Johnson being a bachelor, I was introduced to his only housemate, a terrier dog that closely resembles a lamb, but Mr. Johnson assured me, is of both a gentle and powerful nature. I learnt that the reason for his modest way of living was that the former vestry had been burnt by the Protector's men during the Civil War and that it had never been rebuilt. He himself, he declared, was of simple taste and required nothing more although he said the shadde doth need a new roof. This pleased me much, and I resolved upon return to London to speak of this gentleman and perhaps obtain funds for a more adequate home for him. I reminded that the Member of Parliament for Morpeth, Mr. Dowling, is an old associate and I could no doubt catch his ear in this matter.

I begg'd of Mr Johnson if he knew anything of the story of the Childe or Babe of Bedlington. And at that he seemed summat uneasy. I pressed him as far as decency allowed, and, at fin, he took me to see the carving on the wall of the church of which I had heard. This effigy is on the northwest wall of the church. While Captain Shrewton recounted that it demonstrates the Child in the air, this is not clear. Mr. Johnson said that the image was damaged by the same Soldiers who had stole the box with the Babe's clothes. They had hammered at the statue, hurting it much on grounds it were idolatrous.

Then Mr. Johnson showed me the pit where the residuum from the great rock was put. There was not much to see but a dark set of rock, slightly below the level of the ground. (I took up a small piece to present to the Royal Society.) I then asked the Rev. if he knew anything more of the Babe itself and of the Rawlinson family. He said to me that the subject was so long ago, it was still of great pain to the village and people did not discuss it. I took this as a sign that he would speak no more of this and so I bid him farewell.

I was ready to take my leave of Bedlington. However, after I left the vestry for my horse, the same ancient natural I had seen before accosted me, seizing me by the arm. He asked me, if I wished, if it pleased me, to see something marvelous concerning the Babe of Bedlington as he called the Child. He said he had listen'd at the doorway to the vestry and overheard some of the words I had had with Rev. Johns'n. I did not desire to traffick with this creature, but he importuned me several times. Half speaking, half mumbling. I was almost ready to str:ke this lout, but his constant talk of the Babe halted me. He signed to me that he wished to drink and pointed to an establishment a few furlongs away. We walked there together, but I bade him walk behind me as his stench was very great. He also carried on his shoulder a sack which seemed quite heavy. I went into the inn and brought out for him a pot of small beere, which he drank in one swallow. He signaled for more, which I brought him. Soon, he talked a great while about my going down with him to Newminster Abbey, which were, he said, six or seven mile from Bedlington. I was anxious to start back to Newcastle and from there back to London, but each time the ancient mentioned the Babe, I felt my stummick stir. And he promised if I went with him, he would shew me something that would astonish me.

So, a certain madness took over me, and we set off for Newminster Abbey, the ancient walking and I riding. He told me his name was Raulph Kent, and he claimed to be near one hundred years old. I doubted this as it would make him much the oldest man in Britain. But I noticed that the beere he had consumed made his discourse more reasonable. I asked him how he came to know the story of the Babe of Bedlington. He said to me that now he and I had left the towne, he would tell me his story. Most remarkably he claimed to be Raulph Rawlinson, the sonne of the Reverend Rawlinson, he who adopted the Babe, which I scarcely believed. And I thought he might be a rogue who was playing a trick on me to get money of me. But I said to him that I thought it wonderful that he had lived so long. I begged him to recount the story of the Babe after his father and mother took the Childe to be their own.

As we proceeded on this short journey, which he promised me would be but an hour but which turned out to be nearer two, this was his story. He had no hesitation nor was he a man of few words. And despite his gruffness and foul appearance, he spoke in a kindly and gentle manner with even some education. He told me that he was only in the towne fortnightly to see Rev. Johnson who gave provisions to him. He had just left the vestry when he first saw me. Then he begun telling me the *Tale of the Babe*, as I have called his story.

As Raulph Rawlinson told me, soon after the Reverend and his wife declared at the churchyard that they would adopt the Babe as their own, within a very few days, they were visited by one Rev. Exton, a dependent of Lord Tankerville. Mr. Exton told them they must either give the Babe up to him or leave the parish forthwith and that he, Rev. Exton, would take over the parish. Raulph's father declared it was his Christian duty to shelter the Babe. And so after all things were ready, with much sadness, his father and mother, he, his sister Elspeth, and the Babe, who they named Willielmus, left the Living of Bedlington and moved to Morpeth where they rented a farm with a dairy herd of Chillingham cattle. Raulph, who was being educated in a school in Bedlington, with hopes of attending university some day, and enter the ministry, saw his education end suddenly.

Life was very hard for the family as their neighbors did shun them and few would buy from them, either milk or cheese. However, they were soon secretly aided by a community of five Lollard families in Morpeth. Eventually, they joined this community, and Rev. Rawlinson became the community's leader. The families soon decided that they would all go to the Roanoke colony due to continued persecution of the Lollards.

It was decided by the Rev. Rawlinson that it would not be possible for them to take the Babe, Willielmus, with them to the New World. The Babe was too well known and 'twould be hard to travel with him.

Raulph said that the Lollards, including his father, decided that if the Babe was on a shippe it would probably mean mutinee. So it was sadly decided that Raulph, who was the oldest son and was twenty years of age, would stay on with the Babe, who was then ten years old. Also, Rev. Rawlinson decided to change the family name to Kent, whence the Rawlinsons had originally come from during the time of King Henry VIII.

Raulph said he felt that the events had weakened his father's and mother's mind, and he still could not countenance what they had done. After they departed with the five Lollard families, in great haste, George had one letter of them from Barbados. In this letter, which he shewed me, it promised that they would find a way to bring him and Willielmus to Roanoke to join them. And then nothing. He presumed that they had been lost when the inhabitants of the colony had been attacked by the red Indians. After this, the man was quiet for a while.

We finally reached the Abbey, it being very dark in the woods there. We walked thence amongst the great trees that had grown up in the ruins of the Abbey, and in and out of the fallen buildings themselves. And there Raulph Rawlinson finished for me the *Tale of the Babe*. That he being but twenty years of age was left behind with Willielmus, who was but ten but who had the strength of a grown man and more.

And, he could fly like a bird, Raulph whispered to me. So, he told me, when his brother was frightened, he would leap into the air and fly to the top of any tree nearby. I felt amazed by this but I remembered how the Babe had flown from Rev. Rawlinson's hands to the nearby church steps. T'was a moment before I could speak and then I gave out to Raulph Rawlinson to continue.

The farm, he said, did not thrive. Raulph had no gift for dairying and a few years later, he, even with the help of his brother, could no longer sustain the herd and they quit the rental of the animals and the farm. So he and Willielmus became vagabonds, never straying too far from Morpeth and Bedlington. Willielmus's strength let them be able to maintain themselves. In the spring and summer and in the autumn, they worked on the farms. However, in winter without a house, they lived in the Abbey but in a very poor situation, so that they nearly froze or starved.

Towards the end of one colde season, Raulph went alone to Bedlington and begged some food of the new rector, who gave him some of the new vegetable called the potato, which sustained them till the spring. But labour was plentiful and despite Willielmus's strength, they could get no work. One day the two went to Morpeth for the market, perhaps to pick up some work carting, and there was a local faire with a wrestling shew. There was a champion named Wild Bull Boggy. And there were a prize of £1 for any man who could remain in the ring with him for but five minutes. £1 was more than Raulph and Willielmus could earn in a fortnight.

So, Willielmus urged Raulph to let him fight although he was but sixteen. And he, Raulph, was afraid not that his brother would be hurt or even lose, but that with his strength, something would needs happen, and his identity as the Babe would be revealed. But Willielmus, whom Raulph called Willie, wanted much to fight. And so he went to the ring. Wild Bull, Raulph said, was a truly enormous manne, weighing perhaps twenty stone and above six and a half feet tall. Some said he were the tallest manne in Britain.

After some ado, Willielmus climbed into the ring with this gigantic manne. And, Raulph said, his brother beat the other in less than a minute by the glass. But then, came calamity! After Willielmus threw the giant down and the manne could not rise, Willielmus lifted Wild Bull above his head in triumph and shewed him to the crowd. But then, Boggy twisted in Willielmus's arms and punch'd him in the face. And before Willielmus did realize what he did, he smash'd Wild Bull Boggy to the ring, killing him. And then, in great fear, the lad (nought but sixteen, recall) leaped into the air and flew off!

There were, so Raulph described, screams and panick. And someone yelled out that that was the Babe, the Bedlington Babe, grown to be a man. Without waiting to see what would happen, Raulph said that he fled back to the Abbey and hid in a dry well in one of the cellars. He stayed there hidden through the day, all through the night and the next day. Not till the next night did he venture out. Past midnight he heard a crashing sound nearby. Raulph said it is not imaginable how frightened he was as he thought wildly that some from Morpeth were still out for him. But blessed be God, he said, it was Willielmus crashing down from the skye. Then his brother came and spoke to him and said he had been far away in London. That in but a day he had flew from Morpeth to London and back to Morpeth. And Raulph said he could not close his mouth for astonishment and in fear.

Willielmus then said to Raulph that he was determined to fly first to Ireland and then to Iceland, to Greenland and thence to the New World to find their parents. (Raulph added that he had given Willielmus as much education as he could including in geographie.) He had experienced and learnt much flying to London and back. And that he thought he would leave when the sun rose. Raulph told him this was madness. But Willielmus said no, that he must go.

He then spoke to Raulph of the mother's amulet that had been found on him when he was discovered. The amulet, Raulph told me, was about the size of a grown man's hand. Large as it was, Mrs. Rawlinson had insisted that Willielmus wear it round his necke. But when the Babe was but three years of age, to the amazement of all, he had insisted in his baby voice that his mother should wear it always.

Raulph said that once his mother put the amulet on, Willielemus could always sense where she was. And even across the sea, he always had a vague feeling of her whereabouts. And as he was grown older, that feeling had grown. But until he had taken actual flight, he had no notion to seek out their mother and, hopefully, their father and sister.

Willielmus told Raulph that he was determined to go at dawn. Raulph packed some food for him, of what they had. And, true to his word, after much sobbing and embracing and brotherly kissing, Willielmus leaped into the skie and was gone. Raulph never heard from him or the rest of the family.

In the many, many years that passed, Raulph told me he made a life for himself, as before, wandering about and working and living in the Abbey. About ten years after Willielmus flew off, he approached the Rector of St. Cuthbert's, the man who had replaced his father and begged the man for alms. Rev. Exton had become very old, but still hale. He told Raulph that he felt the Church had done poorly with his family. And that he was willing to give him a weekly pittance. And that was continued for several rectors to this day, including the Reverend Johnson. This explained to me why the Reverend had seemed so unwilling to speak to me.

Then Raulph opened an olde wooden boxe and shewed me what he had brought me to see. It seemed nothing but a piece of cloth perhaps an ell squared in size. It were, he said, one of the wrappings that Willielmus was covered in when he were found. And what a piece of cloth it proofed to be! It was of a dull blue and seemed to be some kind of blanket or robe, but small, for a child. Raulph took it up and told me to try to tear it a-pieces. So strong it was, I could not do it. He said it neither burnt nor did it fade or take dirt. I begged him to let me take it back to London to shew to the Royal Society, but he refused, even after I offer'd him a goodly sum. He said he wished to be buried with this cloth as his shroud.

Soon after that, I left Raulph Rawlinson. I gave him a sum of money to help him. And he thanked me. I arrived quickly back in Bedlington, early enough to set out for and reach Newcastle in time for a fine dinner of a capon and some small fish and a bottle of sack. In the morning into London on the mail packet.

12th. At home after a terrible passage, New Castle to London. The weather were foule and I sickened almost as soon as we left the Tyne. And the young cap'n being inexperienced on this run. He brought us perilous close to the Godwin Sands which he laughingly called the Eater of Shippes. Greeted at 6 in the evening at the door by my sweetling, I being more dead than alive. She fed me on some good brothe, which I managed to hold down. She importuned me to tell her some of my journie, which I did. We dined late on some goode beef and claret. And so to bed.

David Berger's story "Pages Missing From the Diary of Samuel Pepys, Esq." was originally published in Metaphorosis on Friday, 18 September 2020. See magazine.metaphorosis.com

About the author

David is an old Brooklyn Lefty, living in Manhattan with his wife of 30 years: the finest jazz singer in NYC. He's a father and a grandfather. He's been a caseworker, construction worker, letter carrier, teacher, proofreader and union organizer. David loves life, his wife, and the world. He hopes to help us all escape destruction.

Wytchen Wood

Lori Torone

A decade of shavings covered the floor of Lewys's carpentry shop. He didn't bother sweeping any more, although he probably should — wood without magic produces a drab dust that desiccates the throat, shrivels the lungs. He coughed and gulped from his flask, stepping back from his work. Carving the finishing scrollwork on yet another hope chest for the latest bride-to-be in town did nothing to fill his own hollowness.

"Wait for me," she had whispered in the wytchen grove so many years ago, her berry-scented breath caressing his cheek, "I will come back to you." She'd taken magic with her, in the wytchen dust glinting in her sunlit hair as she waved goodbye from the newly-carved wagon. She took his heart as well, but left hope in its place.

Over the years, hope had drained into loneliness, empty and aching, present in the sound of his saw's jagged edge, the taste of his own cough-strained, stale breath, the starkness of his bedroom above the shop. No chance of a bride now, for him, in this small town where he had spurned all coy glances sent his way, waiting for his true love to return.

He wished he hadn't waited.

Still coughing, Lewys threw open the window shutters. He gulped fresh air. Delighted cries of children entered with the breeze.

A pageant wagon creaked into the town square outside his shop, horseless, shedding curls of magic onto the cobblestones from its warped wytchen beams. Children dropped coins into a box attached to the wagon's carriage and scrambled for seats. Eyes widening in shock, Lewys unconsciously dug his fingernails into the windowsill. The wagon's wood was peeling, its stage floor crooked, but it was still the same one. The only one.

As the threadbare curtain opened, more wood peels and sparkling dust showered the stage from the covered wagon's rafters, a natural emission of the enchanted wood, once cut and carved. A princess puppet slumped against a painted forest backdrop. She wore a gown the deep blush of sunset, the falling wytchen dust creating a net of crystals in her golden hair. With the clack of wooden joints, she began a light, graceful dance. A troll, lumbering in from stage right, tore a gasp from the children.

Lewys saw what the audience did not know to look for: The shadow of the puppet master's hands weaving along the stage floor. These puppets had no strings. The wytchen wood itself conjured the play, the magic within the wagon and the carved puppets animating them, their movements directed from above by the puppet master's hands.

After the princess outsmarted the troll, she befriended a dragon, its velvet tongue unfurling like a panting dog. Adults and children alike cheered when she saved a village from a witch.

The curtain closed; the crowd dispersed.

Lewys grabbed his jerkin and dashed outside.

The wagon's damage looked even worse up close. Red rope secured the corners, but it was a temporary bandage for the cracked joints which exposed the wood's inner pith.

The old puppet master emerged from behind the curtain. "Master Lewys, look how well your craft weathered the years. Although, I must admit, some repairs are needed."

"Master Rhodri, you take me for my father," Lewys replied. "He is gone these last ten years. I have his carpentry business as well as his name now."

Hobbling towards him on gnarled joints as the stage boards shifted and groaned, the old man squinted at Lewys. "Aye, I remember you," Rhodri said, beckoning the carpenter to follow him into the narrow living space behind the stage backdrop.

"Is your daughter here?" His lips were dry; his heart constricted with a bare remembrance of hope.

A slow smile deepened the lines on the old man's face. "You remember Roselyn?"

●

The first time Lewys had seen Roselyn, she was sitting on a stump in the wytchen grove, her hair a curtain over her face and lap. He was passing through on his way further into the forest, hatchet slung over his shoulder. "My lady?" he said, approaching carefully, as he would a hare in a thicket, "Are you well?"

She looked up then, and instead of a face smudged with tears as he expected, he saw one smudged with ink from the parchment and quill in her hands. Her eyes were startled, as blue as an open sky. The sun blinked through the branches and transformed her hair into spun gold.

Lewys caught his breath.

"Indeed, I am very well," she replied. "Do you like stories?"

"What? Uh...yes. Doesn't everyone?" he stammered.

"Good!" She jumped off the stump and pocketed an inkwell that had been lying in the grass. "This one is finished. You can be our practice audience." She grabbed Lewys by the wrist and he let go of his hatchet in surprise, dropping it behind him. He spluttered a weak protest — he was supposed to meet his father for work — but the girl tugged him away, into the stand of birch trees that bordered the road into town.

"Audience for what? You don't even know me!"

"Of course I do. Father!" She shouted as they came upon an old wagon pulled into the grass on the side of the road. "The carpenter's son has agreed to see the new play!"

Lewys recognized the man sitting in the grass in front of a small fire, stirring the contents of a pot hanging from a tripod. He was an itinerant toymaker; every girl in the village had at least one of his wood and cloth dolls. Lewys himself had a painted jester on a stand, cleverly rigged to somersault when a button was pressed. It was still on a shelf above his bed, even though he was too old to play with it now.

Master Rhodri looked from his daughter to Lewys and back again. "Roselyn, are you sure..."

She pulled her father to his feet and thrust the parchment into his hands. "Look, I finished! It's the perfect story for the new puppets! Oh, be careful, it's still wet."

"All right, then," Rhodri said, pulling a handkerchief out of his vest pocket to wipe his fingers, "but only if the young man does not mind."

Lewys did not. Roselyn showed him where to sit in the grass beneath a tree, the gentle push of her hand through his shirt sending thrills along his skin. She was a flurry of activity, her bright hair and patched dress swinging to and fro as she fetched the puppets and whispered to her father as he studied the parchment. The puppets were exquisitely carved, like all the dolls Rhodri made, but these had moveable joints and strings, each attached to a cross of wood. Their hair was tangled yarn and their clothes multi-colored swatches of fabric.

Roselyn and her father climbed into the wagon and lowered the puppets into the grass below. The wooden figures clacked as they began to move, and within minutes Lewys forgot about the strings connected to the pair in the wagon above, their hands moving the crosses gracefully. A curtain lifted in his mind.

The story unfolded, wordless but spoken through the puppets' movements. Within Lewys's eyes, the wagon turned to mountain ranges, the grass to a river ford, so real that he could feel the cold wind in the high cliffs and hear the rush of the river. He was immersed in the hardships the brothers faced as they searched for each other. His heart leapt at their final happy reunion. When the puppets bowed, the story's spell over Lewys's mind broke, and he returned with a jolt to his seat in the grass, cooled by the shade of the tree. Roselyn's pleased face smiled down at him from the wagon. He broke into spontaneous applause.

"That was well done," a voice called from further back in the trees. Lewys turned and sprang to his feet. His father approached with his two apprentices. "No wonder my son has shirked his duty for the day." He held out the hatchet. Lewys took it as his father said more quietly, "I was afraid something happened to you, lad." Lewys's face reddened.

"It's my fault," Roselyn said, as she gathered the puppets up. "I did not give him much choice. Please do not be angry with him."

Rhodri came down from the wagon. The carpenter shook his hand, then looked up at the girl, his eyes squinting against the high sun. "Well," the Master Carpenter said, then turned sharply to Lewys, whose color deepened to scarlet. "I can see the appeal of such a play." The apprentices, a few years older than Lewys, grinned and elbowed each other.

"The puppets," he turned back to the toymaker, "are they a new crafting?"

"Yes. My first two. My daughter has great plans for me to make others. She wants a dragon and a witch in particular. And a girl puppet, of course."

The elder Lewys rubbed his chin, dark with beard. "There was something about that play, something quite powerful. I forgot where I was for a while. And I realize that I am long overdue for letters to my own siblings."

"My daughter wrote the story," Rhodri said proudly. "First I had the puppets in mind as another toy, but it was Roselyn's idea to perform plays with them. Do you truly think others will enjoy such entertainment?"

"Truly, but you need a proper stage — a pageant wagon, perhaps, so you can still travel as you do." The carpenter hesitated, glancing at his apprentices, then looked up at Roselyn again. He seemed to make up his mind, and continued, "There is a special wood that I use only for certain projects. I would like to build a pageant wagon for you with this wood. I never take payment for wytchen," he added quickly, when Rhodri blanched. "As I said, it is only for special creations. And I believe this project, and your work, is worthy of it."

Lewys looked at his father in shock. He vaguely remembered the wizened man, passing through town, who had shown his father how to cut wood from the strange trees that no axe could fell before, how to craft an object — for him, it was a staff — with tools and words.

His father had used the wytchen only one other time, as far as Lewys knew, to build a cradle for their neighbor's infant born two months too soon. It was a gift that his father carved in haste, neither eating nor sleeping, in order to finish it by dawn the day after the birth. Within hours after a peaceful nap in the cradle, the child stopped struggling to nurse, and thrived thereafter.

"Come with your daughter to my workshop tomorrow," the master carpenter continued, waving away Rhodri's stammering gratitude. "I'll draw up the plans and we can talk about them over supper." He gestured to Lewys as he turned, a slight smile on his lips. "Let's go. Enough stories for today. Back to chopping wood, lad."

●

The aged puppet master did not answer Lewys's question, but he did not have to. There was no sign of his daughter among the clutter of tools, wood, parchment, and ink pots on the table. Clothes spilled out of a trunk, child's dresses with snippets removed. A torn blanket lay rumpled on the floor. Lewys's heart sank.

How foolish he had been to wait.

The puppet princess was sitting upright in a cabinet with the troll, dragon, and witch on a shelf beneath her. A pile of bedraggled puppets lay at the bottom.

"I'd like to commission you for repairs."

Lewys looked at the rafters and walls, sunlight spearing through the gaps. Rhodri added, "I have the coin to pay you, whatever the cost."

"It's not that, sir." He tried to control his tone, but anger still sharpened his words even after all these years. "There are no wytchen trees left." One of the apprentices, addled with mead in the tavern, had broken his oath and spilled the secret of the grove; news that the master carpenter could release the trees' magic had spread like fire afterwards. The townspeople turned on his father when he refused their foolish requests for wedding rings, pendants, furniture, even an entire house made from wytchen. But the final demand, a flagship, had come from the duke himself in his manor on the coast, delivered with a subtle threat on the carpenter's son's life.

The entire grove was consumed. His father had fallen ill during the ship's crafting and died soon after it was completed.

"But surely you can repair the existing wood?"

Lewys regarded the puppet master, with his bent back and knotted bones, and said kindly, "All due respect, Master Rhodri, but perhaps a warm hearth in a home without wheels would serve you better now."

The old man nodded. "It probably would. But," he gestured to the puppets in the cabinet, "I must continue to tell her stories."

The puppet princess was as finely crafted as porcelain, the warm scent of beeswax polish lingering on her milk-white skin of peeled wytchen wood. Lewys slipped his fingers along the gold cascade of her hair, a silken balm over his callused skin. He had touched Roselyn's hair this way, shyly, so many years ago in the wytchen grove, as his father cut and shaped the wood for the pageant wagon. The elder Lewys murmured words under his breath as he worked, words that he whispered in Rhodri's ear when he handed him small blocks of wytchen.

Coaxed by his daughter, Master Rhodri had fashioned them both toy swords out of plain oak. Lewys and Roselyn pretended they were heroes, fighting trolls and witches, befriending dragons, crafting their own fairy tales from shadows at the forest's edge. Lewys was awkward and reluctant at first, feeling as if he were too old for this play, but Roselyn's earnest imagination captivated him. And it was worth the teases of the other apprentices just to sit close to Roselyn afterwards, their heads touching, as she penned their play into stories for the puppets.

Her lips were always stained blush from the wytchen berries they were not supposed to eat, the red berries marked with stars that she hid in her dress pocket. When the pageant wagon was completed, oiled and shining like the moon, Lewys watched as it rolled away from the grove without need of a horse, Roselyn blowing kisses as she peeked out from behind the curtain. When it was gone, he ate the berry she had slipped into his hand with a whispered promise.

It had flooded his mouth with bitterness, the taste surprising him after a her sweetly-scented breath.

Lewys finally asked the question he had been dreading. "Roselyn is happily married, then?" He tried not to sound bitter, but her name was no longer sweet in his mouth either.

"No. She is not. I wish..." Rhodri took a deep, shaky breath. "Her heart just...stopped." The words were a hammer blow to Lewys, leaving him cold and numb, his mouth drier than bone. His fingers, still caressing the puppet's hair, froze. "One minute she was reading aloud her new story and the next.... It was soon after we left the grove. I don't know what happened."

The old man paused, wiping his eyes with a grimy handkerchief from his pocket. "My wife had died when Roselyn was an infant. My daughter was all I had. My heart lies in that grave with her. To keep living, to keep going...." His voice cracked, and he cleared his throat. "I wanted to save her, to bring her back to life. Impossible I know, but a father will do anything for his child...at least, like this, she can live on in her stories. The stories that she loved, that she lived to write. Her legacy." He reached out and touched the puppet's hair also. "Roselyn and her mother had the same color hair. It is beautiful, isn't it?"

Lewys snapped his hand away, stumbling over the puppet detritus spilling out from the cabinet's bottom.

"You must understand — I could not let her go! But she grew so cold...her hair was the only thing unchanged. It was the only thing still her." The old man twisted his hands, choking back a sob. "Everything I did, all my carving, was for my daughter. *She* was the meaning behind my life's work. She still is. And I have to give her what life I can."

Master Rhodri's struggle to contain his grief echoed in Lewys's own hollow chest. After a moment, he said, "I do understand."

Slowly Lewys collected the puppets from the floor, a mess of small swords and fractured oak limbs. All princes. "Can I fix these for you?" he asked.

Composing himself, shaking his head, the puppet master replied, "They were my gifts, to commemorate her birthdays." He cleared his throat again. "She never got the chance to create a story of true love. I thought perhaps I could write one for her. But the words never came, and the princes never worked right. And I'd find them damaged the next day. If they were made of wytchen, perhaps it would be different, but I used all the blocks your father gave me. Nevertheless, I keep trying, every year."

Lewys was silent for a while, his hands cradling the broken princes. Wytchen dust drifted down from the wagon's ceiling, glittering bright as a promise that had not been broken after all.

I will come back to you.

"I will do something for you, Master Rhodri. And for her."

Back in his room he packed a satchel with a flask of water and food from his meager pantry, then secured a hatchet to his belt. Walking through the bare patch that had once been the grove, he glanced behind him, making sure he was alone before entering the thick forest beyond. He had released the apprentices after the flagship was completed; his destination was a secret only he knew, now.

After an hour, the woodland sloped upwards as the pine trees thinned. He came to a ledge where a single tree grew, slanted trunk and low, leafy branches thriving against the crisp sky: The wytchen sapling that Lewys and his dying father had transplanted here, hidden from human greed. It was larger now, although not as thick and full as the ancient ones in the grove had been. Another sapling, perhaps a year or two old, grew in a sunny spot near its parent. Lewys swallowed the sudden lump in his throat.

He poured water on the roots as an offering, giving some to the sapling as well, and tied a red ribbon around a thick branch as he had seen his father do. Then he sat, the trunk pressing into his jerkin, thinking of what could have been, while the sun painted the sky the color of the princess's gown, of Roselyn's lips, which had never touched his. As the sun descended into the dark forest below him, he hefted his hatchet and spoke his request to the tree.

He hoped he was worthy.

When Lewys came back to the wagon Rhodri was snoring in a corner, blanket wrapped around him and tucked under his grizzled chin. He used the old man's tools, peeling and smoothing the small branch the wytchen had granted him, carving a face, body, and limbs, whispering his father's words to the wood for the first and last time. Rummaging through the trunk, he found the remnants of a white shawl which he cut with a pair of silver scissors to make a doll-size tunic and pants, needle and red thread moving as deftly as when he sewed patches into his own clothing. He painted the eyes and mouth.

Lewys took the puppet princess down from her shelf, arranging her carefully on the work table next to the newly carved prince, staring at her for a long time. He touched her hair again. Leaning close, his lips almost touching her cheek, he breathed deeply. As his lungs filled with her wytchen wood scent, his heart returned, brimming with magic and love as when they had been younger. "Roselyn," he murmured, "I kept my promise too. I waited."

With the scissors he cut his own hair off, and stitched the dark locks to a small felt cap. Uncorking a bottle of pine resin, he brushed the thick glue on the cap and attached it to the puppet prince's head.

Wooden hands twitched, clacked against each other.

Lewys's joints buckled and he flopped to the floor.

●

His name, whispered against his cheek. A whiff of familiar berry.

Lewys opened his eyes. He was sitting in the old wytchen grove under one of the trees, crisscrossing branches spread out above him, and for one disorienting moment he thought the branches were the rafters of the pageant wagon.

Someone was sitting next to him. He turned, and Roselyn's smiling face filled his vision. Reaching out, tentatively, to touch her cheek, he whispered, "Are you real?" His fingers felt strange, stiff.

She laughed. "As real as you," she replied, standing. A pile of berries cascaded from her billowing silk skirts. She pulled him to his feet, and his joints cracked loudly. Lewys pushed the aches in his body aside — Roselyn was here, in front of him, alive and looking more beautiful in a sunset-colored gown than he had ever beheld. Her hair was a curtain of golden strands over her shoulders, a net of crystals holding the strands away from her perfect face.

"I am glad you are finally here, with me, my love," Roselyn whispered, standing so close to him, her eyes sparkling. Lewys folded her into his arms, his heart overflowing, seeking out her lips with his own.

"Not yet," she said, placing her fingers over his mouth. A loud roar sounded from the depths of the forest. Roselyn broke from his grasp. "Father wrote us a story. I don't know all the details, but I know it has a happy ending. We have to work to get there, of course." She gestured to the sword buckled at his hip and, when he stared at it dumbfounded, unsheathed it for him and put it in his hand. The blade was etched with runes. "You're a prince, Lewys."

She pulled a matching sword from a concealed fold in her gown. "I found this one hidden in a wytchen trunk before you came."

Another roar, closer this time, shook the leaves of the trees. Both sword blades began to glow.

"An enchantment! But do you know why?" Prince Lewys asked.

"No," Princess Roselyn said excitedly. "I suppose we will have to figure it out! Remember that friendly dragon? Things aren't always what they seem. We must be clever as well as brave." She smiled up at Lewys, and he had never known such happiness, such excitement.

"We have a new life ahead of us, my love," Roselyn said, and Lewys ached to kiss her. "Are you ready for adventure?"

Magic fell in curls and crystals from the wytchen wood above them. Strange shadows began to move beneath their feet. Lewys took his true love's hand, and together they turned to face the beginning of their story.

●

Lori Torone's story "Wytchen Wood" was originally published in Metaphorosis on Friday, 15 December 2017. See magazine.metaphorosis.com

About the author

Lori J. Torone is an adjunct Speech and English professor at her alma mater, St. Joseph's University in Brooklyn. She lives in New York (both upstate and downstate) with her two teenagers and a small, bossy (but lucky she's cute) dog. "Wytchen Wood" was her first semi-pro rate paid story, an audio version of which can be found in Podcastle. She has continued on to publish stories in *Crow & Cross Keys,* the anthology *Museum Piece*, and 99 *Fleeting Fantasies*, and has some independently published work on Amazon under Lori J. Fitzgerald. She is a member of SFWA and is currently writing a mythic fantasy novel. Lori can be found on Twitter/X @MedievalLit and Instagram @whiteraven829.

The Diary of Thisne Ome

Thomas Ouphe

Fiffnal 08, Third Passage, Moonrise

Warden's Day. Of all the days, she chose Warden's Day. Everyone was at the park; the warden (of course), the teachers from hall, the lower hall children, everyone from upper hall, Krem and all his curls, and (worst luck) mother. Father wasn't there, so I should say almost everyone.

Father hates Warden's Day. It's because the wardens are employed by the Academy and if it weren't for the bloody alchemists of the bloody Academy, we wouldn't need a bloody warden. Those are his words, not mine. The wardens are just normal people. I read in Severn's *Whole History* that the Academy only allows 200 hundred practicing alchemists. There are hundreds of thousands of setins, so there has to be a warden for almost every village near a river. They don't get much money from the Academy anyway, just enough to live on. The Academy wasn't even formed when the setin were created, but father says it doesn't matter, as they're all a bunch of bastards.

I don't talk about Warden's Day around father, because it's the only thing that makes him angry. He didn't even get angry when I left his coat in front of the fire to dry and burned it. But I try not to mention wardens to him at all. I like the warden. I'd like to be a warden and learn everything there is to know about the setins. If you can keep people safely away from the setins, then the setins won't need to eat them. It's pretty straightforward, really.

I like Warden's Day, because Warden's Day is the village's way of saying thank you to the warden. He is out there every day walking the banks, keeping track of the setins, running from house to house if any of them stray from the river.

Miranda says the warden tells the families of people who have been bitten by capius setins where their loved ones have gone. I can't imagine what it must be like for them. The capius are as beautiful as they are scary, their blue skin carving gracefully down the river on undulating yellow frills. Four rows of razor-sharp teeth that rarely leave a victim alive, but turn anyone who survives their attack into one of them. At least, that's how the books describe it. I have never seen a capius. I have never seen a dessius setin either. I am the only person in the whole village that I know who has never seen a setin at all. I bet I know the most about them though.

I prefer setins to mothers any day of the week. Setins may have plagued the village for a hundred years, but you can avoid them. A mother you're stuck with. They may be less deadly, they may even be friendlier, but the real fact of the matter is there's no getting rid of them.

Also, and I don't care how large it is, how venomous it is, whether it's dessius or capius, no setin is ever going to humiliate you in front of all your friends.

I sit here with quill to notebook only because there is no outside world anymore. How could there be, after the incident on Warden's Day?

The girls from my hall were all dressed up in their finest. Even Miranda, whose finest looks like most people's normal. I can't believe I've been stuck with the same group all these years. I was hoping that when we moved from lower hall to upper hall there might be some change of scenery, but it's the same nine girls and seven boys it's always been.

Everyone who still goes to hall has to wear a scarf on warden's day, except the boys, of course. Pater Rother even checks us, which is not fair, because he's only supposed to be in charge when we're in the classroom.

I had borrowed Nana Rose's scarf. Borrowed, mind you, I do not take things without permission. It's a gorgeous scarf: silk with a print of lilies on the river surface and the blue streak of a capius setin just below the surface. You can see the outline of the body, long and fluked, a yellow ribbon of colour about its frills. No hint of the person it once was.

Nana says the scarf commemorates someone that means a lot to her, although she won't say who. Nobody tells me anything.

"Your Mother wouldn't like it if I told you."

She is no doubt correct; Mother doesn't like anything.

I'm not allowed a scarf, because I lost my last one. Miranda borrowed it to carry plums. She says it got juice on it and she washed it, then hung it in the tree to dry. Miranda isn't the smartest and as you might expect, the wind blew it away. Bethan and Kaye have been going on about it ever since. They said Miranda sold it to a hawker for jam tarts and buttons. She does have new buttons and she has got a bit fatter, but Miranda is my friend, there's no way she'd do that. And there's nothing out of the ordinary about her getting fatter.

I borrowed Nana's scarf because I wanted to teach Bethan and Kaye a lesson. The two of them have airs far above their station. Both of their families are moneyed, but neither of them has a scarf as beautiful as Nana Rose's. As soon as I walked through the park gates, they were both green with the not-gots. I think Kaye was just about ready to spew.

The girls of the upper hall had to sing "Oh save me brave". Mater Grierly had us practice it on our lunchtimes for a month. The boys danced, slapping sticks and shins. They all had red rags instead of scarfs. But I saw Krem look at mine. I think I must look pretty wearing it.

We were lined up to thank the warden. The lower hall goes first, so it's a long queue. I made a point of standing between Bethan and Kaye. Kaye had just asked where I got the scarf when Mother came busting out of the crowd with her lips puckered, her brows creased, and cheeks as red as coals.

"Thisne, give me that before your idiot friends trick another one out of you."

She snatched it from around my neck.

"Of all the things to give you," she muttered.

Mother didn't even glance back to see the two of them laughing at me. Or to see me running down to the river. I must have cried for three hours, and not a single setin lurched out of sludge to end my suffering. I'm always hearing tales about capius attacking beautiful maidens to turn them, so their lack of interest just adds insult to injury.

When I got back to the park, the celebration was over, and the warden had left. Thankfully, so had Bethan and Kaye.

Fiffnal 08, Third Passage, Moonrise

I spoke to Father; he says Mother has the right ideas but that she sometimes goes about them in the wrong way. I suppose that's why he doesn't let her cook. If today was her idea of helping, I dread to think what her idea of shepherds' pie would be.

People sometimes say father is funny because he's not from Hessell. People from Hessell are funny like that.

I remember Mater Grierly joking when we were doing sums back in lower hall.

"You talk funny like your father."

Nobody laughed, because you get in to trouble for laughing when Mater Grierly teaches. Everyone hates her and she dresses like a tramp. She says mean things all the time. I'm glad I have Pater Rother now.

Father is from Thinvoll, which is a hamlet. I've never been there but he says it was like Hessell, though without a hall, a park, or even a warden. Only three families lived there, right on the riverbank. The houses weren't spread out like they are in Hessell, but crammed close together.

The setin attack on Thinvoll is famous, it's in all of the books. Father won't talk about it, but I know a few things that I haven't read. I shouldn't really write this down, but I don't suppose anyone but me will read it.

The two types of setin are believed to have been created at roughly the same time by two rival alchemists. The dessius are bigger with ink-black skin. They are more aggressive and stronger than the capius, but the capius scare me more, because of their infectious bite.

A dessius killed my father's sister and he watched both his parents transformed by a capius. They are out there somewhere. Father dreams about them. He screams for them, that's how I know. I wish mother would be more sympathetic, she's never had anything bad happen to her.

Fiffnal 09, Third Passage,
Sunup

I have told mother I am too sick to go to hall for lessons. It's not a lie; I couldn't sleep for worry and stayed up reading last night. My eyes are sore and my head hurts.

She is still making me go!

I shall skirt by the river and give the setins another chance. Given that my other option is abject humiliation, being eaten wouldn't be the worst. I might get lucky and have one of them turn me. If they did, I'd eat Kaye first, she laughed the most.

Fiffnal 09, Third Passage,
Long Shadows

Hall wasn't that bad. Bethan told Krem Barton what happened at the park. He didn't seem to understand why it was important. He just said my mother sounded very sensible. I wasn't sure if I wanted to love him for not caring or be mad that he took my mother's side.

I looked at his beautiful wavy hair and decided I was closer to loving him than hating him, but then I looked down at his unpolished shoes and I wasn't sure how close to loving him I could get. It takes no time to polish a shoe, but the contrast of satin stockings and scuffing is a difficult image to get out of the mind.

He's not terribly smart either and this seems to be a theme with the people I feel affection for. I suppose I must take after my father.

Speaking of stupid people, Miranda was a brick today. She threatened to punch Bethan on the nose and has promised to replace my scarf, given all the trouble it's caused. I thanked her but told her there was no need, but she insisted and after the way she spoke to Bethan, I was a bit too scared to say no.

Fiffnal 10, Third Passage,
Sunup

The old hag woke me up by churning butter. She has no sense of rhythm. I'm not sure she doesn't do it on purpose. When I churn butter, I do it in a gentle melodious way, so that it sounds like waves lapping the riverbank. When Mother does it, it is in a frantic stop-start way that no human ear could find pleasure in.

She's not terrible at everything; if she wanted to wake me up, she can congratulate herself on a job well done.

Fiffnal 10, Third Passage,
Midsun

I still haven't seen a setin. And I'm still the only person I know who hasn't.

It is not for want of looking. Hessell is the biggest village for miles and the Deva River coils around it like a rope. Mother and father travel to sell their barrels, but I've never been beyond the river. Aside from father, I've never met anyone from outside the village, either. Though I know there is a visiting hawker.

Father says Hessell is the prettiest village in the whole of Afon, but like most people in Hessell father has never been more than forty miles. I have read that the whole of Afon stretches hundreds of miles — full of cities and towns; that has to be much more interesting. Hessell is mostly just fields, trees, and houses. There are flowers in the park and a swing, but nothing like the statues or towers you read about in Garsdon. Beyond the Deva there are more fields, more trees, and more houses. If you go far enough north, you can see Garsdon over the Merrisea, and if you go south, you can see the slate hills of Whelston far across the water. I've never seen either. Even I know better than to go to bodies of water that large — I want to see one setin, not an ocean of them.

Mother would never let me go to the Deva as a child, and I am still banned from going alone. I go all time, of course, but I've still never seen one. Everyone else I know has seen scores.

Mother would execute me if she knew I was going to the river alone.

She says, all I need to know about setin is to stay away from them, but it just makes me more curious. After all, Nana had a famous encounter with one — not that anyone will talk about it.

I have hall again tomorrow; it would be nice to get through one day without being humiliated. I still have a headache too and now my eyes hurt. I smell toast cooking, I had better get dressed.

Fiffnal 10, Third Passage,
Blackest Midnight

Our house is decidedly too small. I have been woken by the sound of my parents arguing. That is to say, Mother was arguing whilst Father spoke with the calm tones of a reverend brother ministering to the possessed.

"She's just like Caleb," Mother was shrieking.

I don't know who Caleb is, but he often comes up when they argue, especially when they argue about me. Dorethea in the senior hall had a twin sister who died at birth. Sometimes I like to imagine Caleb is my twin brother and my parents sent him away when I was very young. I keep hoping he will show up and give them something better to argue about than me.

I could hear father take a deep breath. I'm not sure if he's frightened of mother or if he just doesn't have the energy to keep up with her. He spoke slowly, like a ticking metronome:

"She's exactly like Caleb," said father, "It's in her blood. It's in all of your blood."

Father rarely sounds firm, but there was enough certainty in his voice to shut Mother up for at least half a second.

"It wasn't in Caleb's, and it isn't in mine, so it can't be in hers."

I don't know what they'll talk about when I grow up and leave. I bet they'll have hobbies. Miranda's mother knits.

Fiffnal 11, Third Passage,
Long Shadows

I think Miranda may like Krem. Every time I glance over at him, I see her staring at him. My eyes ached after reading and my head felt woozy, so I spent most of hall noticing things.

Did you know that the first mention of a setin in Afon is just after King Humber returned from his expedition to the ice flats? It's longer ago than I thought. Back then, the Academy ran everything and nobody else could read much. They brought in hall just to teach people how to live around the setins. Of all the terrible things the setins have done, eating people, luring them from their families, and destroying homes, making me go to hall must be the worst.

Krem doesn't seem to notice anything. He stares at Bethan. I think he must like her scarf, it's almost as pretty as the one I used to have. I can tell he doesn't really like her though, because she sits in front of him, and he never looks down at her ankles. Lucky for Bethan; they're very boney and I think they would make him sick.

Nobody was in when I got home, and there was a note saying they were at Nana's. I had cheese and bread for dinner, and a whole pot of tea to myself.

I lay in bed thinking about Klem. I hope Miranda gets me a nice scarf. I know her family don't have much money, but I could use the attention. I've never even held hands with a boy. When you add that to my never having seen a setin, you might wonder what I've been doing with my life.

Fiffnal 11, Third Passage, Evensong

Father has come home without Mother. He briefly checked on me. I asked him if Mother was well, and he said she was comforting Nana.

I asked if it was anything to do with Caleb. Father looked surprised but I could tell he wasn't going to tell me anything.

"More to do with Nana," he told me.

If I do have a secret twin, I'll never keep secrets from him the way my parents do.

"Who is he?" I asked.

Father frowned; you could almost see his brain straining to find an answer that wouldn't get him into trouble.

"When your mother's ready, I'm sure she'll tell you all about him."

So, now I still don't know, and I will have to talk to Mother. I consider this the worst of all possibilities.

Fiffnal 12, Third Passage, Long Shadows

Mother is still not back. Went for a walk, did not see a setin.

Fiffnal 13, Third Passage, Midsun

I think there is something wrong with my eyes, I have trouble reading. It can't be that I have gotten stupider. I was trying to get through what should have been an easy chapter on the colourings of dessius setins, but the page kept blurring. If Mother were here, I would complain about it.

I told Father, and he said I might need focus lenses. He said the hawkers sometimes sell them.

Then he made me gut and pluck one of the pheasants he has hanging. He's salted it and is going to cook it for Mother when she gets back. It's a double-edged sword; the pheasant will be delicious, but a delicious meal isn't always a pleasant one.

As I am nearly blind, I asked him to read to me. I gave him my copy of Cordon's *Field Study of Setin Habits*, but he said he could not stand to hear another word about the wretched creatures, and didn't I have any books with stories?

Three years ago, Mother decided I was "too old" for "fairy stories". Father watched whilst mother donated all my old story books to the lower hall, so he knows very well that I don't. We ended up with him reading from a recipe book. It made me hungry for rhubarb and custard, but we didn't have eggs or rhubarb. Father suggested he could look for a recipe for toast.

Fiffnal 14, Third Passage, Mornsong

Father is sending me to Nana's house. He wants me to try her focus lenses. Mother will be there. I think he is punishing me for reading recipes we don't have ingredients for.

Fiffnal 14, Third Passage, Long Shadows

I tried Nana's pince-nez. I am relieved to discover that I am not getting stupider. It is not good news that my eyesight is failing, however. Nana has given me her spare pince-nez to use until I can go to the hawker.

Mother walked home with me. We did not speak much, and I dared not ask her about Caleb. Instead, she asked me about hall. I told her about Bethan's ankles, and she asked which boy I was getting jealous over. I don't believe she will ever understand me.

The pheasant dinner was very tasty. Father made rhubarb and custard for dessert.

Fiffnal 15, Third Passage,
Night

Went to Miranda's house. Her elder brother Iain was skinning rabbits to make gloves. He has very deft hands. He's a similar build to Miranda, but it looks better on him because he doesn't have to wear a dress. Miranda is the only person I know who has any siblings. It's probably why her family is so poor.

I'm not sure what Iain was dipping the skins in, but it smelled even worse than a hanging pheasant. And dead rabbits look unpleasant when they're skinned, like undernourished babies.

He told me Miranda was at the park. He wiped his bloody hands on his leather apron and winked at me.

"You let me know if you want some garters like the ones I made her."

I thanked him for his generous offer.

There was no sign of Miranda at the park. I met Kaye and Bethan by the wrought iron gates. Bethan has a new scarf with a picture of a kestrel. She should wrap it around her pointy ankles.

They hadn't seen Miranda, but they made it very clear they had seen someone else. Kaye said "someone else" in a sing-song lilt that suggested it was someone very interesting.

I wasn't going to take the bait. There are only 16 families in Hessell and none of them has ever been especially interesting before. I bet if you took a ship and left Afon to search all the wonderous foreign lands you still wouldn't find a group of less interesting people. Kaye is just too boring to notice it.

Fiffnal 1, Fourth Passage,
Short Shadows

Sylvia from the lower hall has been attacked by a setin. Her family were fishing on the Deva. Luckily it was a dessius, so she won't turn. I have heard she's quite sick but should get better within a stint. I am quite sick too; here I am at age fourteen and I've still never even seen a setin. I blame Mother for mithering me about keeping away from the river.

I wonder what would happen if Sylvia did turn. Would her family try to visit her? And if they did, would she try to eat them?

Fiffnal 2, Fourth Passage,
Long Shadows

Miranda brought my 'new' scarf to hall. It is quite the most ragged thing I have ever seen. I wouldn't be surprised it weren't one of the rags Iain cleans up rabbit guts with.

As Miranda is my friend, and I know she has done her best, I graciously tied my hair up in it. I might look like a roaming beggar, but that is better than being an ungrateful priss.

Krem smiled when he saw me wearing it, I couldn't tell if he was being polite. Bethan and Kaye both laughed aloud at me.

When I put on my pince-nez Bethan said I reminded her of Mater Grierly. Krem laughed. I have decided that he is beneath my affections.

Fiffnal 3, Fourth Passage,
Night

I loathe it when it rains; the mice in the thatch become frantic and it is difficult to sleep. I have asked Father for a cat. He grunted and pretended to be asleep. Mother told me to get to sleep, they have barrels to coop in the morning. Hopefully, that means I'll be able to buy a new pince-nez soon.

There is an awful musky smell when it rains heavily like tonight and in the flicker of the lamp, you can see damp on the plaster of the walls.

I have been fixed to my window for the last hour. Nana tells me that on nights when it rains very heavily, the setin come inland looking for victims. There was a flash of lightning earlier and I saw something move in the hedges near the gate. It may have just been a fox though.

Fiffnal 4, Fourth Passage,
Long Shadows

I may look like an old woman, but Pater Rother says I was the best reader today. The muddy paths had rendered my dress filthy, but most of the other girls had suffered the same fate and at least two of the boys had managed to push each other over and had little clusters of dirt around their desks.

We had to do an oral quiz. Miranda didn't know the six stages of the capius, and Bethan got three sums wrong. So, all things considered, I shone. I know everything about the stages of the capius except what they look like in real life. Pater Rother has let me borrow a book about dessius. He says I could make a good warden — so long as my eyesight doesn't get any worse.

Mother made me brush my dress and shoes. She and Father have not finished with the barrels yet, so I had to make dinner. They had not so much as shopped and I had to walk back into the village to get fresh supplies. We had potatoes and trout.

I mashed the potatoes, but we didn't have any cream, so I had to add water. The trout was good, even though I wasn't able to filet it very well and now my hands smell of fish guts. I scrubbed them with potato skins, but there's still a smell.

Fiffnal 5, Fourth Passage, Short Shadows

Miranda is no longer my friend. She was talking to Kaye and Bethan and as I approached, she said, "Here comes Mater Grierly."

The outrage! I was only wearing that beggar's scarf to save her feelings. Worst still, at lunch she sat with Krem, and they held hands. I am truly alone in the world.

Two of the lower hall girls, Geraldine and Rhian, saw me crying in the cloakroom. They were very nice and friendly. They calmed me down by telling me all about Sylvia. Sylvia has a patch of scales around the area where she was bitten. The veins in her arms have turned bright blue. This is normal in dessius bites, some people stay that way forever.

She had travelled quite far up the river; her mother is a net fisher. I don't know the spot where she was attacked, but it is supposed to have a clump of willows and a small mooring. Dare I visit it alone? I certainly have no friends to go with.

I may still invite the treacherous Miranda, but to use as bait!

Fiffnal 6, Fourth Passage,
Moonrise

I had to make dinner again. This time I could only make eggs and bread, though my parents seemed happy enough with it. They have finally finished cooping the barrels and looked too tired to care much about anything.

Mother was in a bad mood, which is to say, a normal mood. She found me reading and chastised me for using too much lamp oil. Then she asked what I was reading and why. I told her about the book Pater Rother had lent to me, and how he thinks I could become a warden. Mother snatched the book away and is going to hall to embarrass me tomorrow.

She says she plans on having a stern word with Pater Rother for putting such foolish ideas into my head.

Fiffnal 7, Fourth Passage,
The End of the World

True to her word, Mother barged into hall and shouted at Pater Rother in front of the whole class. It is as well that I have no friends left to lose.

I feel too sick to write and I have no books to read, so at least Mother will save on her precious lamp oil.

Fiffnal 8, Fourth Passage,
Mornsong

Dad has taken pity on me and given me enough money for both a pince-nez and a scarf that doesn't look like it has been used to dust a barnyard.

The hawker visits Hessell every sixth fiffnal. He's a bright-eyed chap who wears a yellow jacket, even in the summer. I have heard people describe him as handsome, but he has a metal nose tied on with a leather cord.

Mother says the metal nose is proof that he must have been handsome once. Father laughed when she said it, but they wouldn't let me in on the joke.

Father replied that he was a well-travelled man, Mother laughed and said he had been to all sorts of places, which they both found hilarious.

Fiffnal 8, Fourth Passage,
Short Shadows

The hawker was not as grubby a man as I was expecting, and aside from the metal, I found him to be both presentable and charming. He was a big help in showing me through a collection of pince-nez, and eventually, we found the perfect pair.

As we were discussing noses anyway, I told him how handsome I thought his own was. It is a bronze alloy that almost perfectly matches his skin tone.

"Thanks. My last one was a touch longer, but I like it well enough. You pay no mind to rumours, I didn't lose it through no wrongdoing or ought," said he.

I had never suggested he did and told him as much but asked how he did get it.

"Let's just say I put it somewhere it didn't belong, and it got stuck there."

His face fell and the tone of his voice dropped with it, so I changed the subject and asked what scarves he had for sale. An instant smile sprang up on his face and his nose sparkled as the movement lifted it and the sun caught it.

"You want to see this one, it's divine."

Reaching into his bag, the man pulled out the very scarf Miranda claimed to have lost.

Why, I thought, of all the deceitful sneaks...

I had lent the scarf to Miranda in good faith, I couldn't believe she had sold it. It's not the scarf, you understand, it's the betrayal of making me wear that awful rag.

"Where did you get this?"

"A bonny lass about your age."

I asked him to describe the girl and aside from the word bonny, there was no mistaking that it was Miranda.

The hawker was most sympathetic to my plight and agreed to give it to me at no charge if I purchased one of his other scarves. It is of a much lesser quality, but it has a rather fetching pattern of red and white stars.

Miranda will live to regret this betrayal, or my name isn't Thisne Ome!

Fiffnal 9, Fourth Passage, Midsun

Mother has spent the morning enraged at my choice of scarf, which she says is too flamboyant and makes me look like a roaming jezebel. I told her about Miranda's betrayal. She was not sympathetic, but instead told me she hoped I had learned the difference between decent people and Miranda's type.

Father asked how much the hawker had charged and then looked surprised.

"You didn't make any arrangements, did you?"

I told him what happened. He laughed aloud when I told him about the hawker's nose.

As if that poor man hasn't suffered enough.

Fiffnal 10, Fourth Passage,
Long Shadows

Sylvia continues to be crowded around and adored in a way that must be both smothering and liable to inflame the mind. But I did finally get to speak to her, by elbowing my way past a lower hall student with a face full of spots. I must say I can see the fascination; Sylvia has a large bite mark on her arm. At each of the points where the teeth of the dessius sank into her skin, there is a green spider web pattern. Dessius toxins can't transform a person but they stay in the blood forever. In *Setin and Their Ways*, Joan Wilts records that people with those marks often dream that they are the setin that bit them; they see through their eyes: diving and hunting in the blackest rivers. It must be more exciting than reading about them.

Nobody has noticed my new pince-nez, which is a tragedy because it has a rather fetching inlaid etching, but I suppose they may have been too distracted by the sudden return of my scarf. Bethan and Kaye were particularly keen to hear the story.

"You mustn't be too cruel to her, her family are desperately poor," said I.

They both giggled at each other and ran off to tell the story to anyone who would listen.

Miranda glowered at me throughout the whole late session of hall. Since I have my pince-nez, I have become more determined than ever to become a warden, and I answered all Pater Rother's questions. I watched Miranda through the corner of my eye, her face contorted with rage. I wouldn't be surprised if Krem hadn't gone off her; she looked quite the ugliest I have ever seen her. I doubt even the hawker would have found her bonny.

After hall, she was waiting for me against the birch in the front garden. I could tell she was waiting for me; she had the determined look of somebody waiting, her eyes scanning each passing face to check that it wasn't mine.

"Looks like she's waiting for you."

Bethan looked delighted by the prospect. She and Kaye seemed to be waiting in anticipation of the spectacle.

"Are you worried she'll try to thump you?" Kaye asked.

I glanced out the window at Miranda. I do not know her as well as I had thought. If I hadn't been worried before that Miranda might try to thump me, I was by then.

I made a show of forgetting some books. Pater Rother was only too pleased to keep me talking about the importance of the volumes I was being allowed to borrow, so I did manage to pass enough time. Miranda had moved on by the time I left. It is worth noting that neither Kaye nor Bethan had left and they were waiting at the gates of the hall.

"Miranda says she'll get you tomorrow."

I walked with purpose and my head held high, but they walked alongside me, continuing with their taunts.

I will pay no mind to them or Miranda. I am the one in the right.

Fiffnal 10, Fourth Passage, Blackest Midnight

I am somewhat concerned that Miranda may attack me tomorrow. She is far bigger than I and from a much rougher family. I am unable to sleep and have been reading by lamplight.

Wilkes has a note about dessius setins that I found fascinating. The bite often kills days after. I think Sylvia is in the clear, but what a trial she must have had. I find myself both in awe of the setins and wracked with fear by them.

It is lucky that she was not bitten by a capius. There is no turning back from that.

Fiffnal 12, Fourth Passage, Estimate

Mother brought my journal to my bedside, I am having a hard time concentrating. It hurts to write and my hand is shaking.

I cannot tell what happened and what is a dream. Miranda has visited me. She cried when she saw me.

I don't know the date.

Fiffnal 13, Fourth Passage, Estimate

This much I am clear on. I have seen a setin and I am no longer sure I will be a warden.

Fiffnal 3, Fifth Passage, Estimate

Days are too bright.

Fiffnal 7, Fifth Passage (I think)

I love Mother and Father. I hope they will know that if I die.

Fiffnal 10, Fifth Passage,
Long Shadows

I ate soup today and was able to stand. Mother will not let me near a mirror, though she changed my sheets whilst I sweated in the wicker chair.

I am starting to be able to tell the fever scenes from real life. Just not when they are happening.

I keep seeing myself in the Deva, I can feel myself swimming. Then I am in bed with a feather scratching through the pillow onto my face.

The warden has been to see me. He says if I survive the next two days, I might be able to live a normal life.

Fiffnal 15, Fifth Passage,
Estimate

I have not been able to write for a while. Three days? It is hard to tell. I don't remember anything but broth and Mother. I suspect she has saved me a second time.

Fiffnal 2, Sixth Passage,
Long Shadows

I must get this down whilst it is fresh in my mind. Or, before I die. There is a thought; death from setin venom is sudden, so at least I won't suffer. By all accounts, it waits in your system, showing no more signs than the bite itself. Then, you just die. Waites speaks of the victims having contorted faces like demons. Sylvia survived. Bethan and Kaye will be beside themselves if a girl from the lower hall survived and I don't. Poor Miranda will never hear the end of it.

Miranda is distraught. She thinks this is her fault, but I am sure that the blame is mine. Even if I had to read back and refresh my memory.

It was the scarf. Miranda stole my scarf and I told everyone. The next day at hall she waited for me in the cloakroom. Her face was grave, her fists were clenched, and she had rolled up her sleeves. It seemed as if she was ready to thump me.

I bit my lip and closed my eyes and waited for the blow to come.

What I felt was Miranda taking my hand. As I glanced down, I could see why she had rolled her sleeves up, they were wet with tears.

"I can't believe you told everyone I stole your scarf."

I was upset. She shouldn't have taken it. I told her so and she fell into a flood of tears.

She had only sold the scarf because her mother spent all of their money on setting up the glove business for her brother. Miranda hadn't eaten anything but a crust of bread in two days.

It is a sad story and at the time I thought, as awful as Mother is, at least she has never let me starve.

Miranda cried some more and begged for forgiveness.

"You don't know the shame of being poor."

Well, she's right — I do not. But I did know the shame of seeing her flirt with Krem.

"It's his stupid wavy hair, I can't think straight around it."

I of course forgave her. Krem's wavy hair seems to affect me in a peculiar manner also. But when she asked how she could make it up to me, I did ask for something unreasonable. I asked if she would help me see a setin.

Therefore, if I am dead by the end of the week, let it be known that it is on my request.

Miranda didn't want to go, not really. I'm too tired to write anymore and feel I may not make it. But I had to set the record straight.

Fiffnal 4, Sixth Passage,
Bright Morning

It would appear that I have survived. Mother will still not let me see my reflection and I want to. I feel I need to know.

My strength ebbed to the point that the village held a vigil. But I am not dead, and I no longer think I will die. I must sleep.

Fiffnal 5, Sixth Passage,
Short Shadows

I have been forced to rest in bed, though the sun is glorious outside and I am feeling well. A strange thing has happened today, I have been reading voraciously but I no longer need the pince-nez to see the words.

I have had a visit from Miranda this morning. She is still giving me peculiar looks. I have asked if she could bring me a looking glass, but she says that she is too afraid of my mother. I can't blame her for that. She keeps saying she is sorry for running away, but what else could anyone expect from her?

There are things I recall clearly from the day I was attacked, other bits of it keep jumping out at me when I'm trying to sleep.

I had followed Miranda up the banks of the Deva. We stood a good distance away from the water.

"It's odd, you can normally see them from here."

I had been to the spot a thousand times and never seen a single setin. I didn't want to go another day without seeing one. So, I just pressed Miranda to take me to the next spot.

She walked down toward the bank and then on to the bridge. It was the most basic route.

"When I last came here there was a dessius in the centre of Deva. I had to run up the bank."

Still, there was nothing to be seen.

After checking two more places, Miranda was looking both surprised and frustrated.

"What about the spot where Sylvia was bitten?"

Miranda was not the model of enthusiasm, but I reminded her that she had promised. I knew I was taking advantage of her guilt, but I didn't care.

We had to pass through a thicket of gorse. There was a small trail leading up a steep hill and then down. The Deva dipped out of sight as we climbed. Then, as we descended, a small rocky inlet became visible.

I had never seen the spot before. The water of the Deva ran more rapidly there. And someone, probably Sylvia's fisher family, had built a small wooden jetty.

I tumbled down towards it, leaving Miranda behind me.

As I stepped out onto the jetty and ran to the far end, I realised my mistake. I felt the movement on the jetty, and I turned to see.

The breath caught in my throat.

A large dessius had climbed on to the jetty behind me. I have read how big they are, but I had not imagined how powerless I would feel when stood in front of one. I felt my legs weaken and then I felt my resolve strengthen; I was not going to die without at least trying to stay alive.

With the jetty blocked I had no means of escape, other than to plunge into the river. I cannot swim, but a chance of survival seemed preferable to certain death.

In the water, I saw the capius. Blue and purple with white frills. I swear I have never seen anything so beautiful. I was transfixed by the graceful movement of vivid colours twisting and brightening in the sunlight. So now my choice was to be eaten by the dessius or turned by the capius.

The capius shook itself, jumping out of the water. Its deep black eyes held my own.

I felt a sharp pain in my leg as the dessius bit me. I crashed down onto the hardwood. I bit my tongue as my skull shook in shock.

The body of the capius loomed over me. I could hear it. A low and rapid set of clicks. The dessius responded at the same pitch but faster. I tried to stand up, but the pain in my leg pulled me sideways.

The dessius bit my arm. Its teeth pressed hard into the bone. I remember screaming and the capius rearing up to attack. As the pressure released, I blacked out.

Fiffnal 6, Sixth Passage, Mornsong

I have some vague memories of movement, of something gentle lapping against my wounds. I am sure it was the tongue of the capius, though that makes no sense. Mother says the capius was still there when she got to me. Which I remember to be true.

She says it 'scarpered' at the sight of her, but that is a lie. I remember hearing her voice, calm but full of pain.

"Caleb. Thank you."

Then the splash of a heavy body returning to the water.

Mother says I dreamed it, but they keep talking as if I'm not in the room. I heard Nana Rose say, "It'll out, blood knows things. You can't believe it's a coincidence."

Mother sounded utterly defeated.

"I'll tell her," she said.

She hasn't, but I know. I can feel him in my veins, see through his eyes. I can talk to him in my dreams. I know he spent years keeping the setins away from me. I know he saved me.

Fiffnal 7, Sixth Passage,
Short Shadows

Nobody has ever had an open wound licked by a capius before me. I am the first. I have a connection that goes beyond any other survivor. And no capius has ever saved a person before, so Uncle Caleb is the first too.

Today I held up the looking glass and saw my face. There is a map of blue lines all over my body. I don't know if I am changed forever.

I look strange but not ugly. It is no wonder I am still friends with Miranda, that is just one of the things that we have in common.

Of course, she doesn't have an uncle who is a capius setin. She can't share his thoughts, feel where the other setin are, or see the setin blood through her skin. But, I suppose I don't know what it's like to be her, either.

Mother still hasn't told me about the day Caleb was bitten, though I have the memory from him — vivid and full of terror. Her, taking her younger brother down to the banks against Nana's will, and what became of him, what would have become of her if Nana hadn't been chasing them.

Poor Mother, it is no wonder she has been so protective. Nobody will have to worry again when I become warden. Here she comes now, bringing me more food. I do hope she hasn't cooked it herself.

Thomas Ouphe's story "The Diary of Thisne Ome" was originally published in Metaphorosis on Friday, 25 February 2022. See magazine.metaphorosis.com

About the author

When Nathaniel Hawthorne was the US consulate, he visited a small village churchyard and scraped the moss off an old stone to reveal the inscription:

Poorly lived and poorly died
Poorly buried and no-one cried

Thomas Ouphe lives very close to the churchyard and regularly goes looking for the stone when he's walking his dog. He's never found it but is romantically attracted to the graveyard because it also contains a lamppost that is said to have inspired the Narnia lamppost and the grave of the first author he ever read — Roger Lancelyn Green (Robin Hood and his Merry Men — in case that's going to nag at you).

He's the sort of person who likes to read and sit quietly. A homebody and bore, were he not so in love with an American woman he might never go out at all; except to walk the dog of course — he's not a monster.

He and his wife have three wonderful children and in addition to a mad Staffordshire Terrier, they also have a sombre and sophisticated cat.

When he's not writing (which to be honest is way more than he'd prefer), he teaches English at a college of further education.

@ThomasOuphe

Escape to Mall B

Theodore Lowry

Brad's first and only memories were of a mall. In time, he came to know it as Mall A, but for most of his life it was simply home. Plastic ferns brushing his face, sofa advertisements dangling overhead, and lime disinfectant squeaking beneath his mother's shoes. Despite the top-ten hits playing in the background, for the first twelve years of his life, Brad hardly noticed music at all. This is the story of how he started listening, and how it cost him everything.

He grew to roam the arcade and toy store, keeping away from his empty home, and later worked in the supermarket to earn mall tokens for Discount Tuesdays in the cinema with candy and other boys yelling along with the latest '80s action flick.

One afternoon, while resting from his labours in the food court, Brad noticed an older boy perched on a nearby stool. He wore a black leather vest inscribed with arcane symbols, and his black boots had left dark traces on the white tiles beneath him. Even from where he sat, Brad caught a rich smell like wet dog, without doggie shampoo.

Brad and his friends had just watched *Too Alive to Die*, starring Chuck Van Willis, and they were acting out their favorite scene. "And then Chuck roundhoused the guy's head into the jet fighter." "Then BOOM!" "Boss goes down!"

Brad stopped listening as the older boy lifted a slender black case onto the square table before him, and slid out a shiny guitar. Brad had only ever seen them in videos. The boy held it, fingers hovering by the strings. The mall's speakers tinkled the current Number 6 song, 'Your Love Hurtz Too Much Much', by The Boyz and Girlz Club. It was slow, but with a dancy chorus. The boy cocked his head, his fingers hovering over the strings.

What came next changed Brad's life forever. The boy played a chord, matching the song. He played another, and yet another, as though he were on stage with The Boyz and Girlz Club themselves. Brad imagined them as tiny people playing somewhere within the mall's speaker system.

From across the food court, a pretty girl glanced over and smiled. The boy looked suddenly shy, and put his guitar away.

Brad blurted out, "How are you doing that?"

"Oh, this?" The boy stopped playing and slouched back in his stool. "Guess you've never been to the Southwest Wing."

Brad rifled through old movie tickets and candy wrappers until he found his bag of mall tokens. "How much do you want for it?"

●

Brad had traded away all his tokens, three months' worth of supermarket work. He couldn't afford movies anymore, so he spent that time practicing the hits on with this precious guitar. It felt wonderful to have these rhythmic patterns seeping through his mind. As night came, and people went to sleep in their capsule beds, the calls of children demanding candy gave way to still hallways. He played more and more quietly, and sang in a whisper. It was then that Brad softly crooned the slow hits.

At first the flow of music was a trickle, like water through a drinking fountain, then a flow, like the fountain in the food court. Music no longer lived only in the mall's tinny speakers; it flowed through Brad's body, like a special power activated in a video game.

One fine evening, he found himself perched on a column above the meandering crowd, playing along with Hit Number 4. Brad wasn't convinced of the singer's claim: 'My baby makes me so crazy I get lazy'. That guy had probably already been lazy.

"Get down," breathed a low voice.

"That's right," Brad sang. "Get down, get on up." He fumbled a G chord.

"Get down *now.*"

Before him was a gaunt face, familiar from many a food-spill debacle. A man who intimately knew every grime-attracting crack of the mall's lily-white hallways. Straddling the top of a ladder, clad in an immaculate uniform, gray hair cropped, Lysol sprayers dangling from two holsters, the Cleaner frowned. "Son, you can't be breathing and sweating up here."

"Why?"

"Moisture breeds mold."

"Mold?" Brad stammered.

"Enemy's first incursion." The Cleaner's hot glare made Brad drop his gaze.

Brad nearly asked, 'Am I mold to you?' But, one: the question was ridiculous. Two: it was obviously true, with the way the Cleaner sneered at him.

The Cleaner's expression lightened. "Pray you never see it, boy. Just keep playing the hits. Y'aint careful, you'll wind up like that good boy who turned into a..." his lips curled, "...*alternative musician.*" In a blur, the Cleaner shoved Brad's foot aside to reveal a smudge, unholstered his weapon, then Lysoled it into foamy oblivion. "You're alright, son. Just don't let that happen to you."

●

Every time Brad sat still to practice, he imagined the Cleaner coating him with Lysol, then wiping him away. Brad didn't really know what the man was capable of. What *had* happened to that older kid who'd sold Brad his guitar?

In between the hits, Brad would sometimes try out tunes of his own. Fumbling, awkward things, but full with possibility. He knew the Cleaner wouldn't approve, so Brad kept moving. He spent the following weeks strumming and humming on escalators, elevators, and stairs. When he did sit down, people would hush him so that they could hear the 'real songs' playing on the PA. His best spot was a disabled person's bathroom. It was spacious, and the acoustics were excellent.

One fine fluorescent morning, he was sitting on a bench playing his most polished song, 'I Love Dat Lovely Luv' by Dang Dem Witches, the current Number 6 hit. Usually he played for the plastic ferns on either side of the bench, imagining them to be cute girls in his peripheral vision. This time he glanced up, and found a group of people staring at him.

He stood. "It's alright, I'm going."

"Long time since I heard live music." An older woman rubbed her eyes, streaking purple mascara. "Look what you've done."

A boy popped a gum bubble. "Can you play faster?"

"Probably." Brad sat down and played the chorus. People gathered like there was a sale on. It was glorious. For a moment, he was in his own music video.

He'd gotten good. He thought to try out one of his own tunes, but they weren't ready, and he thought he'd glimpsed the Cleaner slipping behind a pillar.

●

The next morning, Brad awoke to an odd feeling. Something was different. Missing. He couldn't put his finger on it. His sleeper pod was shiny and cozy as always. He was hungry, thinking to get an egg sandwich in the food court.

All normal enough.

Except that the mall's PA was silent. There was no music on the speakers.

Brad had always awoken to music drifting from the ceiling speakers outside his sleeper pod. His parents always went to work early at the Notary Republic, so it was always the music that had woken him. Now he heard only silence.

Was it the Cleaner's doing? This might be a psychological attack against Brad, like the bad guy in Chuck Van Willis' latest film, the one that Brad couldn't afford to see.

The speakers erupted in a cough. A woman spoke, slow and confident, "This is the Mall Mayor. Paging Brad Ashton. Please report to the food court."

Brad's chest tightened. "I'm being taken to court?" Had the Cleaner reported him for playing the wrong songs?

The voice added, "To play today's top hits!"

●

Brad found himself on a foot-high stage in the food court. He wiped sweaty palms on leather pants given to him by the mayor herself. The guitar was an anchor around his neck, the strings too hard to press.

No one was eating, just staring at him. All he could hear was his own breath. Did they really want him here? This could all be a setup.

"Number Ten," he squeaked into the mic, more gerbil than rock star. "Ten, ten, ten..." like it echoed on the radio. "This one's called, 'Save I Saved my Tears for Years'."

People nodded, watching. There were pretty girls out there.

God, don't let me mess this up.

The A chord came out wonky, his voice thin. The girls looked away. The C chord sounded worse. *Can only get better*, he told himself, and his playing did even out.

At first only a few babies clapped along, off rhythm. Then a pod of football players started singing, and everyone turned on. The prettiest girl sang the loudest.

"Number Nine, nine, nine!" Brad launched into a slow tune, 'Sucky Nights' by Pet Factory.

"Number Eight!" Brad chimed the high notes, swam the sad stretches. "Number Four, Three..."

Number Two was coming fast: 'Your Love's Too Pointy'. This one was tricky. It had this one long, high note at the very end, and Brad had only really pulled it off once. The audience should feel in their bones the cut of his girl's love.

Number Three wound down and he launched into Number Two, feeling exhilarated. He came into that last note ready. Too ready. The note came out happy, like he was a *sucker* for her pointy ways.

The crowd cheered, but not the football players, and not the prettiest girl.

Off to the side, there was the Cleaner, his fingers far from his holster, his grim face satisfied.

Brad was eager to launch into Number One, but the song escaped him. Instead, tinkling, etheric music streamed through his mind. Hardly music at all, but more like the flow from a drinking fountain, mixed with the sound that stars might make as they moved. Not stars as in popular people, but like the ones in outer space in that beer commercial.

A shifting tone trickled from his mouth, another reverberated from his guitar.

The crowd stared at him. The Cleaner's smile fell. The pretty girl looked confused.

Number One landed in Brad's mind. In his voice and his fingers. He started slow and brought it to a messy, gyrating conclusion. The crowd loved it, but to him it sounded mechanical, like a kid pounding buttons on an arcade game.

The Cleaner nodded in approval.

●

A week later, the Mall Mayor was all over the PA system, asking Brad to play again.

Brad was squatting beneath a drinking fountain by a farflung bathroom, arms crossed, staring at a plastic fern. He didn't know why he was hiding; his concert had gone well. They might ask him to play every week. The pretty girls might smile again. If this was everything he wanted, why did it feel like a trap?

"Brad Ashton, we've paged you many times. Brad Ashton, please report to the food court."

Someone stepped in front of Brad, dressed in immaculate white pants. He squatted, bringing his gaze to Brad's level. It was the Cleaner. "No guitar?"

Brad flinched, trying to press himself into the wall.

The Cleaner cocked his head. "Thought music was your big dream."

Brad made himself hold the man's gaze. "Guess so."

"So get up there and play the hits."

Brad looked up. "Is that all…"

"Spit it out, boy."

"I mean, is there *other* music?"

"Like what?"

"I mean, the songs are all kind of like each other. Is there music that... stretches more, tinkles high like stars, rumbles like... and makes you feel..."

The Cleaner scoffed. "Stick with the hits."

"But what if —"

"I said stick with the *hits*." The Cleaner sprayed a caustic stream of Lysol on the floor by Brad's foot. Something invisible had just met oblivion.

●

Brad took to late-night roaming of corridors, trying to get away from the Cleaner. Instead of music in his head, he heard threats and the hiss of disinfectant spraying from a bottle, the click of the cleaning cart's wheels gliding over tiles.

Each time Brad found a place to sit and sing, the Cleaner appeared nearby. He was sweeping up any long hairs Brad shed, or walking backwards and spraying both Brad's footprints and his own. Watching, always watching.

One night, Brad went farther than he ever had, trying to get some time alone. It was there, in a far-off region of the mall, that he saw odd marks on the floor. At first he thought they were stickers leading into a nearby store, but when he leaned down to touch one, his finger came away wet. He flinched, looked around for soap, and only then realized just how far he'd wandered from any bathroom. From anything familiar.

Where was he? He'd never seen that shop selling floral syrups, or that one selling camping food.

His finger smelled like that wet dog, or...

Or like the boy who'd sold him his guitar.

These prints didn't lead into any shop. They lead into a long, empty hallway with green flickering lights.

White foam sprayed out of nowhere, coating Brad's fingers.

"It burns!"

"Purified." With a satisfied grunt, the Cleaner holstered his Lysol. A few blurs of the mop, and the odd marks were gone. He handed Brad a white cloth. "Wipe. It's the antidote."

Brad wiped off his hands. The cloth had been soaked in something. Instantly, the burning subsided. His hands still tingled though, and smelled like someone's idea of lemon.

The Cleaner stared into the dark corridor. "If I had my way, there'd be *no* Southwest Wing."

"What's there?" Brad asked.

The Cleaner didn't reply, and in the silence Brad thought he heard tinkling sounds seeping from the green hallway, sounds like flowing water mixed with stars.

"Time to get you back." The Cleaner smiled thinly, glancing between three visible escalators. "Guessing you don't know your way."

●

For a month, Brad stuck to the safety of the mall, working long hours so he could binge on movies. Then one day, after Brad played the current hits in the food court, the Mayor handed him a bundle of tokens. It was more than Brad could have made working three days in the supermarket. And whenever the Cleaner saw Brad, he nodded his approval.

Brad was safe. More than that, people recognised him in the hallway. A cute girl even told him that he sounded 'almost as good as the radio'.

Yet his thoughts kept returning to the long, storeless hallway. It beckoned to him with patterns of flickering green lights. Each night, he had to pump dozens of tokens into a massage chair just to get to sleep.

In his dreams, the hallway walls were a rich, loamy green. They billowed out and enveloped him with whispered welcomes.

Early one morning he woke up from that dream. Staring at the ceiling of his sleeping pod, it occurred to him that he wouldn't be free from this until he knew what was in that hallway. It was like Chuck Van Willis' wife had said when she'd faced her own sub-main-bad guy: 'You're my nightmare, but I'm your reckoning.' Something like that.

Maybe more like she'd said to their son: 'I love you too much to die. I'll be back.'

That didn't work either. None of the action movie lines seemed to work, which just made Brad feel more unanchored.

Without giving himself time to think, Brad got up and, without even getting breakfast, strode toward the Southwest Wing.

As he descended an escalator, he saw the Cleaner coming up, wiping the black banister as he went. Brad grimaced and pressed on. Later, he saw a flicker of cloth on a tile corner. A mop sliding from view.

Brad wove randomly through the hallways until he was alone again. He entered the nearest elevator and hit a random floor. The doors opened, and the Cleaner stepped on.

"Going somewhere?"

Brad was forced back.

Each day was the same, as though the Cleaner had many forms. He held his Lysol like a gun, his mop like a spear, his cloths like garrottes.

Until one day, while Brad was in the food court wondering why he didn't like burgers as much as the people in the ads, the clandestine hand of fate poked the fabric of reality. A soda dispenser exploded, spraying kids, tables, chairs and customers with liquified chemi-sugar.

While everything around him grew sticky, Brad's thoughts grew clear.

As the Cleaner descended with his arsenal of disinfectants, Brad ran. Sprinted past The Screen Zone and The Perfume Panther. Past where his parents worked in the Notary Republic. He thought to say goodbye, but they'd be busy. He ran past shops selling holiday stuff year-round, then into the strange part of the mall, past dangling antiques and boot insoles color-coded by intensity of wearer's mood.

Sinking in an elevator, running up an escalator. Past where the moist footprints had been, then running, *flying* through the storeless corridor.

Silence, save his own footfalls. He ran alone past flickering green lights and fuzzy walls.

Ahead, he saw a sign scrawled in green ink:

MALL B

The lights went out.

He padded on in the dark.

From somewhere ahead, a deep tone unfurled. Then another, much higher, and a third in between. Was it music? It thrummed his bones, while chimes tinkled his mind. A continuum of strings plucked him to life.

Fear filled Brad's gut like a spicy taco, but he couldn't turn back. He glanced up to see cracks in the ceiling, seeping warm and otherworldly light, like the sunset in a chip ad.

Brad stopped. He'd gone farther than he'd wanted. He could still return to the mall he knew. His parents might be home from work. In any case, the soda machine must be fixed by now, and he could sure use some.

But whatever that sound was, it was close. He saw dim green lights up ahead, and had to keep going. The light came from a window, and in that window was the most beautiful thing he had ever seen. Carved from glistening ocher wood, it sported sleek symbols, ethereal and ineffable and maybe kind of Celtic. This guitar belonged in a music video.

He touched the glass and stared in. There were more instruments: carved shakers, cone-shaped drums, and translucent bowls.

Above the window hung a sign. Curving calligraphy read:

SOUND HEALING SHOPPE

Breath caught in his throat, Brad pushed open the door, just an inch. It chimed, and fragrant smoke billowed out. Mesmerised, he stepped into a realm of dreams.

Crystals dangled. Ceramic fairies danced in pentagrams. Rotating carousels showcased books about telepathic whale guides and helpful star systems.

Feeling faint, Brad fell into a chair. Strings surrounding him strummed his spine with spiraling reverberations. His imagination had only brushed the edges of this place. It was much more.

Someone placed an object in Brad's lap, made of cool metal and shaped like a UFO. He pushed it away, and his touch produced a clear note.

"Play more," said a young woman, stepping from behind the musical chair. She was beautiful and strange, like everything here.

"I..." A few more taps on the UFO, and an exotic melody emerged. Brad couldn't hit a wrong note.

The night was young. Brad played three-reeded flutes with rainbow-painted kids, his feet resting on a crystal-powered machine. The translucent bowls that he'd seen in the window, when stroked, sang like Buddhist angels. As evening became night, he lay still while a circle of singers blessed him with songs from before the mall was built. His body was of earth, formed from stardust. As the singers grew silent, Brad knew his purpose: to help the Earth on her grand initiation into new realms of being.

At one point Brad asked, "Was there ever an older boy here? Slick hair, leather jacket, played guitar?"

"There was," said the young woman.

"Where did he go?"

"No one knows. He left one day, said he was searching for more."

That night, he slept on a reiki table with a mobile of planets spinning overhead. In the morning, the girl gave him a pile of CDs. Their covers were full with words like 'overtone', 'meridian', and 'encounter'.

As he turned to go, she touched his arm and murmured, "Remember what music can be."

●

Brad had never thought of his home as Mall A, just *the* mall. But the Southwest Wing felt like another mall entirely. Going there had been strange, but coming back was stranger. The Healing Shoppe, where he'd been only once, felt like home. He had activated his chakras, had gone on an astral pilgrimage. Now he was back in his sleeping pod in Mall A, comfortable but pierced by loneliness. He hadn't even asked that girl her name.

Later, alone on a bench surrounded by plastic ferns, Brad put *Ancestral Reiki Vibrations* into his discman, slid in his earphones, and closed his eyes. The music drowned out the PA and eased Brad back to the Sound Shoppe.

"Looking mighty content there, son."

Brad yanked out his earphones. "Just the standard amount, sir. I'm loving the hits."

The Cleaner parked his supply cart next to the bench and sniffed the air. "New deodorant?"

"Patchouli, sir."

The Cleaner cocked his head. "Funny, haven't seen that for sale around here."

"Sure is bright today."

"Compared to what?"

"In the supermarket, a light was out."

"Thought I would have known." The Cleaner sat beside Brad and crossed his long, white-polyester-clad legs. "You know, that friend of yours reeked of patchouli, near the end. Stopped looking like the rock star he could have been and..." The Cleaner snatched something from Brad's pocket and held it up. "Had a bunch of shakers, too."

Brad wished he'd hidden it in his pack. "It's from the Halloween Shop."

"Guatemalan, by the look of the engravings on the bulb."

"How do you —"

"Ain't no *Guatemala* in the Halloween Shop." The Cleaner shoved the shaker back into Brad's pocket and lowered his voice so no passing customers would hear. "Don't think I've never been to that place. But you learned the *hits*, boy. You could *be* something in this place." His gaze slid to a tired-looking man toting bags of toys for his son, then back to Brad. The Cleaner's gaze softened. "Don't you want to be a normal father? Someone who can provide for your children?"

●

Weeks passed. Brad longed for another soda explosion, or for drunk teenagers throwing up, or for an overflowing water fountain, or a messy brawl over addictive candies. Anything to keep the Cleaner off his back while he made a break for it.

Nothing. And always, the Cleaner was nearby, hovering, fingering his Lysol.

Well, maybe Brad wasn't meant to be a rebel musician. He could just stay in Mall A. He could be a music-video rebel, well paid and popular. This was his home, wasn't it? He had grown up here, had developed hand-eye coordination playing those video games over there, had learned about human relations in that theater. His very body was built of burritos from Taco Giant, yet he wanted only to return to the nether region of the mall, and to the Sound Healing Shoppe.

Nightmares held him back: Lysol in his eyes, legs scrubbed clean of flesh. Only one thing in the mall was gathering dust: his adventure pack. He had filled it with all the necessities: fruit rollups, cheese strips, kombucha (weird, but recommended by the pretty musician girl), and, of course, his homely guitar.

One night he dreamt of smooth, white walls with spotless tiles crushing him, buckling inward and bashing him in time with hits playing on the radio. Beyond them, green walls folded outward like a blooming flower beckoning in a bee in a nature documentary. The kind of bee that would return to his hive covered in honey. Or pollen. However that worked.

Brad wanted to be that bee. To hear the tinkling melodies of the flower as they made love beneath an open sky. It was crazy. If he stayed here and kept playing the hits, if he had kids, he'd easily be able to buy them bags of toys and tell them they were from Santa, like the other dads. He could have a good life. That was like a sweet flower too, wasn't it?

And if he tried to leave... Brad thought of the Cleaner, fingering his Lysol. If he hadn't handed Brad a cloth soaked in an antidote for Lysol, would Brad even still have his hands?

Better no hands than no heart, Brad thought.

As he got up from bed, defiant dialogue from dozens of action movies flickered through his head. "Over my dead body, punk," he hissed to the air. "Or over yours. Something like that."

Brad bought a variety pack of firecrackers and lit them in the children's cereal aisle.

With crackles and squeals at his back, he sprinted from the supermarket... and from his old life. Had he really just done that? Either way, he kept running, his pack and guitar bounding on his back. Past the Notary Republic with his parents doing some kind of work somewhere inside, then past the strange shops, the stranger ones, and into the empty, flickering corridor with its vivid green:

MALL B

It felt like he was falling. Feet slapping tile, guitar bounding on his back. Chest drumming.

Darkness all around. Running. He'd run as far as before. Still, only darkness ahead.

Sensing something ahead, Brad slowed.

Reached out and yelped, a splinter in his finger. With his phone light, he saw no celestial guitar, no singing bowls, just plywood and an immaculately printed sign.

SHOP CLOSED DUE TO UNSANITARY CONDITIONS.

Brad cried out, "It's spelled S-H-O-P-P-E. It's meant to be fancy." He fell to his knees. "Fancy!"

His voice echoed into silence.

He sat on a chunk of broken concrete, too stunned to weep. He would fall forever with nowhere to land. He had no home.

He managed to cry for a while, maybe a long while.

Frustrated, he plugged his earphones into his discman and picked up his guitar. Celestial harps mixed with singing bowls mixed with chords he'd never tried to play, notes he'd never tried to sing. No one could hear him here, so he sang along like a wailing dog. A wet, smelly, rejected dog. Keening calls. Rhythmic grunts. Songs for angels sprouting from the earth, and for whales swimming through constellations on their way to becoming ancestors. No hits. His own music. The world's music.

When the batteries on his discman ran out, he kept strumming and singing something, stumbling over rubble, running fingers over fuzzy walls. He sipped the kombucha, ate all his fruit rollups, and vowed never to return to the supermarket.

Exhausted, he lay on the dusty floor and stared up, singing in darkness. When his throat dried up, he sang on in his mind.

Above him, he thought he saw filaments of light, a spider-web of bright lines. Faint, and seeming to pulse along with his singing. Maybe the walls were singing along with him, in their own way.

This whole place smelled like wet dog. Something sprouting tickled his arm. The Cleaner had used the word 'soiled' like a curse, but this tickling felt kind of good.

Another voice sang too, at a higher pitch than his own. Sad and clear, it echoed through the empty corridors.

A woman's voice.

Brad sipped the kombucha and managed to sit up. Strumming quietly in tune, he approached the singer.

It was too dark to see her, but he recognized that high, clear voice. As he neared, she fell silent.

"This all used to be forest," she said.

"Like trees?"

"Before the mall. I was born in Mall A, same as you, but my grandmother told me." She kicked the ground. "Thought I'd get out some day."

Brad sat nearby on the cold floor. "My name's Brad, by the way."

"Alta."

He sank back against the fuzzy wall with its doggy smell. "I'm homeless. The Shoppe showed me elders, children, ceremonies, stars..."

"Yeah. Festivals, spirits, worship."

"But I've never seen those things, not even in music videos."

"Me neither, just in visions while we played music."

He strummed sad chords, and they sang laments for old-growth forests and cultures, though he barely knew what he was singing.

When their throats fell silent and dry, the songs echoed through the hallways. He gave her his last sip of kombucha.

"That's gallant of you." Alta sipped, and they sat in silence for a long time.

Then she said, "I have an idea."

"For what?"

She pulled him to his feet and led him through the dark hallway, and stopped in front of what had been the Sound Healing Shoppe.

He said, "I hate seeing it boarded up like this." And that was odd: he could see it, even without his phone light.

"Look up, Brad."

He did, then shrank down to protect himself. Light poured through cracks in the ceiling.

Alta was poking at the cracks with a piece of rebar. "Can you help?"

"You crazy? We don't know what's out there."

"So what are you going to do, go back?"

"I... I blew up the cereal aisle."

Alta made an impressed hum. "Might just get in trouble for that."

"Yeah, there's this guy —"

Alta shuddered. "The Cleaner?"

"You know him?"

She shuddered harder, then looked back up at the ceiling. "We've got to get out."

Brad breathed in deeply, and his out-breath was full of friends he'd never see again, video games he'd never win. All gone.

"Alright, let's do it."

It was dusty work. Brad barely jumped aside as a chunk of concrete struck the floor. The cracks widened. Light flooded in.

"Almost!" Alta pried out a chunk of concrete from above her, then a bigger one. She dropped the rebar, shielding her eyes against the light.

Brad stepped back, shielding his head from falling chunks.

When he could see again, he saw a hole just big enough to fit through.

They piled fallen concrete to make a rough staircase, and climbed up. Bashing, stumbling, prying. With a final effort, Alta shoved up and out.

Brad shrank back. Up above, beyond the hole, a brilliant ball hung in the air, brighter than a thousand fluorescent lights, more powerful than the mall's entire electrical system. Maybe it was Brad's imagination, but he heard it crackling and booming in the sky. Its light warmed Brad's skin, like that time he'd gone too close to a burrito oven.

He turned away and stumbled back down the rubble staircase. The Cleaner was right. Brad should go back to where he belonged. He was a mall baby, not made for a huge, intense world. Brad would return to cheese sticks, pop, plants that didn't smell. If he needed variety, let it be in the slow shift of the hits, as old ones slid from the chart, and new ones came in.

"Brad?" she called down.

"What if it's Tuesday already? Big box of buttery popcorn on me, Alta, what do you say?"

"Brad, get up here!"

"What if they don't have normal food out there? Like if there's just grass and shrubs, like vegetarians eat."

"*I'm* vegetarian."

"Sorry, I —"

"Sunlight, Brad."

"You eat sunlight?"

"No, that's what this is called. I remember my grandmother told me. It doesn't seem so bright anymore. Geez, I can see green grass. And trees. Real trees!"

She crouched, peering down through the hole at him. She looked radiant, terrifyingly free. "See for yourself."

She reached down, and Brad withdrew.

"Knew you couldn't do it, boy," a voice resonated from behind.

The man who stepped from the shadows had no cart, no mop or sprays. Gone was his starchy white uniform, replaced by worn overalls. He held a coil of rope in one hand, which he fingered as he had his spray-guns.

The Cleaner raised a hand, reassuring. "What say we forget this little incident? No repercussions. Teenagers do foolish things."

"I..."

"Throw in a year of free movie passes?"

"You could do that?"

"With popcorn."

"All you can eat?"

"Sure as the sun shines, boy."

Unsure, Brad called to his mind a host of action lines to bolster his resolve. "Your reign of terror ends here and now," he said. "You must face justice for your crimes." It had sounded like such a good line, coming from Chuck Van Willis. It didn't even make sense in this context. He added weakly, "I'd rather die than go back."

"Would you?" asked the Cleaner.

"I mean —"

"Ah, heard it in a movie. Out for your freedom, I got it. But what if you get your freedom and then you die?" asked the Cleaner. "Pretty useless freedom, no? Not much protein out there, boy, grazing with rabbits and deer and other... *vegans.*" He said the last word like a swear, yet with a tinge of sadness in there.

"I'm sure there's popcorn?" Brad hadn't meant it to come out as a question.

"Not a nibble. I should know, I..." The Cleaner gritted his teeth, silencing himself.

Brad was hungry, thirsty. He *could* return. It didn't even matter whether it was Tuesday; every movie was free to him now! Maybe his parents would finally take some time off from the Notary Republic and they could go together.

As if that would ever happen.

He shoved the Cleaner aside and scrambled up the rubble staircase. "My spirit cannot be bound!"

"Just your body, boy." The Cleaner clambered up behind.

Brad burst onto the rooftop and a whole new world emerged. A meadow of brilliant, waving grass, with trees — real trees! — reaching upward. Some were even taller than the roof of the mall, and geez, the mall was so high that looking down made Brad dizzy. That fall could kill him. Birds stroked the sky in murmuring patterns. Clouds streaked farther in every direction than he was able to see. This was better than any deodorant commercial, even better than that ad for potato chips with the great song. The resolution was higher than the newest TVs, and the smells made the Perfume Panther seem... artificial.

Brad murmured a verse from a poem that had always touched him. "From dirty cuts to clean freedom, Fix-cream's got you covered. Live life without fear, ever untethered."

How would he get down from here? He had seen people make bigger jumps in movies... He bent his knees. Didn't they have stunt doubles and ropes to help them?

"Wondering if it's real?" The Cleaner stepped up onto the roof, his short hair ruffling in the breeze.

Alta grabbed a piece of rebar from the ground. "We can fight him."

The Cleaner's gaze settled on Alta. "Thought you were dead, girl." He tipped his hat. "Guess I'm glad you ain't."

She clutched the metal bar, glaring at him. Then her gaze softened. "He was happier, you know."

The Cleaner grimaced. "Don't tell me what he was."

"Who?" asked Brad.

"Don't you know?" said Alta. "That boy who sold you his guitar —"

"Don't say it," barked the Cleaner. "He's not anymore. I disowned him."

Brad stared at his old nemesis. "The smelly cool kid is your *son*?"

The Cleaner's hand drifted to his waist. The rope hanging there was starting to look more and more like a whip. In a flash, Brad realized that all those hours of action movies had not prepared him for a real fight.

Brad raised his hands and motioned for Alta to back away. "We won't fight."

Alta backed away, but kept a tight grip on her metal bar.

"And not 'cuz we're afraid," Brad added. "It's because this new world shouldn't start with fighting."

He stepped in front of Alta, let his hands fall, and faced the Cleaner.

"Well alright, then." The Cleaner unhooked the rope.

Brad closed his eyes and sang a lines from one of the healing CDs. "I sing of love in times of hate, of hope in times of fate. I sing of boats..."

"They're all times of fate." The Cleaner waved toward the roof's edge. "You going to jump off or not?"

"Is that what your son did?" asked Alta.

The Cleaner winced.

Brad's chest tightened. "Why are you provoking him, Alta?"

The Cleaner looked toward the ground, so far below, and his stance softened. "He would have jumped."

With a sigh, he handed Brad the rope. "If you see him, tell him I closed that damned Sound Healing Shoppe."

A long silence opened between the three of them, a vessel that soon filled with birdsong and wind rustling through grass.

Brad took the rope. It was heavy and coarse. "Thank you."

The Cleaner gazed toward the cluster of trees. "And tell him if he does come back, he'd better have stories to tell me."

"I'll tell him."

Alta was looking down over the roof. "I'll go first."

Brad nodded. "I'll hold the rope."

Feet pressed against the lip of the roof, Brad held the rope tight while Alta scaled down. She was heavier than she looked. His muscles strained more and more, and just when they were about to give, the weight lifted.

He looked down to find her dancing. She looked up. "Wait, how will you get down?"

A hand gripped Brad's shoulder. "Boy."

Brad pushed the hand away. "You going to take me back?"

The Cleaner scoffed. "Like the lady said, how will you get down?"

"You won't let go?"

"Only one way to find out."

The way down was terrifying, and Brad nearly clambered back up. The whole time, he was sure the Cleaner would let go.

When he landed, Brad squealed, "This ground's squishy!"

"Called grass, boy. You might have to eat it."

And with that, the Cleaner was gone. Silently, Brad thanked the man.

They started walking. Alta pulled out a Guatemalan shaker, and found a groovy rhythm. Brad strummed a bittersweet chord. They walked along squishy, pathless ground until they saw, there across the waving grass, a boxy building larger than the one they had left. On one wall, a towering sign read:

OAK MALL

The wall below the sign was broken. People streamed out in twos or threes, yelling and singing. Brad and Alta rushed toward them, adding harmonies. They sang for trees, open sky, and for new seeds sprouting from a worn but fertile world.

Theodore Lowry's story "Escape to Mall B" was originally published in Metaphorosis on Friday, 9 June 2023. See magazine.metaphorosis.com

About the author

The mall in which Theodore was born sprung up at the confluence of two rivers, rivers who go on to create one of the eastern great lakes. His family migrated westward, so he sprouted up where vast grasslands crash against the western mountain range. Seeking temples, pilgrimage and clear meanings within messy, colorful life, he traveled to the far east to learn in monasteries there. Seeking to link sky to earth, he returned to his home continent to put down roots among the mycelium and cedar of this chilly rainforest. He writes, sings, draws, and helps others do the same.

storypaths.substack.com

A Yellow Landscape

Sarah McGill

I dream of vast landscapes. The distance bends like cotton on a washing line or a rabbit vanishing down a hole. In my dream, women come, carrying brutally tined forks. Their hands crook around their bodies and somehow they are monstrous and too big. I walk, and I think I'm looking for a better landscape. Or only another landscape. This place is too wide and I pool borderless across it.

A woman draws her fork around her and says, "When I was a girl and I walked on the beach, I found a little house crusted in salt. I sat inside and ate lamprey and mint leaves. At dusk it flooded and I laughed, splashing my feet in the water. I grew into the shape of that house, ancient and mindful."

"My nana's house was a tent," I say and I am very proud. "I want to have walls like she did, but I don't know how to grow into the shape of a tent. She walked barefoot on the mountain with her mule. She made acorn flour and shouted *haloo haloo* to the thrushes in the valley." I am barefoot too.

"Well, it is good to love your great-grandmother. But there are loose rocks on mountain paths and tents aren't houses. They're unstable."

A woman says, "She must have been sad with no doorway to frame her and no walls to hold her. I suppose she was unhappy because she had no house to grow up in and learn to be herself."

I scratch the dirt with my toes and think they're wrong, but I don't know how. I don't know if Nana was happy. And I hadn't known that a tent wasn't a house. I wonder then what walls I can grow up into if not those. I turn around and walk away from their monstrous forks.

●

I lived in a house that wasn't my house, and I lived in a room that wasn't my room. Out the window was a hill the color of clay, covered in scrub. The bed was my cousin Mosi's, even though I slept in it with her. It was obvious it was hers because my blankets were yellow like soil. These were blue, like a bottomless lake. Mosi decided she liked blue when she went to school and the teachers told her the ocean was best. I kept my bird bones in a drawer with her shells and together we built white houses with bone frames and shell rooves.

Downstairs, someone knocked. Out the window, I saw it was a teacher and I hid in the cupboard in Mosi's room. The teacher came sometimes and said I had to go to school, but she couldn't come for me if I stayed in the cupboard. That's what my aunt said. She said the woman would always go away. That sounded true. The cupboard was the smallest place in the house that I could fit. I knelt, folded up over my knees. Sometimes it was suffocating.

My aunt told the teacher I didn't live in the scrubland. She said I lived with my parents in the mountains, even though that wasn't true and they were dead. When the teacher left, my aunt came and knocked on the cupboard. She opened the door and I spilled out. I sprawled, my legs and arms going as far as they could, all the way until they knocked against the walls.

When I went down to dinner, my cousin jostled me out of my seat next to my aunt and I went to sit out of her reach.

"Did you take the mule up to the hill today?" my aunt asked.

I nodded. "I want the hill to be as tall as the mountain Nana lived on."

My aunt served out the partridge's breast meat with pine nuts and pennyroyal. "If it were a mountain, at the top you would find the circle tent in the cloud, just like the hero Oupa did when he went looking for Buzzard. He lives there now and teaches everyone who comes to him."

"Nana met Oupa," I said, clasping my hands very seriously. "She laid down under a blanket and in her dream she was a kestrel and flew to the top of the mountain. Oupa smiled when he saw her."

My aunt pressed her lips together. "She told that story a lot."

"I want to do that. In my dream, I'll be a buzzard." I added pepper and rosemary to my meat.

Mosi laughed, leaning back in her chair to slap the rug hanging on the wall. Every time she slapped it, she grabbed a little thread and pulled, so that someday it would unravel and she wouldn't be embarrassed when her teacher came for dinner and frowned at the black goats leaping over the mountaintops.

"My teacher said that if you jump from the roof, you'll die," Mosi said. "She says it's a lie that Warbler jumped from a gable and learned to fly."

"Birds learn to fly by jumping from their nests," my aunt said, her eyes down. She ate with her fingers, the grease running down her palms. "You used to like the legends about Oupa."

"My teacher said bird meat is dirty." Mosi wrinkled her nose at the plate and wouldn't eat.

My aunt picked over her plate and I wished she'd say Mosi was wrong, but she said nothing.

●

In my dream, the sand is unfamiliar. Each time I kneel, I stand up far away from where I was a moment ago. I hate it.

I'm looking for Oupa. I think, far away, I see a mountain the color of sky. If I find it, I will find him and he'll teach me all the mountain's stories and how to be a buzzard. I don't look at the women when they come up behind me, although the terrible scraping of their forks makes my shoulders rise and my spine tingle.

"The wind is hard on my face," a woman says. "It burns my cheeks."

"You should wear a scarf like my aunt," I say. "It binds up her hair and keeps off the wind."

"Why don't you wear a scarf?" she says.

I put my hands up and I'm startled to find my hair uncovered, whipping around in the wind. "I lost it. I'll get another scarf, when I go home."

"What if you lose that too?"

For some reason I can't answer the question. It's too startling. Instead I ask, "If a tent isn't a house, then why does Oupa live in a tent?"

A woman laughs, so loud that the soil shakes from the mountain in the distance, cascading orange into the sand. The mountain is left bare and I see it's not a mountain, but only a rock, no taller than my hip. "Because he doesn't know anything at all," she says.

A woman spits. "It's too barren. Bring the ocean here."

I hunch my shoulder at the sprawling landscape. "I like the sand." But I reach into the soil where it's damp. A spring pops up as I pull back my hands.

A woman coos, "It makes me homesick. Oh, I miss squid."

●

Mosi came back to the house jumping, kicking up her legs to show off her new hard shoes. They glistened and I asked her if they were made of beetle carapaces.

"No," she said, and then wouldn't tell me what they were made of. She put her hands on her hips. "I'm going to the ocean."

"The mountain is better. In my dreams I'm going to the mountain."

"You don't really go places in your dreams."

I hurled sand over her shoes so they got dirty. "I do." I was so angry I almost hit her. "Just like Nana. I go somewhere else and you're not there."

"I'm going for real. My teacher says I'll like the ocean so much, I won't want to come back."

I crouched down in the sand. "Why did they come here, if they don't like it?" Many people came inland to escape the encroaching shoreline, the floods making the borders on the old maps all wrong, but there were still people near the ocean.

She licked her palms and leaned over to clean off her shoes. "Because they want to teach us to be good. The mountain people don't know how to be good. But if I go to school on the beach, I can be better."

"It'd be a long walk back in the evening."

She laughed and it was like the women with their forks laughing. "I wouldn't come home in the evening."

I held my hands in a cage at my belly, horrified. I didn't want to sleep in a house that was nearly empty, the wind rattling the loose windowpanes, or eat with just my aunt and the dripping dishes. "You aren't going."

She wrinkled her nose. "Yes I am."

"I said you can't go."

"I don't care." She clapped her hands in my face, like my aunt did when she was angry.

I pushed her hands away. "Your mama won't let you."

"It doesn't matter what she wants."

I lunged, grabbing her through her sweater. She hit me in the nose as we fell and she screamed about dirtying her uniform. I squeezed her around the waist. I imagined the empty house again and shook all over. I didn't want Mosi to leave me. I tried to map her body to mine, to match her concave belly over my hip, her spine around my arm. But she squirmed too much and when she hit my ear and set it ringing, I let go.

She scrambled to her feet, dust scrubbed into her uniform. Tears tracked down the dirt on her face. "I'm going to the ocean and I'm not coming back. No one can make me come back. I'll go to school there and be better than you." She turned and ran inside.

I curled up my knees and pretended I was in the cupboard, with the dark and the smell of pigeon. But it was too small, like I would never get out and would always be its cramped shape. I didn't want to grow into the shape of the cupboard. I sat up and wished a tent were a house.

My mule came around the house. She gnawed on the white shrubs beside me until I reached up and rubbed her flank. Her mane was full of dust. "Mosi doesn't mean it," I told the mule. "She won't leave. She'd miss the drawer with her little towels and the pegs to hang her shoes. The ocean is too wide and terrible for her." My mule gummed my hand.

When I came into the house, dirt up and down my knees, my aunt sighed. "I've told you not to jump on Mosi like that."

"She said bad things to me."

"What did she say?"

I didn't tell her. It would be more true if I said it. I would keep the words in my belly and make Mosi a liar. I sat in the corner and pretended it was a little house just for me.

"Can I sleep in the attic?" I asked while she stoppered the sink and poured in water. The attic had once been a dovecote. Doves were very sacred on the mountain, but I'd never seen one. "I'll sleep on a rug and hang walnuts and garlic like Nana did in the mountain."

My aunt shook her head. "I want Mosi to be in the room with you."

"Why? She doesn't get scared at night anymore. Not since her teacher told her Owl doesn't come at night to steal children's tongues. She says owls are stupid and crabs are better, because their shells are their houses and they fit inside them perfectly."

My aunt muttered something I didn't understand, which sounded ugly and mean. "She's still very young."

"She doesn't like me sleeping with her. I want to sleep in the dovecote." The dovecote roof came to a point like a tent. But it wasn't a tent so it could be a good house where I could learn how to be myself.

She handed me a dish and I just held it. "I need it for storage," she said.

She started soaping the dishes and I held the plate tighter. "But there's nothing up there. Just old rugs and baskets."

She made a *tch* sound with her teeth that meant she was done arguing.

I set the plate into the water, holding it with the tips of my fingers, hoping it would float. It didn't. I scrubbed with the heel of my hand. I felt bad for being upset and hoped I could make my aunt smile. "Were there really doves?"

She put her hand on my shoulder. "A long time ago, when I was a girl. We ate dove when there were guests and to celebrate the day my father came down from the mountain. He said coming down was a good decision. The traders liked him, even though he didn't eat their fish."

I set the plates up to dry on the rack. "What happened to the doves?"

"When I was eleven, I told my teacher I didn't want to go to school anymore. She said I had to. Until I was sixteen, I would go to school. But I wanted to stay home and tend to the doves. My teacher came for dinner and she said we shouldn't eat bird. It made our bones brittle. It scared papa and he got rid of all the doves. Lots of other families were told to get rid of their doves too and soon all the doves were gone."

I rubbed my thumb on the tines of a fork and made faces at it. "Why would everyone give their doves away?"

She crooked her chin into her shoulder and whispered, "I found a dove with a bullet hole in its belly."

"What happened?"

"Not everyone agreed to get rid of their doves." Her shoulders lifted gently, with a kind of long-drawn weariness.

"Was Nana upset that you didn't have dove for her when she visited?"

She clattered a cup into the sink. "Very angry. She called papa a weak son. She said he didn't respect his family's traditions. That's why she took me out of school and brought me up to the mountain, even when the teachers sent men after her to bring me back. We stayed away from them for three years."

I smiled. I'd never lived in the mountains. My mother was a little girl when she came down with her family. I thought sometimes that nothing would be the same if I'd been born in a bed, with walls to hold me like a second womb. Or if I'd been born in a cave, held by stone and a sheet of rain across its mouth. But I was born in a gully and I tumbled out like water from a pipe. The shock of me spilled over and soaked the landscape. I was a flooded road, shallow and clear and so still it was like a hole into the sky.

My aunt's stories about the mountains made me proud and jealous. I wanted to climb a mountain because it went on forever like the scrubland, but it had caves and cliffs and crags and definition.

She put her hand on my head. "Where's your scarf?"

"I lost it in my dream. The wind blew it away. Can I have one of yours?"

"You put it on the windowsill and left the window open, you mean. That was very clumsy."

I scowled. That wasn't what I meant.

She sighed. "Now I have to buy another."

"I'm sorry."

"If we were in the mountains, I would invite a woman to dinner and she would make you a good scarf."

"I'll go to the mountain in my dream and get a scarf."

She shook her head and I snuck guiltily out of the house with her green scarf that showed the coils of my hair underneath. I took my mule to the hill. Maybe I'd run away to the mountain to get another scarf. That was a bad thought, because I lay down in the heather on the hill and stood up hours away, the squat village like rocks among the yellow bushes. But the mountain was still far away, just a tear in the horizon.

My mule snorted as I mounted up. It took us a long time to get back. At the edge of town, a woman looked at us out her window and came out around the front of her house. I tried to turn away, but she came out too fast.

"Good evening," she said. It was the teacher who wanted to take me to school. "Not many people around here have mules." She leaned down and scratched my mule's jaw. "I hear they're not very cleanly."

I held tight to my mule's mane. "They're tenacious. She loves me and takes me where I want."

The woman flicked her fingers like she was dislodging dust and gnats from under her nails. She smelled like fish. "Are you from around here?"

I wanted to say yes. It was my town and I knew it very well. "No."

"Where are you going?"

"I'm riding through."

She smiled, her eyes pinching. "Haven't we met before? I remember. You said you were riding through then too."

"I ride through a lot."

"Mosi's mother wears a scarf like that."

"She got it from my mother. My mother makes these scarves. No one else makes them like this." I remembered then that my aunt had bought the scarf in town and flushed with fear.

The teacher locked her fingers together. "Perhaps you'd like to come in for supper."

I shook my head.

"I insist. You must be hungry. I have red tea, fresh from the fields, and sole fillet with mint."

"I don't like fish."

"You don't know how good it is. This is what happens, when you grow up on birds. Everything else scares you. You're flighty."

"I have to get where I'm going." I dug my heels into my mule's side, jerking her away from the woman. The woman watched me go, her stance trim and disappointed.

I rushed inside when I got to the house. It was dark and the walls stretched away into a terrifying vastness. It was like they weren't there at all. I climbed into bed with Mosi. She didn't like me holding her at night, but I squeezed up against her, staring until I found all the corners in the room.

●

It isn't my dream. Or I think it's not. The sands unravels behind me and I stand on the ocean shore. The water goes on forever, dizzying. It's unfair that I should find the ocean, when I can't find the mountain.

A woman stops beside me and jams her fork into the sand. She takes a deep and satisfied breath. *Ahhh*, she breathes.

"I'll send the ocean away," I say.

She gazes up, the skin crinkling around her eyes. "This is home, sweetheart."

I shake my head hard.

Her coat is like stone. "If your cousin goes to the ocean, you could go to school with her," she says. "Then you wouldn't miss her."

"But I would miss my aunt."

"If you were in a schoolhouse all day, you would be better. You would always sit in the same seat and know where you should be. And there's a drawer in the desk for you to keep your things."

"Can I lock it?" I've never had a thing before that I could lock.

"Good students can keep locked boxes inside their desk. If you went to school, you could bring your friends to the house and say, 'This is my home. This is where I live.' "

I like the idea. Then I could tell the teacher I live here and I'm growing into the shape of my house. "What about the mountain?"

Tsk, a woman says, *tsk*. "The mountain is a bad place to live. It's dangerous. There are no houses, so everything is unstable."

"Oupa lives in a big tent. My aunt says that's his house." But I don't feel very certain about it.

I try to imagine Oupa on the waves, kneeling in a boat, crouched on a reed mat with the sea birds and the white seashells. But it's impossible. My dream cracks around my waist, nearly breaking in half with the impossibility of it. Oupa can't come here, not ever. If he saw me now, he'd say I was the wrong shape and he couldn't teach me. I hold onto a woman's coat, wanting to step into the black recesses that are like tall walls, so that I don't crack all the way through.

●

My aunt stood with her hands hovering over the open cupboards. She stared at the lemons and the pepper and the barley flour. Her hands rested on a tin of red tea leaves, which she bought in the summer and said were very expensive. Her hands slipped to the dried mutton and salted pheasant.

I watched her from the doorway, my toes up against the lintel.

"If only I had a scrap of fish," she muttered.

Goosebumps ran up and down my arms and I put my hand on the doorframe so I wouldn't find myself a great distance away. "Should I kill a chicken?"

Her hands scrunched, fingers folding up tight against her palm. "Yes."

I killed a chicken outside and plucked the feathers, putting them in my pocket for pillows. Mosi came and crouched nearby, squinting. Her hair tumbled down her back, whipping over her mouth.

"My teacher's coming for dinner," she said. "Are you going to hide in the cupboard?"

I shrugged, even though I didn't want to go into the cupboard. There was a stiffness in my throat and I was afraid if I went in there, I would cry. It wasn't a good shape.

"How do you do that?" she asked

"Nana taught me." She died when I was young, but I remembered plucking birds was important. I held out the chicken and Mosi crept forward. I showed her how to grasp the feather so she wouldn't tear the skin.

When Mosi's teacher came, I didn't go to the cupboard. I sat in the closet under the stairs where I could look through a crack in the panels, and sucked on my fingers. If I decided I liked the teacher, maybe I could come out. The teacher came in a flower printed skirt, which flapped against her knees. She smiled and took my aunt's hand with only her fingers.

"I hope you don't mind," she said. "I brought a little something for dinner. I came home early today and I had extra time. I thought, wouldn't it be nice if I brought something to share?"

My aunt nodded, small. She picked up the chicken, which we'd cooked into a thick stew with bay leaves.

"Oh, no. I didn't mean to supplant your own meal." But she let my aunt take the stew away, and replaced it with her own plate. It was a fish of some sort, large and white and stuffed with sweet-smelling pears and apples. It smelled good.

The teacher insisted everyone wash their hands in the sink, scrubbing between their fingers before they ate. Everyone sat very quietly. My aunt didn't eat with a fork usually and she grasped the handle with her whole hand. The teacher held the fork with the ends of her fingers so that it dipped gracefully. She smiled at Mosi, who blushed and looked very proud. It made me jealous.

"Your daughter is a wonderful student," the teacher said.

My aunt nodded.

"You mustn't be concerned that I'm coming with bad news." She spoke with her hands, holding them out like she hoped my aunt would grasp them warmly. "Don't look so worried. I don't have one bad thing to say about her."

Mosi grinned at her mother, who didn't look at her. "Yesterday," Mosi said, "We learned about the new houses they're building on the coast to withstand the flooding."

Her teacher smiled encouragingly. I imagined building a small house out of seashells and the teacher looking at me like that. Maybe I could learn good things at the school and then grow into the shape of the house instead of its cupboards and closets.

"I'm very excited," the teacher said. "You see, there's a lovely boarding school by the seashore. Very safe, of course, and not too near the water. I went to visit last month. It's cleaned every day and the students can play on the beach. There's fresh fish in the morning and once a week they go fishing."

My aunt chewed fast, like she was trying to swallow before the teacher could finish speaking. But the fish went back and forth in her mouth and she couldn't seem to swallow.

The teacher beamed. "We'd like to send your daughter there."

My aunt coughed, spitting up a half-chewed piece of bone and fish.

The teacher jumped. I did too.

"I'm sorry," my aunt said. As if to remedy her fault, she cut off another piece of fish and put it in her mouth.

"That is to say," the teacher said, her hand on her chest, "all the students will be going there, eventually. But we'd like to send your daughter sooner."

"Mama, I have to go," Mosi said, hopping up onto her knees. A shock of horror went through me.

My aunt waved her back and Mosi slid down on her seat. When my aunt swallowed, it was like something huge was going down her throat, bulging the skin tight.

The teacher put out her hand. "I know it'll be hard for your daughter to move so far away. But you can visit. Or you can move to the shore, even. We'll help you buy a house and find a job, maybe skinning fish or somesuch."

"Yes, mama," Mosi said. "Come live with me."

My aunt stared at her daughter, her eyes wide and confused. "I've lived in this house my whole life."

"Your daughter told me that your father came down the mountain as a young man. Wouldn't it be following in his footsteps to move to the ocean?"

My aunt blinked at her. It was as if the woman had slipped her father under her nails like slivers of wood. "I could see Mosi then?"

I put my face against the panel, the wood smell strong in my nose. I thought of yelling to her that she couldn't go because then I would be alone. My body would spill over the scrubland and I'd vanish.

"Of course. It is a boarding school, so she'll sleep over. But she can visit you on the weekend, if she chooses."

My aunt set aside her fork. "I don't see any reason why she should go earlier than the other students."

Mosi gripped her fork, bits of fish still caught on the tines. "Don't you think I'm a good student?"

"Of course you're a good student," my aunt mumbled.

"Your daughter will benefit by going early. It's a better school."

"I don't want her to go."

The teacher folded her fingers together, poised over her fork. "There's another thing." She glanced around the house, frowning at the rugs on the walls, the sunflower seed oil on the counter, the unwashed dishes. I shrunk back into the closet. "Your niece."

"She doesn't live here," my aunt said automatically.

The teacher sighed, her shoulders heaving up in exasperation. "We've played this ruse for a long time. We've let you get away with it and we shouldn't have. We know your niece lives here, and it's illegal to keep her from school."

Mosi glanced at the stairs and squeezed down in her chair, shoving fish into her mouth. I was terrified that the teacher would stand up and thrust her hand into the closet and drag me to school right now. I wouldn't go to school if they meant to send me to the ocean.

"The next semester starts with the rainy season. Mosi will go to the school on the shore and your niece will start school here. It'll be better for everyone."

My aunt shook her head, but said nothing. The teacher wiped her mouth and popped up cheerily. "Thank you so much for supper. Please, keep what's left of the fish. It's my gift to you."

When she was gone, my aunt slid down until her head sunk into her arms. Mosi sat still, staring at her mother collapsed across the table. I leaned against the closet door, the doorknob pushing painfully into my hip, needing someone to say it wasn't true. Mosi stood, clenching her hands opened and closed, and left the room.

●

In my dream, the wind ripples the ocean waves, hushes, holds still. But then the tide gushes up the beach, washing over my knees, and I slosh out with the water, tumbling over the waves. I'm drowning. I catch my throat in my hands and bubbles pour of my mouth. There's nothing here to hold me. I spill until I am so big and thin that it's like I'm nothing at all.

●

I got up early so Mosi couldn't leave for the ocean without talking to me. My tongue was thick with salt. My aunt stayed inside, putting chicken stew into small pots sealed with leather caps. She moved slowly, stopping often to stare out the window. Mosi sat outside on her suitcase, rubbing her nose red.

"Do you think it'll be cold?" she said. "What if my sweater is too thin?"

"Wear a scarf over your hair." I scuffed my heels in the dirt.

"It's not allowed at the new school."

But she wore a scarf now, which she hadn't done in months. It tucked neatly under her sweater collar, crafted into a perfect curve against her back.

"You could wear it if you weren't being stupid and going," I said.

She stiffened. "I have to go."

I wrinkled my nose at the road winding toward the school and the car that would come for her. "I've never slept alone before."

"They'll make you go too."

I scratched my wrists and rammed my toes against the step. "Nana would be angry."

"Nana's dead."

I shoved her and she grabbed my hand, holding tight to my wrist. She looked at me and squeezed and squeezed. "Ow," I said. But she didn't let go, just kept squeezing until my wrist cramped. "Ow!" I shouted, jerking away.

She clasped her hands and stared down at her lap. "I wish you'd come."

"No. I hate the ocean. I hate it."

She buffed the side of her shoe with her wrist. "You've never seen it."

"I want to go to the mountains."

"What if there's no one left there anymore?"

I pushed my heels hard against the step. "They're still there. They'll teach me how to set up a tent and whenever I'm afraid of how big everything is, I'll set up my tent and sit inside."

Under her breath, like she was saying something forbidden, she asked, "Can you dream about the ocean and visit me?"

The sky spun and I had to sit down. I put my arm around her. "Yes."

She flushed and straightened her cuffs. "I'll write letters."

The door rattled and banged, catching on the frame as my aunt came out with a pot for lunch. Mosi put it in her bag. My aunt crouched behind us and fiddled with Mosi's scarf.

"What if we ran into the mountains like me and my grandmother did, when I was a girl?" my aunt said, very quiet.

I squeezed my hands shut. I wanted that very much. But my aunt would never go.

Mosi patted her bag, checking that everything was there. Then she stood, brushed off her uniform, and grabbed her mother around the waist. She held so tight her mother gasped and her hand fluttered indecisively over Mosi's back.

Then the car came and she left us standing alone on the stoop.

●

I sit in the surf, water dripping down my back and my clothes soaked through. When I twist out my hair, a river spills away. The ocean waves beat against my chest. I'm so angry I want to cry. All the ocean does is take people away. Nana wouldn't have gone. She knew the mountain was where she should be and was happy in her tent. Why couldn't a tent be a house? It was as much a house as anything.

The mud sticks and scrapes when I stand. But when I'm on my feet, I see something caught on the waves. I run to it and when I snatch it up, it's my scarf, the one I lost in my other dream. I wring it out and bind it over my hair.

●

In the morning, it started to rain. As I tucked my hair behind my scarf, I realized it was the scarf I found in my dream. I went into the kitchen and found my aunt opening drawers loudly. She hadn't slept. I'd heard her moving around all night, stacking plates and pouring water and then sitting at the table, the chair creaking when she shifted.

"You'll go to school today," she said.

I shook my head.

She rubbed her face, holding herself up on the counter with her left hand. "You have to go. I'll be arrested if you stay here."

"I'm going to be a buzzard!"

She stared down at her hand. "I'll still tell you stories about Oupa in the evening. We'll sit outside and look for his home in the clouds."

"They'll send me to the ocean." My arms flopped over the table like awful cooked fish. "I went to the ocean in my dream and I drowned."

Her hands went over the sink, rubbing and rubbing so it said *shush, shush*. "You didn't go anywhere. You just dreamed about it because you were thinking about the ocean."

"I found my scarf in my dream last night." I held up the scarf to show it was true.

She snapped her hands together. "You lost it under the bed or stuffed it into the bottom of your chest."

"No. Nana went places in her dreams."

"No she didn't. It was a good story. She couldn't do that." She grabbed a plate and set it down in front of me. Honey pooled over yesterday's bread.

I stared at her as she sat down and started eating. She didn't look at me. The corners of her mouth were firm and angry. I didn't understand how she could say that about Nana. It was the most impossible thing she'd ever said.

"You can't travel places in your dreams," she said.

I knocked against the walls. I spilled out the open door and the window. I drowned in the arid air.

I didn't finish breakfast. I packed lunch and extra food because I'd always eaten when I wanted and I was terrified of being told I could only eat at a certain time. Outside, through the drizzle, I searched for Oupa's circle tent in the clouds. It began to rain so hard the world turned grey and brown. My scarf plastered to my hair. I splashed through water, looking for my mule. Everything vanished into the downpour.

The house was dim and hazy. All the lamps were out and it was floating at sea, vast and empty. My heels sank into the mud and I was floating too. My skin crawled. The house was a bad shape. If I went in it again, it would crush me with its twisted rooms and slippery stairs and bent doorways. It was the wrong shape.

In the mountains, I would find a cave and the cave would hold me until the rains passed.

When I found my mule, I packed the saddlebags and mounted quickly, urging her on to the slippery road. The town was blue, vanishing in the coming tide. I could be anywhere, or nowhere. Water ran down my back and chest and my pants stuck to my thighs. My aunt would stay here forever, drifting aimlessly. I watched a buzzard fly under the clouds, its feathers black with rain. It was going toward the mountain. When it got there, people might see it and then tell how Oupa and Buzzard became friends. They would tell it inside their tents and they wouldn't mind that the walls flapped in the storm, because that was the shape they'd grown into. If I were there, I'd grow into that shape too, instead of a rigid, crooked house.

I pulled my mule around, digging my heels so hard into her sides that she leapt. She landed at a gallop and we pounded out of town.

"We'll go to the mountains," I said into her ear, mud from her hooves splashing against my shins. "Our family lived at the rim of the mountain and they weren't hard to find. Oupa will teach me to be persistent like Buzzard and strong like Nana. I'll sit in a tent and grow into it and it'll be my home. I think maybe tents aren't houses, but they can still be homes."

In the evening, the rain cleared. The mountains were white and red slips on the horizon, cutting out a small space for themselves in the sky. By morning they were bigger than even the women with their forks, and I could see smoke from cook fires. I imagined Oupa when he first came to the mountain, watching in wonder as Buzzard flew up and up and up and yet never seemed to reach the top. When Oupa finally reached the foothills, he put his hips and knees against the mountain crags and found that he fit. I reached the mountain that evening and as we went up the rocky paths, the peaks rose up like tents.

Sarah McGill's story "A Yellow Landscape" was originally published in Metaphorosis on Friday, 5 April 2019. See magazine.metaphorosis.com

About the author

Sarah McGill has published fantasy short stories in *Strange Horizons, Metaphorosis, GigaNotoSaurus, Not One of Us,* and elsewhere. She studies Medieval literature, but her favorite time and place is post-revolution France at the height of the Death Cabarets, mostly because the bohemians really did walk their lobsters in the rose gardens and pretend hydropathes were Canadian animals whose feet were made into drinking glasses. You can find her occasional ramblings at sarahmcgill.com.

The Last Duty

Dawn Lloyd

The fireworks rocketed past the jagged remnants of the palace's roof, soared above the razor wire, and then cascaded down behind the wall. The gunpowder boomed. The first four nights, my eyes had jerked to the remnants of the roof still clinging to charred rafters. I was sure the concussion would shake the last pieces lose, crushing me. But I had not been so lucky, and tonight I closed my eyes to shut out the lights.

Huddled in the corner, Petrov shifted. I opened my eyes to see him struggling to pull the wool blanket tight against the snow. Only two weeks before, the gold-rimmed dome of the palace's great hall had cast a yellow tinge on the empire's largest silk carpet. Now we sat on rubble and slush. The rebels who thought they could rule better than him had looted the gold.

"Are you awake, Jerov?" He asked.

"How could I not be?" I tried to keep the edge out of my voice. I had nothing but the highest regard for the man who had crushed the Charter Rebellion and held the islands together through the bread riots. I closed my eyes yet again, this time against the images of waves crashing over the torn and broken bodies our soldiers had hurled from the cliffs. The images grew still stronger with my eyes closed. There were reasons I was glad I had been Minister of the Finance and not a general.

"I was just thinking," he went on, his voice quiet and shaky, "that the map to the caves where the desalination plant designs are kept surely burned with the rest of my office."

"I have no doubt it did," I assured him.

"You were always better at maps than me," he continued. "Do you think you could sketch it?"

The last sketches I'd seen had been shoved in our face yesterday. The tall palace guard who usually whistled "The Mourners' Revenge" laughed when he waved the cartoons of the rest of the royal family at us. Petrov's wife, my sister, had been stripped naked, the artist exaggerating her breasts and lips absurdly. The first drawing showed her standing by the stocks. The second, with her innards strewn across the barren ground. The last, a flock of vultures vomiting after eating them. The guard had assured us the first two were true, and the last would have been if the rioters had left anything for the birds.

It was my fault. The rioting had increased when we lengthened the period of compulsory military service. Apparently we were supposed to somehow protect the islands without an army. We'd executed over two hundred of the rioters, plus their families, but it hadn't stopped them. The rioting advanced until we heard them at the palace gates, and then the palace itself. Petrov had handed me his own knife and begged me to see to his family if it became necessary. Then he bolted out the door to command the guards, but the quaver in his voice made his intent clear.

I had raced up the steps to where my sister clutched the curtain overlooking the courtyard. I was no fool, nor was I naïve to the mob's intent, but when she turned to me, her eyes begging protection, my hand froze. How could I slice her neck and watch the blood spurt like a common soldier's?

Thankfully, Petrov's voice pulled me from the memory. "The map, Jerov. Could you reconstruct it?"

I snorted. "You think they'd let us buy our lives with that?"

"Don't call me a fool." His voice was soft, quiet. I hadn't called him a fool. I'd only thought it. "We're the only ones who knew about the map, and they won't be able to build any more desalination plants without the designs in the caves. When we die, the plants go with us."

"Right," I muttered, relishing our last revenge.

The night sky flashed blue and green for a moment, tainting the snow the same color. The boom came instants later.

He took a slow, ragged breath. It sounded hollow against the explosions and the cheers. "The aquifers will run dry in less than twenty years. They'll need to be able to build more plants, and without knowing where the caves are, they won't know how to design them."

"If they didn't kill us, we could keep producing water for them. Murdering swine." It had been my own great grandfather who had sponsored the inventor and then suggested we maintain a monopoly on the plants for just this day. Why should the people have them if we were dead?

His dark outline turned to face me. He pulled his legs up, and the blanket around them. "They'll never find that cave on their own."

The blanket slipped from my own shoulders. Cold air slashed across my arms, but seconds passed before I noticed. "You can't be serious. Not now. Not after all this."

"This isn't the people. The people wouldn't turn against me. It's heretics provoking them."

I didn't know how to respond. Was it a greater cruelty to remind him of the crowd chanting for our deaths, or to let him go on with his delusions?

"Heretics that your own people wouldn't even fight. And it wasn't the heretics who did this." I waved at the blackened beams and razor wire shadowing the sky.

Silence settled around us. Through the clouds, the hazy circles of the two moons stared down, cold and indifferent.

"Jerov," he said at last, "you didn't carry out my last request. Do this, at least, for me."

If I were not so weak, I would have had my hands at his throat no matter his station. "Don't," I growled, "don't even start with that."

"Because it's true?"

"Because," I snapped, but stopped.

He didn't press. A cough penetrated the darkness, and for a moment I thought he was crying again, trying to choke down the sound and hide it. But a flash of red lit his face and flickered to yellow. His lips were drawn in a tight line, his face hard.

There was no purpose in arguing with that expression. I took a deep breath, staring up at the gray sky as if it would release me from the truth. I owed him whatever I could repay, not just because of his station, but for my sister. Why did helping our murderers have to be his last request? Nevertheless, the longer I thought of protests, the more map lines and ridges squiggled into my head.

"They'll never believe it even if I do draw a new map."

"They will if we make it look like we were trying to hide it."

"Of course," I let the sarcasm drip from my voice. "Fine. I'm sure the guards will be happy to give us the paper." I went to the door and called, "Hello?"

From down the corridor, close to where his forefathers' portraits hung, where his should have been placed at his death, came drunken laughter.

"Hello!" I shouted again, louder.

"What d'ya want?" a voice slurred back.

What could I say? That we wanted to help them, truly. Their impudent revolt, the murders, the destruction, were all trivial. We still wanted to be the good and caring rulers that we always had been and to protect them from themselves.

"I need help," I tried.

Hoots pierced the darkness until a blue shower and another explosion drowned them out. I turned back to Petrov, triumphant.

He still faced the place I had been sitting. "We're next to the library. You could climb out and get paper from there."

I sighed and retraced my steps.

I spent the next 30 minutes rolling and stacking stones against the wall. My head fell to my hands when I finished, and he spoke.

"I'm sorry. I know you don't think they deserve it."

"I feel our last night would be better spent in prayers."
Or better spent in anything.

"When Naimat was a baby, and he fell and cut himself,
and then hit the nurse because he didn't want her to put
ointment on it, did you abandon him to let the wound
become infected?"

"That's different."

"How?"

"They aren't children."

"Of course they are. If they didn't think like children,
they wouldn't have tried to overthrow us."

"Tried?" The word stuck in my throat.

He didn't answer, just pointed at the top of the wall
meaningfully.

I braced one hand against the wall and began
climbing, placing as little weight on any single stone as
possible. At the top, straining, I could just reach a handhold
where the wall had cracked, but I wasn't strong enough to
pull myself up.

He lurched towards me on his good leg. I wanted to tell
him to stop. My job was to serve him, not for him to help
me. But the truth was, there was nothing more I could do
without help.

He reached the pile and braced a shoulder against the
wall, making a step for me with his back.

I couldn't.

He took a breath. "Go on. I can't stay here forever."

And so I went, forcing my foot to touch his shoulder
and then searching the rocks until at last something jutted
up beneath my palm. It was a carved leaf of the grape vine
that had latticed the ceiling. I cleared the snow off it and
leaned my weight back, testing it in the way I had when, as
boys, we had dared each other to climb the lighthouse
overlooking the Duralaman Cliffs.

The broken rocks tore at my clothes and skin as I
pulled myself up, but I didn't feel it until I panted from the
top and looked down the hall. The guards leaned against
the table, boots propped against the remnants of portraits
clinging to the wall. The nearest one sat with his back to
me, waving a crystal and gold goblet in broad, drunken
circles as he spoke.

Petrov waved me down, and I realized I was just as visible to them as they were to me. I swung my legs over, found the emptiest place on the floor, and jumped, tumbling forward onto my hand.

Bookcases had fallen, crushing centuries of books beneath them. Others lay scattered on the floor, fragile spines torn. I picked my way through, resisting the urge to straighten and restack the books. Petrov had always scoffed at my love of them.

I was creeping towards the scroll room, having decided they would be the best for a map, when the door opened near my destination and torchlight quavered. I crouched behind a bookcase, lying low to the ground. A pile of books slid under my hand. I grabbed for them, but they slipped anyway. I froze, hoping he would think it was only the weight of the books against each other.

The torch raised higher, moving from side to side, but it came no closer. I realized I had stopped breathing, then wondered why. Was I afraid he would kill me?

Minutes passed before the wooden legs of a chair scraped against tile and the jaunty notes of "The Mourners' Revenge" lilted out to me. He must have sat down by the door.

I had no other choice. I couldn't lie there behind the bookshelf all night, and so carefully I crawled backwards, arms bent, belly barely above the ground, like an alligator reconsidering its route. Wending my way around sprawling piles of books and broken bookcases, at last I reached the far wall and sat up. The guard sat less than ten paces from the scroll room. If I had continued walking my current route, I would have had to pass directly in front of him. Now I needed to squeeze down the corridor by the wall and then dart into the room when he wasn't looking.

The bookcase sheltering me from his vision lay tipped against the wall, allowing me to stand with my head ducked. I crept forward, hand stretched out to guard against the darkness, until at last I reached the end. The door to the scroll room stood four steps away. If he looked away, it would take less than a second to bolt in. If he looked away.

Seconds and then minutes ticked by. My legs began to ache from the tension. If I had something small, I could throw it to distract him, but the books scattering the floor were too big. I had nearly despaired and given in to the idea of sprinting in front of him when a gust of wind from the empty roof made the torch flicker. He looked up at it, and in that moment, I leapt. My feet seemed to pound the ground as I careened around books to hide my footsteps from him. If he heard through his drunkenness, he did not come to investigate.

Once my heart slowed, I reached for the first scroll I saw. The desk back in the corner stood surprisingly well intact, and I took a pen from the corner and a still-intact bottle of ink from the top drawer.

Hiding in the shadow of the door, I waited for perhaps half an hour, wishing I could simply draw the map there. It was too dangerous to wait there long enough for the ink to dry before carrying it back, though, so I watched for an opportunity to repeat my dash to the shelter of the bookcase. At last, his torch burned low and he stood, stretched, and disappeared back through the door.

The return trip was easy. All I had to do was make myself force one foot after the other down onto the books. The bookcases made an easy staircase up the wall. I tucked the scroll under my arm, and deposited the ink and pen in my pocket. What did stains matter now?

From the rock pile, Petrov watched me. I mimed tossing him the scroll, then did so. He caught it with the same deftness he had shown even when we fenced in our youth, and I lowered myself to his side, testing my weight on the rocks that shifted and rolled as I dropped onto them.

At last I sat, resting in front of him.

"You were gone a long time. Did you have problems?" he asked, as if I might have stayed there for the joy of it. Of course, under other circumstances, that might have been true.

"A guard, the one who whistles all the time, came to look. I had to dodge him."

Petrov grunted. "I suppose it wouldn't have mattered if he'd seen you."

"Except I wouldn't have anything to draw on." I stopped, for the first time wishing I had let the guard drag me back.

He just grunted again, opening the scroll and squinting against the shadows to see it. "Which one is it?"

I shook my head. "No idea. It came from the science wall."

"You can draw the map after sunrise? Before the guards come?"

"I should be able to." I shrugged. "But you still haven't told me how you're going to get them to believe it."

He was silent for a time, then. "We could tell a guard to leave it in some unique place. Let him think we expect someone to come. He'd try to sell it instead."

"Tell?" I corrected.

"Yes." Then, softer as the realization sunk. "Yes, I see your point." He paused and my mind worked against the problem when he went on. "A bribe, perhaps?"

Etiquette and years of respect kept me from snorting. "Bribe him with what? The stones we sit on in our final hours?"

His voice raised as if issuing orders. "Outside the western wall, behind the boulder that marks the beggars' grave, is a smaller stone. Under it is a small cavern. He is to leave the map there. If he returns the following night, he will find his payment. We still have friends. His efforts will be well rewarded."

I nodded into the blackness. "That could work."

"It has to."

●

Through the night, as the snow fell between us, I watched him. He did not move, but I don't believe he slept, either. Twice he tipped his head up as if he could see the stars through the clouds, and sat that way until the snow turned his face white. The hours rolled on until the sky tinged orange.

I had completed the inking and was blowing it dry when the bar grated upwards and the door opened. It was, yet again, the whistler.

Petrov raised his chin and waved the guard closer.

He came.

"I have a task for you," Petrov announced.

I had assumed his tone in outlining the plan to me was only habit. I had assumed he would speak it as a request. I had assumed he would not think to give orders.

I had assumed wrong.

"Behind the beggar's grave is a stone. You are to leave this map under that stone.

The guard stopped. "I am to do *what*?" He spat out the "what" in a fashion I doubted had ever been used to Petrov's face.

Petrov continued unflappably. "If you return the next day, you will find your payment in the form of melin shells. My associates will make it well worth your efforts."

"Melin shells? You think I'd help you for money?"

"It will be enough that you can buy yourself a high seat in the..." his voice quavered for just an instant. Perhaps the guard did not notice, "in the new regime."

"Would it be enough that if I had it now, I could buy the privilege of holding the sword?"

Petrov took a deep breath. "It would be enough, yes."

The guard walked over to where I stood, still holding it flat to dry. He yanked it out of my hands, and I fought down the urge to strike him for his impudence.

"I'll see that your map is taken care of," he muttered, rolling it and undoubtedly smudging the ink before he stalked out.

The door closed and the bar pounded into place before Petrov spoke again.

"He won't do it."

"No," I answered, fighting down guilt at my triumph. "But we had no other choice. There won't be any other guards in here today before..." There was no point in actually saying the words.

Several breaths passed. "We don't have time to make another. We'll have to draw attention to it when we're taken out."

I sighed. It was our last morning. There were better ways to spend it.

"When they take us out," he spoke slowly, formulating the plan as he went, "whether it's together or separate, we will each pick someone at random and tell them the guard has it. Loudly. It will need to be someone at the back of the crowd so we can shout it to them. Tell them which guard has it, and that he took it when we were trying to hide it."

"All right," I muttered. A few hours from my death, it was not worth debating.

●

The sky remained gray when the door scraped open. Two new guards entered wearing the absurd red armbands the rebels had adopted. "Him first." The short one pointed at Petrov, not even granting him his name or title. "We won't be able to keep the mob under control much longer if we don't give him to them."

Petrov stared back at him, refusing to acknowledge them unless they addressed him properly.

"Do we get to drag you out?" The taller one sneered, pulling off his armband in what I can only assume was intended as some sort of inane threat. But in the moment of death, threats lose their power.

Petrov stood slowly, dropping the blanket to the ground with a quiet. "Go with them peacefully when they come for you, Jerov," he said, granting me the dignity of following his orders, not theirs, when my turn came.

I always had the romantic notion that great leaders somehow had profound last words. The final words written in books were always weighty. But in that instant, I realized that final moments are still just moments, and no more likely to be inspired by divine insights than any other moments.

"I will go," I said, "and I'll do as you wish, out of respect for you."

The guards exchanged nervous glances and the taller one yanked him towards the door. The shorter one closed it behind them, staying with me as if they could prevent us from whatever strategy we might be initiating in our last seconds.

His gaze rested on me for a moment, then he turned to run a finger along what was left of a carved ivy leaf above the door.

I finally broke the silence. "Don't you want to watch your king be killed?"

"Why would I want to watch an execution?"

"I thought that's what you all wanted."

He didn't look back at me, just continued to trace the ivy, running his finger in oblong circles again and again. "We want a country where people aren't executed for speaking against the rulers. Your soldiers made me watch when they hung my father for saying we could survive the drought if we had more desalination plants. Why would I want to watch something like that again?"

"We are surviving the drought," I said, pulling my blanket tighter around my shoulders.

"Tell that to the mothers who bury —" His words were cut off by a cheer outside. He didn't repeat himself and I didn't press.

He bent to pick up a piece of the ivy that had fallen, pressing it into the jagged hole in the wall. "Your turn," he said.

I followed his instructions, resting a hand against the wall to brace myself. "The guard who whistles, he has a map to the designs for building more desalination plants," I said. Was I following Petrov's wishes or my own?

He didn't say anything. Maybe he didn't even believe me. He just opened the door and stepped aside when the tall guard grabbed me. Outside, the slush-covered grounds were no less dismal than the roofless palace. A split second later, a roar went up. "Kill him twice," someone shouted, and another yelled, "For my son," just as a brick hit my arm, stabbing pain through my shoulder.

I raised the other arm when the guard shoved me and I fell forward. I lifted my head and searched the crowd for a face I could call Petrov's final instructions to as backup, but another rock hit the back of my head and I couldn't see through the blur of pain. I gasped, throwing up my arms to block when something slammed into my side. I rolled sideways as the blows continued.

I could hear the people cheer, but through the dirty cobbles, all I could see were the stained paper shreds of once-bright fireworks. For a moment, I wished I could cheer with them.

Dawn Lloyd's story "The Last Duty" was originally published in Metaphorosis on Friday, 16 August 2019. See magazine.metaphorosis.com

About the author

Dawn Lloyd is an American who got bored and set out across the world looking for adventure. Nineteen years, four continents and six home countries later, she's returned to the US to find adventure as a principal in the Alaskan bush where she is currently the principal of the Newtok & Mertarvik schools as the village of Newtok (total population ~300) is relocated 9 miles across the river to the new site in Mertarvik.

She's chased lions on foot, hung out with mountain gorillas, summited Mt. Kilimanjaro, survived a suicide bombing and lost a number of friends in that and other bombings, lived in places where temperatures of 50+C/120-130F were normal, lived in places which only had a few hours of electricity every few days, lived in places with full daylight at 1 am and darkness at 11 am, and a host of other experiences that she feels very fortunate and privileged to have experienced. Many of these make it into her writing in one form or another. More information about her adventures can be found at

sites.google.com/site/dawnlloydwriter/home.

Koehl's Quality Impressions

Tim McDaniel

Early Wednesday morning, not much past 10:30, I wheezed my way through downtown in my old '31 Ford. Down to White Center, where the city sprawl collided with the suburban rents, resulting in rows of dingy cheap apartment buildings, absentee landlords and the retreats of the old or underemployed. I found the place easily. A building of wooden clapboard, still advertising 'covered parking' even though those parking spaces were filled with rusting Chevys, discarded washing machines, and mildewed mattresses.

I parked along the street and walked up to the front door, then leaned on the button next to the peeling paper with 'Linaman, Manager' penciled on it.

After a long while there was a muffled voice.

"Yeah?"

"Mr. Linaman?"

"Naw, he left months ago."

"You the manager now?"

"Yeah. You a cop or what? No one here been making any calls."

"Nothing like that. I have a small business proposal that you might be interested in."

"A business proposition, huh? So there's money involved?"

"There's money involved." I'd met plenty of guys like him in prison.

"Well come on up, then, I guess. 203."

The door opened, and I climbed the stairs. The thin carpet, perhaps originally a beige sort of color, was held together by stains, and the narrow staircase exuded the tang of cat piss.

Mr. Manager was, as I would have guessed, dressed in an old t-shirt and a pair of sweatpants, and smelled a lot like the staircase. I explained my needs, he articulated his, and we reached an agreement.

I checked out the deceased woman's room next. It was tiny, and the windows didn't open. There were a few sticks of shabby furniture, and one yellowing photograph on a wall, of a young man in a uniform standing in a desert somewhere. The room at least smelled a little better; a lavender-kind of scent lingered there. I closed the door behind me when I left to go back downstairs.

I left the building and took a deep breath. At least the apartment was still vacant. I wouldn't have to make any more deals on behalf of my client. Vampires, we called them, but not the blood-sucking kind. I made a commission on each deal, but they still made me feel like I needed to shower.

●

"Koehl's Quality Impressions" was stenciled in black gothic letters on the glass of my office door. A little crooked. All it needed was a cheesy little "While U Wait" card taped under it. Well, in this building, this neighborhood, I couldn't expect the clients I used to get at First Impressions; over there, Pichrenn's name still brought in the classy set, even this long after his death.

Was "Quality" accurate? Well, it's not bragging to say that I can raise ghosts with the best of them. I can make latent ghosts visible, clear as day, short-term or long. At least I can when I can afford to lay my hands on quality equipment. The gear I use now is so shoddy I'm lucky if Fred and Mary can even recognize dear jowly Aunt Greta.

So, yeah, clients were not lined up outside my door. I came in every day, though, in at nine or maybe ten or eleven and out at five or maybe four, when I wasn't out on a job. I couldn't afford to miss any walk-ins. I got the occasional referral of a double-booked or cheap client from my old friend Nol at First Imp, and some job orders from a few regulars, vampires, some of whom I knew from my prison days. But walk-ins, impulse buyers, were my main source of income. Sometimes people do act on whims. I stayed in the office daily, watching TV or reading or surfing for obits or drinking until I could justify the return to my apartment.

The glass on the door was at least frosted. A classy touch. Most of my clients didn't particularly want to be seen from the street, no more than I wanted passersby to see my empty reception room.

Empty it was, when I got back from arranging the vampire feeding. I hung my jacket on the rack near the door.

Ah. There was a new message for me on my computer. I went to the desk and jabbed the button.

"Hello, Koehl." I was sitting in the chair, and I didn't remember sitting down. Lindsay. "I have a job I'd like to discuss with you. I can come by tomorrow about eleven, if that's good for you."

I hadn't seen her since... when? Oh, yeah. Not since the trial.

God, how I wanted to see her again. And I also really wished that, tomorrow at eleven or so, I could be somewhere else, far away.

●

"I need you to come see me." Pichrenn's voice on the phone had been thin and uneven, air forced through rusty valves. I was in the middle of a job, taking the impression of a young couple's son, four years old at the time of death, but this was Pichrenn, so I called Nolan to take over for me.

This kind of thing wasn't unusual. The job I was doing was routine, though never tell a family that, and Pichrenn often called me away from those to attend him on more interesting cases. Or more high-profile. I figured, and hoped, he was grooming me to take over once he passed on.

I apologized to the couple, saying I had a family emergency, and took a cab over to the address Pichrenn had given me. I found him in one of those huge, lavish condos on 12th, squatting in the corner of a bedroom. The equipment was still boxed, lying in its contoured foam.

The room was dominated by an immense bed, brass. A window took up most of one wall, affording an impressive view of the city and the mountain, and ostentatious abstract paintings garnished the other walls.

There was another bit of apparent abstract art on the peach carpet, a dark red Rorshach image, all that physically remained of the room's former occupant: a bloodstain like an obscene starfish that had been crushed into the floor. There were additional random splashes and splatters on the mussed bed, and even on one of the walls.

Well, this family wasn't shy about displaying their money, if they could afford to keep the condo, untenanted (so to speak), for four and a half months after the murder of the husband. No wonder they could afford Pichrenn himself.

He stood up and looked down at the carpet stain, back straight, perfectly still, but his hands, jammed deep into his jacket pockets, were twisting and pinching the material. He did that a lot, as if his hands were the only vents for whatever emotions roiled within.

Lindsay was next to him, sitting on a clean part of the bed, composed and quiet. Her eyes were on Pichnrenn, but she was breathing a little too heavily.

"The Dudanna murder," Pichrenn said. I raised my eyebrows. The story had been a big one.

"The wife was the one who did it," Pichrenn said. "Made it look like a robbery, or tried to."

"Yeah," I said. "I saw it on TV. Hi, Lindsay."

She nodded at me, her eyes flashing secrets over Pichrenn's lowered bald head.

I said, "Our client, then, must be the dear departed's murderer's sister, is that right?"

Pichrenn smiled. "Right. The sister of the killer. That's what makes it interesting, isn't it?"

I squatted on the floor next to him and surveyed the scene. He was waiting, I knew, for me to see it. Our job, if we did it well enough, would be both a reflection on the murder, and a comment on the client. And of course we had to please our client while doing so, which sometimes meant hiding or disguising our own comments. We were portrait artists. Well, that's how we thought of ourselves. We wanted to do more than get a snapshot of a corpse. Our equipment amplified the energies embedded in the walls, the floor, the air, to reveal not a carcass, but the shade of a living man.

"Not a happy family, I take it," I said. "I mean between the sisters."

"I'd guess not."

"The wife got away with a slap on the wrist, as I recall. The best justice money could buy."

Pichrenn said nothing.

"Sis is, of course, married herself. An older gent, if I recall."

"Very happily married. There've been no reports of trouble."

"Right. And so there would be no jealousy of the sister who snagged the young movie-star-handsome millionaire, no sexual tension at family get-togethers, no younger-sister resentments or buried bitternesses."

"These people were the top predators of the social jungle, Scott. We're not talking about trailer trash."

"Course not."

"Would it make a difference if they were trailer trash? People all do the same things to each other, no matter their positions," Lindsay said. "Cheat on each other, sneak around."

I decided to ask Lindsay what she had meant the next time I was alone with her. But I knew I wouldn't. Betrayal was not something I wanted to discuss. And anyway, Lindsay had a way of making me forget scruples, even as they clearly gnawed at her.

But I had to say something. Something safe. "Sure it would," I said. "They couldn't afford us. They'd have to make peace with their dead and move on."

We were all silent for a time, then I stood up and squatted down again next to the box of highlighters. I took the first one out and stood up, looking the room over again. Then I crossed the room to the bedroom door and extended the tripod. After setting it in place, I put another highlighter just behind and to the left of where Pichrenn still stood. He observed my choices.

I pulled a third highlighter out of the box and placed it just in front of the window. I punched in some settings. Then I looked down at Pichrenn. He cocked his head.

"There was a lot of emotion flying around here, before and during," I said. "The whole area is bound to be saturated."

"Then we wouldn't need three highlighters," Pichrenn said. "I can almost see the remnants without the use of even one."

"You're sensitive, so you don't count. I've set up these two —" I pointed at the one near the door and the one near Pichrenn — "with complementary frequencies. They'll nearly cancel each other out, with just enough bleed-through to give us something to work with. As you say, it's so thick in here that even that amount should be plenty."

"Ummm."

"And the third one, near the window, I've set much lower."

"To pick up the background."

"Right," I said. "With only one, and with all the other energies flying around, all it'll probably pick up will be ghostly half-images, like something seen out of the corner of your eye."

"You did that at the Joshi place," Pichrenn said.

"Are you accusing me of repeating myself? But these will probably be a little weaker, more ghostly. I've been thinking about getting the chance to try this since the Caceres job. There, the energies were so weak there that half-images were the best I could get, but I did think the effect was an interesting one."

Pichrenn nodded. "And why here?" he asked. "A neat effect is just so much dazzle without a purpose to it."

"The energies released during the act," I said, "will be powerful, and I'm sure they'll be compelling as all hell. But they're all of violence, and terror, or its aftermath. We're sure to get some striking images. But what interests me just as much is the underlying tension. I doubt the victim was entirely shocked by his wife's deed."

I chanced a glance at Pichrenn, but his gaze remained focused on the floor, his brow creased. I would have given a pinkie to know his thoughts just then, to know why he wanted me there. Just for the job? Or was he sending me another message? "He knew, he must have known," I said, "that she was on the edge. He probably enjoyed baiting her, flirting with the sister, making her feel unwanted, bullying her, whatever. I don't know. But I'm sure there was something there. If we can display some of that, even as — or especially as — ghostly after-images behind the main action, I think it'll be something worth looking at."

"Hmmm," he said. Lindsay was nodding along.

"And I was thinking. They specified suppression of sounds, knocks, smells, temperature variations, I suppose?"

Pichrenn nodded.

"I don't know if it's totally ethical, but if we allowed a little of the subsonics to leak through..."

"Yes," said Lindsay. She looked over at me.

"Unsettling." Pichrenn got up, bones creaking, and shook a leg that had apparently gone numb. "Very interesting, Scott," he said. "You have a good grasp of things. I believe I'll leave this one in your hands."

I kept my face blank. There was no way he could have found out about what Lindsay and I had been up to. He had called to say he'd be late for a meeting up at his cabin, and things had just happened. And then they happened again, in other places at other times.

"The client paid for your personal attention," I said. "She's bound to be upset."

"I'll smooth things over with her," he said. "If she wants to pay for my judgment, she'll have to accept my judgment that you're the best one for this job."

Maybe that was all there was to it — that he thought I was best for the job.

It kind of makes me sorry that I killed the old guy.

●

Lindsay settled into the chair and leveled her eyes at me. Lindsay Ingham, Charles Pichrenn's former lover, or at least the final one. And mine. She used to breeze through the outer offices on her way to his inner sanctum, slim, elegant, and moneyed, with glossy black hair that bounced off the small of her back.

After Pichrenn's death, she'd pretty much disappeared. At the funeral it seemed to me, at least, that an understanding look had passed between us, an acknowledgement that I was still part of her world. But I had been out on a job when she came by the studio to pick up her mementos. She called me twice. I put off answering. But when she heard that I had taken Pichrenn's impression, she vanished. Felt like I'd betrayed him even unto death. Or maybe it was just guilt that she felt, however unwarranted. Our affair hadn't killed him.

Then the law finally caught up with me, and I saw her in the witness box at the trial, and there was prison. She didn't visit.

And now here she was, in my own little studio, in one of those new skirts that's tight in some places and loose in others, and a black blouse with ruffles around her neck. The air was low in oxygen just then, and my gaze stole back to her face, tracing the line of the chin, her cheeks and eyes and hair, whenever she looked down.

"So. Welcome to Koehl's Quality Impressions," I said. "It's uh, good to see you again, Lindsay."

Lindsay looked around her at the decor — the faded carpet, the Degas print on the wall. "Nice," she said. She didn't say it was nice to see *me* again.

"Yeah," I said. "High class all the way."

"Do you keep your equipment here?" she asked.

"I got a closet. This place came with every convenience. So, what have you been up to?"

"I remember you used to only use the best. You know, Charles really admired your ability to keep all of it in such top shape."

So she didn't want to get personal. No old friends and lovers catching up crap. "That's the trouble with the best stuff," I said. "It's temperamental." Like people. I waited for her to talk.

"Charles used to say you were the best in the studio," she finally said, not looking at me. "No knocks, no temperature swings or stopped clocks when you did a job."

The second mention of Pichrenn. "I miss him too, you know," I said, opening and closing a desk drawer for no reason. "I was there with him from the beginning."

"I know. Until the end. Well, if you miss him so much, stop by his place. You can see him anytime there, right?" Her voice had shifted out of neutral, but not in a direction I liked. "Sorry," she said. "I know you didn't mean... I mean, that you never wanted..."

"Don't worry about it. I'm past that. So what's up, Lindsay?" I leaned back in my chair. It creaked a little. I thought Lindsay had perhaps changed her perfume, but I couldn't be sure.

"I need a job done, Scott."

"And you came here? As far as I know they're still taking commissions at First Impressions. They're the best. And I know you always did like the best." I couldn't look too long into her eyes.

"If you're fishing for a compliment, I've given you too many already. Do you want to take the job?"

"I need to hear a little about it first," I said. A lie, but I didn't want her to know how far I'd sunk and how desperate I'd become. Oh, when I first got out on probation, I was the talk of the town, the indispensable impressionist and party guest. Offers both personal and professional came in the daily email. I had turned them all down; they had all been just a different kind of vampire, getting their jollies with a touch of death. But my fifteen minutes had ended.

Back to business. I clasped my hands on my desk. Clients liked it when you seemed to give them your full attention, and going to an impressionist is a little intimidating to some, like going to confession, or revealing your dirty little secrets to a psychiatrist. People take death seriously, even if it's not their own.

"It's my mother."

"I don't remember you talking much about her."

"No. We didn't have a lot of contact the last few years."

"So you had a fight. Teen angst, I suppose?" She didn't say anything. "But now you decide that you want to raise her. Planning to enact a little posthumous make up session, a sort of after- death mother-daughter heart to heart? You know it doesn't work that way." I don't know why I was being such a bastard.

"Look, I just owe it to her. There's nothing else I can do for her."

"'For her'? How's that? It's just a damn ghost, Lindsay. It's got as much self-awareness as a black and white photograph. Your mom, she's gone."

"Call it a gesture, then. It's too late for anything else." She looked down at the floor, as if the topic were too personal for her to go on. I didn't believe that for a second, but I let it ride. I didn't need to talk myself out of a job.

"OK. You're the customer." I slid a brochure over to her. Nice how desktop printing can make your hole-in-the-wall look like a real-live business. "Here are the rates."

She took it, but she didn't look down at the brochure. At least she didn't crease it; I could use it again next time if she didn't stick it in her purse. "I came to you because you're good. I don't want the effect spoiled by second-rate equipment."

"I don't really have the resources I once did."

"With the advance I'm prepared to pay, you can afford to get some of those resources again." I liked the sound of that; I missed the feel of properly tuned and maintained equipment, its quiet, even hum and ozone smell. The garbage I used now tended to sputter, and the focus kept going out unless you constantly kept on top of it.

Also, an advance that big could pay some of my less important bills, too. Rent and food came to mind.

Lindsay began tapping her code into my paypad.

I forced myself not to look. I pulled up an empty file on the computer, and started filling it out. "I'll need your current address." She took one of her cards out of her purse and passed it to me. I saw that nowadays she was employed at EarthTenders, Inc., a non-profit environmental umbrella. Part-time, no doubt. It was just the kind of feel-good job an over-indulged rich girl would have. It shouldn't have made me so bitter. If she spent her time suckling endangered wildebeest puppies, what was it to me?

"Any other legally interested parties?"

"Mom's latest ex has signed off on it. That satisfies your legal requirements, I believe."

"Sure does." I kept typing. "Visual, audio, olfactory?" Most people want only the visual, even though it's more work to suppress the taps and moans and temperature swings.

"Just the visual."

"Short-term, long-term, or permanent?"

"Short-term."

"OK." I stopped typing and looked at her, but she was doing her stare-at-the-floor act again. I saw a few wrinkles on her face that hadn't been there all those years before.

"I really just have to say goodbye," she said. "I don't need an endlessly repeating exhibition, for people to gawk at." Another little dig at me for raising Pichrenn. So I guess the guilt still gripped her. But I'd show her that nowadays I was immune to that kind of subtle reprimand. I was a businessman now, not some overpaid artiste.

"Short-term it shall be. Cause of death?"

"Her heart."

"OK, good. Place and time of death?"

"June 19th, this year. It was a Saturday. At 9:10 p.m. At 7th and Bell."

I typed. Then, "If the death occurred on the street itself, or in any public area, we'll need all kind of permits."

"That's not a problem. She actually died in a restaurant there, Grasso's. They've already given their permission." She fished some papers out of her purse and passed them across the desk. Standard release forms. The restaurant probably figured a ghost would be good for business, and maybe they were even right, at least for the short term. But I doubted it. "When can you do it?"

I pulled my appointment book out of a desk drawer and made a show of flipping through its blank pages. "How about this Thursday? Say one o'clock."

"That would be fine."

I didn't suppose the restaurant would object to that hour of the day. The raising of a ghost would be good entertainment for their lunch crowd.

After Lindsay left I sat in my chair, blinking. What the hell had I done? She'd reached out — clumsily, indirectly, but she had made contact. And all my defenses had shot up. I'd needed her, on many levels, after Pichrenn died. My friend, my mentor. According to the law, my victim. And I'd had no one to lean on, because she was dealing with her own issues.

I could still smell her. I didn't know if it was a perfume or just her, but now I knew it hadn't changed from back when. The office was suddenly small, dingy, dark and close. I had to get out.

I had to visit Pichrenn again.

The apartment building was now owned by a foundation that had agreed to allow suite 612 to remain vacant. They rented out the other rooms, and probably not one in ten of the current inhabitants knew that the former occupant up there on the sixth floor had not really left.

The doorman knew.

"Mr. Koehl. Good to see you again." Jacob removed his hat and put it under an arm. I noticed that his hair was graying, the tight curls looking like ash.

"Good to see you, Jacob."

Jacob turned to open the door for me. "Time for the renewal, Mr. Koehl?"

"No. Just a visit."

"Ah." Jacob led the way across the plush lobby to the bank of elevators. "Well, that's important. Remembering." He gently pressed the elevator call button, and the doors opened immediately.

"Yeah, I guess so," I said. We entered the elevator. "Many tourists come by lately, Jacob?"

"Not so many. There was an old lady eight, ten days ago, and some art student early this week."

The elevator car stopped. We paced the cream carpet down to 612. Jacob turned the key in the lock, then stepped back. "Have yourself a good visit, now, Mr. Koehl."

He never came in.

"Thank you, Jacob." I opened the door.

Usually he was in the big easy chair, head up, one hand touching his chin. He must have done that a lot, for it to have imprinted so strongly; he couldn't have planned a better portrait.

And, I must admit, I had done well with the material. Nothing flashy here, nothing avant-garde, not for him. A quiet study of a thoughtful, gentle man. I'd let a sound of even breathing come though. The legs were almost invisible, mere suggestions of lines and the drape of his trousers. But his body became more substantial as you moved up, and the chair back was nearly completely obscured by his torso. The head was preternaturally distinct, the dark eyes burning.

God, I missed him.

The foundation kept some equipment in a closet. I set it up the way I always did, going through the motions, and renewed the imprint. It wasn't time yet, I just needed to do something with my hands. Then I sat in a chair for a while. It doesn't do any good to talk to a ghost. I never know what to say, anyway.

●

I shouldn't have set the appointment for Thursday. It gave me three days to wait. Sure, I had wanted her to think I was busy, but I could've claimed a sudden cancellation. She'd have seen right through me, but then, she almost certainly already had anyway.

There was one thing I could do. I fed her check to my computer. Now I had the money, I could stop using the shoddy broadcasters that spit all over the spectrum, and the tuneless highlighters and the touchy suppressors. Now it would be topline stuff, paid for in full with Lindsay's advance.

At the shop they greeted me like an old friend who'd killed someone — fair enough. But once we got to going over the equipment — oh, the way those new suppressors squelch noise! — all awkwardnesses and discomforts were forgotten, and I walked out of there with the best stuff I'd ever worked with, and slaps on the back.

Then, of course, I had to go to the scene of death, to scout out the territory. I hoped my car still had some juice in the bat.

It was in a good part of town. A very good part, in fact, where I stuck out like a zombie at a wedding. Grasso's was the kind of place a Mafioso would kill to be murdered in — all indirect lighting, widely-spaced tables, dark reflective wood, candles, and hovering waiters. And expensive.

Conscious of my old jacket, my shoe with the loose sole, I didn't want to go in.

I knocked on the glass door anyway.

A guy in a billowy white shirt, his tie undone, peered out at me. I flashed him my business card, which should mean nothing, but flash any sort of ID when you aren't being asked to and people just start thinking police or Homeland Security. He opened the door.

"I'm afraid we're closed," he began.

"Yeah, I figured. Lindsay Ingham asked me to stop by."

"One moment, please." He disappeared into the bowels of the restaurant and soon came back with a Mr. Sarkouhi. Apparently there was no Grasso.

"Ms Ingham mentioned you would come to see the site, Mr. Koehl. Thank you for visiting before we open for dinner." Mr. Sarkouhi, comb-over plastered to his wine-colored skull, a thin moustache drooping against jowly cheeks, nodded me inside. "When you have prepared everything, of course, then we will go public, as they say. The table where it occurred is just through here."

Nothing special about the table. It was against one wall, a painting above it. But I saw some interesting possibilities, and the setting was appealing — death and money, death and elegance; these were and remain powerful combinations. They pushed buttons, and I found myself getting excited by the work ahead. Such a change from that which I had been getting lately.

I made some mental notes. Places I could shoot from, surrounding material resonances. I forgot that Mr. Sarkouhi was hovering behind me until he delicately cleared his throat.

"I'm almost finished, Mr. Sarkouhi. Just figuring the angles."

"Of course, Mr. Koehl. The passing of Ms Mehrer in our establishment was, I'm sure you understand, quite a shock."

"I'm sure it was."

"What I mean is, Ms Mehrer was more than a customer here. She was here so often, and she enjoyed a close relationship to those here, the staff and the other diners."

I could see what he was working up to. "Do you suppose they'll enjoy seeing her here again?"

"It might be disquieting to some."

"And yet Lindsay told me you agreed to the raising. She showed me the paperwork."

"Yes, that's true. It's just that, well…"

"I know. I guess you don't say no to Lindsay." I never could, for different reasons. Or maybe they weren't so different. "Mr. Sarkouhi, she's asked for just a temporary raising. I'll make sure it's as tasteful as I can. I don't know what else I can tell you."

"Thank you, Mr. Koehl. And my thanks, again, for coming when we are closed between lunch and dinner. I appreciate that you are trying to minimize the disruption."

"No problem." Actually, I hadn't even thought about the restaurant being open or not.

As Mr. Sarkouhi turned away, a thought struck me. "Mr. Sarkouhi. On the night in question, was Ms Mehrer dining alone?"

Mr. Sarkouhi's face flushed a deeper red. "Ah, no, Mr. Koehl. She was dining with her husband."

Her husband? Lindsay hadn't shown me any paperwork from him. And I would need it. As she well knew.

●

Back in the office, I called up the news stories about the death of Ms Mehrer on the computer.

Alicia Mehrer had indeed died of a heart attack on June 19th, at 9:10 p.m., at Grasso's. According to witnesses she murmured something, stood up, took a few steps and then collapsed, dying a few moments later.

I wondered at the last name. I looked up Lindsay's bio. Skimpy. She must have paid someone monstrous sums to keep her bio so short. But it did show that her dad, Joseph Ingham, had left the family when she was just seven. The mom remarried two years later. The second husband had died. Cancer. Then mom had married Joseph again, and divorced him again two years after that. Well. Sounded like an interesting family. Money and death, and Lindsay's family had a lot of both. But with a divorce on record, at least I wouldn't have to meet the old man to get a signature.

My computer search turned up plenty of gossip concerning the late Alicia and her ex Joseph. Curiosity got the better of me and I expanded the search a bit and came up with some charming hospital records. All of the sources agreed that Mr. Ingham had been one real bastard. The kind of guy a jury would wink at you for killing.

And yet, even after the abandonment and after the divorce, Alicia had kept coming back for more pain. Again and again.

Sex and death is another powerful combination; the oldest and the strongest of them all.

And why had Lindsay neglected to mention that her dad was with her mom at the time?

Closet skeletons can make a raising a lot more interesting.

●

Thursday. The restaurant door opened, and Lindsay entered with the grace of a predatory eel, dressed all in satiny black. She stood and watched me work for a while. Of course, a small crowd had already gathered; the equipment summons them as reliably as it summons ghosts. Mr. Sarkouhi stood prominently in the center, his arms folded in pride, surveying the crowd.

Lindsay came closer. "How's it going?" If she was so cool and commanding, why did her fingers clench her bag?

"Just finishing up the underlays now." I tightened a tripod leg, then checked the broadcast shadow.

"I've decided to go long-term, Scott."

I looked up. "What?"

"I said I've decided to go long-term. With an option for permanency."

I looked at Mr. Sarkouhi. "It's all right," Lindsay said. "Mr. Sarkouhi has given us permission."

"I'll need to see that for myself."

"Of course." She opened her purse without looking at it and took some papers out. She held them out to me.

"Why the change in plan?" I left her holding the papers and picked up another broadcaster.

Lindsay was silent for a short time. "Does it matter?" She allowed her hand to drop to her side, the papers slapping against her tailored slacks.

"No, I guess not." I extended the tripod legs on the broadcaster and set it up at a 45-degree angle to the first. I'd put a highlighter just between the two. "You just wanted to say goodbye — wasn't that the purpose of this raising?"

"Maybe I just thought I would need more time with her." I didn't even pretend to look convinced, and she continued, "She *was* my mother, Scott."

I flipped the test switch on the 'caster and checked the levels as it hummed. "Not a very private place for getting in your quality time with mom." I adjusted the levels and checked the output. I looked up at her.

Lindsay looked at me, her eyes just slightly narrowed. I knew why she had chosen me for the job. Not because I was the best, but because she knew that I would do it, that I would gratefully touch things more reputable studios sneered at.

Or there was another reason, but I veered away from that thought.

"Well, if you change your mind, remember I do collapsings, too," I said. "In fact, I lay more ghosts than women." It was a standard joke, and she gave it the response it deserved.

"Are you ready?"

"Another ten, fifteen minutes."

"Fine." Lindsay passed the papers to Mr. Sarkouhi and greeted some oldsters sitting at a nearby table. Mr. Sarkouhi stood there, one hand on his moustache, not looking at anything.

"I guess you'll be getting a permanent tourist attraction, right here at table eight, Mr. Sarkouhi," I said.

"Permanent, maybe." Sarkouhi looked less than thrilled.

"None of my business, but it seems to me that what might attract a crowd for a short while might grate on the nerves of your diners, if it's constantly in view. Of course, you'd be a better judge than me of what might pique a person's appetite."

Sarkouhi narrowed his eyes. "If you talk me into withdrawing my permission, Mr. Koehl, you'll lose the job."

"Last thing on my mind, Mr. Sarkouhi."

"I could revoke permission, though, at a later date. Couldn't I? I read the contract."

"Yeah, maybe. But Lindsay might try to sue if you try it. The lawyers would have to decide what your contract actually says. Better to just curtain off the table."

Sarkouhi met my eyes briefly, then nodded thoughtfully.

●

Memories intrude like unwanted ghosts.

The day Pichrenn died, I'd gone to see him at home. That memory was a persistent visitor. He'd been sick for some time, and he'd had his bedroom outfitted with all kinds of medical equipment and monitors. The place smelled of disinfectants and futility, and Pichrenn lay in his huge bed, looking over at me with eyes too bright in a head become too large.

His voice was as weak as his body, but he could still speak, was still coherent.

"Art," he told me. "That's been my life, Scott, these last thirty years."

"And you've done well," I said. "You know how impressions were looked at before you got into the field. Dodgy at best. You made a whole new artform. I guess not many can claim that distinction."

Pichrenn smiled sickly, not falling for the flattery, sincere though it was. "And now this." With an arm little more than papery skin stretched over knobby bones, he gestured at the IV feeds, the machine that beeped his heart along. "They tell me I could live ten more years like this."

What could I say to that?

"They're making advances all the time."

"So maybe I'll only lie here for eight years, or six. That's no way to be, Scott. But the law says I can't take the easy way out, with ten 'good' years ahead of me. Damn Republicans."

I looked away.

"Help me, Scott." He whispered it.

And then, "Make me a work of art."

"Huh?" But I knew.

There is no kind of death that can compare with a properly-conducted suicide. Despair, desperation, pain, a reckless courage, and even a strange sort of hope: that someone will stop you, that you'll be delivered into heaven, whatever. It makes for one hell of an impression.

And it's almost as hard to kevork as it is to do it yourself. Sure, lots of laws make it all right to kill someone, if they really want you to, and if the doctors have signed off on the sign-off. But that's not what Pichrenn was asking for, a sterile room and a certifiably painless fade out. My way would be less clinical.

But afterwards, I made the impression, and it's still drawing the occasional connoisseur. Maybe Pichrenn, or part of him, thought he was doing me a favor, giving me so much pain to work with.

●

Lindsay came over, ushered by a hostess. "Everything's ready?"

"Yep."

"Fine. Let's do this."

Sarkouhi raised his eyebrows at me. I nodded.

"I think your host would like to get everyone here for the unveiling," I said. "That's his payoff, right? That he can show this off to his customers."

"Who knows why anyone does anything. He gave his permission. That's all I needed."

"Still, we can give him a minute to get his people assembled." I made some final, unnecessary adjustments. "I have to say that I don't feel this will be representative of my best work, Lindsay. The image is fairly clear and sharp, but the background hum is, at best, just..."

"I don't need art. I just want to see Mother."

"Well, then everything's fine."

Sarkouhi, all smiles and broad gestures, led a small group of his well-fed and overdressed patrons into a semicircle around the table. I showed them where they could stand for the best view, then stood before them. I waited for their gossiping to slow to a trickle, their eyes to wander to me.

"Before I unveil this, I'd like to clear up a few common misconceptions about my craft, for those who may not be as deeply involved in the netherworld as I am," I said. I saw that Lindsay was annoyed with my delay, but hell, this was too good a chance to pass up. I just might pick up some high-class clients.

"First, what this is not." I started passing out business cards. "Ghosts are not self-aware, they're not beings. They can't see you or hear you. They're simply impressions, imprinted on the local area by the trauma of death. Or by other trauma, or other emotion. That's why you sometimes see ghosts of the living." I'd passed out all my cards. Time to wrap it up.

"The impressions are often of the moment of death, but not always." I went back to my equipment. "Dominant feelings, commitments left unfulfilled, unsaid messages, all these things can and do show up, and it's up to the artist to see that they do. And that's all I have to say. Let's see what we can see."

I checked my viewer. Yeah, I was satisfied with what I had called forth. I flipped the final switch.

At first there was nothing, except for the low hum of the 'caster. The smell of ozone grew in the air. Slowly an image started to form, in mid-air next to the table. It started as a grainy mist, like fine television snow, a vague human shape. It slowly intensified and clarified as the highlighters brought more of the energy out into visible forms, kicking it to the focusers. All this was needed to get the image formed in the first place — although of course natural ghosts do form, usually of an inferior quality, and with odd, annoying, aural and temperature effects — but once it was there, it would stay until properly laid, as long as it got boosted now and then.

The image continued to clear, and soon we were looking at a woman. It was a loop. Not uncommon. She moved, in jerky, uncertain movements, from the table to a spot a few feet away. Then suddenly we would see her lying on the floor, face down. Then she would be up again, moving around, as if confused. Her death had obviously come as a shock to her.

Her body, her clothes, were not too distinct — vague suggestions of a matronly form, decked out in some kind of conservative dark dress. Maybe the neckline was a bit lower, the dress a bit tighter, than society would choose to dictate. Was that a string of pearls around the fleshy neck? It was hard to tell.

But none of that mattered. Because the face — the face was clear, very clear. Real.

It was an aged face, but not heavily lined; Lindsay's mother would have been happy to hear that her face-lifts had survived her death. The forehead, fringed by curled white hair, was nearly smooth, the cheeks still full, the chin small and weak but still single.

You could see all that eventually. But it took time to take in, because what caught the attention were the ghost's eyes. They were startlingly blue in that papery face, and as the woman paced they sought something, something to be wary of. You could almost see a hunched form, a shadow, a dark aura, hovering at her back. And the expression in Mrs. Mehrer's eyes —

They were imploring. That's the word. But why? Was Ms Alicia Mehrer asking for mercy, for freedom? Or for understanding, compassion? There was shame in those eyes, too.

Even in death, she remained in thrall to her husband, bound to him by pain and need.

I couldn't have manufactured such a thing. But an impressionist can choose what to highlight — lives are complicated things — and I'd made sure that sick dependency came through. Call it art, showing a truth in place of the prettified picture that was asked for. Call it a stab at Lindsay. I don't know.

Maybe it was just what Lindsay had wanted to see. I had to look over at her. Her expression was at first smug, then horrified, lips parted and wide-eyed, but soon a mask slid down over her face. Her eyes narrowed and the right edge of her mouth curved up slightly. She coolly surveyed the onlookers; before her eyes met mine, I quickly looked down.

Then I looked at the crowd. I'd seen the same reactions a hundred times before. Some looked on in horror, lips curled, and clutched at the arms of those next to them. Some tried to avert their eyes, as if embarrassed, but their gazes were continually drawn back to the apparition before them. And some few leaned forward, drinking in the death.

●

Sarkouhi was watching the crowd, too. He seemed less than pleased. He saw me looking at him and walked over to me.

"Is this normal?" he asked in a low voice. "I mean, will it do anything else?"

"Some few do seem to react to things near them. Some look like they are trying to talk to you — the impressions can react to the impressed energies of those still living. Some act out the worries on their minds at the moment of death. Sometimes they even communicate what that was. Or try to. But, to answer your question, no. This is it. It's a fairly short action loop this time. She wasn't here long enough to lay down much more narrative."

Sarkouhi looked back at the impression, his face sour. I began packing up my stuff. Sarkouhi looked back at me.

"You're leaving?"

"Yep. Job's done."

"And this will just go on, repeating here in my place?"

"That's right." I folded a tripod and laid it gently in its foam-lined case. "I've pumped a lot of energy into the floor and walls, enough to keep it going for at least five or six weeks. And after that, I'll come back and pump it up some more. Can I use your phone? I have to call to have this stuff picked up." I couldn't just toss equipment of this caliber into my trunk, but it was humiliating to have to ask.

"Of course." He handed it over and I turned to the wall to give the man a moment, and sure enough, Sarkouhi went to talk to Lindsay.

Their conversation apparently didn't last too long, because when I clicked off and resumed packing, Sarkouhi was over by the other restaurant patrons. I guess he was trying to put a good face on the show, but the diners weren't buying. Several had already left, and a few in the back were realizing that they would have to pass uncomfortably close to the ghost to get to the door.

"Mrs. Sorensen!" Lindsay called, and one of the biddies looked up. A much younger man, his hair still dark, put a protective arm on her shoulder.

Lindsay made no attempt to get closer to her. "Enjoying the show, Mrs. Sorensen?"

"It's, ah..."

"Not sure? Perhaps your latest young man has an opinion — what's this one's name?"

The man scowled, whispered something to Mrs. Sorensen, and they turned away. Then she pulled away from him and looked back.

"I didn't know, Lindsay. I swear, I didn't know what he was doing to her." She turned and walked away.

Lindsay looked after them, her mouth fixed in its smile, her eyes full of hate.

Then she blinked and looked back at her mother for a moment. She strolled over to me. "Good work, as always."

"Thanks. And the rest of the money will be in my account when, exactly?"

"Oh, how you've come down in the world, Scott." She fished around in her purse and then started writing out a check.

"Yep. All the way down to the bottom line." I swiped her check through my reader. "Pleasure doing business. Please remember me whenever a loved one dies on you." I went back to the packing.

"This is my mother, Scott. You make me sound like one of your ghouls."

I folded a tripod and lay it gently in its foam. "The term is 'vampire.' But you're right. I know that you had me do this out of the love and respect you hold for your dear mom."

Lindsay moved in front of me, and spat her words. "You, of all people, have no right to judge me. I paid you for the job, and you did it. You didn't complain."

"I'm no judge, Lindsay." I closed and locked the lid on the case. I stood up. "They are, though." I nodded over to the last of the restaurant patrons. "You've given them a good show." I couldn't resist. "Was it the one you wanted?" I really was curious about that.

"You're done here, I think," she said, and walked out of the restaurant, almost striding through her mother's image.

Lindsay, Lindsay, Lindsay. Our shared betrayal of Pichrenn had eaten away at us both. Maybe my time in prison had given me a chance to let it go just a little more than she had, had convinced me that she was now out of reach, a subject of wistfulness and what-if. And how did she feel, now? No way would she think of me as out of her league; she could scrape me off the sidewalk any time she felt like it. But having me in her life would just remind her of what we had done to Pichrenn, how our relationship had been tainted from the start by that duplicity.

Sarkouhi headed over to me. I was getting downright popular. "This," he said, "is a bad business."

"Disappointed with the show? You're not alone."

"Oh, Mr. Koehl, I'm sure you have done an excellent job. But this is... It's not dignified."

"Death usually isn't."

He looked at me. "This isn't just death. How can I serve food, with this obscene thing here?"

Dear, dead Ms Mehrer continued her routine.

He hadn't thought of that before? Just what kind of idiot was he? Or, more to the point, what had Lindsay done or said to him? "You'd be surprised," I said. "This kind of show does bring a certain subset of the population. Not like your current crowd, though." I waved a hand at the people. "Like I said, you can always withdraw permission, Mr. Sarkouhi. These things are a lot easier to collapse than they are to bring out. And I work for reasonable rates."

"Ah. Mr. Koehl. As you reminded me, Lindsay Ingham has very many friends."

"She can make trouble for you, is that it? Not just legally."

"That is it."

"Looks like she's making trouble for you, anyway, Mr. Sarkouhi."

"That she is, Mr. Koehl."

As I climbed into my car I saw Lindsay watching the ghost through the window of the doorway, smoking an actual cigarette, the smoke making her features a little unclear. You can't do that in a restaurant. It's slow suicide. That wouldn't bother anyone, but even worse, it's public suicide.

●

The next day I was sitting in my office, staring out the window. I felt like shit. With the money and new stuff, paid bills, I should have felt like a pop star. Instead I kept seeing Ms Mehrer's face, and I felt like a whore.

The phone buzzed. I picked it up, and there was my vampire, Justin Hoben — excuse me, "John Robertson". The idiot called himself that, and then paid me through his personal account.

"John."

"You said to call today. You said that you would scout out the, that job we talked about."

"Yeah, John."

There was a pause. "Well?"

I didn't know why I was giving him a hard time. Lindsay's money would only last so long, and the bills would come due again eventually. So I roused myself. "Yeah, John. I checked it out. The manager is willing to go along, except he wants a cut. The usual amount, three hundred, and there's my fifty negotiating fee, on top of the baseline costs."

"Yeah, that's fine. When?"

I made a show of looking at my watch, although he wouldn't see it. "I guess I could squeeze it in late this afternoon, say four o'clock, if that works for you."

"Yeah, that would be good for me. Four o'clock."

I hung up. Sure, Mr. Hoben, that time works for you. I figured it would. Your wife thinks you're still at work, your office thinks you've left for the day. That works for you just fine.

It was sacrilege to use the new equipment for a job like this. Wiping grandma's priceless china with a rag made of old underwear. I could just as easily dig out my old stuff. My Mr. Robertson deserved no better.

But the lure of using that fine new gear was just too strong. My breath actually quickened as I thought about it. I felt like a pervert at a schoolyard. But I got it out anyway, and by three I was on my way.

Once there, it didn't take long for me to set up. Everything snapped into place just as it ought to, just as it used to. No sputtering, no loss of definition or control or focus, no stray signals. I played with the fine tuning, bringing out effects and details I hadn't been able to play with in years.

The old woman had died in the chair, just slumping further down, further down. No drama, just death. Her image flickered at the edges a bit; I toned it down, then brought it back up just to the edge of sight. She kept her eyes half closed, and she seemed to be mindlessly staring at something, probably a television set that the landlord sold off when the body was found. She wore a gray blouse, and a necklace of fat glass beads, red and brown. She also wore some fading blue jeans. She was barefoot.

Some current celebrities say in their wills that their houses or places of death should be destroyed, to forestall this kind of thing from ever happening to them. The rest of us can't afford that kind of protection, though there are restraint policies that are supposed to prevent the kind of thing I was doing. The very poor, though, are wide open to the predations of vampires after death.

My vampire knocked at the door. I opened it. "John."

"Mr. Koehl." Justin Hoben's eyes barely brushed me before they focused on the dying woman. His breath caught in his throat.

"I'll be outside." I went down the stairs and I heard Justin close the door and lock it.

I sat in the open door of my car. It's a shame I never took up smoking; it would pass the time. I watched the traffic go by, the single occupants of single vehicles. An hour or so later Justin came back out. His shirt was no longer tucked into his pants, and there was drying sweat on his flushed face. He walked up to me, and didn't look at me as he slipped me his check.

But after he turned away, he spoke.

"You're a genius," he said, his voice thick with emotion. "That was the best — the best I've ever had. Amazing." Still without looking at me, he said, "Thank you," then hurried away.

So the new equipment had an endorsement.

I went back upstairs, and put down the ghost.

●

Afterwards I drove slowly past Grasso's, though it wasn't on the way home. Grasso's didn't look to have many customers. I laughed, and went home, wishing I had eaten something so I could vomit it back up.

●

The next morning Lindsay was already in my office corridor when I arrived.

"Where the hell have you been?" she greeted me. She stubbed out her cigarette in her pocket ashtray. "It's almost noon."

"Hello, Miss. Did an appointment slip my mind?"

I unlocked the door and Lindsay followed me inside. She sat down, a firm line to her mouth and a hard look in her eye.

"Have a seat," I said. I seated myself behind my desk and rested my chin on my hands. "Something I can do for you?"

"More like something you did to me."

I leaned back. That gaze was a little too intense. "I don't understand, Lindsay. I did what you asked. The ghost hasn't collapsed, has it?"

"To hell with you, Koehl."

"Yep, anyone with one good eye can see the sick relationship she had with your dad. It's all there for everyone to see. And that's exactly what you wanted."

"It's disrespectful, mocking her like that. I wanted a tasteful —"

"In a restaurant. Yeah. Please, Lindsay."

"Go to hell." She folded her arms, looked away, and began to sniff.

"Cut the act, Lindsay. We both know what you wanted. You wanted to leave a bitter taste in the mouths of all her society friends. You hated them for not stepping in, or you hated them for leading perfect lives within calling distance. You hated her for what she allowed your dad to do to her, and you couldn't resist a little public humiliation. And I gave it to you. Just like you knew I would. Because I've got the eye to see it, and the technique to show it, and the desperation to accept the job in spite of all that."

She ended her pretense of crying, and just sat there. I wondered what she wanted, why she was here. To justify herself in my eyes — Oh, I never expected to see *that* — or to gloat with me over her triumph over her mother?

Gloat with *me*? Did Lindsay have no friends?

Did I care? "You always were a little self-centered. Justifiably so. But hardly blind — did you think the relationship obvious to her old friends would slip past me? I do know my work, Lindsay."

"Your work! Raising ghosts for perverts!"

"Don't worry. I don't discuss my clients with anyone."

I should have seen the slap coming. Maybe I did. Then Lindsay stood up and turned her back to me.

The inside of my cheek had been cut by a tooth, and I tasted blood.

"He hated you, you know. Towards the end. That was his parting shot — saddle you with a murder charge."

"Manslaughter." I kept the disinterested tone in my voice, but her words rang in my head. Pichrenn had hated me? I had practically been his son.

And yet — it rang true, also. It didn't come as big a surprise as it should have.

"He taught me well. I owed it all to him. He had no reason to resent me."

Lindsay turned back to me. "Idiot! It wasn't your skill he resented!"

"I never —"

"You didn't need to."

She glared at me, expecting me to — what? Kiss her? Slap her, like Bogart in some old movie? Explain away the thing we'd had behind the old man's back, when I'd been the favored son and it was clear that Lindsay would be free after the old guy had passed on?

I knew that there are ghosts all around us, hovering just at the edges of sight, on the fringes of our minds, as we go about our lives. I made my living revealing them. Now Lindsay was showing me others.

"Why do you keep renewing him, Scott? Why don't you let him fade out?" Her voice was flat.

I had no answer.

"He's gone, Scott. And you blamed me. You never returned my messages."

Had she left messages? I'd told myself for so long that she had cut me loose. But yes, she had left messages I had brushed off. After killing Pichrenn, how could I just go on, take up openly with his lover?

I couldn't think of anything to say, and Lindsay stalked out. Was I supposed to call her back?

Had all this been her way to get through to me?

●

I've always had trouble with moving on. Maybe everybody does. But I thought a lot about what Lindsay had said, there at the end. I sat in my apartment in the dark, the TV on with the sound turned low, and decided that maybe it was time to act, and maybe even time for Lindsay to take another peek at the sunlit world.

Me too. I not only have trouble moving on, I have trouble going back. Lindsay had reached out to me, coming to see me about a ghost; she had made contact, however awkwardly, and maybe that's the only way she could do it. Still, she had done it. She had tried to show me herself at her most vulnerable, most unappealing, most venal, and most real. I could, too.

●

I had no idea if she would show up or not. The message I'd left hadn't given her any details, any reason to see me, just the time and place. I watched Pichrenn in his chair, and tried not to think about it. About where she was now, what she was doing, that she was still in the world even though she wasn't in mine.

The door opened. "Scott."

Lindsay stood there.

"Lindsay."

She entered hesitantly. "I'm not sure what I'm doing here."

"Yeah. Neither am I. But I'm here."

She nodded as if that made sense. She crossed the room to the window. She hadn't looked at Pichrenn. She wasn't wearing black this time — light blues and yellows.

I joined her. "I need to tell you something, Lindsay."

She nodded, but didn't say anything.

It was easier talking when she wasn't looking at me. "It's like this. Yes, I killed Pichrenn. He asked me to do it, and maybe he had more than one motive. I don't know. But I know that I've never forgiven myself, for that and for — you know. Us. And afterwards I pushed you away, like it was your fault or something. But I'm tired of pushing."

She turned to me. Her eyes flickered to the impression, then back to me. "You don't have to —"

"Yeah, I do. I really do. Since I got out of prison, since even before that, I've been moping and cynical, and it's got me nowhere. Maybe I've been a little too much in love with death. Maybe that's a job hazard. But I'm tired of it. Finally, I'm just *tired* of it."

I went to the closet and pulled out a single piece of equipment. I didn't even need a tripod. I could just hold it and point it at the apparition.

"Scott — you're..?"

"Time to say goodbye."

I pointed, and pressed the button, and Pichrenn vanished.

Lindsay looked at the chair where the impression had been. I couldn't tell what she was thinking.

I held out the defocuser to Lindsay. She looked at it as if she didn't recognize it, but didn't take it. I put it on the chair.

"If you ever want it, here it is," I said. "It's easy to use. Runs on batteries. Just point, and push the nice red button." I walked to the door. Lindsay still hadn't moved.

At the door I turned. "I usually have dinner weeknights at a little place on Fifth, near Pike," I said. "Rommie's. It's easy to find. I'm usually there from seven-thirty to eight-thirty or so."

I walked out.

Maybe Lindsay was tired of death, too. Tired of looking back.

I'd have to wait and see.

Tim McDaniel's story "Koehl's Quality Impressions" was originally published in Metaphorosis on Friday, 27 April 2018. See magazine.metaphorosis.com

About the author

Tim McDaniel started his career in education in the 1980s, as a Peace Corps Volunteer, teaching English in a small village in Thailand. Later, he taught at Khon Kaen University in Thailand,, and — in the US — at the University of Washington as well as at several community colleges and refugee/immigrant programs, and has been teaching at Green River College, not too far from Seattle. for almost 20 years. His short stories, mostly comedic, have appeared in a number of SF/F magazines, including F&SF, Analog, and Asimov's. He also has a collection of skits for ESL students, The Playbook, up on Amazon. Tim lives with his wife, baby daughter, and dog, and his collection of plastic dinosaurs is the envy of all who encounter it. His author page at Amazon.com is www.amazon.com/author/tim-mcdaniel and many of his stories are available at Simily.co.

It Thaws in Spring

Brittany M. Perkins

Lena lived under the ice. She might have always been there, or perhaps she had lived on the surface once. It didn't matter. Lena could not remember a time when she had not floated in the still waters below the frozen pond, a time when she knew things other than damp and cold and dark.

The under was a vast expanse of water, which, with an effort of great concentration, could be molded into ghostly rooms or objects, though these structures were easily dispersed with a wave of the hand. Impermanence was the way of the under, and it was the way of the ice children as well. There were only four of them now (Lena and Edna and Rebecca and Julian), and every winter began with the uncertainty of how many would remain.

Winter was all Lena knew, all she could experience and remember. She never saw the pond melt in spring, although Edna assured her that it did. Edna never saw this either. Instead, Lena and the others awoke each winter, the ice above them firmly intact, aware that time had passed, but unsure what had happened in the interim. And sometimes, when winter came, someone would be missing.

There had once been more of them, but Lena had not seen Raymond in four winters and Matteo in seven. Lena didn't remember much past twelve winters back, but she had heard other names, of children who had disappeared before her memories began: Cindy, Lola, Isaac. After Raymond hadn't come back, the other children grew more and more distant, until the under became a silent place, and Lena worried that one day he too would be only a name to them.

Lena was drifting through the under, thinking of those who were no longer with them when she spotted Edna, sitting in a chair. A swirling current that had not quite solidified made up its curving frame, and an elaborate tea set was suspended in the space in front of her. Many winters back, before it had become just the four of them, Edna had often talked with Lena, but, lately, Edna rarely acknowledged her at all. Lena approached the girl who had once taught her how to spin up towers and tea sets from the water around them. In the old days, Edna would brighten at Lena's approach and immediately invite her into a story or game she had come up with, but that never happened anymore.

Today, Lena hovered beside Edna, studying her, while the other girl hardly seemed to notice. "Can I join your party?" Lena asked, conjuring a chair of her own, more solid than Edna's, and sitting across from her former friend.

Edna glanced at the teapot and the cup in her hand as though seeing them for the first time.

Lena waited a moment before continuing: "What are you playing? Are you a princess? Or a society lady?"

Edna looked at Lena, opening her mouth as if to speak, but no sound emerged.

"Why don't you talk to me anymore?" Lena asked. "Why don't any of you ever want to play?" Lena rose from her chair, and the structure dispersed into the depths around them. "You used to be fun," she said. And then, softer, "You used to like me."

As Lena withdrew from the girl she had once considered a friend, she thought she heard Edna speak, a barely audible rasp: "I'm sorry."

●

One of Lena's earliest memories was of Matteo, and it was really more of a feeling than a memory. The memory was a single image of Matteo, pushing a ball made of water toward her. He was laughing. And the feeling was of excitement and joy. That was the best way to describe Matteo: joyful. But the winter before he disappeared, something had been different.

Once, that final winter, Lena had approached the watery rocket ship where Matteo had resided for going on three days. She crept through the half-formed hatch, careful not to disturb the structure's fragile architecture, and inched upward toward the boy who had once filled the underneath with such light and laughter. As Lena neared him, she could see that Matteo was in constant motion, wafting back and forth across the small space at the top of the rocket.

"Matteo?" Lena called up to him.

He did not answer, an eerie smile dragging up the corners of his mouth, as if against their will.

"Are you alright?" she asked. "Do you want to play a game?"

Matteo floated in a slow circle to face her, and although his eyes met hers, they were cloudy and seemed not to see her at all. Then his right hand shot out, grasping for her. Lena couldn't remember what had happened next, but she knew that she had left, and the next thing she could picture in her mind's eye was talking to Raymond.

None of the ice children knew how old they were, but Raymond had always felt older than the rest. So when she told him about Matteo's unresponsiveness, Lena expected an explanation.

Instead, she received a shrug. "That happens sometimes," Raymond said. "Matteo is very social, and it's been hard on him not having new children to play with."

"But I asked him to play, and he wouldn't talk to me," Lena said. "Why does he need someone new if I'm right here?"

Raymond sighed, not meeting Lena's eyes. "I don't know, Lena," he said, the slightest edge of frustration creeping into his voice. "I've tried to tell them — all of them — to be grateful for what we have here, but they always want more. I can't make them happy, and I just..." Raymond clenched his fists so hard and fast that a small current swirled around them. Then he looked at Lena. "You're happy, right? Even with just the six of us?"

"Of course," Lena said, though she wasn't sure that was true. She remembered that feeling of joy from years ago, but she couldn't think of the last time she'd felt it. "I'm very happy, Raymond."

When Matteo didn't come back during the following winter freeze, Lena had been confused. She was the only one who hadn't seen it happen before. Lena had searched for Matteo, and when she was nearly sure but not quite believing that Matteo was gone for good, Lena had asked Edna where he was. She received only a slow shake of the head in response before Edna drifted away, leaving a trail of silt in her wake. Lena soon learned it was taboo to talk about the disappearances, which was why she only had the whispered names of those who had already gone. But Raymond was different. Raymond would talk.

One night, Raymond appeared beside the bed Lena had willed together out of water droplets. The ice children never slept in winter, but they did rest, and sometimes, they dreamed. Lena had been dreaming. In the dream, a girl, whose face Lena could not see, hovered above her, near the ice. Lena was falling away from the girl, as though sucked into an undertow. The girl's hand reached toward Lena, and Lena reached out in return, but their fingers never met. As the distance between the two increased, Lena saw a sunray peek around the girl's head, but she soon faded away, leaving Lena staring into the blaring sunlight.

As Lena tried to call after the girl, she felt algae tickling at the sides of her mouth. She thought it was only part of the dream, until a hand lightly brushed across her shoulder. The coldness of Raymond's skin, which was blue with chill and slightly slimy, like they all were, startled her. Before she could call out, Raymond put a slender finger to his lips. "You want to know what happened, don't you?" He did not wait for Lena to respond. "Do you ever feel alone, Lena?"

Before she could think through the action, Lena nodded.

"We all do, and sometimes we feel so alone that we can't stand it. Sometimes during spring, we get so lonely that our ears are searching, even if we are not. And sometimes our ears find them: the children of the surface.

We might hear a laugh or a splash, but it's enough, enough to wake us and call us upward."

Lena's eyes moved back to Raymond's. "Does that mean the others went to the surface?" She sat up, sending loose bubbles and mud flying as her pillow lost form and dispersed. "Is Matteo up there now?"

"We used to have many children," he said. "And for a long time, it wasn't like this. We were happy. We played games. We weren't just... quiet."

"But if they were lonely, why did they leave their friends?" Lena's bed flittered into nothing as she floated upright.

"They were bored with just us," he said. "They needed *new* children — new friends. They got greedy, and now they're all gone."

"Are they on the surface?" Lena's voice was pleading.

"No. We can't live up there. We can't go back, not once we're here."

"Go back?" She thought of the girl from her dream, reaching out to her from the surface.

"More of the surface children used to play on the ice in winter. They would skate and sled, and sometimes, they would fall through. After a while, I guess they decided it was too dangerous."

"What happened... when they fell?" Lena thought she knew, but she didn't want to. She wanted to be wrong. At the edge of her memory, she heard the scrape of blades on ice.

"The ice children would save them. But to save them, we'd have to *change* them, get rid of who they were before. When the surface children stopped coming in the winter, the others still wanted to save them. But that doesn't work in the spring. It only works with the ice. In the spring, they just drown, or they swim away. And if we go after them, we disappear." He took a deep breath, and the water swirled around his mouth. "We're barely here in the spring, not even ghosts, and when we go up there, we're nothing."

"What if we go up in the winter?" Lena asked.

"We don't."

"Why not?"

"Because of the ice." And he turned and drifted away.

●

Lena was lonely, under the ice. She missed Raymond and his stories about how things used to be. She missed Matteo and his games and high spirits. And it was on a very lonely day, when the sun breached the ice and lit up the underneath, that Lena first heard it: a child of the surface laughing.

Lena soared upward, the water's temperature seeming to rise as she ascended, and stopped just in time not to hit her head on the ice. As she arrived, something thumped above her, and she saw a blurred shadow cover the ice above like a rug. Then the laughter came again, followed by a faint call: "Claire! Claire, get back here. It's too dangerous. Come back to the shore." The caller's voice was like an icepick driving into Lena's brain, and she suddenly felt scared and cold.

"Okay." This voice was closer, clearer, and somehow warmer as well, taking the edge off of Lena's fear. This voice came from the shadow, and as Lena realized this, the shadow moved, became smaller, and began to recede toward the edge of the pond, the water cooling in its wake.

Lena followed the shadow as fast as she could. Claire's shadow quickly outpaced her and was gone, taking the laughter with it. Lena continued her pursuit until she came to the pond's edge. She pressed a hand against it, mud wafting around the point of contact. She tried to grab a chunk of the muddy bank, but it was too tightly packed. Lena let go and wandered back toward the middle of the pond.

When she returned, Lena saw two structures, and she could see the occupants of each through the water that comprised them: a cottage with missing bricks and a crooked chimney (Edna) and a ship that was cracked down the middle, with only half a flag dangling from its too-short mast (Rebecca and Julian). Lena burst into the cottage where Edna sat in a one-armed armchair, a plate balanced on her lap, in front of a fire that would have been roaring had the flames been more than water held in shape by Edna's wishes. When Lena reached her, she stood in front of Edna's chair, blocking her view of the heatless flames. "So, what do you think happened to Raymond?"

Edna choked on her water droplet toast. "What do you mean?" she rasped. Edna looked older than Lena, but not by much. Lena knew Edna remembered longer, though, and knew things the others did not.

"I mean, where is he? And Matteo? Where did they go?"

"It's best not to —" Her voice was clearer now, though still sharp around the edges.

"Raymond said they got lonely and bored and that you think they go to the surface and evaporate."

"Lena."

"I saw someone today."

Edna's eyes brightened for a moment. "Where?"

"She was skating on top of the ice. A surface child." Lena paused, deciding whether or not to go on. "Raymond said there used to be more of us. He said surface children would fall through the ice."

Edna closed her eyes. "Yes," she said. "That was the way. But not anymore." Edna placed a hand on Lena's cheek. "You used to be so warm," she said, and Lena felt a chill run through her, though she wasn't sure if it came from Edna's touch or her words.

Lena recoiled and turned to face the fire, wishing it and its heat were real.

"I wish you still were," Edna said, reaching toward Lena again, her fingers barely brushing Lena's forearm before Lena fled, not wanting that chill to spread elsewhere on her body.

Lena hovered briefly above the cottage, rubbing her cheek. Then she entered the ship, where Rebecca and Julian were clapping their hands together, chanting nonsense rhymes and giggling. The two moved their hands in a circle and spun up three small dolls from the bubbles around them. The dolls hung near Rebecca's head, and she giggled again.

"What are you playing?" Lena asked, moving closer to the pair. "Can I play too?" Lena could remember a time when she had played with the two — Edna called them twins — but that was long ago, when Matteo and Raymond still occupied the underneath. "When you clap like that," Lena added, still feeling Edna's cold handprint on her cheek, "how does it feel?"

The twins did not look at her. "Did you hear something?" Julian asked Rebecca, not breaking the rhythm of their clapping. Neither seemed to wince or react in the slightest to the other's touch.

"It's the dollies," Rebecca said, inclining her head toward the bubble creations suspended to her left. Lena wanted to reach out and slap one of their hands to answer her own question, but instead, she departed the ship. Once free of the twins' rhymes, Lena willed herself her own structure: a twisting tower, like you would find at the top of a castle, but without the castle.

Lena surged to the top of the tower, which nearly brushed the ice, and as she sometimes had over the past four winters, closed her eyes, and spoke to the only friend who had ever been truly honest with her. "Raymond," Lena said. "I saw someone today. It was a surface child, and she was on top of the ice. I heard her laugh, and I heard someone calling her, and then she got away. I tried to catch her, but she —" A voice seemed to call from somewhere deep within Lena, jerking her sideways and sending pieces of parapet flying. It was the voice that had called Claire, except it was calling for her instead. As Lena shook away the imagined sound, something drew her eyes upward. She looked from the ice to her hands, feeling like they had not always been blue, and almost, but not quite, remembering what warmth felt like. *Claire would be warm.* The thought came, unbidden, and pulled Lena's gaze upward again. Claire would come back. She had to.

●

After what could have been three weeks or two months — Lena had never been good at measuring time — the light shifted overhead, and Lena felt the slightest kiss of sunlight on her cheek. She flew toward the surface, and, through the icy blur, Lena thought she saw skate blades gliding overhead. She watched for a moment, in awe, and then panic set in. What if this was her only chance to have a friend again? Dizzy at the thought of losing Claire forever, Lena raised a shaking fist and rapped on the ice. In what seemed like an instantaneous response, the figure above collided with the ice with a thud. The shadow filled the patch of ice above Lena, but this time, there was no laughter.

Lena was quick. She pressed her face against the ice to one side of the shadow. Lena rarely ventured this high in the pond, and the solid dryness of the ice always surprised her. "Hello?" she said. "Claire?"

For just a moment, Lena saw blurred eyes in a dark face. Then she heard a muffled scream as the figure jumped up, and the shadow quickly receded toward the shore.

Lena pursued, this time keeping pace for nearly twice as long as before, but still, when the figure reached the shore, Lena could not follow. Lena buried her face in the muddy bank and screamed. As she did, she again heard someone calling her name. It was less of a call and more of a shriek. And then it was all shriek and no words.

●

The possibility of seeing Claire — she was sure it had been Claire — again filled Lena with such desperation that her stomach ached. The other ice children either ignored her or took from her, but Lena sensed that Claire had something to give, and Lena had not been given anything in a long, long time. Lena thought that if she could talk to Claire, a bit of warmth and joy might make its way into the under, and maybe things could be how they once were. So she hovered under the patch of ice, waiting for Claire's return. She did this every time she could see sunlight, and did not retreat until all light drained away, occasionally scratching or tapping on the ice above to feel closer to Claire and the surface. Lena wondered how many ice children had waited like this. She wondered who had waited for her.

She was engaged in such thoughts when the shadow returned. A soft thud sounded above Lena's head, and she moved as close to the ice as she could.

The blurred face appeared above her. "A-are you still there?" It was Claire's voice.

"Claire?" Lena said, and Claire recoiled. "Wait. Don't. Please."

Claire's face returned. "Sorry," she said. "You're a little bit scary." Claire paused. "Say, how do you know my name?"

Their conversation was muted, as through a tunnel, but Lena could understand her clearly. "I heard someone calling you," Lena said. "The first time I saw you." She paused. "You didn't see me that time."

"Oh," Claire said. "That was my mom." Every word Claire spoke was like a little ray of warmth through the ice, and sometimes, the warmth burned.

The burn at the mention of the screaming woman from their first encounter was too much; Lena needed to change the subject. "Do you like to skate?" Lena asked, and she could almost feel herself gliding smoothly over the ice.

"What? Oh, yes. I do."

These words muted the heat, now more of a comfort than a burn.

Claire continued: "It's just my mom thinks it's dangerous. She doesn't trust the pond to hold out, says I'll fall through."

Lena heard a cracking sound from the corner of her memory and winced again, but it was less intense this time. "Are you afraid?" she asked. "Are you afraid you'll fall?"

Claire laughed, and Lena moved closer. The ice between them made the laugh sound far off, like it was coming from somewhere Lena couldn't quite reach. "No. Nothing scares me. Well, except you." She paused before adding, "But not anymore." Claire's shadow shifted. "Besides, I just come when she's sleeping. Mom sleeps a lot during the day, actually."

Lena didn't know how to respond to any of this. She was overwhelmed and excited and somehow afraid of what Claire might say next.

"I'm sorry. What's your name? I didn't even ask you."

"Lena."

"Huh," Claire said. "My mom had a sister named Lena."

Lena shuddered.

"They used to live where we do now. We moved to the cabin to help when Grandma got sick. She died a few months back."

The feeling of lying under a quilt, safe and warm, filled Lena's mind for a moment until the face of an older girl invaded the vision, scorching it around the edges. "What's your mom's name?" Lena asked, inching closer to the flame of Claire's voice.

Claire's shadow shifted again, and Lena worried that she'd upset her, that maybe she'd leave now. "It's Margaret," she said, finally. "But everyone calls her Maggie."

The name set Lena's thoughts afire. "What... happened... to... her sister?" she asked, needing a break between nearly every word.

"She died. Or they think she did. She must have. They never found a body, though. Mom was a lot older, and she was supposed to have been watching her. Mom and Grandma fought a lot after that." Claire trailed off before asking, "Hey, what *are* you?"

"I — I don't understand."

"Like, how did you get down there? There aren't even fish in this pond anymore. Are you a mermaid or something?"

Raymond had told Lena that there used to be fish. They had disappeared a long time ago, though. Even Raymond hadn't known why. "I'm just down here," Lena said. "I've always been down here. I — I'm an ice child."

"An ice child?" Claire asked. "I've never heard of that." Claire moved her face closer to the ice. "I can't see you very well," she said.

"Not much to see," Lena answered, dragging a fingernail across the underside of the ice and sending a curl of frost receding toward the pond's floor. She didn't want to explain herself anymore. She didn't want to tell Claire about the other children. She just wanted Claire to keep talking, because even though the warmth of her words hurt, they made Lena feel more *real* somehow, and Lena needed that.

"Listen," Claire said, "I have to go. Mom will be up soon, and she'll never let me out of the house again if she knows I've been here."

"Wait —" Lena started. But Claire was already on her feet, skating for shore.

●

"Do you remember that surface child I told you about?" Lena asked.

Edna was silent, still as the water around her.

"She talked to me, asked how I got down here."

Edna closed her eyes but made no move to speak.

"Was I one of the children who fell? Like they used to? Claire's mother had a sister: Lena."

Edna opened her eyes, pain filling the icy blueness of them. "You were mine," she rasped. "Yes. You fell too. You were skating, but it was too thin." Edna's voice caught a bit. "It shouldn't have been so thin, but it was."

And as she said this, Lena could almost remember. It felt like remembering the feeling of a dream, but not knowing what it was about. "And you saved me."

"Yes. To save one, you have to take out the warmth. They can't live down here with that. But with the warmth goes the memory. Everyone starts over down here."

Lena took a breath. "Did everyone come from the surface? All of us?"

"I think so," Edna said. "I can't know that for sure. I can only remember the ones who came after me, and most of them are gone now. But I remember you, and I remember Rebecca and Julian. They came down together. I remember when Matteo fell. I don't remember a time before Raymond. I think he's the one who saved me. But that was long ago."

Lena still could not remember. Only the shrieking was left, but excitement quickly overtook it. "Maybe Claire will fall," she said.

Edna's eyes brightened. "She might."

"Claire would be new. She could make things good again."

"Would you do that?" Edna asked. "Would you save Claire for us?"

"Of course," Lena said. "I'm tired of alone."

●

Claire spread out on her belly on the ice. She had not visited in what seemed a long time, and Lena had been antsy. "Sorry," Claire said.

The single word left Lena slightly singed, and she wanted more.

"Mom's been having a hard time. She always does in winter. I think it's —"

"How old are you?" Lena had not spoken to anyone since her conversation with Edna, and her voice came out rushed and clipped.

"Uh, twelve, but I'll be thirteen next month." Claire paused, dragging a gloved finger through the frost covering the ice. "How old are you, Lena?"

"I — I'm not sure..." At the fuzzy edge of something like memory, Lena saw an older girl, someone who loved her and protected her. "Say, how old was your mom's sister when she...?"

"Well, Mom was nineteen, I think, so that would've made her sister eleven."

Lena felt herself swoon slightly, certain now that she was also eleven, and that she had been eleven for a very long time. "Are your friends twelve, too?" she asked a little breathlessly.

Claire sat up, her blurred face blending into the rest of her shadow. "I don't really have any," she said. "They just kind of stopped coming around once my grandma got sick."

"But they could visit," Lena said, nervously scraping the ice with a nail. She imagined how warm they would all be, Claire and her friends. "They could skate with you. You could be friends again."

Claire's shadow shifted slightly. "I don't think so."

"Why not?"

"It just doesn't work like that," Claire said. "We don't talk anymore, and I had to change schools. And Mom doesn't really like visitors. Even before everything... happened, she liked to keep to herself."

Lena was overwhelmed with the feeling of a shy, reserved presence. She sighed, working the edge out of her voice. "That's okay," she said. Then a thought occurred: "We can be friends, then."

Claire shifted again, hesitating. "Th-that's sweet of you."

"You should visit more often." Lena paused, as though deciding something. "It's lonely when you're gone."

"Is it just you down there?"

"Yes," Lena lied. "There used to be others, but they went away."

Claire's shadow was still for a moment. "Lena, did you ever have a sister?"

Lena shrank back from the ice. "No."

"It's just, my mom's sister, she drowned, and I was wondering —"

"It's just me," Lena said. "And I've always been here."

"Listen, I have to get back. Mom will be waking up soon." And before Lena could respond, Claire's shadow began to move away.

When Claire was completely gone, Lena again slid a fingernail along the underside of the ice. Pressing harder this time, she scraped off a thin mist of shavings. Claire didn't understand how important it was for them to be friends, but she would. And so, Lena lingered there, scraping at the barrier between her and the warmth of her new friend until the sun was gone.

●

That night, just as Lena was nearly to dreaming, Edna appeared at her feet. Lena sat up, dispersing her sleeping mat and waiting for the other to speak, but Edna floated silently, staring down at Lena.

"Edna?" Lena said at last.

"Yes," Edna said, her voice a slowly clearing rasp. "Did you see her today? The girl from the surface?"

"I did."

"And will she be back? Do you think she'll fall?"

"I — I think so," Lena said. "I told her we could be friends."

Edna's eyes widened, a hungry look growing in them. "When will she be back?"

Lena shrugged. "Edna, is it okay to... to *help* them fall?"

Edna's blue-tinged ear twitched. "Do you mean to thin the ice?"

"Uh, yes. I guess so. Would that — would that be bad?"

Edna moved closer, close enough to touch. "We used to do it sometimes, just when we needed more friends. Matteo did it a lot. Raymond was always very mad when we did."

"So, it is bad, then?"

Edna looked away before placing a hand on Lena's forearm.

Lena shivered.

"My hands are colder than yours," Edna said. "Did you know that?"

Lena shook her head.

"You think that we don't talk to you because we don't want to, but really we can't remember how."

"I don't —"

"Raymond said that the other ice children disappeared because they were lonely, that we saved the surface children because we were bored, but that was never it. He didn't understand. You don't either, Lena, because you're the newest, but you will, soon."

Lena retreated slightly, putting distance between herself and Edna.

"I don't remember how to start talking anymore. Someone has to talk to me first, and then I can, but I can't start it. Rebecca and Julian — they were twins before, on the surface, always together — they can only remember how to talk to each other. To save a surface child, we have to take away their warmth, and the longer we're down here, the colder we get."

"And with the warmth goes the memory," Lena said.

Edna nodded. "Yes." She advanced toward Lena. "Do you remember that you used to sing?"

Lena gave her head a single shake.

"You did. All the time, but now it's gone. Sing me something."

Lena tried to think but could not find what singing was. "I can't," she said.

"Because you forgot. And you'll forget more, the colder you get." Edna began to drift back and forth in front of Lena, as though pacing. "Matteo and the others didn't leave because they wanted to bring back children; they left because they were so cold that they forgot they couldn't go. You can't be warm and live down here, and once you're here, you can't go back.

"The reason we saved those children and helped some of them fall was because new children help us remember what it's like to be warm. When the new children stopped coming, we couldn't remember anymore. But Raymond always said it wasn't fair. Not fair. Not fair."

Lena drew her limbs close to herself, as though afraid that Edna would take them from her. "If Raymond saved you," Lena started, "then he'd have to understand."

Edna shook her head. "He was different. Raymond was always different."

"Who saved Raymond?"

Edna shrugged. "We never knew, and he wouldn't say. I think maybe Raymond saved himself. I think maybe he was the first."

"But Raymond left. He must have been cold too."

"Maybe," Edna said. "Or maybe he knew what he was doing. Maybe he didn't want to watch us forget anymore." Edna closed in on Lena again, grabbing her by the collar. "You have to save Claire," she said. "We need her, Lena. You have to save her. I — I'm cold."

And it was true. Lena could feel the chill through her frayed shirt.

"You're the newest, Lena, which means one day you'll be all alone. Alone for real. Things didn't used to be like this. We used to have fun. We used to be happy. You're still warmer than I am, Lena, but touching you is like remembering my name. Touching a surface child would be like remembering who I am. Claire can help all of us."

Lena pulled back, breaking Edna's loose grasp. "Okay," she said. "I'll save her."

"Thank you," Edna said, and she wrapped her arms around Lena tight enough to hurt.

Lena felt a chill run through her, a chill that she was sure would stay there now, for always, although she couldn't remember why.

●

Whenever the sun broke through the ice, Lena raced toward the surface to wait for Claire, and each time Claire did not arrive, Lena worked at scraping the ice. She would drag her nails back and forth, shaving off the thinnest layers until by the time Claire returned, their patch of ice was noticeably thinner.

Claire arrived this time not in skates, but in boots, and she squatted over the patch rather than lying on her belly. "Sorry, Lena," she said, and her voice sounded hoarse, not quite warm enough to burn just yet, and Lena ached to get closer to her. "Mom's been really bad lately. I think she knows I've been skating on the pond. She won't say anything, but she hid my skates."

As Claire said this, Lena almost felt that it had happened to her instead. Lena had found her skates, though, hadn't she?

"Listen, Lena," Claire started, "I don't think that I'll be able to come back. It's getting late in the season, and Mom's probably right that it's not so safe now."

"No," Lena said. "You have to come back." Lena remembered falling on the ice, someone carrying her, a sprained wrist. She remembered an arm around her shoulder and a kiss on her forehead. "If anything happens, I can save you," she said.

"That's very kind, Lena," Claire said, but her voice did not have the same warmth as her words. "I just don't — Oh no."

"What is it?"

"I think my mom is outside the cabin. I think —"

And then Lena heard it, the screaming woman: "Claire! Claire, come back!" Lena imagined that voice — Maggie — calling her own name, ordering her down from a tree branch or away from a ravine.

"I have to go," Claire said, straightening up.

"No. You can't leave. I have to save you."

The light shifted as Claire turned to go, and Lena pounded her fist against the ice. A sickening crack echoed through the under, and with the crack came a flood of heat. In seconds, Claire was submerged in the water, Lena catching her in her arms. Lena could feel Claire's warmth, and she suddenly had the urge to sing. She knew what singing was now. And then Lena felt a hand tugging at first one leg and then both. Lena looked down into the depths to see Edna's hands around her ankles.

The heat from Claire's body was almost unbearable, but Lena could feel it draining, little by little, and as Claire became colder, Lena began to fill with warmth. She looked at the girl in her arms and saw not Claire but herself, and Edna holding her. Lena remembered the struggle to break through to the surface and the fear as she was pulled down. Someone above was screaming, but that too was fading as Lena descended into the depths, Edna's hands leaching the warmth from her body.

That was when she heard it.

The shriek.

Maggie screamed for Claire, just as she had screamed for Lena back then.

Lena looked at Claire's face and saw her lips beginning to go blue, and she felt the tug of the other ice child at her ankles again.

"Let go," she said, kicking at Edna.

"Save her," Edna rasped.

Save her. She would save her, but not for Edna and the ice children. She would save her for Maggie, Maggie who had always looked out for Lena but still couldn't save her all those years ago.

Lena closed her eyes and kicked against the water. Edna fell away, and Lena felt the light and warmth of the surface. And then she felt air and snow-covered ice. She thrust Claire's body onto the ice and pulled herself out. Lena could feel every part of her wanting to float away, as though she, like most everything else in the world beneath the ice, were formed from fragile water droplets. She willed herself together and scooped Claire into her arms. Lena began to sing. She couldn't remember learning the song, but still, she knew every word: "Oh my darling, oh my darling…"

Lena walked. She pointed herself in the direction of the shore, and she moved. "Oh my darling, Clementine…" Lena felt her feet begin to fade away and saw that her hands were losing color and shape, but she willed her arms to stay together, just for a bit longer. "You were lost and —" she could see the woman on the shore, frozen to the spot like she had lost her own warmth as well " — gone forever."

What was left of Lena's feet stepped onto the shore. "Dreadful sorry…"

"Claire," the woman breathed, interrupting Lena's song. Then she followed the arms holding her daughter. "Lena?"

"Maggie," Lena said. And as her legs and arms and face dispersed, she remembered all of it.

Brittany M. Perkins's story "It Thaws in Spring" was originally published in Metaphorosis on Friday, 10 November 2023. See magazine.metaphorosis.com

About the author

Brittany M. Perkins currently resides in the southern United States with her three well-behaved cats and one terribly-behaved cat. She began her writing career at the age of five after returning home from kindergarten to inform her mother that she wanted to write a book. She's been writing ever since.

When not writing, she can be found cuddling a cat, doting on her niece and nephew, or creating LEGO structures with her boyfriend.

Leiprenese 101

Jason A. Bartles

I scrambled to find the arm hole in my gown as I ran toward Zorah's office apartment. Synthetic fabric should not get this twisted, but the wind tested my best efforts to arrive precisely on time. Zorah lived in the central Administration Building that towered over Mount Leipren University. They occupied the second-highest floor, but unlike the Chancellor right above them, Zorah invited their students and coworkers inside. I untangled the gown and situated the cap, trying to catch my breath. Then I checked my watch. A minute to spare. As I waited for the elevator, I reviewed my mental checklist for the final interview that stood between me and tenure.

My blood pressure rose with each passing floor. An MLU professorship was not a job for the lazy, the purposeless, or even the decently competent. Imposters and flakes were weeded out. It was tenure or bust, admission into the inner circles of academia or irrevocable banishment from this campus and this career. I could not fail now.

The elevator chimed, and at exactly six o'clock the doors opened to reveal — *you've got to be kidding me* — not Zorah, but Rafa.

"Good morning, Charlie!" Rafa practically burst with self-satisfaction. They had been waiting in front of the elevator to gloat. I could have sworn I had reserved the earliest office hour. I wanted to set the bar high, to become the standard against which others were compared, but Rafa had outmaneuvered me. "Good luck," they said insincerely and squeezed past me to take the elevator down.

I shot them a fake smile and stepped into Zorah's foyer.

"Come in," Zorah called, and a door opened at their command. I shook my wrists and took a deep breath before proceeding to their study.

"Good morning, Zorah. Thank you for meeting with me so early," I said. I had planned that greeting, but after Rafa's surprise attack, my words took on a double meaning.

"Never mind about Rafa," Zorah began. They had anticipated my reaction. "Everyone assumes going first gives you a leg up, but the truth is," they leaned forward and gestured for me to sit, "the patterns of the recent past are no guarantee of the present."

Zorah was dressed in the finest regalia. They sat behind a grey marble desk. On either side, bookshelves lined the walls. They were crammed with old lesson plans, monographs overflowing with sticky tabs, and personnel files. Somewhere in there, I thought, must be Zorah's field notes for the first English-Leiprenese dictionary and countless other treasures. Behind them, floor-to-ceiling windows opened onto the Appalachian ridges that wrapped around the campus.

The view from this elevation, and Zorah's reassurances, washed away the disappointment and most of my nerves. They had a way of making the world feel right again.

"Let's get down to business," said Zorah. I took a seat, while they opened my file. Zorah skimmed the summary of my publications, peer evaluation scores, and the data collected about my work-life balance. They mmhmmed and appeared to be quite pleased with my performance over the past decade. Then they tapped the page with their finger and looked at me over the rim of their glasses. "This says you have a new essay forthcoming. A report on the influences of Leiprenese on Earthling languages?"

"Yes. It will be published next month."

Zorah gestured for me to explain the work. This was an interview, after all.

"Right. Leiprenese is a pidgin language developed by the Renner to facilitate the colonization of Earth. At first, the Renner envoys used it to communicate with Earthling leadership about commercial matters. For the Renner, Leiprenese was an undignified but necessary mode of speech."

"Some of your peers would disagree with that statement," Zorah interjected.

"Well, they would be mistaken. There is a somewhat popular, but unfounded, notion that the Renner cherish Leiprenese for its simplicity. However, such scholars fail to distinguish the moral value the Renner assign to efficiency from their own yearning to be respected by the Renner. It's pure solipsism."

"Let's assume that's true. How, then, do you explain the Earthling desire to borrow from a language of such low esteem?"

"Earthlings are banned from learning any of the Renner's native languages while on Earth. The Renner have always insisted on maintaining a certain distance from their colonial subjects," I explained, and Zorah finally nodded in agreement with something I had said. "On Earth, Leiprenese was, and still is, the only possible means of communicating directly with the Renner. Speaking the language provides a way to improve one's station in life. For those born around the time of Earth's discovery and who came of age just as the Renner reconstructed the economy to ease its entry into the galactic marketplace, Leiprenese became associated with the progress and prestige of the Renner and their Homeworld."

"You're speaking of my generation."

"Precisely. In fact, I analyzed many of your early speeches."

"Is that so?"

"Yes, as if overnight, you stopped using gendered language."

"That was intentional. The Renner practically demanded it. Are you arguing that all of the changes were conscious?"

"Of course not. Most occurred over time as the result of code-switching, of constantly living between the two languages. Over a span of ten years, you adopted new vocabulary and even smoothed out some of the harsher consonants not used by the Renner. The *th*, for example, became an aspirated *h*."

"And?" Zorah prodded.

"And the hard *k* softened into sibilants."

"When I think back to how I used to speak, these changes seem drastic," said Zorah. They traded the steely gaze of peer review for a more wistful expression. "But I suppose those born into this world never knew anything else."

"Now you're speaking of my generation," I replied with a wink.

"And speaking of your generation, I have to say I'm quite impressed. With two of you anyway. You and Rafa can count on my endorsement."

"Thank you, Zorah, that means a lot." I could have melted in relief.

"You've earned it," they added.

"What about you? Is there any news about your ascension to the Homeworld?"

"You never know about these things," Zorah said cryptically. Without a doubt, they were the most qualified candidate. Every year, the Renner chose one professor from each planet in the empire to retire among them. Zorah had been favored for last year's opening, but at the eleventh hour, the Chancellor received word that the Renner had suspended all ascensions due to unforeseen circumstances. Something about the collapse of the housing market on a distant planet. Zorah stood and turned toward the windows. "But I try to remain optimistic," they said and invited me to join them.

"I'm sure this will be your year," I said as I approached the wall of glass. "I can't wait to be where you are. I lie awake most nights and dream of escaping this backwater planet."

"I take it you've watched the latest video of the Homeworld?" Zorah's gaze rose toward Renner Hall as they spoke, and mine followed. Perched on the highest peak, the site where the Renner had made first contact almost fifty years ago, its gold-plated facade reflected the sunrise over the entire valley. Originally, the building had been reserved for Renner envoys, until they stopped visiting the planet in person. Ever since, the hall had taken on a ceremonial role, housing the person chosen to ascend for their last night on Earth. The rest of the year, it looked down on the campus as a comforting reminder of the Renner's promise: Paradise awaited those who worked with passion and perseverance.

"Who hasn't? Rethinking your plans now?"

"Absolutely. I had always wanted to stay in the capital. I love living in the mountains, but I thought for my retirement I'd try something new. The sprawling city with its glass towers and plastic-lined boulevards. The personalized pods to carry you to the Anthropological Museum of the Galactic South and then to the beauty spa for a quick chemical peel. I'd watch the sunset in one of those open-air wine bars in a heated pool near the coast. But that train, is that what you would call it?"

"I suppose. There weren't any tracks, or at least none I could see."

"It made me rethink everything. Having your own private car while touring the planet," Zorah's voice soared with their imagination. "The quartz canyons, the cloud forests, the petrol rivers."

"I had no idea those even existed."

"No one did. And being granted permission to study the local languages as you pass through each region."

"It's a dream come true for language nerds! Any favorites?" I asked.

"I'm partial to Milonian. I find the short, shocking phonemes to be an irresistible challenge for my palate."

"Hacher would be my choice."

"The language of austerity," they added. "It all sounds marvelous."

"I wish they'd allow for more opportunities to visit the Homeworld. You'd think if people got a taste of that lifestyle, they'd be more motivated to develop their own planets."

"I'm sure they have their reasons," cautioned Zorah.

"Of course," I agreed and shifted the topic. "It's exciting to think I could get tenure the same year the Renner choose you to join them."

"That would be nice." They spoke in hushed tones, as if another line of thought were running under the surface. "You're following closely in my footsteps."

"I've had a fantastic mentor in you," I said, at risk of crossing that line between gratitude and groveling.

"But best not to get ahead of oneself. There's still plenty of work to do here."

I watched as Zorah traced a finger over a hairline fracture in the window. The gesture was unassuming, as if out of habit, but it left me uneasy. I couldn't help but imagine the entire pane shattering into a million shards and pelting the ground below. I took a step back from the edge and returned to the other side of the desk.

"Look at the time," Zorah said as they turned toward me. Their voice helped shake the irrational vision from my mind. "I have eight more interviews to complete, and you have a class to teach."

"Thank you again." I bowed in deference and left Zorah's study. For a moment, it felt as if everything were lining up just as I had planned.

●

The students in my Leiprenese 101 class were arranged in their mobile desks like ten little bowling pins. It was my job to knock them down in order to build them back up. Now that I had secured Zorah's endorsement, I could focus on defending the record I had set years ago as a student in this very classroom. Today's unannounced oral exam was designed to do just that.

"My value is my work," declared Student 1, leading the repetition of the weekly motto. Rankings were all that mattered at the introductory level. Scores were tied to biometrics, and only the top twenty percent would survive the first year. Only then would I bother with their names.

"My value is my work," said the other students in unison.

Student 1 had been Student 1 for almost a month, which gave me until the end of the week to depose them. They knew I would be relentless to them in defending my title, while lobbing easy questions at their competitors.

There were no friends in that classroom. Only ten adversaries. And I had all the power.

"Today, I will assess your understanding of pronouns," I said. "Student 1, are you ready?" I had switched to Leiprenese, and they knew resorting to English would move them immediately to the back of the class.

"Ready," they responded.

"Student 1, fill in the blank: The employee is late. *Blank* lose ten percent of their wages."

"*They* lose ten percent of their wages," they affirmed with annoyingly accurate pronunciation.

"Correct. You earn one point." I pursed my lips.

"Student 2," I said, slowly and in English, freeing them to respond more easily. "True or False: *I* is the first-person singular pronoun."

"Umm."

"Student 2, you have three seconds."

"False?" Their voice cracked with uncertainty.

"Such a maynard," mumbled Student 1. "Pathetic."

"Wrong," I said in disbelief. "Did nothing trickle down from my recorded lectures? Minus four points."

At my command, the scoreboard in the front of the room docked four points from Student 2, who became Student 4, though they deserved to be in the back of the class. As always, I had been too generous. The desks rearranged themselves, moving Student 2 back a row and sliding Students 3 and 4, who became 2 and 3, into higher-ranked positions.

Just then I noticed Rafa lingering in the hallway, checking to see if Student 1 had outperformed me yet. Time to strike.

"Student 1," I said, returning to Leiprenese, "Fill in the blank with the proper first-person plural pronoun: *I* am the foreman. *They* are the Manager. *Blank* always reward efficiency."

"*They*, wait —" the student's eyes popped as they began to self-correct. I had my opening.

"Sorry, Student 1. The correct answer is: *I and they*. Minus —" I turned to look at the scoreboard. Student 1 was now in the lead by twenty-four points. "Minus twenty-five points."

The star student became outraged at their failure to best me. While the chairs for Students 1 and 2 swapped places, I walked toward Rafa, winked, and shut the door in their face. I would count this as payback for the little trick at Zorah's office.

"You'll just have to try harder, Student 2," I said as I turned. It was better they learned how the world worked under my guidance than on the job. This was for their own good.

●

The day of the Promotion Ceremony had finally arrived. I and Rafa and the other eight candidates for tenure waited behind the auditorium with luggage in hand. Anyone not tenured would be escorted from campus immediately. A lucky student had been assigned to usher me and the others through the loading door and into the wings. In the audience, the tenured faculty were arranged by rank in the shape of an inverted pyramid that pointed toward the stage. At stage left, the Chancellor teetered behind a podium, while Zorah oversaw a folding table draped with purple fabric. It bore the MLU sigil of a black bear under a maple tree. I counted two golden sashes and two flower crowns.

I and the other candidates drew lots to decide the seating arrangement on stage. I drew a front-row seat, and Rafa, poor thing, would have to sit behind me. As they settled in, their shoe kicked my chair. It was not an accident. I was used to the spats, the little digs at every turn, the subtle, but not unnoticed, affronts. It would be a long road beside them, but then again, every Arguedas needed their Cortázar. Rafa's disparagement drove me to new heights, to push harder than I ever imagined as I worked to outshine them.

The Chancellor tapped the mic. They praised the faculty for their increased output and commitment to student success, but then they deviated from the perennial format of their speech. "This year, I'm proud to report a special honor bestowed upon the campus." The auditorium brimmed with anticipation. This must be Zorah's moment, I thought. Zorah took a step toward the podium, and a hush fell over the crowd. "Mount Leipren University," the Chancellor continued, leaning toward the mic, "finally pushed into the number one spot for most accumulated unused vacation days on the entire planet."

The faculty cheered as a wave of ceyah washed over the room. Such a frugal loan word from the Leiprenese. It named a feeling that had become prominent under Renner tutelage. Ceyah is similar to pride, but without the enduring sense of satisfaction, because no record is ever unbreakable, no limit impossible to surpass. Ceyah is that brief moment you celebrate before going back to work.

"Now, on to the final event," they said.

The faculty were caught up in their own success, but I kept my eyes on Zorah. They would not ascend yet again this year. They appeared sullen, as if something had broken, as if they had known it would slip from their hands but picked it up regardless, only to watch helplessly when it crashed to the floor. As the lights dimmed, they stepped back to the table and tried to put on a brave face.

Suddenly, my chair began to move. I and Rafa and the others swirled and rotated around one another at center stage. The big reveal had begun. My chair pulled me upstage, and my pulse pounded in the side of my neck. This was the wrong direction. I felt the blood drain from my cheeks, and Rafa rolled beside me. The others enjoyed the view from downstage. I stared at Rafa, and they at me. An uncharacteristic nervous sweat had beaded around their brow. At least if I were being banished as a failed professor, I thought, so were they. But to my relief, the bigger group was then split in half and dragged toward the wings. I and Rafa were pushed through the open space between them, and in a reversal of fortune, the undeserving eight were swept from the stage entirely. I dared not turn around for a final look at my former colleagues.

The spotlights landed on me and Rafa. I stood to receive a handshake from the Chancellor and my sash and crown from Zorah. Rafa received the same in reverse order. This was the moment I had been working toward my entire life. On paper, it was my greatest achievement. I was happy, or I would be, I told myself, once the reality sank in.

Still, there was no denying this competition had taken its toll, and it was far from over. Earning tenure had been a simple sprint. Now, I would need to adopt a new regimen if I wanted to beat Rafa — and if I hoped to avoid Zorah's fate — in this marathon toward the Homeworld.

●

I unclenched my toes and let my head drop onto the pillow. Rafa rolled off my bed and rebuttoned their shirt.

"That was productive," they said, hopping as they pulled their too-tight and too-short pants up to their waist. "What are you going to work on tonight?"

I usually experienced a renewed clarity as soon as I and Rafa finished, sometimes even a hurried need to start drafting a new lesson plan before they were out the door. But my mind felt mushy.

This rivalry paused twice a week. Wednesdays I visited them, and Saturdays they visited me. The calendar was marked for a strict twenty minutes. I and they toasted to recent accomplishments, in this case tenure, and allowed for a quick release.

"Afraid I'll steal your next great plan?" Rafa prodded.

"Please, you couldn't scoop any idea of mine."

"Then tell me." Rafa almost knocked over a stack of journal articles piled on the nightstand as they bent over to pull on their socks.

I didn't know what to say. For the first time in my career, a blight had spread over the vines where my upcoming ideas usually ripened and waited to be plucked. "Didn't you —" my voice trailed off as an impossible idea skulked around the corners of my consciousness.

"What?"

"Expect the Chancellor to announce Zorah's ascendance last week?"

"The thought did cross my mind."

"They should have ascended last year. To be passed over twice is incomprehensible. If Zorah can't make it, who can?"

"I can," declared Rafa. They never missed the chance for self-promotion.

"Seriously, the Renner have to realize Zorah is unsurpassed in their generation. No one at those old-world Ivies even comes close."

"That entire generation began to slack the minute they got promoted. I and you both produced more plans and better research than Zorah last year. The way I see it, none of them have earned the right to get to know the Renner in person. They were just lucky enough to not have serious competition."

"Still, I wonder —" I sat up and pulled on my undershirt. There was a tear in the seam under the arm. I would have to get this mended.

"Out with it, Charlie. The clock is ticking."

"Maybe ascendance isn't worth it."

I watched their mouth droop a bit. The thought had never crossed Rafa's mind, and it ought not to have crossed mine either. The mere doubt in my voice approached the treasonous.

"That's absurd," Rafa scowled.

"I just mean —" I tried to backtrack. "I thought this would be Zorah's year."

"Yeah, well, it wasn't."

My proposition had been outlandish, mindless, even violent. If I were Rafa, I would have been over the moon, plotting the best strategy to reveal my great mistake.

"It was a dumb thought. Don't pay me any attention."

"Sure thing," said Rafa as they opened the door. They chose not to confront me in private. Their energy would be better spent on a whisper campaign that would slowly erode the high hill on which I currently stood. For now, they shook their head and slipped out the door.

I should have been panicked, or angry, or rushing to preempt Rafa's next move. Right then, for a reason I could not explain, it just didn't seem to matter. The calendar alarm sounded, but instead of getting back to work, I sat on the edge of the bed and stared blankly at the reflective poster of the Homeworld hanging over my desk.

●

A sea of purple caps and gowns with golden doctoral stripes packed the roof-top deck of the Administration Building. I stood with my back to the party, sipping champagne, and stared out at the campus. The valley shone under flood lights on this chilly evening. Going into the New Fiscal Year, I had to reclaim my sense of purpose.

Looking for inspiration, I turned toward Renner Hall, but the campus lights had imprinted on my vision. I lowered my eyes, blinking away the glare, and noticed a crack in one of the deck boards. It appeared to be quite deep, like a fault line on the verge of fracturing. I traced it as it zig-zagged beneath my colleagues' shuffling feet, but I couldn't see where it led.

I was taking another sip when a hand landed on my shoulder. I recoiled, and champagne dribbled down my gown.

"Charlie, hi, sorry, didn't mean to startle you," said Zorah. They reached for a cocktail napkin and dabbed at the wet spots.

"No worries," I said. "It won't stain."

Still, they folded the napkin and patted at the spot once more. "Why are you standing over here all alone?"

"I'm just in my head tonight."

"I know that feeling."

They noticed the doubt in my silence.

"Seriously," they said, getting quieter as they rested their lower back on the bannister and crossed their arms.

"Did something happen?" I asked cautiously.

"The Chancellor informed me the moratorium on ascensions has been extended indefinitely."

"Let me guess, another unprecedented crisis on the other side of the galaxy means Earthlings have to tighten their belts?"

"Pretty much."

"And by indefinitely, they don't just mean a year or two, do they?" I turned to look back at Renner Hall as I asked. Zorah should have been spending their last night on Earth over there, waiting for the shuttle to pick them up first thing in the morning.

"It could be five, ten years. Maybe never. Who even knows?"

Zorah turned around with me. As their words echoed in my thoughts, the future I had imagined, the one the Renner had promised, slipped from my fingers like a balloon from a child's hand.

I felt dizzy and braced myself on the bannister. "This champagne is strong."

"I don't think it's the champagne," replied Zorah. "A little birdie told me you're also having some doubts."

My face burned, and my shoulders went stiff with the thought of Rafa's version of the events. I tried to strategize a counterattack, still unsure of Zorah's motives. Before I could muster the energy, they reached out and rested their hand on my upper back. Their touch, friendly, released some of the tension and quieted the growing sense of abandonment.

"Rafa, blissfully unaware, approached me the day after your accidental revelation," Zorah said, laughing a bit.

They stood beside me and waited, patiently, as I debated what to say next. Even if this was a trap, I thought, even if confirming Rafa's accusations meant some sort of punishment, I decided to risk it. I couldn't hold back any longer.

"I can't explain it, but this —" I looked around.

"Doesn't seem worth it?"

I almost dropped the glass, so I set it on the bannister. "How did you know?"

"Because, Charlie," they sighed and paused. Exhaustion settled in the crow's feet around their eyes. Meanwhile, Rafa kept to the opposite side of the deck. The busybodies kept buzzing around them, perpetually reconfiguring the dynamics of the swarm. "It's not worth it. Only a handful ever made it to the Homeworld. And the rest, what did they get? What did I get? What will you get? I'll tell you what. Nothing."

Zorah's words confirmed a fear I had so far kept from surfacing.

"The Homeworld is a lie," I mumbled, still concerned I might be overheard. Worse, I realized, is that I would never get the chance to prove to the refined and upstanding citizens of the Homeworld that I was an elevated example, if not an exception, to the human race.

"The Renner withdrew long ago," said Zorah. "Yet, they control every dimension of this little planet from a distance."

"So they don't have to get their hands dirty?"

"Yes, and also to avoid being blamed for the world they built. Today, Earthlings discipline and drive other Earthlings. As professors, I and you play a key role in churning out the managerial class that keeps this system humming along. One of the strategies the Renner developed was to prohibit the use of Earthling languages in the workplace. They believed they could prevent, or at least slow, any nascent sense of solidarity by alienating the workers from one another. Of course, the crushing debt they acquire just to make ends meet and the lack of alternatives keep most people from stepping out of their assigned role. Not to mention the threat of being sent to the mines. Meanwhile, the Homeworld keeps those who are better off shut into the system, running in circles to achieve a vague promise of another world, another life."

"Not just running, but constantly trying to outpace everyone else," I added.

"Right. The Renner never force you to run faster, technically speaking. They don't crank some knob. The faculty here do it to themselves. All in pursuit of a dream that was imagined by another. Meanwhile, the Renner sit back and feast on the fruits of Earthling labor. And every time the Renner move the goalposts, everyone accepts this as a greater challenge. Look at Rafa."

"Between my blunder and your failure, Rafa couldn't be more motivated."

"You can't blame them. I've been in their shoes and acted no differently. Everyone is playing the same game here. But I think, Charlie, like me, you're growing tired," Zorah offered.

"I am."

"You know, you and I really are quite similar."

"Do you think —" I started to say. "Wait." The word order was wrong. "What did you say?"

"You heard correctly, Charlie." Zorah smiled and took my hands in theirs as the unnoticed anagram unscrambled itself. "You and I," they repeated.

Zorah's words sprouted before my feet. Their syntax went against everything I had believed, everything I had been taught. Yet somehow it perfectly described one of the many sensations that had been surfacing since the Promotion Ceremony. I let my toes inch their way toward that new growth. It was soft and squishy, like a bed of moss. Zorah, quite literally, had put me first. Not their work, not their own interests or ambitions, but someone else. I felt light as air and stood tall.

"Yeah, you and I," I repeated slowly. "You and I." I had to untrain my mouth to break the deeply ingrained grammar, but with practice, the words would take shape, and one day I might be able to return that generosity or pay it forward.

Zorah squeezed my hands once more and then, as the final seconds of that year wound down, left me to make a decision for myself.

●

"In the year 2035," I recited in slowly enunciated Leiprenese, "the Great Navigator discovered a primitive culture with the potential to be molded." I paused. The students, arranged before me in two opposing lines, furiously transcribed my every word. They were competing to reproduce the most accurate text in the least amount of time.

In the interim, Zorah's "you and I" kept rattling around my brain.

I read the next sentence. "Upon contact, the Renner demonstrated the benefits of cultivating a highly intensive culture of achievement."

Such a clunky phrase, "you and I". A more succinct way to express that idea, that connection, had to exist. It was on the tip of my tongue.

"The Great Spaceship dropped through the atmosphere to the wonder of all Earthlings, who freely offered —" I stopped the dictation mid-sentence and looked out at the obedient students. I had to stop repeating the Renner's lessons. This could not go on.

One by one, each raised their head wondering why I had paused for so long.

"Professor, you may continue," the student currently in first place informed me.

I would not go on. There were no words, in Leiprenese or any other language, that could reach across the void and explain to the students I had trained so well what I was about to do. Out of habit, I gathered my notes from the podium, tucked them into my briefcase, and walked silently out the door.

I could hear the disbelief in my wake. A few sat frozen. Others buzzed with gossip, and one suggested they follow me outside.

Renner Ridge surrounded me. Even from my relative elevation at Leiprenese Hall, it was impossible to look off into the distance. There was no horizon here, only a barricade sealed by Renner Hall. If someone happened to let their gaze wander beyond themselves, their work, and their rank, the building's shiny walls would grab their attention and redirect it toward thoughts of the Homeworld.

That was where I needed to go.

The Hall could only be accessed by a narrow staircase. I hopped the gate. Before my little stunt, no one had imagined a need for greater security. The minds of each member of this campus blocked access better than any physical barrier.

My gown whipped in the wind as I plodded along. I clutched my cap reflexively, but then I ripped it from my head and tossed it over the railing. It soared above the campus for quite some distance before landing in a thicket. A student, still playing by the rules, rushed over to retrieve it.

Higher and higher, I climbed until I finally reached the launch pad next to Renner Hall. For a second, I saw myself from the outside. I laughed at the absurdity of it all. Here I was trespassing on consecrated grounds during a workday for no apparent reason.

Up close, Renner Hall did not look the same. The façade was scratched, and the shiny surface only coated the walls that were visible from below. The others, made of concrete, were covered with mold and old growth. I had an urge to smash the windows, but I changed my mind when I noticed they were made of plexiglass.

For the first time, I saw Renner Hall for what it was. A vacant tower. A few crumbling walls coated in fool's gold. A monument to deception and exploitation. A cardboard box left out in the rain.

I walked back to the stairs, peered over the railing, and saw bodies pouring out of every building. They gathered around a central figure — Rafa — who steered the swarm's bewilderment. They directed outraged hands and fingers to point in my direction.

A corrupting influence on such impressionable minds!

A defender of society hiding in plain sight!

Meanwhile, the briefcase tugged with the weight of the world below. *Why was I still holding on to this?* The lesson plans and ungraded essays begged for their release, so I popped the clasps and dumped out the contents. Pages and pages burst from their folders and fell out of rank. As the papers hung over each stunned student and staff member, time itself lurched to a halt.

An irreversible first strike, for those below. From here, a moment to contemplate the slow beauty of my disruption.

The sheets fluttered in the wind. Some drooped toward the crowd and caught in treetops, while others glided into the distance. I dropped the empty briefcase and stripped off the gown as I walked to the other side of the launch pad. There, I climbed on the railing and sat with my feet dangling over the far edge. My idleness occupied a forbidden space and time. But it also revealed a horizon that had been missing from my life.

A hand touched my shoulder, and I steeled myself to be cuffed and dragged back down the mountainside.

"Charlie," said Zorah.

"Don't try to talk me out of this," I shouted, but they shook their head.

"I had no such intention." They climbed on the bannister, took a seat beside me, and removed their cap. They had not come to stop me. They had been waiting for me to join them. "You and I sure are going to give them something to talk about today."

"*You and I.* My mind resists that phrase at every syllable, and yet it feels somehow right to foreground you instead of me."

"*I and you* wasn't always the grammatical order," Zorah explained. "It was imposed by the Renner in the early days, and I thought, just maybe, you'd have noticed in that last article you wrote."

"Oh really? No, there are no oddities in the use of pronouns in your recorded speeches."

"In the ones that still exist. Many documents from the first years were purged, and by the time you were born, those changes had already taken hold. They were taught to you in school and in every interaction. They even reflected the hierarchies and values built into the environment all around you. But language cannot be controlled completely from above."

"It was so disorienting, and yet freeing, when you said 'you and I'. You named this thing I couldn't quite put into words, this thought I didn't know how to express. I sensed there had to be more than this competition, this life of working without rest. There had to be more than my little academic achievements."

"See, you get it."

"You're the one who invited me to hop off the treadmill. There was no going back after that."

"Indeed."

Zorah took a deep, renewing breath.

I did the same.

It was quiet here, calming. There was an ease to it all.

Mountains stretched before Zorah and me. I could have stared at those blue ridges for days. No roads or trails pointed the way. No rope guided my descent. Only a steep drop, and beyond that, the open woods. Not long ago, the thought would have terrified me.

"What now?" I asked. The timeless questions had resurfaced. "How do we undo all of this? How do we build something better?"

"*We*, Charlie. You do know that word after all."

"We!" I shouted in surprise at myself. The ancient pronoun had crept up from the back of my mind. Not *I and you*. More than *you and I*, even — Zorah and I became *we*.

The word echoed in the distance. So elegant and unassuming. It joined, not through isolating chains of conjunctions that mark order, but by allowing individuals to come together in a collective syllable.

We sat here together. We were exhausted and burned out. We let ourselves, *ourselves!* We let ourselves rest, shoulder to shoulder, and for a moment, we chose not to do anything at all.

Our collective inaction sent a shudder through the campus behind us. We had opened a hairline fracture in the foundations of this place. We had cracked open a door. There would be no guarantes, of course. It would take more than two to change the world, for we could easily be discredited, cast out, and replaced.

Yet, for us, being tired together formed the strongest bond we had ever known. This was our first real lesson, one we were writing together. Ours was a small offering, intended as only one of many more to come. For now, though, we would wait here on the cusp of something unforeseen as long as we could. We would invite others to take a seat beside us. To rest and linger here for a while. To contemplate a new sense of time, one that did not consume, but endured.

And after that, we just might have the strength and the stillness of breath to speak with one another and imagine where we go from here.

Jason A. Bartles's story "Leiprenese 101" was originally published in Metaphorosis on Friday, 21 May 2021. See magazine.metaphorosis.com

About the author

Jason A. Bartles (he/him) is a queer SFF writer and academic. Originally from West Virginia, he now calls Philadelphia home. He is a Clarion West '23 alum. As a researcher of Latin American literary and cultural studies, he published *Arteletra: The Sixties in Latin America and the Politics of Going Unnoticed* (Purdue University Press 2021). This book received an Honorable Mention for the Best Book in the Humanities Prize by the Southern Cone Studies Section of the Latin American Studies Association. He has authored numerous essays on literature, film, philosophy, and video games. As a creative writer, his short stories have appeared in *Daily Science Fiction*, *Utopia Science Fiction Magazine*, and *Little Blue Marble*, in addition to his debut paid publication in *Metaphorosis*. In 2024, his debut novel, *A Valley to Harness*, will be published with Two Doctors Media Collaborative.

I Will Go Gently

Susan McDonough-Wachtman

They sat in their deck chairs, watching their son fish. "Has he caught one?" she asked, gently rocking.

Walter squinted out at the lake. "I don't think so."

"I think he did."

"Did you *see* it?" Ellen had the sight, but to Walter's constant exasperation, she made no distinction between things she saw and things she *saw*.

"No."

He looked at her. Her eyes were on her knitting. "How could you know, Ellen? You're not even looking at him."

"I just know."

"Hogwash." He resumed his contemplation of the lake. He pointed. "A coupla loons." He glanced over at her and saw her half smile. "I didn't say *we* were the loons."

Her smile widened. "Did you see the otter?" She pointed with her needle.

"No. Where? Now?" He looked where she indicated.

"No, this morning, early."

"Why didn't you say so?" Fifty years they had been married and still she didn't tell him things right away. She said it wasn't necessary, because he could see *back*, but still. He made a swiping motion with his hand and looked into the space he had made, a little viewpoint into the past. His heavy features lightened with pleasure. "Huh. You're right. Good, maybe there are more." He watched for a moment, hopefully. They had moved to inland Nunavut to escape the rising sea but had worried about the spread of pollution from the flooded cities. It was still a concern, twenty years later, but an increase in the otter population would be a good sign. "Mmm. Don't see others." Disappointed, he closed the vision with a wave. "How did you see it? You don't get up that early."

"I do lately."

"Hogwash. You've never been a morning person."

"I sleep very lightly these days, Walter."

He looked at her, frowning, worried. "Hog —"

" — wash, I know." She smiled again, a gentle creasing of her wrinkles. "I know you don't want me to die. But I'm not afraid."

"I am." He muttered it low, but she heard.

Her eyes went back to her knitting. "You'll be fine."

He stood abruptly and slammed his hands against the railing. He winced. His hands weren't as tough as they used to be. And his leg ached. He had broken it falling off the barn roof. She had warned him not to go up there.

"Have you *seen* me fall?" he had asked her.

"No, I just saw a shadow over you."

"Well, I'm not going to leave the roof unfixed because of a shadow."

Now he was using a cane and probably would for the rest of his life. His leg hurt. He was no use to anyone. Getting old was shitty.

They had both aged quickly these last twenty years. They had left the benefits of society behind and had survived with hard work but insufficient health care — just like any other pioneers. Someday, she said, more people with gifts of power would be born into their little community, including seers and healers. Their Inuit-related tribe had always produced them, but sporadically, and no one knew how or why. Their own son was "ungifted" and apparently content to be so.

"I think Julian's coming back."

"Oh, good, fish for dinner." She set her knitting in the basket at her feet. She knitted only a few minutes at a time these days before her hands cramped and she had to stop. "Do you remember when we moved here? You said he'd never be happy out here at the end of the world."

"And he wouldn't have been, if Penny hadn't come." She had *seen* the others coming, but she hadn't been sure there would be someone for Julian. The visions of seers were sporadic, uncontrollable, and sometimes unreliable. The future could be changed. "But she did, and they'll be marrying soon. They'll have children."

"Have you *seen* it?" He looked down at her frizzy white hair. Her thin, veined brown fingers were like the driftwood twigs on the saltwater beach where they had grown up. That beach had long since disappeared under a rising sea. It had been Ellen and the other seers who had warned their people first, even before the scientists from Down Below. But many had chosen not to listen. Just as he had chosen not to listen to her warning about working on the roof. If you put your hands over your ears and said, "la la la," all the bad news would go away.

"Some things I know without seeing," she said.

He barked out a laugh, startling the birds in the garden. "You don't know. You just — you're just — an infernal optimist."

She giggled. That sound took him back. He swiped at the air and smiled at his memory of her, sitting on another deck, long ago, her hair a thick, dark mass caught into a long braid down her back, her slim, clever hands busy making a dreamcatcher.

"Come back here," she ordered, in the present.

"Why? Why should I?" He rubbed off the tear running down his cheek. With a wave of his hand, he dismissed his hovering vision of the past.

"Because I am still here. And because he needs you."

He looked down at the beach, where their son was tying the boat up to the dock. "Don't be silly. He's done that by himself since he was ten. Besides, I'm no help to him these days." He tapped the cane hanging on the railing beside him.

She shook her head. "I don't mean right now. I mean when I'm gone."

"What about me?" He knew he sounded childish. He couldn't stop himself. He stared out at the water, not wanting to face her.

She sighed. "It won't be long —" He could hear the creak of her chair as she shifted.

"Please stop saying that."

"Let me finish."

The snap in her voice took him by surprise. He turned around.

"I was going to say," she continued, "it won't be long before you join me."

His hands gripped the railing behind him. He was younger than she was, and stronger, and healthier. His mouth opened, but he couldn't get any words past his teeth. Everything he thought to say got stuck there, like gristle.

She was looking up at him, calm again, with that calm which had always infuriated and delighted him. At many of the worst times in their years together, she had regarded him with just that expression of peace and a faint sense of humor. He always got the impression she was laughing at him, just a little. He hated it. He loved it.

"I haven't told you before," she said softly, "because I wasn't sure if it would help."

"What ..." He cleared his throat, turned and spat over the railing. "What do you mean by that?"

"Will you miss me enough to be glad to die?"

Silence for a moment while they both listened to these words, and felt them weighing down the air between them.

"Glad to die? Why would anyone be glad to die?"

"I am." She smiled sadly. "I'm tired and in pain all the time. You know this."

"Yes, but —"

"I know. You want me to 'rage.' But, you see, I know the light isn't dying." She waited a moment. "We can talk about this later, if you want to."

"If I want to? If I *want* to?"

Their son came up to the porch, carrying his basket of fish. He considered each of their faces in turn and sighed. "You've upset him again, Mother." He bent down and kissed her cheek.

"It's what I do," she said. "Are we having salmon for dinner?"

"Indeed. How would you like me to fix it?"

"Brushed with dill and butter, please, Julian."

"Grilled?"

"Yes, that sounds lovely."

"Father, you look like a plum. Do you want some salmon, too?"

"She... she..." Walter tried to unclench his jaw, then grabbed his cane and stomped down the stairs and across the garden to the beach.

"I'll take that as a yes." Julian turned to his mother. "What did you say?"

"I told him I'm dying. Which you both already know." She smiled up into his brown eyes. "You will marry that girl soon, won't you?"

He squatted next to her and took her hand. "You *know* I will. But that isn't why he was so upset."

"No," she sighed. "I told him something I probably shouldn't have. I probably shouldn't tell you, either. I hope you get married soon."

"Yes, so you've said, even though you've also told me that we will."

She touched his broad cheek. "Seeing the future and being sure it will come to pass do not always go together. Especially when one's emotions are involved. The observer influences what she observes, and not always for the better."

"Yes, Mother," he said. "Come to the kitchen and tell me how much dill to use." He stood and held his hand out to her. She took it and stood, slowly and with a grimace of pain. "Shall I make you some of your tea?"

"Yes, please."

●

The kitchen was made of split pine, as was the furniture. It had been the first room they had built and was still her favorite. Walter had done almost all the work by himself. Ellen had spent most of her time establishing the garden, while Julian fished and hunted small game to sustain them. It had been hard, and lonely for Julian. Ellen had *seen* that more people would join them, but she had not seen any particulars. She had been optimistic, but not sure, that there would be a wife for Julian. She was still optimistic, but not sure, that there would be some with the genetic trait which resulted in powers. It had always been a fickle and unpredictable occurrence in their far northern part of the world.

As Julian settled her at the kitchen table, Ellen said, "He will be tempted to look into the past. All the time." She rubbed the worn wooden surface, scarred from years of hard use.

"Yes, I know." He put the kettle on and got out her favorite mug.

"You must not let him."

"Yes, I know."

She scowled up at him. "You know, for the first time I understand what your father means when he says I'm too agreeable."

"That's good!" he exclaimed, falsely hearty. "A real breakthrough in your relationship."

"I don't appreciate this new sarcasm, either." She rubbed her aching hands.

"Do you want an extra teaspoon of willow bark?"

"Yes." He put the mug in front of her, and she sat back and sipped her tea, remembering. She and Walter had come here when Julian was thirteen, and they had been alone then. She had enjoyed that, the solitude. Seeing the future for three was much easier than seeing it for a village.

"Feel better?" asked Julian after a bit. He had cleaned the fish and was slicing it. She admired the sure movements of his big, brown hands. She had always hoped her vision of only one child would turn out to be untrue. "Mother?" Julian turned around.

"Yes. Yes, I am. Just remembering." The others had trickled into this valley, settled here on the shore of their little, landlocked lake. Walter was right. Julian had been much happier when Penny had arrived with her little sister.

Julian smiled. "That's Dad's job."

"Yes. I used to be a little jealous of that."

Julian put down his filet knife and washed his hands. "Jealous? Of Dad? Why?"

"Of seeing the past. So much more comfortable than seeing the future."

"But not as useful." He drizzled melted butter with lemon across the filets.

She shook her head. "That depends on the circumstances. Your father still has a part to play." Julian glanced at her, surprised. "At any rate," she continued, "people often enjoy remembering the past. They don't really want to know the future. They think they do, but they don't. Even good visions seldom turn out to be what you think they'll be."

Julian sprinkled dill on the salmon. "Enough?"

"More."

He smiled. "I better plant more dill." He crumbled and sprinkled the herb, put the salmon in the oven, and sat down at the table beside her. "I'm pretty sure Dad's been jealous of you."

"I know. Are you sorry you weren't gifted, Julian? You were angry about it when you were young. Then, when you were about twenty, you told me you were glad your life wasn't complicated by, I think you called it, 'hocus pocus.' How do you feel these days?"

"I feel I have enough to take care of with a regular life, and I don't know how you ever managed to balance your sight with everything else."

"I don't either."

They heard voices outside. "That sounds like Penny," said Julian, surprised. "And Maria."

"I don't think there's enough salmon for five. You'd better make some pilaf."

Walter entered, looking much happier than he had thirty minutes before. "I found treasure." He ushered in the two young women, both stocky, dark-haired, and round-cheeked. The elder went immediately to Julian and kissed him.

The younger went to Ellen and examined her carefully. "How are you?" she asked, her tone much older than her eleven years.

Penny turned in Julian's arms and said, "Maria insisted we come. I'm sorry to intrude so close to dinner."

"You know you're always welcome," said Julian. "Help me make some pilaf and join us in eating it."

Ellen faced the serious child with an equally intent gaze. "I am fine, Maria. Are you well?" Wisps of fine, black hair obscured the little girl's brow. Ellen brushed them back, gently smoothing out the furrows. "Did you *see* something, sweetheart?" Her quiet question seeped out into the room, a ripple of change.

Walter straightened up with an involuntary, "No." Ellen made a shushing gesture towards him.

Maria's chin trembled. "I saw you sick. I saw you — gone."

Walter sat down heavily. Julian, who had been checking the fish, turned around, blinking steam out of his eyes. Penny put a hand to her chest and murmured, "Ohhh."

"It's all right, Maria," said Ellen calmly. "I know all about it. It's all right." Maria sobbed and threw her arms around Ellen, who hugged her tightly, suppressing a grimace of pain as the child squeezed her. "Shh, shh, shh. Shh, shh, shh."

●

Ellen refused to discuss it until everyone had eaten. She ate very little these days herself but refused to see freshly grilled salmon sit untouched. The pilaf never happened, but they made do with leftover cornbread and salad. Ellen sipped her tea and prayed for strength.

"Now can we talk?" Walter pushed his plate away. "Did you *see* this, Ellen? Couldn't you have warned us that Maria would develop the sight?"

"You know I don't see everything. I can't demand it." Ellen turned to Maria. "This is a difficult thing that you have been called to do. I wish I could say different words to you. I wish I could promise to always be here to help you through." She shook her head. "I cannot."

"Do I have a choice?" whispered Maria. Her eyes were the color of the split pine walls.

"No. The visions will come. But you will have guidance in how to deal with them."

"And who will be doing that?" demanded Walter.

Ellen smiled, almost laughed. "You will." She looked around the table. "You all will."

Julian and Penny were holding hands, Penny's eyes shining with tears. "How, Ellen? How can I possibly help her with this?"

"Well, you've made a good start by falling in love with my son. He has a lifetime of watching me process visions."

Julian tilted his head inquiringly and opened his mouth.

"Don't be ridiculous, Ellen," burst out Walter. "Watching isn't enough."

Ellen turned and lifted one hand to touch his cheek. "I know how hard all of this is for you. But you must be strong and courageous. For Maria."

Walter glanced at the child and lowered his eyes. "I just don't understand," he muttered.

"I think Mom can explain things, Dad." Julian rolled his eyes. "She's just doing it in her own good time, as usual." He glanced around. "That was supposed to make you all smile."

Penny tried to smile at him. "Maybe... maybe Maria should go out and say hello to the goats for a few minutes," she suggested.

Maria looked at her sister, torn, desperate to escape all this tension, but also desperate to know.

"Let us figure things out, chick, then we'll talk, okay?" said Penny gently.

Maria's face lightened. "Okay." She touched Ellen's arm gently. "You'll be okay?"

"Oh, yes, sweetheart, I'll be right here for a while yet."

Maria stood up, hugged Ellen again, and rushed out the back door.

The adults drew breath. Penny sobbed, Walter cursed. Julian hugged his fiancee and said, "Am I right in assuming that Dad is going to be remembering a lot over the next few days?"

Ellen smiled. "Are you sure you don't have the sight?"

"Ellen, please." Walter closed his eyes. "When you foresaw the flooding, it was so —" he searched for words " — so hard to cope. How are the three of us going to be able to help a child like Maria if she should have a vision as difficult as — as that was — without you?"

"You'll have my memories, Walter. You and I are going to make sure you have everything you need."

●

They began the next morning, while they were still in bed. Walter opened a window into the past, and she helped him find the memories she believed would help Maria. He had not often been called to use his gift in this way; he had to "mark" the remembrances so that he would be able to find them again, when they were needed. After her death.

They began with Ellen's earliest recollections of her own first visions. Her parents had found a seer to help her understand and develop her gift. There had been hundreds of people in the community they had grown up in, and several seers. Their warnings about the crisis to come had not been appreciated. When the sea level began to rise, and the visionaries told people they would have to give up their homes and their saltwater lives, some had turned on the seers. Walter and Ellen and their young son had fled from the violence of their panicked neighbors.

In this new little village, which now homed fewer than a hundred people, Ellen and Walter had been the only gifted ones. Until now.

After breakfast, they continued their work. "You know," said Ellen, "there may be another child out there. One with your gift. There's never been any predicting it. Even for those with the sight."

They were sitting on the porch again, watching their son working in the garden. He was harvesting for a feast. The wedding date had been brought forward. Ellen had told them it needed to be, if she were to attend.

Walter grunted. "Let me get this one sorted first." He pulled his chair closer to hers and swiped at the air. "Here's when you were fifteen, and you *saw* your grandmother's death. I was with you that day. You cried a lot. I was only twelve, and I didn't know what to do."

Ellen smiled. "You did fine. You took me to Megan, which was just what I needed."

"Yes, see, that's what I mean. We don't have a Megan to take Maria to. We won't have you." His voice cracked.

"Yes, you will, Walter. You'll be able to take Maria to Megan. She'll get a vision of Megan, so she'll hear exactly what I heard. You and Julian and Penny just need to provide the physical part. Hug her and kiss her and tell her everything will be fine."

"Everything won't be fine."

"Yes, it will. It may take a while, but it will."

"You're an infernal optimist."

"A cockeyed optimist!" she sang, with only a slight tremor in her voice, "I'm only a cockeyed optimist, immature and incurably green!"

They didn't have movies anymore, but sometimes Walter opened a window to the past and played one for her. ("A blasted parlor trick," he called it.)

"You've never been immature," he said. "Not even when you were fifteen."

"I just didn't seem so to you, because three years younger is such a lot in teen years."

Walter sighed and marked the memory. "What comes next?"

Ellen's eyes sparkled mischievously. "I foresaw our first night together."

"But didn't tell me about it."

"Well, not then. How could I? You were just fourteen, and I was a very sophisticated seventeen. I went straight to Megan and begged her to tell me the future could be changed."

He paused in opening the window to this memory and said, "You never told me that part."

"No?" She closed her eyes. "Well, it was a bit much, you know. Walter, I think you and Julian and Penny should review these memories together — before they are needed. I think it will help you to help Maria if you are all forewarned about how it may go."

"And what if it doesn't go this way?"

"All the more reason to be forewarned. Oh, Walter, it will be close enough. Young women mature along a fairly predictable timeline. Megan managed."

"Megan had the sight!" Walter pounded his fist on the arm of his chair. His raised voice caused his son to look up from his work in the garden.

Ellen groaned and seemed to shrink in her chair. "Walter, what can I say? This is the best I can do."

He slid out of his chair and knelt at her feet. "I'm sorry," he whispered. "I'm sorry. I'm just so frightened, Ellie."

She stroked his white hair, still so thick and soft. "I know. But Walter, you're so much stronger than you think you are. There's never been a time when you weren't able to do what was needed."

●

In bed that night, he held her gently. "Tell me," he said slowly.

"Yes?"

"Tell me why you begged Megan to change the future. I mean, I saw what you said to her, but still —" She shook in his arms. "Are you laughing?" he demanded.

"Yes. I'm sorry." She kissed his chest. "I had never had sex, Walter. I had never even kissed a boy."

"Well, I should hope not. Whom would you kiss?"

Silence.

"You didn't kiss —"

"I am not going to discuss with you who I did or did not kiss before we were married." She was shaking with laughter again. "Not at this stage of my life. My point is, that seeing the experience of an orgasm with a boy who was, to me at that time, a snotty fourteen-year-old, was an existential shock. I panicked. And Megan helped me, as always, and she will help Maria, too, if such a thing should happen to her."

"Oh," said Walter with a groan. "Oh, Ellie, I really, really can't handle this."

"Yes, you can."

"No, no, I can't."

"Yes, yes, you can." She tickled him and he jerked. "If it makes you feel any better, I've seen you dead before Maria is seventeen. That's why you need to be sure to share all the remembrances with Julian and Penny."

He stared into the darkness. "No, no, I don't believe that makes me feel any better." His arms tightened gently around her. "But... it doesn't make me feel any worse, either." He sounded surprised.

"No raging?"

"No raging."

"Hogwash." Her voice smiled in the dark. "You'll rage. When I see you again, I'll know you immediately, because your spirit will be plum-colored."

"Have you *seen* that?"

"No." She shook her head, her wispy hair brushing his chest. "But I can depend on you, Walter. In all the chaos we've endured, I've always known you would be there for me, raging on my behalf."

He smiled. "Well. I can handle that."

Susan McDonough-Wachtman's story "I Will Go Gently" was originally published in Metaphorosis on Friday, 14 December 2018. See magazine.metaphorosis.com

About the author

Susan McDonough-Wachtman has been a high school teacher for most of the past thirty years. She is also a writer, mother, wife, gardener kayaker, cat lover, and book addict. Susan enjoys throwing her intrepid heroines into unlikely situations: a Victorian woman on a spaceship, a medieval woman kidnapped by a dragon, a woman from a future matriarchy in a forced marriage to a chauvinist playboy, a typical teen as the savior of an alien world. *Snail's Pace* placed second in a contest by Publishing Online and was published by them in January 2000. (They subsequently went out of business — surely unrelated events.) *Arabella's Gift* won the Los Angeles Romance Writers' Best Bet for Bestseller and was to be published by Wordbeams, but they went out of business...oh dear. *Matriarchs: Eliza's Revenge* placed first in the Pacific Northwest Writers' Association genre novel contest. The Association, happily, still exists.

Twitter: @SusanMcdW; Facebook: www.facebook.com/susanmcdonoughauthor; Instagram: @suewrite

susanmcdonoughwachtman.wordpress.com/

Time's Arrow

C. Heidmann

In 2130 the Nelari began resurrecting the dead. In 2133 Talia's father called for the first time in five years.

"You want to bring her back, Dad?" *After all this time, after what you did?* Talia wanted to add, but didn't. Couldn't. Not to his face. Not anymore.

She barely recognized the white-haired, eighty-three-year old figure; the holo-projectors in her quarters relayed every etch-mark of time, his still-bright blue eyes peering at her out of a sagging, heavy face.

"Don't you?" He looked… hurt. Like when she was small and had uttered an expletive. How could she, his perfect little girl, have said such a thing? "But she's your *mother.*"

"Have you thought this through? How it will be for her? For all of us?"

He rubbed at his left eye and blinked a couple of times. "You think I haven't? Ever since I got that notification, I can hardly think about anything else."

Talia's notification about the offer to reanimate her mother had arrived the previous day. Half-knowing it wasn't going to go away, she'd ignored it; until her father's call woke her in the middle of Copernicus Station's artificially maintained night.

"She deserves another chance, Talia."

Yes, but did he *deserve another chance with her?* She clamped down on the retort.

Twenty-three years earlier, Talia had lost her mother and learned of her father's infidelity in one afternoon. He'd been away on another 'business' trip which couldn't be put off even in the face of his wife's terminal cancer. When Talia tracked him down and gave him the news, he'd been heartbroken. The shameless display of grief had enraged her.

The pause lengthened as she concentrated on not fidgeting.

What could she say that would convince him she didn't want to talk? Not about bringing her mother back from the dead. Not about anything. She didn't want to get caught up again in the emotional turmoil of his dredged-up pain, his guilt, self-justification, or whatever new form his latest plea for absolution would take. It was part of the reason she lived off-Earth, as far away from home, from him, as she could get.

Her father's hologram fragmented as interference rippled it into multi-colored snowflakes, granting her a reprieve.

"Do you know how lucky we are?" he said as the holo-emitters recomposed his image. "If we'd not had her buried, if we'd had her cremated instead..."

"I know, Dad."

For their own mysterious reasons, the Nelari had revealed their technology in stages. Initially, only people who had been cryogenically preserved, a full body or a head, could be reanimated. Then the Nelari taught human scientists techniques for reviving the interred. Now families of the cremated lived in fervent hope that it might become possible to resurrect even those who had suffered complete body-loss.

"I thought you were opposed to the Nelari, Dad. You said you didn't trust them, that you don't believe in benevolent beings from the stars. Now you're ready to roll over and take their offer?"

He scratched his lip with his thumb. "I did say that. And I still don't trust them. There's no such thing as something for nothing." He shook a crooked forefinger. "One day those damned aliens are going to want something in return and payback's always a bitch."

She resisted the urge to roll her eyes. "They're not like that, Dad. In all their time here, they've not once demanded anything in return for their generosity."

"Then why don't you want me to take their offer?"

She rubbed at her rat's nest of hair. "I don't know if it's the right thing to do, I don't —"

"What do you mean not the right thing? Don't you want your mother back?" She didn't react to his accusation but the hardness in his eyes pushed at her, shoved like a playground bully.

"What about the rehabilitation? It will take weeks if not months, and you realize there's a chance she might not retain all her memory or personality when they revive her." Some reanimations had not gone well — people failing to re-integrate, like a graft not taking. Unable and unwilling to face life again, having never expected to be resurrected, they ended up in mental institutions or chose to end their lives again — with a stipulation to never be revived again.

A glint of moisture filmed her father's irises though he pretended it wasn't there. "I read all the literature. I know there's a chance we could lose her all over again."

"But you're not going to let that stop you, are you?" Certainty of his answer, his total conviction, sat like a lead brick in her stomach.

"You can't expect me to walk away."

"Why the hell not, Dad? It's what you did last time," she spat, instantly regretting it, suddenly tired and wanting to get this over with. She massaged the beginnings of a headache at her temples. "Why do you want my approval when you've already made up your mind?"

"Because that's what your mother would have wanted — us, united as a family."

"Since when did you care what she would have wanted?" The sound of her voice rising a few octaves spurred her on. "You were the one who broke up our family. You walked out on her when she needed you the most." Ignoring the bounds of the holo-pickup fields, she gesticulated wildly, punctuating her words, slashing the air, decimating the millions of miles between them.

"I can't believe you're still holding on to that pain —"

Blood whooshed in her ears. "Her dying gave you an excellent way out of the mess you'd made of your marriage. You think she'd want to come back to that? To you?" She dreaded the return, hated the idea her mother would have to face it all again, her own tragic end, her husband's betrayal, the pain he'd caused her and the rifts it had opened in their family. Why couldn't he see that?

"Talia," he cast around him as if searching for his words, "listen to me. You don't know what it's like to lose a partner, a... a soul mate." His eyes tracked left to some point in the virtual distance, somewhere she could never see.

"Everyone who's lost someone wants them back, it's part of mourning. But we have to let them go, learn to live without them. Hasn't Mom suffered enough?"

She stepped back from the holo, folded her arms across her chest and became aware of her rapid breathing, accelerated heart rate. Finally, she'd run out of words, weapons to hurt him with.

This time his voice rose. "She *has* suffered enough, that's why I have to bring her back."

She had started it, but he wasn't going to let it go. She strove to keep her voice low. "Dad —"

"It's okay, I get it." He nodded as if he'd read her thoughts. "You don't want your mother back because you don't want *me* to have her back." He choked to a stop and lowered the accusatory finger he'd been brandishing. "You want to make me pay again." He was pointing his thumb at himself.

He was right. She wasn't denying her mother, she was denying *him*. But she clenched her mouth. Time had worn him down to a wrinkled, shrunken version of what he'd been, a badly made puppet of his former self. She'd said more than enough hurtful things to him over the years. This time had proven no exception.

In her father's world, a buzzer sounded. The evening mealtime call for the residents of Raintree Retirement Village. His eyes flicked to his right, then avoided hers.

The buzzer sounded again. "You'll have to excuse me, I have to go." He rolled his chair away, an old man not wanting to miss his dinner.

"End connection," she told the com and headed for the medicine cabinet. She slipped a medi-film strip onto her tongue, let it melt into her palate. Within seconds, her headache disappeared, but the chagrin, the bitter aftertaste of their argument lingered. No instant medi-film remedy to soften that.

Did she really want her mother to remain dead just to punish him? She'd mourned, accepted the loss, and moved on. How could she go back on it now? How could her father expect her to retrace those painful steps?

Her mother had never yearned to be brought back to life and cured. And she couldn't be asked if she wanted to come back or to be left alone. But if obtaining consent was impossible, did that make it irrelevant?

Never before had it been necessary to deal with questions like these. When people died, that was it. End of story. Time's arrow had always pointed one way. Death followed life, not the other way around. Until now. Until the Nelari.

In a few short months, she would have to face the reanimated version of her dead mother. What should she do? she wondered. What would she say to a mother she'd already buried?

●

"Hi Mom," was all she said.

The regenerated version of her mother smiled as she came into the waiting room. She looked incredible, radiant, and almost too beautiful. But her face didn't hide the shock, the disbelief, the pain and the disappointment when she saw how time had changed Talia and her father. She recovered and revealed nothing more as she greeted them in turn, asking the appropriate questions, keeping everything normal, calm, as if nothing untoward or overly emotional, were happening.

Talia had gone numb. When her mother hugged her, it didn't feel real. It was like holding a doll, an automaton. Who was this perfect imitation they'd been given? Why did she want to outright reject this manifestation of her mother? Why did she feel she had to keep her own emotional distance? Was it because she'd perceived this... this... ghost of her mother, as doing that?

She'd been coached, Talia told herself as she watched the apparition of her mother; prepared for weeks ahead on how to cope.

Her father was a mess. He began weeping the moment his past wife emerged. More than two decades of pain and guilt, and of mourning her, came out and pulped him, mashed him up like a losing boxer. He failed to stay upright on his new Nelari-gifted cyber legs. They had to help him into a chair, get an aide to give him something to calm him.

Juxtaposed against Talia's decrepit father, her stunning, young 'mother' kept smiling, fussed over him in an over-caring, and to Talia, false way.

"Did you want to come back, Mom?"

All eyes in the room — including those of the bot-assistant who'd been facilitating the meeting, turned to Talia. No one moved.

"I... I, yes, of course, darling."

"Really? You wanted to come back?" Talia flung her forefinger towards her father, "to *him*?" Back in his mobility chair his tear-filled gaze pleaded with her.

"You remember how he hurt you? Abandoned you? Right when you needed him the most?"

"We can talk about this later, okay, Honey?" The manifestation of her mother tried to soothe. Was this her mother? Weren't they supposed to reconstruct enough of a person's personality to be indistinguishable from the original, assimilating every scrap of information left behind by, or about that person?

The resurrected woman's words seemed to de-immobilize everybody. Everyone started talking and moving at once. Talia barely heard them.

A timer display in her left vision flashed. "I have to go," she said in a loud voice. "My ship leaves in an hour. We talk now, or not at all."

They didn't talk then.

Outside, she blinked in the mid-afternoon sun, her space-accustomed eyes smarting in the harsh light. The trip to the spaceport was a blur. The whole way, she cried for her mother. Before her mother had passed away, she'd never spoken to Talia about what her father had done. She'd let Talia believe she'd accepted her impending death early on; that she'd been coping and that at the last, suffering and in pain, she'd wanted it to end, for herself and for all of them.

"Talia, wait."

It was her.

Almost through the departure gate, Talia paused. The reanimation of her mother stood alone, on the other side of the crowd, waving at her. Talia hesitated before weaving through passengers clamoring to get ahead of the line.

"I did want to come back," her mother started, out of breath, "despite everything. I... I mean, if I could have, you know, had a choice." Her cheeks were flushed, two distinct red patches on either side of her face, like Talia remembered.

Her mother had never been good with words, had had difficulty explaining herself. For the first time, Talia felt sympathy for her. Here was a woman scarcely her senior now, facing the prospect of going home with an eighty-year-old man, thrust back into a world she didn't know anymore. How would she pick up the pieces of a life death had made her leave so long ago?

"I'm... alive." Her mother's eyes shot full of tears. She shuddered in a breath and gulped. "I mean I'm glad I'm alive again. I can go travelling now like I always wanted to..." Her mother offered a smile. "I understand you live on a space station? I would love to see it, I mean, to see you... I mean, to talk... some time." Her mother hooked an imaginary strand of hair behind her ear. Despite her new short hair style, she repeated the action two or three times as if she still had the shoulder-length hair she'd lost to cancer and its medications so long ago.

The jittery little gesture triggered Talia's memories, countless instances when she'd seen her mother repeat exactly that nervous tick, always when her mother had been anxious, emotional. Talia's heart melted. It sounded like her mother, looked like her mother, *felt* like her mother. She grabbed her. "Oh, Mom." Her tears spilled unabated.

They hugged until the final boarding alert flashed red in Talia's vision.

●

Her mother went home with her father to the house bought back for her at great expense. Refurbished and re-decorated to as close as possible to the way it had been when she died. The pitiable, harmless-seeming gesture of a guilt-ridden erstwhile cheat and widower.

Talia wasn't surprised when they broke up.

It took about six months for everything to unravel before her mother found a younger man and moved away.

Talia's father died shortly after.

Her mother was still alive, of course, carrying on with her new life and her new beau. She might even outlive Talia now, might even be brought back from the dead again someday, like Talia would be.

But when the Nelari offer came to revive her father, Talia discovered that despite his insistence on resurrecting her mother, he'd neglected to specify his own wishes. He'd left the reanimation decision to his next-of-kin.

Her mother was hesitant.

"I... he said he didn't want to live without me. I... I feel bad... about the way I left him. But that house, the way he... I know all he was trying to do was atone, but I couldn't take it..." Another person hovered in the holo behind her mother, too far out of range to be rendered in detail.

"I felt like a ghost, like I was haunting him," The person in the background moved into the holo-frame and squeezed her mother's shoulder. She squeezed back. "What I mean to say is, I have Antonio now, and... maybe... your father deserves another chance at life too." She spread her hands, as if opening the best possible outcome.

●

At the resurrection and rehabilitation center, they let Talia in early.

She paused in the doorway to her father's room. He didn't notice her right away as two bots helped him upright out of bed. She eyed the figure of her dad.

Still eighty-three, still white-haired, he looked... invigorated, sprightly. Gone were the sunken haggardness, the slow movements, and the pallor that had washed him out. His cheeks had a rosy glow, almost like the cliché Santa Claus figure, and despite still being a little unsteady on his feet he had a quickness to his movements, a new sureness. Restored to the peak of health for his age, he should have another thirty, forty odd years of good quality life. More, probably, at the rate of Nelari-gifted medical advancement.

"You had me brought back." His soft words broke her reverie. Her mind had drifted. He took a step toward her, bots hovering either side in case he lost his balance. "Does that mean you've forgiven me?"

She opened her mouth. Had she? She bit her lip. She wasn't sure. But she was willing to try. In the post-Nelari world of selflessness and compassion, disallowing his resurrection would've been tantamount to purposely keeping him dead. She couldn't live with that; with herself.

C. Heidmann's story "Time's Arrow" was originally published in Metaphorosis on Friday, 6 July 2018. See magazine.metaphorosis.com

About the author

Originally from South Africa, C Heidmann writes from Auckland, New Zealand. Indistinguishable from a local after a number of years on the Outer Rim, she grew up on an entirely different galactic arm and relishes the idea of secretly being an alien.

Sanctuary

Chris Cornetto

The sentry's voice carried from the tower, filling the courtyard below. "Someone's coming! Open the gate!"

Abby dropped her basket and raced up snow-dusted stairs to the palisade catwalk. She leaned from the wall, bracing against the chill to peer into the storm. She wasn't meant to be up here, but no one stopped her — a privilege of being the Patriarch's favorite.

Beneath her feet, the wall shuddered from the rumble of unseen machinery. With a groan of protest, the gate yawned open. The wind lulled. In the distance, a shadow formed in the swirling white, a ghost drawn from the veil.

"It's Orphiel," someone shouted, and the cry spread from voice to voice. "Seeker Orphiel returns!"

A second form appeared behind the first, staggering through the knee-deep snow. "Look!" Abby called down to the crowd. "He's not alone!"

Her heart raced. It was a Homecoming, the first in five years, the third in her life. Not only had Orphiel survived the wasteland, he had found lost kin among the savages — a new life for the city, with new blood for the revival of their race. It was cause for celebration, and, for one unfortunate, cause for despair.

But it wouldn't be her. With her golden eyes and perfect silver hair, with the spurs of bone protruding from her back, she was *necessary* — not just to Father, but for the rebirth of the world. It was a humbling thought.

Below, the Patriarch waded through his eager flock, shining in his golden raiment like the sun among stars. "What are you waiting for?" he thundered. "Greet them." At his command, the crowd dispersed to put on their finest clothes, to gather gifts for their new kin.

Abby came down from the wall and picked up her basket. She had no need to change, as all her clothes were fine, but they were hardly warm enough for standing on the palisade. She huddled in front of a thermal vent and hugged herself for warmth.

Salome came over to join her, likewise shivering. "You must be mad, going on the wall in your condition. It's freezing out there." Though her hair was more blonde than silver, her eyes were finest gold. She, too, had little reason to fear.

"My condition, nothing." As if she couldn't handle a little nausea. She wasn't even showing yet. "I'll be fine."

Salome arched an eyebrow. "Say that to the Patriarch, why don't you?"

Abby waved her off and joined the re-forming crowd. Her people lined the avenue, resplendent with their blazing torches and best attire. Though only a shadow of the seraphim hosts of old, the sight still made her ache with pride.

Sanctuary, the last spark of civilization in a shattered world. How nervous, how excited their new Returned must be.

●

Abby shut the door behind her. She bowed her head lower than humility required to hide the grinding of her teeth. "You sent for me, Father?"

She knew why she'd been summoned. In the week since Martina's Homecoming, not a thing had gone right. The woman's sulking had cast such a cloud over the festivities that Father ended them early — and because it was Abby's task to make the newcomer welcome, she'd been dogged by the cruel smirks of those eager to see her fall. Being the favorite had its perks, but it painted a target on her back.

The Patriarch set his cup on the table. He rose and stretched his twisted wings, deformed but magnificent, before hiding them beneath his cloak. "I did, Abigail. Come here, child."

Across from him, Seeker Orphiel remained seated, one hand on a bottle of sparkling blue glass. Abby tried not to stare, though she'd never seen its like.

The Patriarch inspected her. "You are well, I trust?" His pale blue eyes, a defect inherited from his mother, bored into her.

"Yes, Father. Thank you for asking." She tried to pretend his concern was for her, but she knew better. She envied the child inside her; the Patriarch's interest in *her* waned by the day. It was for that reason, to prove herself the dutiful daughter, she had volunteered to be Martina's keeper.

What a mistake that had been.

He waved his hand. "Good. I need you to deal with Miriam again. She's not adjusting well, and there is no place in Sanctuary for idleness."

"She doesn't like that name, Father. Perhaps if we let her keep–"

The Patriarch silenced her with a glare. "What, keep her old name? Invite the taint of the wasteland into our walls? Don't be impertinent, girl."

Abby trembled. She looked to Orphiel for support, but he refused to meet her gaze. Flush though he was with the Patriarch's favor, that most precious currency, he wouldn't squander any to help her. "I only thought–"

"No, you did *not* think. Question me again, and I'll send you with her to clean the light-harvesters." Though it was an idle threat, his cheeks flushed an angry crimson. "Now, can you manage this *simple* task before I give it to someone more capable?"

"Yes, Father," Abby stammered. She retreated to the door, and all but ran to the women's barracks. Why did she keep sticking up for the useless woman?

Barracks #6 was farthest from the Patriarch's manor, and its residents furthest from his grace. Abby knocked only briefly before throwing open the door. "Miriam? Are you in?"

"Don't call me that," came a blanket-muffled voice. "I hate that name."

Abby went to the woman's bunk and peeled back the covers. "I know, I'm sorry. I wasn't sure if anyone was listening." She sat on the bed and ran her fingers through Martina's hair — its gleaming silver sheen left no doubt how the Seeker had found her. Despite the dark rings around her eyes, she was an attractive young woman, at most three years Abby's elder.

Martina brushed Abby's hand away and climbed back under the blanket. "Here to send me to sweep the snowfields? Or has the almighty Patriarch decided which of his stock I'm to be bred to?"

There'd be no reasoning with her in this mood, so Abby tried a different tack. "Have you had breakfast yet?"

●

Even in her warmest coat and scarf, Abby shivered. The light-harvesters needed constant sweeping, and it hadn't been hard to find someone willing to trade duties with her. Most of the residents of Sanctuary dreaded leaving the safety of its walls, even the short distance to the solar field.

Abby kept a nervous eye on the wall. Those Seekers not scouring the waste acted as the Patriarch's eyes — and the firm hand of his law. He would not be pleased to find the bearer of his child outside the walls.

For that matter, it didn't please Abby to be there, either. She shivered and swept and waited for Martina to speak.

After twenty or so minutes, Martina broke the silence. "Why are you here?" she snapped.

Because you're a fool who doesn't understand the bounty you've been given, Abby wanted to shout. *Because you don't see the glory of Father's plan, or the honor of being part of it.*

And because, when I make you see reason, Father will notice me again, her heart whispered. *He'll appreciate me for myself, and not just this child inside me.*

But she said none of these things, and settled on a neutral remark. "Because the machinery needs light, to keep the city warm."

The woman rolled her eyes and stopped sweeping. "That's not what I mean. I've heard the rumors. You're carrying the Patriarch's child. There's no way he sent you to freeze out here."

Called out on her scheming, Abby flushed. "I... I thought you could use the company. I worry that you're unhappy here."

"Unhappy?" Martina snorted. "And you enjoy being cattle?"

Abby cocked her head. "Cattle?" It wasn't a word she knew.

Martina gave an exasperated sigh. "Livestock. Animals kept and bred for their labor."

So they were creatures from the wasteland? She'd always been fascinated by the outside world; as a child, she'd pestered old Seeker Malthus for stories of its terrors. "But is that so bad? To survive, we all must labor and breed."

"It's not that simple. I hate the way Old Hunchback orders everyone around like he's some kind of god."

"Don't call him that!" Abby snapped. The woman's endless sulking was bad enough, but she had no right to insult Father. "Besides, he's not a hunchback."

"Not a–"

Abby dropped her broom and took Miriam's hands, guiding them beneath her coat to the spurs on her shoulders. To where, if the god was willing, her son would have wings. "Don't you understand? He's our Father, the greatest of us all. He's the closest to a seraph the world has left!"

Martina's eyes went wide. "You're telling me seraphim are real?"

"Didn't Orphiel explain why you're special? Chosen?" How ignorant *was* she?

"I didn't take him seriously! I get that my hair's odd, but it's just a quirk, isn't it? I assumed the old man was eccentric, and fancied a certain look." She paused and chewed her lip. "He really has *wings*?"

How could a woman of the blood, who had seen the wasteland with her own eyes, not understand the urgency of Father's project? Only by the return of seraphim could the world be reborn from its ashes. "If you didn't believe Orphiel, why *did* you come to Sanctuary?"

Martina looked at her feet. "It was a place to run away. My husband was killed by bandits, my home burned to the ground. I came because I had nothing left."

●

Martina passed Abby another plate to dry. "Why do you call it the wasteland?" she whispered.

For several days, Abby had been swapping chores to keep Martina company — and so far, bless the god, the Patriarch hadn't noticed. The two had arrived at something of an understanding, in which Martina tried to fit in so long as Abby didn't rush her. Abby had even come to like the woman, a little, despite her irreverence toward Father. Their candid conversations had become her guilty pleasure.

"Because everything was destroyed in the Cataclysm. Wasn't it?"

"Well, yeah, more or less. But that was hundreds of years ago." Martina plunged her hands into the basin and scrubbed the next dish.

Abby wrung out her towel. She set it down and hoisted herself onto the counter. "So isn't it terrible out there? Plagues and hunger, poverty and war?" She had heard all about it from the Seekers. "Didn't you want to get away from it all?"

Martina stopped washing. "I... thought I did. But I was wrong. I miss my home."

Abby's jaw dropped. "Miss *the wasteland*?"

Martina chuckled, her mouth quirked in a hint of a smile. "Have you ever looked around you? *This* is the wasteland. Nothing but mountains and ice as far as the eye can see." She paused a moment, looking thoughtful. "You've never been *anywhere* else?"

To her surprise, Abby felt stung. She knew as well as anyone there was nowhere *worth* going, but the way the woman spoke... "I've been to the lower village," she blurted, though it made a poor boast. Most of her kin called it the Dungheap. "It's... not a nice place."

"I think I passed through it on the way here. Crude little village, tucked in a valley about a day's walk down the mountain?"

Abby nodded. "That's the one." *Crude* was kind; it was where rejects were sent to huddle in stone huts, to scrape the dirt until they starved. "The people there don't have much. When there's a Departure, I sneak them some fruit from the greenhouse."

"Departure?"

On the walls, the crystal-lights flickered and dimmed — a warning that curfew was approaching. Abby cursed and jumped from the counter, and the two began scrubbing at a furious pace. "It's the rule," she explained over the clatter of wet dishes. "Seven-score and four. That's Sanctuary's capacity. The seraphim built it as an outpost, not a city."

"But what do you mean by 'departure'?"

"Well, if the population grows, someone has to leave, right?" Abby shrugged and grabbed another dish. It was an uncomfortable topic. She didn't worry for herself, but Martina... "There'll be one soon."

Martina stared at her. "What, so now that I'm here, someone gets kicked out of Sanctuary? Thrown away like trash? That's awful."

Abby winced. Departure was slow execution by hunger and cold, but it was also how things had to be. So why did she feel so defensive? "We hold a feast to thank them. And we walk them all the way down to the village."

"Oh, how noble." Her voice dripped bitter sarcasm "So who's the lucky winner?"

While most departed were picked for their weak bloodline, some were chosen for holding... dissenting views. Despite Abby's efforts, the current odds were two to one on Martina. "My guess is Michel, the engineer's son." It wasn't quite a lie. With his thin blood, and without his mother's aptitude, he was certainly at risk.

"But why not let me go home? Then Michel could stay..."

And let all my work go to waste? It was a selfish thought, but Abby couldn't help it. Besides, without ample provisions, there was no way for Martina to survive the trip back to the wasteland.

The lights gave a final hum, dimmed, and went out. Abby struck flame to a lantern, and they put away the still-damp dishes. It was too late to finish drying them, but at least they were clean. "Help me with the basin?"

Together they lugged the washbin outside, careful not to slosh water on the ground. The outdoor vents shut off at night, and spilled water meant ice in the morning. They dumped the soapy water behind the building.

Abby went back inside for the lantern, though it was hardly necessary in the crisp starlight. She locked the mess hall behind her, already shivering in the biting cold. "Can I walk you back to your barracks?" she asked through chattering teeth.

Martina hugged herself and nodded. "Gods, I hate it here. So damned cold."

Abby leaned close to Martina for warmth, frost crunching beneath their feet. "It's not cold where you come from?" She'd always pictured the wasteland with a blanket of ice, its people huddled in rude huts to keep from freezing.

"Ha! I used to complain of the heat. Silly, right?"

Abby shook her head. Her scarf slipped loose, and the wind raked chill claws down her neck. "So there wasn't much snow there?"

"In Sunhome?" Martina arched an eyebrow. "Never. We got enough rain for the crops, more or less, but that's the worst of it. Most days, the skies were so clear you could see the cathedral from my parents' vineyard."

They reached Barracks #6, but curiosity made Abby linger. She squeezed her hands to coax warmth into numb fingers. "Cathedral?"

"Like a big temple. Imagine the Patriarch's manor, but ten times bigger, and a hundred times more beautiful. My father would take me there when we brought our wine to market."

Abby studied the woman's face, but saw no hint she was teasing. Could a wonder like that exist in the wasteland? "And what's wine?"

Martina paused, and, for the first time, actually laughed. "Gods, girl, don't you know anything? It's a drink, made from grapes, sunshine, and a little bit of heaven."

Despite the cold, Abby flushed. *Did* she know anything?

●

Abby set the basket on the table. Steam rose as she peeled back the cloth, filling the room with the scent of fresh biscuits. She arranged the Patriarch's breakfast on his platter, set out his fine cutlery, and stepped back to wait. The blue bottle sat on the table, corked and half empty.

Most days, Abby's stomach would rumble in anticipation of her own breakfast; today it churned. She leaned against the wall, shifting her weight from foot to foot.

Uncomfortable minutes passed, followed by more. Just before she caved in and ran outside to vomit, she heard the tread of the Patriarch descending the stairs — followed by another. She hurried to pull out his seat.

"I'll get that," Salome said, reaching it first. Her dress was disheveled, and her blonde hair in disarray.

What was *she* doing here?

The Patriarch tugged his robe over his shoulders, smoothing it as best his wings allowed. "That will be all, Salome. We appreciate your zeal to serve, but I must speak with daughter Abigail now." He placed a hand on her shoulder and steered her toward the door.

Salome turned and dropped a neat curtsey. "As you will, Father. Goodbye, sister Abigail." She gave a coy smile and waved, showing a flash of silver on her thumb — a new ring, in a pattern of woven vines. A treasure scavenged from the wasteland.

Abby gritted her teeth. She hadn't merely lost Father's affection. She'd been replaced.

The Patriarch ignored her while he ate. When finished, he wiped his mouth and waved her over. "Come, child. Let's have a look at you."

Though fuming inside, Abby obliged. He lifted her shirt to place a hand on her belly, as he often did, but today her flesh crawled at his touch. She thought of Martina's favorite name for him — *the old lecher*. It had a nasty sound that fit all too well.

"My son is well?"

Abby nodded. Always *his*, as if she were a mere vessel.

The Patriarch furrowed his brow. "And you wouldn't be risking him by staying out late? By going out in the cold after curfew?"

That traitor Salome must have whispered about her! Abby's irritation twisted into fear; she prayed they didn't know she'd been outside the wall. "I've been working on Mar... Miriam, as you asked, Father. I helped her wash up last night. I think she's coming around."

He arched an eyebrow, and his frown eased just a little. "Very well. But be more careful. This child is my triumph... maybe even my heir. Think how honored you'll be as his mother — and how *terrible* it will be if anything happens to him."

Abby tried to control her quaking knees; she knew precisely whom it would be terrible for. "Yes, Father. Will there be anything else?"

The Patriarch picked up his cup and gestured to the blue bottle. "A drink, if you would."

Abby turned away to hide her fear. She wrangled the cork until it twisted loose with a pop. As she poured the ruby liquid, she caught an aroma of fruit and flowers. "What is this, Father?"

The Patriarch drank it down. He lowered the cup and wiped crimson from his lip. "A barbarian novelty, brought home by Orphiel. It would not interest you."

"Yes, Father," she agreed, though he was very wrong. She could guess what it was, and it interested her very much.

When he finished with his meal, the Patriarch rose from his seat and put on his gold-trimmed coat. "You may continue your work with Miriam, but I suggest you act quickly. I've put off this Departure long enough. It's time her faith was tested." Without waiting for a reply, he went outside.

Abby cleaned up from the meal, placing the dirty utensils in her basket. Still piqued about Salome, she also took the wine.

The greenhouse was the largest building in Sanctuary, and also the warmest. The citrus-scented air hummed with the drone of vents and honeybees. It was Abby's favorite place in all her tiny world, and the best in which to shake a bitter mood.

Martina spread her arms and closed her eyes. "I can almost pretend I'm home."

It had taken a few white lies to get Martina on greenhouse duty with her, but it was worth it. It was also less risky than leaving the walls with Salome snooping on them. "Is your home really so lovely?"

"All this and more. We have orchards that stretch as far as the eye can see, and the fruit... What I'd give to taste it again."

After checking that no one saw her, Abby twisted an orange from the nearest tree. "So now we're alone, will you tell me what's bothering you?" She peeled the fruit hastily, hiding the rind in her basket.

Martina breathed a heavy sigh. "I've been trying to take your advice, trying to keep my head down and make myself useful. But I don't know if I can go through with this."

Abby handed her half of the orange. "Go through with what?"

"I've been assigned to Orphiel. I found out this morning." She bit into the fruit and crinkled her nose. "Ugh, sour."

Abby tasted her own half; it was the same as any orange she'd eaten. "What's so bad about Orphiel? He's passing handsome." He didn't have the best traits, of course, but a Seeker had to blend with the savages. He had also become quite influential, as his acquisition of Martina had placed him high in Father's esteem.

"It's not that." Martina tossed the rest of her orange — a waste so extravagant, Abby couldn't believe it.

"That's *fruit!*" she whispered harshly. She picked it up and brushed off the dirt. "We shouldn't even be eating it!"

"Huh. Sorry." Martina gave a sheepish frown. "I guess I wasn't thinking. Back home, a small, sour orange like that wouldn't have sold for half a copper."

The more Abby heard of the wasteland, the less it sounded like one. "So what's the problem with Orphiel?"

"I don't like him. Those weeks on the road, between Sunhome and here, he barely talked. Just watched me like a hungry wolf. I was almost surprised he didn't try to... Well, I guess now's his chance."

"If you don't like him, why'd you come with him?" She ate a segment of the dirty orange. There was no sense wasting it.

"I wasn't thinking. My grief was so fresh, so intense, all I could think of was fleeing my ruined life. By the time I wanted to turn back, we were too far from the world I knew. I was afraid of him, but I was more afraid to cross the wilderness alone."

Abby squeezed her friend's arm; Martina's troubles made her jealousy of Salome seem a petty thing. Thinking of her rival brought to mind her stolen prize. "Oh, I know what might cheer you! I brought you something." She dug the blue bottle out from her basket and held it up triumphantly.

Martina's eyes went wide. "And you told me you'd never heard of wine?"

Abby handed her the bottle. "I hadn't. I sort of... borrowed it from the Patriarch. The Seekers bring him things from the wasteland. Orphiel must have given him this."

As the woman looked the bottle over, her lips trembled. She closed her eyes.

Abby frowned, worried she'd done something wrong. "Don't you like it? Is it bad wine?"

"No," Martina said through gritted teeth. "It was a kind gesture, and it's very good wine. It's just... a painful memory. This is Sunhome wine, from the Vianello vineyards. Bertholo had been saving a bottle of the same vintage for when... for when..."

The woman broke into tears, and Abby hugged her close. "Oh, dear..." Not knowing what to do, she patted her back.

"I was going to be a mother," Martina whispered through sobs, "but I lost the baby. I'm so sorry, Berto."

Abby squeezed the woman. She could imagine the Patriarch's wrath if she failed to carry her own child to term, and her muscles clenched in sympathetic terror. "I'm so sorry. Your Patriarch must have been furious."

Martina stopped sniffling and looked up at her. "We don't have a damned Patriarch," she snapped.

Abby drew back, startled. "So there's no one in charge? Everyone does whatever they want?"

"It's not that." Martina shook her head and rubbed her puffy eyes. "There are laws, sure, and the abbot expects his tithes, but it's nothing like here. There's no one controlling every detail of your life — telling you what to think and who to love."

It still sounded like chaos to Abby. "Then who assigned you to have a child with Berto?"

Martina laughed through her tears, a sound absent of mirth. "What a pair we make. I should be the one to pity you. Don't you know anything of love? Of family? *I* chose Berto." She tugged at a leather thong around her neck. "We said our vows, traded rings, and pledged our lives to each other — not because we were ordered to by a nasty old fool, but because *we loved each other*." At those words, the tears welling in her eyes again overflowed. "And now he's gone."

Abby had no idea what to say, so she held the woman's hands in silence. She had never imagined any way other than the Patriarch's. The idea of having no one to order her life was terrifying... but also strangely enticing.

"I can't stay here," Martina said at last. "I can endure the loneliness and drudgery, but I won't be part of that filthy lecher's breeding project. If the gods see fit to send me another child, it'll be on my terms, to be raised with love. Not enslaved and bred for stock." Her face twisted in disgust. "A child deserves better."

Abby placed a protective hand over her belly. What did *her* child deserve? "What will you do?"

"I don't know. Does it matter?" She threw her hands into the air. "I guess, next time I'm sent to the solar field, I'll run off."

The Speculative Teachers' Lounge

"Don't be foolish," Abby gasped. It wasn't a plan; it was a quick, icy death. "The Seekers would drag you back before you made it ten paces. And even if you could outrun them, you'd freeze after sundown!"

Martina slumped against a tree. "Why do you stay here? A woman can endure much, but what mother would wish this prison on her child?"

Again, Abby brought her hand to her belly; already it swelled with the life growing within. She took pride in her favored status, and her child would be greater still, but Martina wasn't wrong. Beyond the cruel whispers and resentful glares, the price of that favor was the constant, gnawing fear it would be withdrawn. Her son's life would be governed, from cradle to grave, by the whims of the Patriarch.

All her life, she'd drawn no distinction between servitude and survival; she assumed there was no other way. But what if she were wrong? If Martina spoke true, Sanctuary's walls didn't keep the wasteland out — they kept her people in, slaves to the Patriarch's will. Yet somewhere beyond them, down the mountain and across leagues of trackless wilderness, people lived *free*.

Her head spun with the implications. She could hardly imagine what freedom was like, or what one did with it. What would she change about her life if she could choose?

There was one thing.

"Where you come from," Abby whispered, "can mothers keep their children?" It was a guilty thought, unbecoming of her, but it tugged at her more with each passing week.

"You mean..." Martina's eyes flashed with sudden anger, and she forced her words through gritted teeth. "That settles it. I'm leaving this place, and *you're* coming with me."

●

The Underworks rumbled like a sleeping beast, making Abby's skin crawl. Even coming from the greenhouse, the heat of the dim, damp tunnel was unbearable. It was not a place she went by choice.

"You're mad," hissed the engineer. "I should report you to the Patriarch."

The threat held weight. It was what any sane person would do when asked to participate in rebellion, and what the Abby of a few weeks ago would have done in her shoes.

But Martina had changed her. Abby was sick of the endless jockeying for Father's approval, of the bitter distrust it caused. It was a tense, lonely way to live. Only Martina seemed outside the game — which made her the only person in Sanctuary safe to call a friend. She couldn't let Martina down.

"You won't," Abby told the engineer. "We hunger for his love and fear his wrath, but you hate him as much as I do." She nearly shouted to be heard over the clank of metal, the whistling steam.

The engineer looked away but made no denial. "Perhaps I should report you anyway, just to see his pet fall from grace."

Abby thought of Salome and her ring, and she flushed with anger. She placed a hand on her belly. "*This* is his pet. I'm just its husk." She had never spoken those words aloud, as if her silence could deny them truth, but they were true, regardless. "So, will you help?"

The engineer looked at her, her ill-concealed hatred giving way to the sympathy of one outcast for another. Still she shook her head. "I can't. As much as it would please me for the girl to escape his grasp, I can't risk it."

Abby wrung her hands. "But what about your son?"

"Michel will be fine. Everyone knows Father's going to pick Miriam." The woman's brow wrinkled when she frowned, and her nut-brown hair was shot through with gray — the fast aging another sign of her thin blood. "If she wants out so badly, just wait for the Departure."

"I can't." Abby mopped the streamers of sweat from her face. How did the woman stand it here? "We need to smuggle out supplies, a lot of them. We're not staying at the lower village — we need them to reach the wasteland."

The engineer arched an eyebrow. "We? You're going with her?"

Abby nodded mutely. She didn't belong in Sanctuary. The only thing keeping her here was fear of the outside world, but with Martina as a guide...

"You're not mad, you're suicidal. Where will you go? How will you survive?" She shook her head in disbelief. "There's nothing out there."

"But there is." It wasn't just Martina's stories that convinced her — she had seen the evidence. "The Seekers bring home things we could never make here. There's got to be more to the world than we're told."

The engineer shrugged. "Maybe, but what does it matter? You know he'll hunt you, even to the edge of the world."

"That's why we need you to give us a head start. Think on it. Even if Miriam gets picked now, what happens when my son is born? Michel is still at risk." Though she had little choice, it felt wrong to exploit the woman's attachment to her son. She used to think it unnatural, but now, with a life growing inside her, she understood.

The engineer chewed her lip, hesitating. "I just need more time with him. Once he grasps the machines a little better, shows how useful he can be..."

It was Abby's turn to shake her head. "And you'll teach him in, what, a mere six months, what took you a lifetime of study?" She squeezed the woman's calloused hands. The machinery was ancient, older than the Patriarch, and it took a rare genius to keep it thrumming — a genius Michel didn't have. "Let me leave. More room in Sanctuary means more time for your son."

"But your death–"

"Will not be on your conscience. I choose this." She couldn't explain the feelings rising inside her, how living only to serve the Patriarch would never be enough. Martina had opened her eyes, and there was no closing them again. For herself and her baby, she had to risk the wasteland.

The engineer slumped against the wall, defeated. "Fine, damn you. Second bell after sunrise, to give you as much daylight as I can. But you'd better reach the lower village by nightfall. Mark my words — a storm's on the way."

Maybe the woman *did* get it. It had been so long since anyone called the engineer by anything but her function, Abby didn't even know her name.

●

In the distance behind them, the alarm bell clanged.

Abby and Martina dragged the sled onward, unable to see anything through the blinding fog. The damp air sapped the warmth from their skin and frosted their clothes.

As promised, at second bell the engineer had overheated the main boiler and jammed the manual shutdown. Crews spilled through the gate to drag sheets over the light-harvesters, cutting off power, while others scrambled to open the vents full-blast. Steam met snow, blanketing the mountain in the thickest fog Abby had ever seen.

It was through that fog that Abby stumbled. The deep snow grabbed at her legs, pulling her to the ground.

"Come on," Martina shouted, hauling her to her feet.

Though there was little risk of being heard through the chaos, Abby still cringed. "Where's the track? I don't see it."

"We've already lost it. Just keep the sun to your back until we clear the fog."

Abby brushed herself off. She searched the sky for a hint of brightness, a smudge of silver amongst the white, but it was hard to be sure of anything. They took their best guess, and together they tugged the sled back into motion.

As the minutes stretched into hours, the bell grew fainter and eventually ceased. Abby trudged onward, each step an act of will. She ached with the effort, her muscles freezing through the heavy Seeker coat, but she didn't dare rest. In the best weather, for one who knew the way, it was a day's walk to the lower village. At their current pace, they'd never reach it by nightfall.

The fog followed them down the slope, but after another half hour it began to thin. A few minutes later, the sunlight cut through the haze. Martina, too weary to curse, pointed south and frowned.

Abby saw what she meant. From a different spur, divided from theirs by a deep ravine, the track snaked into a chasm. It was the only way down from the high plateau, and they'd have to backtrack to reach it. Uphill.

There was no use complaining. In this icy void, words were nothing but frozen mist, meaningless against the lonely silence of the mountain. They yoked themselves to the sled and trudged back the way they came, plodding one weary foot before the other until time ceased to have meaning.

When they reached the chasm, the sun had already passed its peak. Gray, billowy clouds scudded in from the horizon, devouring the sky ahead. The wind howled a warning of the storm to come.

And from behind rang the mournful note of a hunting horn.

Abby looked over her shoulder. Beneath the lifting fog was every Seeker in Sanctuary, racing down the slope in snow-gliding shoes. She froze like a hunted hare.

Martina shook her by the shoulders. "Snap out of it! We have to run!"

Abby nodded, and they tugged the sled into the ravine.

The winding track slowed their progress to a crawl. In some places, drifts piled so high they had to dig their way past; in others, rocks jutted through the snow to trip feet and snag the sled's runners. They couldn't see their pursuers, but each blast of the horn drew closer than the last.

As they struggled on, the first flurries danced through the air like mocking sprites. The flakes clung to Abby's coat until it was white as a burial shroud. The storm had come early.

With so many miles left, trapped between one doom and another, there could be no escape. If they weren't captured, dragged back to the city in shame, they would freeze to death in the snow. At the thought of her warm bed, tucked snug in the embrace of Sanctuary's walls, Abby sank to her knees and cried. "I can't. We never should have run away."

Martina slapped her, hard. "What, you thought this would be easy? Pity yourself later. Now get to your feet and pull!"

The vicious sting brought a flush of warmth to Abby's frozen cheek. She rose mechanically and picked up the tether, pulling the sled with flagging strength while Martina pushed from behind. Each step became a stumble until she pulled on all fours, head down like a beast of burden.

Though Martina huffed for breath, the woman kept her focused with constant chatter. Abby closed her eyes and fled her body, lost in stories of bustling markets and shining palaces. Of a cathedral, light gleaming from glass of every color, towering above a sprawling city. Of acres of fruit trees, not trapped in a greenhouse, but spread across the hills, warm in the generous sun.

Could it all be true? Had the world, once fallen into ruin, grown back without the seraphim? And if so, why did the Patriarch keep them in ignorance? She was too weary to process it all.

After a time, the sled halted. When Abby looked up, her heart caught in her chest. Before her, the canyon opened to a panorama of the slopes below. Though the sky was now full gray, painting the snow to match, there was another color far, far in the distance.

In a little valley, sheltered from the weather and biting wind, was the brownish-green of grassy fields.

Behind her, Martina cried out in alarm.

Abby whirled around to see her grappling with a Seeker, trying to writhe free of his grasp. They fell, skidding down the slope, and the heavy sled careened after them.

Too late, Abby noticed the harness tangled about her shoulders. It jerked taut, ripping her from her feet and dragging her with it. She clawed at the ground, but the icy scree gave no purchase. The attempt sent her into a spin, tangling her worse in the grasping cord. She skidded along with no sense of direction, curled instinctively into a ball to protect her belly.

A rock caught her foot and whirled her about; another struck her head with the force of a hammer. Stars exploded across her vision, and the world went black.

●

Abby drifted from one nightmare to the next, until she found herself lying on her back in a dark and frozen hell. Large, feathery snowflakes settled on a face barely warm enough to melt them. Only the pain in her head suggested she was alive.

She couldn't see through the blackness, but felt the sled rumble beneath her, heard it hiss along the snow behind the crunch of footsteps. How much time had passed?

She tried to move, and panicked when she couldn't. She thrashed harder, felt her body shift. Thank the god — she wasn't paralyzed. As sensation returned to her numb limbs, she felt the cords binding her to the sled.

So that was it, the abrupt end to her ill-fated plan. She was captured, dragged home to face her people's scorn, her Father's wrath. As battered and helpless as she felt, it was almost a relief. Of course, whatever happened to her, it would be so much worse for...

"Where's Martina?" Abby gasped.

"Hush. The Seekers are close on our trail."

Martina?

Abby slipped in and out of delirium until she couldn't tell the waking world from dream. Had she and Martina really escaped? Where were they, even? She caught a slight gleam in the sky as the moon tried and failed to pierce the thick, gray clouds. The world was nothing but snow.

Some time later, the sled ground to a halt. The air held a hint of smoke, but how could that be?

"I'm sorry," Martina rasped. "This is as far as I can take you."

The cords holding Abby went slack, and she felt the woman's arms around her torso, hoisting her. Her head throbbed as if it would burst.

Something creaked, and a foul draft wafted over Abby. A deeper darkness swelled around her, but it was warmer now, and out of the snow.

Martina lowered her onto a soft, prickly floor. "I'm going to lead them away from here. I'm sorry there's no food to leave you. When your child comes, give him my love."

Footsteps rustled. Something creaked again, and the darkness grew complete.

●

Abby woke in the dark to a throbbing head. She itched all over, but when she moved to scratch, lightning shot through her aching skull. She gave up and clenched her teeth, trying to ignore the crawling sensation she could do nothing about.

She was in a dark, reeking room that stank hardly less than the composter. She was cold, too, but not frozen — which came as a surprise as the memories trickled back. Where was she? Where was Martina? Her brain said to panic, but her body was too sore and weary to comply. She shut her eyes, useless anyway in the black, and slipped into a fitful sleep.

The next time she woke, a faint seam of light traced the outline of a crude but heavy door. The wind whistled an eerie tune through the cracks. She fought through the pain and eased herself upright. "Martina?" she whispered.

Something rustled in the darkness.

Abby strained her eyes until the room slowly came into view. The walls were unmortared stone, piled thick, and the floor was heaped with chaff. The shadow in the corner shifted again.

"Martina," she croaked through a parched and swollen throat. "Wake up."

The shadow crept closer, accompanied by the dull clank of an iron bell. It stepped into the streamer of light that trickled through the door, and Abby recoiled in horror.

It was a four-legged demon from some nether hell, with curving horns, a tuft of beard, and soulless yellow eyes. She scuttled away until her back pressed against the far wall.

Hot breath puffed against Abby's neck, making her skin crawl. Slowly she turned, barely daring to look, dreading what she might see.

There she was, face to face with a second demon, with nowhere to flee. Abby crumpled to the floor, overcome with terror.

She didn't realize she was screaming until the door burst open.

A man barged in and leveled a hayfork at her chest. He had silver-white hair and a thick beard. In Sanctuary, few could grow beards, and none did willingly — save a Seeker on assignment.

"On your feet," he ordered. "Come where I can see you."

Abby's blood ran cold. "Where's Martina? What did you do with her?"

The hayfork dipped, and the man squinted into the shadows. "You okay there, girl? Looks like you took quite a knock to the head."

"You're not a Seeker?" Abby brushed her scalp and found it tender to the touch. Flecks of dried blood clung to her fingertips. "Where am I?"

The man stuck his fork into a pile of hay. He gave a low whistle. "I'll be. No wonder I didn't recognize you. You're from up the mountain." He nudged the snuffling demon back from her, and it fell to munching dry grass. "Let's get you into the house."

Suddenly, realization dawned. The beasts, the beard, the crude stone hut... She had reached the lower village. But how? The dim gray light caused her head to throb, making it hard to think.

The man held out a hand. "Come on. Breakfast is still in the pot. Warm up, eat, and then we'll talk."

Abby let the man help her to her feet. She followed, her legs trembling beneath her.

●

"So how far along are you?" the woman asked. Brown-eyed and raven-tressed, she hardly showed the blood at all. She bounced a child on her knee, a dark-haired baby boy.

Dressed in her shift and a borrowed coat, Abby dug into her second bowl of thin barley gruel. It had little flavor, and, if there was any scent, she couldn't smell it over the burning peat. Above the firepit, the kettle had been set aside to make room for her drying clothes. "Three months, I think. Is it so obvious?"

"A mother knows these things," she said with a wink.

A mother. In Sanctuary, her son would have been taken from her, her purpose served once he was born. But here in the wasteland…

"Another bowl?" offered the woman. Her face was lean with hunger.

"Oh, I couldn't," Abby protested. She *could*, but the woman hadn't eaten, and the pot was near empty. She nodded to the baby. "Is he your first?"

"Second," she said, but her lips drew tight. "Second to live, at least. My eldest, Tiri, is taking the goats to pasture." The baby drowsed, and she set him in the cradle.

Abby looked around the little cottage, with its dirt floor, its walls of mud-daubed stone. Wind gusted through the chinks, stirring the smoky air. "It must be a hard life here."

"It is," admitted the woman, "but we make the most of it. We have each other."

The door opened, admitting the chill air of a crisp morning. The man came in, shook the snow from his coat, and wrapped his arms around the woman.

"He's your… husband?" Abby asked, recalling Martina's word for Bertholo.

"Aye," she said, "and I his wife. I hear they do things differently up the mountain?"

Abby nodded.

The woman took her husband's coat and hung it by the fire. "It must be a hard life there, too."

Abby had pitied the lower villagers for so long, the woman's sympathy caught her off guard. "In a different way, perhaps. But yes."

"It must be," the man said, "for you to have run away. Feel any better?"

"I do, thank you. But I came here with a friend. Have you seen her?"

The man and woman looked at each other, concern etched on their faces. It was the man who spoke. "A party from up the mountain passed through here during the night, and returned not long before dawn. I don't know if they caught her or gave up in the storm."

He didn't add the third possibility — that they had found Martina in no state to bring home. Abby prayed to the god that she was somehow safe, somehow still alive, but the prospects were bleak. "What if she's hurt? I need to find her!" Or at least find what happened to her.

The woman turned to her husband. "You'd best go with the lass. Let me worry about the fields until you're back."

The man nodded and draped his still-damp coat over his shoulders. "Alright, just don't overdo it. I'll hurry back."

Abby wrung her hands. "I could never ask that of you..."

The woman smiled, her eyes sparkling with tiny flecks of gold. "There's no need to ask."

There was no thought, no hesitation. Their generosity shamed her. "How do I thank you?" she whispered, trying not to cry. "I don't even know your names."

"I'm Davyn," the man said, "and the wife's Tarah. And think nothing of it."

But she couldn't. Overwhelmed by their kindness, Abby did cry. They had taken her in, given her food they couldn't spare, even though they had nothing.

No, not nothing, she realized. Abby saw with envy how the woman leaned against her husband, their child squirming in the cradle. They had something worth more than the safety of Sanctuary's thick walls and steady rations. They had a family.

⬤

Despite the snowfall, it wasn't hard to follow the Seekers' tracks. There had been eight, maybe ten of them in the group. It wouldn't surprise Abby if Father had emptied the city of Seekers to hunt her down.

As the sun rose, lighting the sky like frozen fire, Abby paused to lean against a stunted tree. She fumbled with the pouch of dried leaves Tarah had given her — featherfoil, the woman had called it. She didn't like the herb's bitter taste, and wondered if her nausea wasn't a little worse this morning, but at least it took the edge off her aches.

Davyn climbed a rock to peer above the thicket, searching the landscape with a frown. "It can't be far now. Not if they went this way."

When, a few minutes later, they broke free of the short, scrubby brush, Abby saw what he meant. The land fell away in a cliff so sudden it made her stomach lurch.

"Careful. It gets slick here." Davyn caught her elbow and steered her away from the edge. "Looks like they turned right, toward Giant's Nose."

A sudden gust tugged at Abby, yanking her coat and scarf, and she clung to the man who, a few hours ago, had been a stranger. Even in daylight, the track along the rim was daunting; she could hardly imagine how terrible it had been for Martina, alone in the dark. Where had her friend gone? "Is there a path down, ahead?" she shouted over the wind.

Davyn didn't answer. They marched on, crunching the snow's icy crust beneath their feet. A hawk wheeled and screamed; from far away, another returned the cry.

The path came to a headland, jutting over the valley below. The tracks formed a cul-de-sac in the snow, where the group had milled around before turning back. There was no way down — none that a person could survive. Had they cornered Martina here and captured her? Or...

Abby crept to the edge and peered over, her heart thudding in her chest. A cry escaped her lips.

Far, far below was the sled, dashed to pieces on the cruel rocks. Beside it were two bodies. Except for the blood, they looked like broken dolls, discarded by a careless child. She drew back in horror.

Davyn closed his eyes. His jaw clenched, and he swallowed hard. "I'm sorry for your friend. I'd feared the worst, but it's something else to *know*."

Abby sunk to the ground, numb with shock. The bitter wind pulled back her hood, teased her hair into streamers, but she barely felt it. She had abandoned her people and failed her only friend. Save the child in her belly, she was utterly alone.

Davyn took off his hat and twisted it in his hands. "Listen... Why don't you come back to the house? We can–"

"I have to see her." She wasn't sure why, but she did. She wanted to say farewell, maybe build a cairn. Martina deserved better than to be left for the carrion beasts. "How do I get down?"

The man gave a heavy sigh. "There's a rope we use to haul up peat from the valley, but it's not safe for a person. The wind could dash you against the cliff."

She'd given up safety when she left the stout walls of Sanctuary. She could skulk home once Martina was buried, but not before. "I'll risk it."

They backtracked half a mile, to where a rope was coiled beneath the snow — one end secured to a boulder, the other tied to a wooden basin. Abby stood in the bucket and gripped the rope for dear life as the man lowered her down. Though it swayed and rocked with every gust, she reached the bottom without disaster.

From there, she followed the cliff wall, climbing across shifting piles of scree. She nearly stumbled over the bodies before she saw them.

Up close, she recognized the other corpse. Joriel. He was the youngest Seeker, barely more than a boy, and eager to prove himself. She realized he was the one who'd caught them on the mountain slope, and the puzzle pieces shifted into place.

For a second time, Joriel must have rushed ahead of the pack. He'd caught Martina at the ledge, and, rather than be dragged back to Sanctuary, she'd flung them both to their death.

Had the other Seekers, mistaking Joriel for her, given her up for dead? What if that were why they'd turned around? It could take them a day or more to recognize their error, time she could use to get a head start... But to where? She had lost her friend, her guide. How would she survive the wilderness alone? Abby knelt beside Martina's broken body and wept, sobbing useless apologies.

Through her tears, she noticed something clutched in the dead woman's hand. It was a leather thong, torn from around her neck. Abby pulled it free of her grip, and stared at the mystery dangling from the cord — a silver ring, in a pattern of woven vines. Salome's ring.

Why would Martina have stolen it? When had she even had the chance?

Abby held the ring up to the light, awed by the workmanship. It had to be from the wasteland. The smiths of Sanctuary were adept at forging tools, but they brought no art, no beauty to their work.

It was also smaller than she expected.

On a hunch, she tried it on for size. Though Salome had worn the ring on her thumb, it was too tight for Abby's. She found it snug on her third finger.

There was no way Salome's hands were so tiny; the ring wasn't hers, but its twin. So what did it mean that there were two? What was she missing?

As Abby studied Martina's face, almost peaceful in death, her friend's words came back like an echo. *We said our vows, traded rings, and pledged our lives to each other.* Understanding struck her like a bolt from the sky.

It was no coincidence that Orphiel had found Martina just as her life had been destroyed. To persuade her to come to Sanctuary, he had first needed to isolate her. Bertholo's ring, the bottle of wine — they were a boast, grim trophies of the hunt.

Orphiel had killed a man, and for what?

She knew the answer. It was the same thing that drove all her people, had driven her. Father's approval.

Abby turned aside and retched.

Even in service of the cause, how could a Seeker do such evil? Did Father know the cost of his prize?

Deep, deep down, beneath the thoughts she allowed herself to think, she knew the answer. The great cause justified anything, even atrocity. Father would stop at nothing to breed seraphim back into this ruined world, because that was the only way to save it. The Seekers, as extensions of his will, would do the same.

Martina, her, her son… they were nothing but tools to be used and discarded. But what if the Patriarch were wrong? What if the world didn't need seraphim? What if all his plans, all his schemes, were nothing but the crazed obsession of a wicked old man?

There was only one way to learn the truth.

●

They left the next day, in the pale gray before dawn. Davyn led a goat laden with supplies gathered from around the village, while Abby followed. Everyone had chipped in.

Abby didn't question the villagers' kindness anymore. It made sense now. For people with nothing but each other, working together was a matter of survival, a way of life.

Together they cut through a small, scrubby forest, more brush than trees, until the village disappeared from sight. The wind was fresh, and the sky brightened to liquid gold.

Some time after noon, footsore and hungry, they stopped for a quick rest. "Are you sure I can't persuade you to stay with us until the child comes?" Davyn offered. "Space is tight, but we'd make the room."

Abby scratched the goat's wooly beard. "I know you would. You've already done too much for me." She cringed to think what would happen if Father found them hiding her. And besides, she'd find no answers in the little village.

His mouth cocked into a half-grin. "Tarah made me promise to try."

By evening, they came to a jutting outcrop of rock. Davyn left the goat and scrambled to the top. "This is it," he called down to her. "The farthest I've been. It's guesswork from here."

Abby climbed up behind him and took in the view. The landscape rippled with shadow-dappled hills, endless steppe — and beyond that, who knew? She felt the walls of her tiny world expanding, giving her room to breathe. She sucked in the frosty air.

"Feels good, doesn't it?"

"It does," she agreed. The vast expanse, full of danger and possibility, thrilled her. She was done being told how to live, what to believe. Never again would she be the Patriarch's creature — and god willing, her son never would be. Their choices, right or wrong, would be their own.

Abby closed her eyes and pictured Martina scaling the slope those few brief weeks ago — from freedom to prison, from life to death. She imagined herself treading those very steps in reverse, each footprint a guide and a gift.

"Thank you, Martina," she whispered to her absent friend. The words would never be enough.

Chris Cornetto's story "Sanctuary" was originally published in Metaphorosis on Friday, 19 March 2021. See magazine.metaphorosis.com

About the author

Chris Cornetto is a physics teacher by day and writer by night, time and coffee permitting. He likes exploring ethical questions through fantasy settings, and enjoys long walks with small dogs. In addition to *Metaphorosis*, his stories have appeared in magazines such as *Wyldblood*, *Hypnos*, and *DreamForge*, and his "Shadow and Full Dark" was a finalist for the Baen Fantasy Adventure Award. His novella, *The Door in the Mountain*, is available through Of Metal & Magic Press.

He can be found online at cjcornetto.wordpress.com and cjcornetto.bsky.social.

Rooks on Sundays

Jack Neel Waddell

"You never liked to play chess with me," she says.

The board lies on a tray across her bed. Pillows prop her up slightly, just enough to see the pieces.

She reaches out a wrinkled hand, skin both pale and blotched brown, like the flesh of an apple left out too long. She grabs a rook that she carved, perhaps twenty-five years ago, from purpleheart wood. Today she remembers how it moves.

"I know how much you love it, Mom," I say, the word still feeling awkward in my mouth. It took me weeks to even say it.

We play until the end of visiting hours. She frowns as a nurse comes in. She weakly tries to push him away as he hooks her oxygen mask back over her face, clasping the straps behind her head within the milkweed-seed wisps of her hair.

I walk out of her room and toward the door of St. Agatha's hospice.

"You have to sign out, ma'am," calls the registration nurse after me.

The log book is open, with the heading, "Patient: Ella Reilly."

I sign Katherine Reilly, the only name on the list going back every Sunday for pages.

I've hidden the case in a park a few blocks away. A few cherries are blooming, but a chilling drizzle drives away any strolling couples.

I press the button on the front of the case to return.

I tuck the case back under the bench in my garage shop. Then I get inside my Corolla and drive.

There's one other place I go on Sundays.

It isn't raining here, now. The sun shines with vernal tenderness through the willows onto a pair of monument stones, dated only months apart. I place butter-yellow mums on my dearest James's grave, the one on the right. Kay, our daughter, buried in the other, never cared for flowers.

She injured her back when a Land Rover drove her into a ditch on her way to the coffee shop. She was taking an extra shift to pay us rent, which I imposed when she refused to sign up for classes at the community college.

The doctor gave her pills, which ran out. She found more, then she took too many.

James always blamed me for the gulf between us and our daughter. He left me after Kay's funeral, but his heart gave out before the divorce was final, whether from grief or stress or coincidence.

I wish I could take my case back to one or any moment during that time, to pull them back to me. Or, if not that, just to have them again as I push them from me — an arm's length away is closer than six feet deep. But the past is Hermetically sealed, even to my machine.

I've already purchased the bare plot to the right of James, but I won't need it for twenty-eight years. Now I'm saving up for the Catholic rest home in town, the best in the county, since I will have no one to tend to me but myself, and only on Sundays.

I drive back to my shop. Small blocks of exotic wood lie scattered on the workbench. I reach for a piece of purpleheart I rounded on the lathe, then hesitate. Instead, I select ebony. I pick up a gouge and carve.

Slivers of the past fall away with each splinter. Soon I think of nothing but the piece hidden in the grain and, after a while, I finish the crenellated parapet of a rook.

●

"What's this?" she asks as I hand her the box. It's wide, long, and thin, like a box of chocolates.

"A gift, Mom," I say. "Open it."

She pulls the ribbon and lifts the top. Laid out in four rows is the chess set I've made over the past month, of ebony and olivewood. She picks up the kings of each color.

"They're beautiful, Kay," she says.

She smiles, eyes beaming, and it warms my heart.

"You made these?" she asks.

I nod, with a strangely proud smile spreading across my face. But her eyebrows draw together in suspicion. She turns her eyes up and left, as if she's trying to call something elusive to mind.

"Mom?"

She looks at me, and I see something change in her.

She puts the pieces back in the box and places it aside, then leans out and places a pale hand on my own. She looks into my eyes, and I into hers. I see the peanut-brown of her irises, not the forest-floor hue of Kay's, and I know she sees the same because within her eyes shines a spark of recognition. A spark that fades into sorrow.

"You're so good to visit me," she says, voice breaking. "All we've got is each other."

Jack Neel Waddell's story "Rooks on Sundays" was originally published in Metaphorosis on Friday, 1 November 2019. See magazine.metaphorosis.com

About the author

Jack Neel Waddell is a Southern writer, physicist, and educator who lives with his wife and daughters in an old, white house nestlec among the bones of the Ouachita Mountains. He has been a semi-finalist in the Writers of the Future contest and his fiction appears in the *Strange Economics* anthology published by David Shultz, the *SQ Mag Best of the Year* anthology, and an upcoming issue of *Fantasy and Science Fiction*.

Till All the Hundred Summers Pass

J.A. Legg

"*Spindle*, this is *Sky Castle*; come in, *Spindle*."

Aurora grabbed a handhold and pulled herself to the front of the command module as the voice came through her headset — the first signal from home the ship had received since travelling back through the wormhole. The first word from Earth in over a year.

Her pulse quickened as she pressed the button on her mic. "This is *Spindle*," she breathed. "Aurora King speaking; how soon until you can bring us home? Over."

She heard the cold slap of palms against rungs in the ladder shaft that led down to the spinning gravity wheel. It was Fairburn, come to relieve her at the end of her seven-hour shift. He thrust himself up the tunnel and grabbed a headset hanging near the entrance. He was a few minutes early, and she thought about clocking out, but Commander Grimm could be pretty rigid about time stamps. She pulled up the map on the monitor in front of her, trying not to look at him. Her muscles tightened.

Fairburn nodded. "Talking to someone?"

"*Sky Castle*," she nodded. "We're in home space. Just short of Neptune's orbit." The *Spindle*'s blue dot blipped toward a green light on the far end of the screen. *Blip. Blip.*

"Almost home," he breathed.

Home. It seemed strange to Aurora, after all she'd been through, to describe Earth that way. Especially since the one thing she had missed — the one thing she really wished she could come back to, the one person that really felt like home — wouldn't be there.

Phil.

The engagement ring he had given her still hung around her neck, and she'd clipped a photo of him to the glass on her ship's berth. They were good reminders — but just reminders. Shadows. Cheap copies of the real Phil. They weren't enough.

Especially because he was *supposed* to be here. On the ship. With her.

"Where's Grimm?" Fairburn asked.

"Dinner break," she answered flatly, careful not to turn her head. "He'll be back soon, I'm sure." She reached down to the communicator clipped to her belt and clicked the pager button. The commander would want to be here when the next word from *Sky Castle* came in.

Fairburn glided through the module's null gravity, then coasted to a stop beside her at the control interface. She fixed her attention forward, away from him.

"*Spindle*, we have a lock on your coordinates and we're sending you our information," came the voice in their headsets. "Can you confirm your trajectory?"

Fairburn scanned the information. "Confirm, *Sky Castle*." He took his hand off the button, then paused before speaking again.

"Will you tell?" he asked.

Tell what you did to him, Fairburn? she thought. *Tell how you took him from me?*

"No," she said at last. Even if she did, it wouldn't change anything. Phil would still be gone.

More silence.

"He's long dead now, you know," Fairburn said.

Aurora glared at him. Her fingers clenched into a fist. "Do you have to?" she rasped.

He turned back to study the interface.

"Look at me," she said, louder.

His finger traced the ship's trajectory across the monitor. He drummed against the edge of the control panel in time with the blue dot flashing on the screen. Her shift ended.

"*Look* at me."

Aurora wrenched his shoulder back so that he faced her, away from the starboard wall. He stared and let the uncomfortable silence hang in the air. She studied him closely, searching for a hint of remorse. Nothing.

Unbelievable.

Somewhere in the back of her mind it registered that Commander Grimm could come back at any moment, but she didn't care. She had had enough. She kicked off from the edge of the control panel and pushed him hard against the far wall, teeth clenched. Fairburn collided with the metal, his face still hard as her blow sent her back toward the module's other side.

"You got what you wanted. I'm here. You're here. And he's not. Isn't that enough?" There was a crack in her voice. *Damn it.*

"*Spindle*?" asked the headset. "Looks like you'll be crossing into our orbit in another twelve hours. We're adjusting course to meet with you then. You'll be home soon."

Fairburn kicked toward the interface. "Confirm, *Sky Castle*," he said. "See you then."

He looked out into the void. The sound of hands on rungs came up again through the tunnel. Grimm was back from dinner.

"I didn't get *every*thing I wanted, Aurora," he told her at last, levelly. "You know that."

Didn't get everything I wanted. She thought back to the offer he'd made her, back on the planet. It still made her stomach turn.

You didn't get me.

"Yeah," she said. "Yeah, well, neither did the rest of us."

The commander emerged into the module. Aurora ignored him and made for the exit. She pushed past Fairburn, past Grimm, swung her body toward the tunnel, then dropped feet-first toward the floor below.

"Not even close."

●

Aurora had been eleven when she'd first studied NASA's launch of the *Dove* and *Olive* probes through the wormhole nearly a century before. She'd been working on a school project with her dad; he was an amateur astronomer himself, and he knew how to talk about science so that everyone in earshot would love it like he did. Especially Aurora.

She listened in rapt attention as he explained the physics behind the wormhole using one of her mother's crochet needles and a Post-It note. "A wormhole," he said, poking the needle through one side of the paper, "bends space and time so we can travel vast distances and back again quicker than we would ever be able to do without it. Like this." He bent the note around the needle and poked it through the other side. "So fast," he added, "that time actually passes slower on the way through the wormhole than it does on Earth." She'd used the same illustration with her class the following day.

She was thirteen when the probes' data came in to the research base stationed on Triton. *Dove* and *Olive* had sent back a host of new discoveries — chief amongst them a new exoplanet, the fifth in orbit around the star NASA had dubbed Perrault. By the end of five years, the astronomers had reached a consensus: Perrault V could support human life. Nearly every condition necessary for human colonization was in place, from temperature to gravity to distance from its star. The planet boasted an ample water supply and thriving plant ecosystem. While oxygen levels in its atmosphere were minimal, preliminary simulations had predicted successful terraforming over the course of only a few generations using comparatively simple breeding techniques. Discussions were already under way to send a crew to the planet that could bring back its native plant life, to splice the DNA the probes had found with that of native Terran vegetation. Aurora swore she would be a part of it.

For the next four years, she learned everything she could about space travel. At age fourteen she did a science fair report on the launch of the first moon colonies. At fifteen, she aced 12th-grade physics. At graduation she walked across the stage to shake hands with her beaming science teacher amid the applause of proud parents. Next stop: MIT.

Two months later came the car crash. Dad had been crushed under an overturned roof. Mom died in the ER eight hours later. She grieved them, then pushed her grief to the side and kept studying. She convinced herself it was what they would've wanted.

Aurora was just finishing the first year of her undergraduate degree when NASA announced plans to construct the first manned interstellar spacecraft. The project would be helmed by the esteemed astrophysicist Dr. Pyotr Chekovsky, who had named the ship the *Spindle*. It was shaped like a gigantic wheel, rotating on an axis to simulate gravity in its rim, and driven by a long propulsion shaft that stretched behind the central hub, like a *Spindle* without thread. The vessel would bring seven astronauts and a handful of robot aides through the wormhole to land and survey the exoplanet beyond. Once there, they would spend a full Earth year collecting plant samples and conducting a series of experiments on Perrault V's surface before returning home. If all went well, the *Spindle* would emerge from the wormhole to a fleet of cryoships, ready to carry whole colonies of frozen humans (and the first crop of plant hybrids) to the virgin world.

Soon after finishing her degree, Aurora came onto the project as an astroengineer. As a graduate student, she'd been commissioned to design an elbow mechanism for a robot intended for use in the ship's construction. Several months later, an email confirmed her place at NASA, engineering landing gear for the *Spindle*'s suborbital craft, *Odyssey*. The job was a dream come true — the moment she saw the subject header, she grabbed her roommate from in front of the TV and danced her around their apartment for joy. It wasn't just a job with NASA; it was an opportunity to help contribute to the most ambitious step in space exploration to date. One that would soon be looking for a field engineer.

From the beginning, she gave the project everything she had. Every second in the laboratory was well-spent, as she pored over readouts and tinkered with blueprints to optimize the lander's design. She spent hours of overtime testing new ideas and running the simulation programs like an addict with a drug.

Sometimes the lab would receive a visit from a group of clean-shaven men with gray suits and lapel badges, scribbling down notes about her team's progress. Sometimes those clean-shaven men would interview team members about their performance. The rumour spread that they were looking for candidates for the ship's maiden crew. Aurora's heart skipped every time she saw one of them gesture in her direction. For anyone else, the pressure would have been crippling. Not for her. She wouldn't *let* it be.

She was getting on that ship.

●

It was two weeks into her work on the *Odyssey* that Aurora first met Phil. It was late, and she was hard at work on one of the lander's main gear actuators. Something was wrong with the computer simulation, and she wasn't willing to let the glitch sit untouched for an entire weekend. After a quick caffeine boost, she figured she'd be able to get the program working by midnight.

She ducked out of her office, keys in hand. Her footsteps echoed through long, empty hallways, clicking a steady beat across the linoleum. Presently, though, she heard another sound between her steps: a loud, deep, expressive voice singing at the far end of the hall. She recognized it: he (yes, definitely a he) was singing Aerosmith's "I Don't Wanna Miss a Thing". Aurora followed the sound through the maze of corridors to another office door, cracked ajar. The name plate read: "Chekovsky: Astrophysicist".

She was curious. She'd heard Pyotr Chekovsky speak in briefings and lectures before, and knew the voice serenading the empty halls couldn't be his. The graying physicist's voice, though strong, was that of an old man — far from the young, vibrant voice that echoed Steve Tyler across the abandoned building.

Aurora pushed the door open on the sight of a young man about her age spinning in his office chair, his fingers picking across an air guitar. He swivelled to face her and broke off from the music, a startled look frozen on his face.

Their eyes locked. Brown eyes, she noticed. Handsome features. A shock of auburn hair.

He flashed her a grin; embarrassed, playful. "Hi," he said perkily.

Aurora smiled back and tucked her hair behind her ear. Her stomach fluttered. Without breaking eye contact, his hand slipped over to his computer keyboard to the volume button. The 1990s-era crooning grew quieter.

"Most people use headphones," she said.

"Sorry. I'll keep it down."

"No, it's... it's fine. You sound good." She pointed to his name plate. "Chekovsky?"

"Phil Chekovsky, yeah."

"Related to Pyotr?"

"His son. And you are?"

"Aurora King. I'm in the astroengineering department."

"King?" he asked. "I've read some of your work. Your preliminary designs for the *Odyssey* landing gear are really impressive."

"Thanks," she said. She felt a swell of pride, and at the same time, wished her hair looked a bit neater. "Working late tonight?" she asked.

"Yeah. You headed home?"

"Actually, I was gonna go for a coffee run before settling in for another couple of hours." She hesitated. "You wanna come?"

"Sure," he said, grabbing his jacket. They made for the exit.

"So Aerosmith, huh?" Aurora remarked. "Old song."

"I like old songs," Phil shrugged. "I'm impressed you recognize it." He held the door as they left the building, then led her across the parking lot to his silver Toyota.

"My dad read me a lot of old sci-fi when I was a kid," she told him. "With all the wormholes and exoplanets showing up in the news, he wanted me to understand what it meant that the mythology of the past was becoming real in our lifetime. Read to me every night before bed — Herbert, Clarke, Heinlein. We watched a lot of old movies too. I saw the one the song was written for."

"That why you joined NASA?" he asked. "Science fiction with dad?"

"Something like that," she answered. Phil opened his passenger door, and she thanked him and ducked inside. He gunned the car's engine.

"I get it. When I was a teenager, I saw my dad looking over some of the data the probes sent back. He was bent over the table, pages open, morning sun streaming through the windows with Mom's pot roast still on the table. Cold from the night before. It was a big deal to him — how close we'd just gotten to actual interstellar expansion. It became a big deal to me too, I guess. All the more so now that we're about to launch the *Spindle*."

Aurora bit her lip. "I'm — I'm going to be on it."

"Really?" Phil pulled out of the parking lot. "Like, you've already been accepted for the crew? I thought that wasn't going to be finalized for another few years."

"No," Aurora corrected herself. "Not yet. But I'm determined. It's what I've been working toward ever since they announced the project."

"Isn't your dad gonna miss you?"

She hesitated. It wasn't something she liked talking about, especially with new people. She traced mental fingers over the throb of old grief.

"He died," she said at last. "Both my parents did. Car crash, years ago."

Phil braked to a halt at an oncoming stop sign. He looked across at her. "I'm sorry," he said. He was, too; she heard it in his voice, that sense of loss that so many people tried to fake when they heard her mention the crash. Not Phil. She could tell almost immediately — Phil wasn't fake.

"I know they're proud of me," she said. "My dad gave me this dream. My mom taught me I could reach it. I'm going to be on that ship."

"They sound like pretty great people," he said. "And honestly, you might make it. Like I said, I've read some of your work. Your parents have good reason to be proud." He checked the traffic and turned onto the street-lit road.

"Thanks," she said. "How about you? Would you join, if you had the chance?"

"Hey, if I apply, I won't need anyone else," Phil joked.

"Yeah?" Aurora raised a playful eyebrow. "You're going to pilot the ship through a wormhole, leave her in orbit, camp out alone on an alien planet for a year, run a series of complex atmospheric, botanical, and microbiological tests, adapting to any and all problems you find along the way, and then come back with the appropriate plant samples — by yourself?"

"Totally," he said.

Aurora chuckled.

"Honestly, I dunno yet if I want to ride the *Spindle*," he said, more serious now. "I probably could. I'd miss everyone back home, but my parents would be proud."

"But?"

Phil held his breath, deciding whether or not he should say any more. "I feel like a lot of people think I'm only here because my dad's in charge. I don't want to give them another reason to think that. Like I'm inheriting a kingdom or something."

"But you're not."

"I hope not. I wanna work for it. Just like anybody else."

"Okay," Aurora said. "So, you're not at NASA just because your dad got you a job. The project is clearly something you care about. If you were in my situation, you'd apply, right?"

He glanced across at her. "Definitely," he said. He checked his mirrors.

"So why?"

"Because it's the next big quest," he said. "The next leap forward in the human journey. Like we're looking for something, on orders from deep down in our collective gut. It's something... almost primal, I think. Like the first time somebody rubbed two stones together to make fire. Or the day you moved out of the house because it was time to grow up."

Aurora nodded.

"And this isn't just your leap, or mine, but everyone's. Once a few of us do it, all of us can do it. You know what I mean?"

"Yeah," Aurora whispered. "Yeah I do." She nudged his elbow with hers. "I think you should go."

"Yeah?"

"Yeah. I'd fly a starship with you. Who cares what anyone else thinks?"

"Sounds like you want me to care what you think."

She rolled her eyes, but couldn't hide her smile.

He nudged her back. "Hey. Maybe I will," he said.

Questions and answers bounced back and forth between them ("What's the first thing you would do once you touch down on the planet's surface?" "What do you think will change the most on Earth during the voyage?" "If you could take one famous dead scientist to Perrault V, who would it be?"). Phil was smart, she found. Smarter than most of the guys she'd met in college. Funny. Confident. Inventive and curious. Any silence between them during that evening didn't last long. Aurora was almost disappointed when they reached the drive-thru and put their conversation on hold while the speaker box took their order — and sighed, only half in frustration, when Phil insisted on paying for her coffee.

They returned to the research building, and a small, responsible part of Aurora thought that would be the end of it. She'd go back to her lab, he to his office, and both would have a productive evening. They reached her door, still talking, neither quite willing to part ways, until one or the other realized they'd been standing there for almost three hours. It was two-fourteen in the morning when Aurora drove home, her glitch still unsolved, remembering what Einstein had said to explain time dilation. "An hour sitting with a pretty girl on a park bench passes like a minute. That's relativity."

Phil asked her to dinner the following week.

●

By the end of that year, Phil had gotten his PhD, and both of them were candidates for the *Spindle*'s maiden crew. Aurora was ecstatic. The following September, the project coordinators shipped Phil, Aurora, and the rest of the relevant personnel up to the *Sky Castle* space station for further trials and training. The selection process would conclude in orbit.

Aurora could still remember the day she'd first seen *Spindle* in her *Sky Castle* dock — almost-built, glimmering white in the sunlight, drifting out from Earth's shadow in the launch station's slow, graceful ballet-orbit around the planet. Technicians and construction droids hovered in and out of her shadowy edges like dragonflies over a pond, edging the proud vessel nearer and nearer completion. She hung on Phil's shoulder as he pointed down the *Spindle*'s propulsion shaft, where her lander blueprints had begun to take form. He wrapped his arm around her waist and pulled her close.

"See that?" he whispered to her. "That's *yours.*"

●

Aurora and Phil met Malcolm Fairburn the day after their arrival. He was one of thirteen other candidates for the mission — an astrophysicist, like Phil, who'd served as a critical consultant for military spacecraft. He had angled features, a patch of beard over his chin, and focused, iron-gray eyes that never missed an atom.

"Chekovsky?" he asked, on hearing Phil's name. "Like Pyotr?"

"He's my father."

No response.

Fairburn was smart. Solitary. He'd been working in space a few months longer than Aurora and Phil had, and his experience made him a prime candidate for the crew. But something about him irked her. His curt manner with the other contenders, maybe, or the way he studied her in the mess hall without a word.

Training on the *Sky Castle* was intensive. Space exploration had come a long way since the early years, but the candidates still needed to learn how to manoeuvre the craft. They logged hours together piloting space suits and operating maintenance equipment, running and repeating drills and tests for every situation they might encounter. The purpose was to give each of them a well-rounded practical fluency with all the ship's operations. Should anything happen to one of them, the others could still make it home.

Aurora noticed Fairburn's approach to the program early. He was competitive. Incisive. Any perceived mistake on the part of his fellow candidates, no matter how invisible to anyone else, and he'd slice into them like a scalpel — without anaesthetic. Actual *kindness* seemed out of his reach, like a skill he had never learned before.

Maybe no one's ever been around to teach him, Aurora thought.

Only she seemed exempt from Fairburn's snide remarks. Phil thought he knew why. "He's in love with you," he said, one night over dinner.

The words made Aurora cringe. While Fairburn's rage never settled on her as a target, there was something else in him that did; a silent, hungry attention that made her edge to Phil's other side every time she caught Fairburn staring at her in the dining hall.

Even Fairburn's attempts at friendliness, especially to Phil, were seasoned with a tone of subtle but unmistakable condescension. It was especially potent in the nickname he chose for him: "Prince." *So much for not inheriting a kingdom*, Aurora thought.

"He's projecting," another candidate, Dr. Basile, told Phil after a particularly tricky exercise.

"What do you mean?"

"He was working on a project for the military before this," Basile said. "Project Diablo. I heard his dad was the project director. I doubt he really *worked* his way up here."

Aurora wasn't sure. Fairburn might be an asshole, but he was also smart. And he wasn't the only other qualified candidate under consideration, either. Dr. Basile had applied as the crew's geologist. Dr. Kavita Tennyson was a veteran biologist who had been researching Perrault V fauna from the beginning. Dr. Percy Forrest had been a child prodigy, designing parts for the *Spindle* when he was seventeen years old. Aurora wasn't sure how she and Phil could compete. And if only one of them was destined to reach the new world, she knew that they couldn't remain a couple forever.

That was the problem with time dilation. Relativity. Time on the voyage would pass slower than time on Earth. The seven explorers who set out on the *Spindle* would have to leave everything behind — their homes, their families, their whole lives — with little remaining on their return. Aurora's only living family was an estranged aunt living in Alaska — but her attachment to Phil wouldn't so easily dissolve. If she boarded the *Spindle* without him, or vice versa, their relationship couldn't last.

She'd tried to talk to him about it already, on Earth. Four times she'd screwed up her courage to do it. Twice she'd let the opportunity slip. The third time she'd gotten distracted; he'd cooked them dinner, stubbed his toe on a corner at his house, and spilled spaghetti sauce all over the floor. She'd laughed. He'd started a meatball fight. By the end of it all, they'd given up and ordered Chinese.

And the fourth time — well, the fourth time she'd asked him. Out loud. He'd changed the subject.

But Aurora was resolved to talk about it before the final roster was revealed.

Phil took her to the observatory tower the night before Director Walter was scheduled to make the final announcement. He'd brought two ration packets for dinner, and together they hovered in front of the bright-strewn glass dome, gazing out at the glittering promise of faraway starlight. Deep purple gas threaded its way across the porthole. Phil reached for her hand and wove his fingers into hers.

Please God, let them send us both.

"Hey, Phil?" she said.

"Yeah?"

"What happens," — he cocked his head, waiting for her to continue — "tomorrow, I mean," — her pulse quickened, screaming at her not to ask the question — "what happens if they only take one of us?"

The words hung heavy in the weightlessness.

"I hadn't thought about that," he said at last, with a theatrical nod. "I figured they'd just — *give* us the mission and tell everyone else to stay home."

"I'm being serious, Phil."

"So am I," he said. "I don't need six crewmates to make it through a wormhole and back." His fingers stretched, then tapped against her knuckles. "Just you."

She paused.

"What if I can't go? What if they send you and not me?"

Phil let go of her hand and rotated himself around her, his back to the glass. She stared up at him, meeting his dark eyes against the backdrop of the stars. He took her hands in his, and she felt him pull her up towards her, like gravity, like the beginning of a dance. His hands were warm.

"You're the youngest person in the running," he whispered, "and the smartest person on this station. You'll be the first one on the roster. Trust me."

"But what if —"

He shook his head. "No. No what ifs. No backups. Whether we're on one side of the wormhole or the other, you're the only crewmate I really need."

She nodded and smiled. *Man.* Those brown eyes. *Please, God.*

He rotated again to look up through the inky veil of gaseous whorls to the stars on the other side. "One more night," he said. "And then we leap."

●

Aurora woke the next morning to find Phil already out of bed, clicking through his messages.

She unclipped from her berth, slid open the glass partition, and scrambled forward, desperate with anticipation. She touched her hand against his back and ran it up under his arm, wrapping him in a close hug. She inhaled deeply, stretched herself upward and glanced toward the screen from over his shoulder.

He spun around to face her, blocking her view of the monitor. He rolled his bottom lip back against the edge of his top teeth — Phil's telltale sign of disappointment.

"Did we make it?" she whispered.

When he didn't respond, she raised her eyebrows. "Come on. Don't joke about this."

His eyes darted around the compartment. Other candidates, bleary-eyed and slow, began to unclip from their berths. Fairburn glared at him as he emerged from behind his glass. Phil said nothing. His eyes began to water.

"Phil!" Aurora said, as she tried to push him away from the monitor. "Did we make it!" He reached behind himself and grabbed the underside of the keyboard in an effort to steady against her push. She pushed harder.

"Answer me or get out of the way, Philip Chekovsky. Are we on the *Spindle*?"

He shook his head and bowed low. "I'm sorry, Aurora," he whispered. He pushed up toward her, his arms outstretched in a comforting hug. She heard a catch in his throat. She shoved him away from the keyboard to look at the screen.

She scanned the opening paragraph and down to the list of names. Her mind barely registered most of them. But there, in professional black font, in a column with five others, were the names "Chekovsky" and "King."

Phil sputtered a mischievous giggle and floated to his berth. Aurora checked the list again, praying she wasn't dreaming. Andersen. Basile. Chekovsky. Grimm. Forrest. Tennyson. King.

They were going. *Together.*

Aurora turned to Phil and grinned, then shot toward him and pressed him against the bunks. They locked eyes, and she grabbed his arms to pull herself close.

"Hey," he said, grinning. She felt him poke at her stomach and looked down.

There was a small felt box in his hand, open.

"Will you marry me?"

A white diamond sparkling against the black. Like starlight.

"I kinda want to say no now," she said, smirking through the tears.

"Would you say yes if I got down on one knee?" He grabbed a handhold and tried to edge himself lower, fumbling an attempt to remain kneeling. He stared up at her, weightless.

She savoured the tension as long as she could, but in the end, couldn't stop the laughter. "Yes," she said. "Yes, I'll marry you."

He pulled his fist back in triumph, then pushed upward.

Aurora shot a playful blow to his abdomen. His torso crunched forward, and he gave an exaggerated *oof*.

"Don't do that again," she lilted. Whatever shock Phil had felt from the hit had vanished, replaced with a wide smile. She grinned as he pushed himself forward, and pulled her close, his hand on her back.

Then she kissed him.

●

The clock read 4:23 am. Three hours before wake-up call. Four before departure. Aurora unlocked the glass partition and pushed out from the berth. She hadn't slept.

She slipped on her jumpsuit and floated to the observation deck. The Earth spun beneath her, cities radiant in the shadowy blue.

Another planet. She was going. The most important journey in human history, and she would be a part of it.

And the *Spindle* was only the beginning. Once they made it back through the wormhole, the colony arks would be close to finished. Research into cryonics technology had already begun; the hope was that this would make it easier for the colonists to board their ships *en masse*, as well as conserve supply storage space on board. On reaching orbit, the colonists would remain frozen, then be thawed in waves as the settlements grew in population capacity. With any luck, in only a few decades after their arrival, Perrault V would have a thriving human colony on a breathable new world. For Aurora, the morning's launch would mark a new beginning for the human species — the dawn of the interstellar age.

And she and Phil were going to be a part of it. *Together.*

She admired the ring against the starlight.

A few hours and a wash later, she made her way to the dining hall for breakfast. Basile and Forrest greeted her as she gulped down her rations. Phil wasn't up yet. By 7:42 she still hadn't seen him — under half an hour before launch.

She drifted into their quarters and found him lying still in his berth. She tapped her fist against the glass.

"Phil."

No response. He looked sick.

"Phil!"

His eyes, half-opened, were rimmed with fatigue, and the rest of his skin was an inflamed red. At first Aurora thought it was the light in the berth — but no, after a closer look she could see something was wrong. She pushed toward the exit and saw someone blur past.

"Dr. Tennyson?" she called into the corridor. "I think something's wrong with Phil!"

Dr. Tennyson grabbed a handhold, turned, and floated into the sleeping quarters. She peered at the body beneath the glass.

"How long has he been like this?" she asked.

"He was fine last night."

"Anything he could've eaten? Any change in his schedule that might have let an infection into his system?"

Aurora shook her head. Her stomach turned with every question. The station's crew had been under rigorous hygiene standards since their arrival — Earth's germs were a far more serious threat in orbit, to say nothing of whatever microbes they might find in the alien star system — but there was no mistaking it. Phil was sick.

"You need to get to the medical bay," Dr. Tennyson said, pushing Aurora into the corridor.

"But Phil —"

"We'll take a look at him once we've got everyone under quarantine. We're going to have to push the launch back a few days at least, no stopping that now — but Director Walter will still want to limit the delays as much as possible. If we can figure out how the disease got into his system, we can still salvage the mission."

Aurora knew she was right. A deep space voyage would weaken the immune system and strengthen diseases in ways that could prove fatal if the dangers weren't addressed as quickly as possible. They couldn't afford unnecessary risks. They notified Director Walter, and after a brief consultation with the medical crew, Aurora and the rest went into quarantine. Until they could be sure that no one else was contaminated, the *Spindle* project was on hold.

Aurora lay strapped against the infirmary bed, cringing under the medprobes and trying not to ask for news of the others. She knew the doctors were doing the best they could, but the suspense was growing unbearable. They'd come so close to beginning the journey, and now they faced a danger that could halt the whole project.

Phil. Where was Phil?

She tried to sleep, with little success. Another doctor came in to run more tests — blood scans, micro-x-rays, psych evals. She pressed him for updates, but got nothing. Finally he sent her to wait with the others. Silent stares haunted the room as they waited for the ordeal to end.

By morning they were free to move about the station. Phil's berth had been decontaminated, and he'd been transferred to a medical station for further diagnosis. The rest were given a clean bill of health. Director Walter met with them that evening to brief the remaining crew.

"Research into what happened is ongoing," the director told them grimly, "but we're confident the disease is contained." His attention bounced from one crew member to another. "What that means is that we're going ahead with the *Spindle* mission — but we're going to do it without Dr. Chekovsky."

Aurora's stomach knotted.

"We need an astrophysicist," Dr. Andersen pointed out. "We can't complete the mission without one."

"Dr. Malcolm Fairburn will serve as Dr. Chekovsky's replacement."

"There's no chance waiting for Phil to recover?" Aurora asked.

Walter shook his head. "It's still too early to know how long that would take," he said. "That's why we're sending Dr. Chekovsky Earthside to recover. But we can't afford to wait. If we do, the Earth's orbit will carry us away from the wormhole. It'll cost us precious time and resources."

Aurora wanted to hit something.

"I know you two were close," the director told her. "I'll give you until tomorrow."

"Phil?"

"Hey," he breathed. Even in her headset, he sounded different from the man who had proposed to her less than 48 hours ago. Weaker. Aurora's stomach turned.

From the communication tower, she could see the bright white of the medical station hovering over the tinted horizon, falling forward into the Earth's grim shadow. How had things gone from so right to so wrong in only two days?

"How are you feeling?" she asked.

"Pretty tired," he replied. "Doctor says my fever's at 103. Last few trips to the restroom have been kinda brutal. They're sending me home in a few hours."

Aurora nodded. "We're going ahead with the mission," she whispered.

The medical station began to fall past the sunset.

"I heard."

"We didn't decide what would happen. If one of us couldn't go."

"Didn't we?" Phil's voice cracked.

"You said you wanted me to be your crewmate," she whispered. "That whether we were on one side of a wormhole or the other, I was the only one you'd really need."

"Yeah," he said. "Yeah, I did." His voice gave way to silence — a burning, heavy silence, buffering the next painful word like the wall behind her buffered the fury of solar radiation.

"So now what?" she asked.

"Well," he said, "I think you get on that ship, and you bring us back some plants."

Aurora shook her head. "I can't."

"Can't what?"

"Can't leave a day after you asked me to marry you. I mean — I love you, Phil. I can't abandon you after that."

"You also can't pass up this opportunity."

The silence was uncomfortable.

"You need to get on board that ship, Aurora," he said. "I'll be here when you get back."

If only that were true, she thought. "I can't."

"Alright," Phil said. He took a deep breath. "Then, Dr. Aurora King," — God, she loved how her name sounded on his tongue —"I'm breaking up with you."

She gave a bittersweet laugh.

"You're just no good for me," he continued. "You're smart, and beautiful, and *awesome*, and bound on a journey through a wormhole to an alien star system. And that's just not the kind of woman I can, in good conscience, tie down. So I'm leaving you."

"I'm leaving *you*," she said, wiping a tear from her smile.

"Hey, promise me this," Phil added. "Make sure you're the first to touch your foot to the new planet. And say something good."

"I love you, you know," she whispered. "I'll always love you. Make a girl really happy for me someday, okay?"

"I will," he said. "I love you too." The words sounded casual, like he was just leaving for a night and would see her again in the morning.

If only.

●

Aurora saw almost no one else until the pre-launch briefing nine hours later. She felt their eyes on her, heard the whispers when her back turned, and endured the silences that told her how little they felt they could say. She sat through the briefing, hardly listening to any of it, praying, instead, for one last chance that Phil might be well enough to go with them after all.

But the crew boarded the *Spindle*, and Aurora and the others watched from the observation deck as Commander Grimm unlocked the ship from her docking bay. The launch sequence blurred past in what seemed like minutes. She didn't try to savour it. All of the excitement she'd expected to feel as the *Spindle* broke away from *Sky Castle* seemed forced and insincere the moment they actually detached. How could any of it matter, without Phil on board beside her?

The crew slept in shifts. With no sun to distinguish between days, a preset twenty-four hour schedule served as its replacement. Aurora woke every cycle feeling sick, loss churning through her insides like machinery. Sometimes she wished it would end. Other times she dared not let it. It would feel like betrayal, letting her memory of Phil float out into the void. Like he hadn't really mattered to her. And no matter how much the loss of him hurt right now, she refused to admit that he had not mattered.

For most of the voyage, she cut herself off from the rest of the crew. Dr. Basile tried to keep them occupied as best he could — the man had an endless supply of games and anecdotes — but Aurora found it difficult to stay interested. She secluded herself for days in her quarters, combing through the selection of books and movies on the *Spindle*'s mainframe. Sometimes recorded a few video greetings to send home. No one ever replied. And in the silence between the stars, her grief howled.

The others worried. All of them had had some idea of what Phil had meant to her, and most had been there for the proposal. Dr. Tennyson noticed the ring around her neck, and tried talking to her about it once or twice. Aurora brushed it aside. As kind as the thought might be, Aurora was perfectly capable of doing her job without a breakup counselor. She could deal with loss, she insisted. She'd done it before.

Soon everyone's concerned looks gave way to indifference. She'd join them when she wanted to, they reasoned, but until then, pressing her was futile. Eventually most of them got used to her absence.

She wondered if Phil had gotten used to her absence.

It wasn't just grief that drove her further from contact with the others. It was Fairburn. The distance from Earth had increased his irritability. Whereas Aurora kept to herself as often as possible, Fairburn hovered right on the edge of nearly every activity, silent — until he saw the opportunity to mock someone. His insults grew sharper, crueller, followed by deafening silences as everyone realized that shooting back would waste oxygen.

Once, at dinner, she heard him mutter something about moving on. "It's not like they were evenly matched, after all," he said. "*She* made the roster on merit."

Aurora couldn't take it any longer.

"You talk as if Phil were some third-rate hack who just lucked his way into his candidacy," she rejoined. "Like you think mocking him will make us forget the truth. But it won't. We all know you were second choice."

Fairburn glowered, and she knew she had struck a nerve. *Good*, she thought. She kept on. "And if you really have a problem with nepotism, I think it's time you looked in the mirror. Everybody knows how you got to be on the *Spindle*."

"And how was that?" He raised an eyebrow.

"Wasn't your dad the director of some military project?" she asked. "Project Diablo? Pretty easy to get a position like this when your father's willing to pull strings for you, I bet."

He paused. It was the first time she'd ever seen him hesitate in responding to someone. Then he smiled, a harsh, self-satisfied smile.

"Project Diablo was a disaster," he said. "It was a waste of precious time and manpower, and the military cut the funding for it early, on my advice. Since the director of the project resigned in disgrace, I don't see much point in asking favours from him." Not *my dad. The director.*

His glare, unbroken, forced her to retreat back to her dinner. But she went to bed that night thinking on it, and realized that at last she had found a chink in his armour. A weakness — one she wouldn't soon forget.

It wasn't until the *Spindle* reached the entry to the wormhole that Aurora began to take a real interest in the mission again. The call went out across the ship; Commander Grimm's firm German voice woke the few sleepers, and everyone filed into the command module. Aurora crowded in with the others, strapping in and grabbing a handhold on the far wall.

The wormhole gaped before them on the other side of the glass. Distant stars and gases warped along its rim like shadows on the ripples in a pond. Aurora felt a lump in her throat as she thought about what they were seeing. They were already farther away from Earth than any human being had ever been. And now, there it was: that sphere-shaped gravitational anomaly tunnelling through spacetime and across the observable universe. The one she had been chasing since grade school, the one she'd left behind everyone and everything to find. The crew tethered themselves into place as the ship arced around the tunnel, orbiting toward it in a long, silent fall.

"Hold on, everyone," Grimm said. "Here comes the drop."

The spatial shimmer began to twist and elongate like a rubber band. Aurora felt her stomach turn inside her. Her teeth clenched. She heard something rattle at the back of the module, something that she hoped was tied down. Another rattle. She felt vomit burn the back of her throat and prayed the ship would hold together.

She looked back to her fellow crew members. Fairburn's head was tipped upward, wide-eyed in a silent expression of terror. Basile held his head in his hands. Tennyson had gone unconscious. She wasn't sure how long this went on, but then, everything went still.

Aurora relaxed. Her stomach heaved, her head ached, but it was over.

"We made it," Grimm said.

Aurora breathed a sigh of relief as others whooped around her. She unstrapped herself and floated forward, hardly daring to believe it. They were through.

●

The *Spindle* entered orbit around Perrault V about two months later. The clouded white atmosphere veiled a world of virginal ocean blue, patched with continents of dark red deserts, snow-capped mountains, and blue-green forests stretching low and deep through waiting ravines.

Aurora made Grimm promise to put her on the first landing mission. If something went wrong with *Odyssey*, she argued, it would be good to have an expert aboard. Tennyson and Andersen went with her, while the other four remained in orbit.

Dr. Andersen winged the *Odyssey* lander toward a grassy clearing at the mouth of a river, near where the long-dead *Olive* probe had landed to conduct its atmospheric tests centuries before. The three women felt the landing gear unlock, then touch down gently on the alien turf.

Aurora felt Tennyson's hand on her shoulder, and the biologist mouthed "Well done" under her helmet glass. The astroengineer smiled back. Then the boarding hatch opened with a slow *vvvvt*, and at last Aurora saw the alien world.

"This is for you, Phil," she whispered into her oxygen mask, though no one heard it on the official recording. It wasn't 'One small step for man,' of course, but she didn't care. There was a victory in that step, even if it felt bittersweet. A step violated for being taken in Phil's absence.

The ground was damp after heavy rain a few hours before, and glistening water droplets clung to the edges of tall blue-green grass. Her suit's readout confirmed the old probe's findings: the sliver of oxygen in the air was too sparse to breathe, but still detectable. *We'll change that*, Aurora thought. She inhaled deeply, and thought of what it would feel like to set foot outside on this planet without an oxygen tank on her back. *One day.*

The rest of the crew arrived several days later to set up camp. The planet was astonishingly well-suited to human life; its days were about eighteen hours long, its gravitational pull was comfortable, and there was a vast landscape to explore. Aurora and Basile spent the following weeks mapping the surrounding area, cataloguing plants and animals, taking soil samples, and testing the water supply. After a month, they traded the ship's rations for food native to the planet: large, egg-shaped fruits that tasted halfway between an apple and a peach. Dr. Tennyson took DNA samples from Perrault's vegetation, and spent days poring over the data in the lab. Fairburn spent the evenings in isolation.

Aurora was reading in her room one night, though, when his silhouette appeared in the doorway. She looked up from her book and swallowed.

"What do you need, Dr. Fairburn?"

He stepped inside. "Call me Malcolm."

"Why?"

"We don't have to go back with the plant samples," he said. His voice was hard. "The air filtration system in the habitat would provide enough oxygen for the two of us for a long time. After the others leave, we could wait here for the first cryoship." He walked further into the room and stood at the foot of the bed. "We — you and I, I mean — could give them something to find when they arrive."

A sense of unease crept into her at his words. "Something like what?"

"A colony."

Aurora was incredulous. "You're asking me to have your children?"

"With Chekovsky gone —"

"You took his place on the ship. That doesn't mean you have a right to take anything else."

"It wouldn't have worked out, you know. You and Phil. It never does."

"Get out, Fairburn."

Fairburn was silent, but didn't leave. Fine, then. If he wouldn't leave, she would make him. She knew by now what would make him uncomfortable.

"Is that why you boarded the *Spindle*?" she asked. "Something didn't work out? A breakup, maybe? Or a divorce. Or maybe you just realized that no one on Earth would miss you. And you don't know how to change that — so you tell other people that no one really cares about them either. For you, that's all there is left."

He bristled, but said nothing.

"Is that what your dad did to you?" she continued.

"My dad didn't do anything to me."

"Did he do anything *for* you?"

Fairburn glared.

"So he left," she guessed. "And you found him again. Or someone did, anyway. In charge of a flashy new experiment for the US military."

His silence told her it was true. For all his talk, Fairburn never denied the truth when someone else spoke it. Especially now. He couldn't.

"Beloved father and husband to a great big happy family," he finished.

"But not yours," she realized. There it was. Fairburn's wound. She eased up. "I'm sorry, Fairburn."

Fairburn didn't seem to notice her apology. "He was a decorated soldier who failed the only thing he was ever good at," he said. "Dismissed from his new post in weapons development because his own son tanked his idea. Because he was too proud to admit who I was. Even to his other family." There was contempt in those last two words.

"And now his own son's made history," Aurora finished. "In a way he never could. He can't claim credit for that without acknowledging who you are."

Fairburn nodded.

"I'm sorry he hurt you, Fairburn," she said at last. "But that doesn't change how I feel about Phil."

"Still?" Here, too, there was contempt. Bitterness.

"Still."

"Decades have passed on Earth. Even if he survived the typhoid, by now there's nothing left."

It was her turn, now, to feel the wound throb. Damn you, Fairburn. *Just when I start to feel sorry for you, you show me why I shouldn't.* "I thought I told you to get out," she said.

"Aurora —"

And then she realized.

"Who said it was typhoid?"

Fairburn looked like a deer in headlights. "The doctors — the medical personnel said —"

"No one said it was typhoid." Her feet slid off the bed and she stood, glaring. "We left before the final diagnosis."

Fairburn said nothing. She felt the old scar of Phil's absence bleeding anew, and the blood turned to venom in the silence. She stepped closer. "You bastard."

"We cured typhoid long ago, Aurora."

She cut him off with a cold slap.

Fairburn let out a trembling breath. "I didn't kill him."

"'Decades have passed'," Aurora spat. "'By now there's nothing left.' God, how did you even get the virus onto the station? You must've been planning it for ages, just in case you didn't get in."

"You won't tell," Fairburn said. "You can't prove anything — and our mission can't afford to lose a man if something goes wrong. You need me. They all do."

"Get out," she ordered, "and I won't tell anyone."

He glowered and obeyed.

●

Fairburn kept his distance in the weeks after she rejected his proposal. He had to. He knew, by now, how much she hated him; how nothing in the world would ever reverse what he had done. *Fine*, Aurora thought. *If that's what it takes.* Hatred was the language Fairburn understood best.

He tried to pretend it never happened. Avoid unnecessary contact. He knew she knew the truth, and that she would always know the truth. It was true that telling anyone right now would cause further division in the crew, and they might still need each other to return home safely, but once they did, she wouldn't need him anymore. If he wanted her to keep his secret once they arrived home, it was in his best interests to behave himself. Yes. That, at least, was a barrier Fairburn would respect.

But there was no healing in this. Knowing the truth, warding him off, didn't bring Phil back. She felt it all the more now, in fact. Phil was dead by now, probably; and if he wasn't, he would be before she got home. She thought of her parents all over again, the way she had wept at their funeral as they lowered the coffins into the ground. They'd been killed by a drunk driver. She'd seen a photo of him once online, and had felt sorrow for him, more than anger. He'd done a bad thing, but he probably hadn't woken up that morning with murder in his heart. But Fairburn had planned this. He'd *wanted* to take Phil from her.

She felt empty. Like the wormhole. After Phil's death at Fairburn's hand, that emptiness was the only thing left.

Little changed for Aurora in the final months on Perrault V. Dr. Basile kept taking soil samples. Dr. Tennyson continued her survey of the planet's greenery. By the end of their stay, they were confident the biology teams on Earth would be able to engineer a strain of Perraultian flora to terraform the planet's atmosphere. Their tenure on the planet ended, and at last, the seven explorers returned to the *Odyssey* lander, docked with the *Spindle*, and began the long trek home.

●

Aurora woke to a knock on the door of her quarters. It was Dr. Tennyson. Several hours had passed since contact with the *Sky Castle*, and she was here to announce their docking with the station. The ship had stopped spinning, and dozens of astronauts, scientists, and executives were waiting on the other side of the airlock, eager to hear the details of the voyage. Aurora dressed and followed her colleagues through the airlock, dizzied with new faces beaming smiles.

She was shipped to Earth with the rest of the crew and met with a triumphant welcome at NASA headquarters. The new director called a press conference, and ushered them down a hallway lined with photographs of directors past (Walter's and Pyotr Chekovsky's among them — Aurora noted the dates printed beneath each one with a twinge of grief) and into a room filled with shouting reporters, cameramen, and public sponsors, eager to learn all they could about Perrault V.

After the commotion had died away, one of Aurora's attendants tried to explain what had changed in her decades of absence. Private corporations had begun to expand their reach beyond the moon's orbit, and asteroid mining had made great strides in the construction of a colony fleet. The first ten colony arks were nearly ready, and they could expect to begin human migration in less than two years. Cryostasis had been successfully tested soon after her departure, and with the data the *Spindle* crew had gathered, everyone was enthusiastic that plant breeding could begin in the labs of the colony ships.

The *Spindle*'s crew spent weeks in a cycle of briefings, board meetings, and talk show appearances as people clamoured for insight on what was next. Aurora found it difficult to keep up. She found it difficult to even want to. Eventually she requested a year-long sabbatical. She needed distance from the busyness of the world. She would use her time off for research; to catch up on the various advances in astroengineering that had occurred since her departure. When the year was over, she could then resume her work preparing for mankind's next great leap.

Once the new director granted her request, Aurora bought a small home in Orlando and began her research. It was a welcome escape from all the media attention — and gave her something to do aside from thinking about Phil.

After all, for all his cruelty, Fairburn had been right. Phil was long gone now.

One morning, though, Aurora heard a knock at her door.

"Dr. King?"

The woman was tall, with curly raven hair and mocha skin, dressed in a gray pantsuit and carrying a briefcase. There was something about her eyes that looked familiar — something Aurora at first couldn't quite identify.

"Yes?"

The woman offered her hand. "I'm Dr. Penelope Chekovsky," she said. "I'm a medical researcher at the University of Miami. It's an honour to meet you."

Aurora furrowed her brows. By now Phil, if he had still been alive, would be 108 years old. The middle-aged Penelope was too young to be a wife. "Like Philip Chek —"

"His niece," the researcher corrected her. "His younger brother Troy was my father."

"Oh," Aurora nodded. They shook hands. "Dr. Chekovsky, I don't know what they told you about me and Phil, but —"

"Everything," Penelope interrupted. "They told me everything. Your first date. Your work on board *Sky Castle*. The proposal. And the day after, when he got sick and you had to leave him behind." Her mouth curved upward in a kind smile. "You told him to make a girl really happy someday."

The memory of her own words stabbed.

"What I can do for you, Doctor?" Aurora said. Whatever else happened, she wasn't going to break down in front of a stranger at the front door.

"I'd actually like to do something for you, Dr. King," Penelope said. "There's something of Phil's that I'd like to show you." She nodded toward the ring, still hanging around her neck. "Is that the one he gave you?"

"With all due respect, ma'am, that was a long —"

"Please," Penelope insisted. "Do you still love him?"

Aurora didn't know what to say. It all flashed through her mind again: boarding the ship, crossing the wormhole, her first step onto the planet. The bitter night with Fairburn, and all the anger and confusion that had come after it. And then the return to dock with *Sky Castle*. It all felt so hollow. Marred by his absence. A full year of her life — the one she'd spent her life working for — and he hadn't been in it.

Did she still love him?

"Yes."

"Then come with me."

●

It was sunset when Penelope's SUV pulled in front of their destination a few miles out from Orlando: a wide gate in a high chain-linked fence with thorns of razor wire lining the top. The guard at the toll booth waved them through, and Penelope led Aurora into a lifeless gray building, with tinted windows and a handful of cars in the parking lot. Aurora followed, trying to understand what all of this had to do with Phil.

Penelope had refused to address her questions during the drive. "I'd rather show you than tell you, Dr. King," she'd answered.

They walked past the secretary and down a few labyrinthine hallways to an elevator waiting for their arrival. A black scanner stared from the wall, and Penelope pressed a key card to it.

The elevator began its descent. Penelope hummed a familiar tune under her breath, and Aurora strained to hear it. Gradually she recognized the melody. In a hundred years, she could never forget that song.

"Aerosmith?"

"I heard that was how you met."

Aurora nodded.

"You haven't asked about him," Penelope remarked. "Philip, I mean."

"Is that a question?"

"Yes."

"I meant what I said. I really did want him to move on. Continue his work. Fall in love." She paused. "I just didn't want to have to think about the man I loved — the man I *love* — wasting away over long years with someone else. I didn't want to think about him dying." She stared at her blurred reflection in the elevator door.

"We've cured typhoid, Dr. King."

"Can you cure time?"

"Maybe."

The elevator stopped and the doors slid open to a well-lit medical examination room. The place was set up with a heart rate monitor, defibrillator, hospital bed, refrigerator, and various other medical instruments. On the far side of the room lay a long box of padded gray, waist-height, topped with a long near-opaque white glass cover the length of a full-grown man. A circular light along the side glowed white, and along the floor a series of cables fed into the box's underside.

Aurora approached the box like a pilgrim approaching a shrine. The blurred outline of a face stared out at her from behind the glass. She drew her fingers over the surface. It was cold.

"Philip Chekovsky wasn't just an astrophysicist," Penelope said. "After his rejection from the *Spindle* mission, he went back to school. His work in cryonics is a big part of the reason the Perrault colonies are now possible."

Aurora looked to Penelope in awed disbelief. "You mean he's —"

Penelope nodded. "A little cold, maybe, but he's in there. He's been waiting for a long time." She pointed to a fingerprint scan beside the white light on the side of the cocoon. "It's coded to you. You want to wake him up?"

Aurora's heart quickened.

Alive.

Phil was alive. Dreaming. Right in front of her. A fingerprint scan away from waking up.

She pressed the scanner.

The bar of light rolled up and down the screen. There was a beep and then a click, and then the glass cover slid off the sarcophagus with a steamy hiss. She heard short gasps of breath spurting out from an ancient respiratory system.

Aurora peered inside.

Dark brown eyes looked up at her and blinked. Squint. Blink.

"Phil?"

She touched her palm to his frozen cheek. Breath steamed from his mouth, warm to her touch compared to the cold of his skin. A hand reached up and grabbed the edge of the coffin. Phil pulled himself upward, shivering, his face still caked with ice. He wiped his hand across his eyes and stared at her. Another blink.

"Aurora?"

The voice. His voice. The one she'd heard echoing Aerosmith lyrics through the halls of the research building so many years ago. God, she'd missed that voice, the one that should have filled all the silences she'd travelled since their call before the launch. Aurora grinned and wrapped his frigid hand in hers. For all the weakness his body had endured during cryosleep, she felt the strength in those fingers as they closed between her own.

"You're alive," she breathed.

The icy Phil nodded. "I promised you I'd make a girl really happy someday."

She kissed him, and it was as if all the years that had stood between them melted away in that kiss. He was here. Here, and alive, and young, and *hers*. Her lips remembered the taste of his, eager and lively even under the cracks that had formed in frozen years. She smiled between each caress of his mouth with a delight far greater than she had ever expected to feel again. His kiss woke something in her, and promised it would never again have to sleep.

"I love you," she gasped between kisses. "I'll always love you."

"Always," he replied.

Finally they pulled away. Phil staggered to his feet. Penelope found him a blanket, and together they checked his vitals. Fifteen minutes later he sat on the hospital bed, eating a ration packet.

"What was it like?" he said. "Perrault V, I mean."

"Do you want to see it?"

"Go there?" Phil asked. "With you?" He reached behind her hair to unclasp the ring from around her neck.

She nodded, moving her hair out of the way. "They're projecting only five years before the first colony ships launch," she told him. "You ready to make the leap with the rest of the human race?"

"Yeah," he said, smiling. He took her hand and slipped the ring back onto her finger. "I mean... I've got the only crewmate I'll ever need."

J.A. Legg's story "Till All the Hundred Summers Pass" was originally published in Metaphorosis on Friday, 10 September 2021. See magazine.metaphorosis.com

About the author

Jordan Legg is originally from Oshawa, Ontario, and holds a degree in English and Creative Writing from the University of Windsor. He is an amateur cyclist and sketch artist, as well as an avid reader and writer of speculative fiction. He currently teaches literature and history to preteens and teenagers at a private school in South Asia, where he's lived for several years.

@TheJordanLegg

Rosalind Dreams of Aersea

Travis Burnham

Rosalind was eleven when she got her first hammer, an 8-ounce, Estwing ball-peen. She thought it was the most beautiful thing she'd ever seen, though her Dad had frowned the whole time she unwrapped it. Rosalind's father's first disappointment had been that Rosalind wasn't a boy — he was a carpenter who'd dreamed of a son to follow in his manly footsteps. Rosalind couldn't remember a time when she hadn't wanted to be a carpenter — to be a builder, a maker of places people could call home.

When she was thirteen, she ran the third leg of the 400m relay at the State Track Meet. Second only to carpentry, she loved running — the warm burn in her muscles and the feel of air brushing against her skin. And she loved the companionship, telling wild stories to her teammates, the shared training and hard work. The team was depending on her points for the meet. On the starting line, her toes were tingling — she thought it must be nerves. But at three hundred meters, her left foot went numb to the ankle and she stumbled to the track surface. Scraped and bleeding, she pulled herself up and hobbled across the finish line. It would have been easier to bear if her teammates or coach had been angry.

That night, she had her first seizure, opening a gash in her forehead on the way down to the yellow kitchen linoleum. Nearly the only thing she recalled of the experience was the gentle voice of her older stepsister, Muriel, trying to talk her through it. When, five weeks later,

Rosalind was diagnosed with Taeka-Storovski Syndrome, she was told she'd be lucky to make it to her 17th birthday.

This was Rosalind's father's second disappointment — and he didn't stick around for a third. Rosalind's mother stayed, but was never quite the same after. She'd always been somewhat mousy, and the abandonment drained something vital from her, making it seem like everything she did was just going through the motions.

As Taeka-Storovski dismantled Rosalind's body, she raged against fate. She cried, she screamed into her pillow, she shattered plates in the kitchen and smashed her favorite 'Dark Side of the Moon' record. One morning, she woke to her throat still raw and her vision bleary from crying the night before. She could barely feel her right hand. Down in the kitchen, she poured some milk into her Lucky Charms with her shaky offhand and looked over the room with exhaustion. Her eyes fell upon the fold at the top of the milk carton: SELL BY 10/26/23. This milk would go bad in five days. Her eyes fell back to her soon-to-be-soggy cereal as she realized she, too, had an expiration date, and would most likely be dead in three years, maybe less.

She didn't want to spend her remaining days in complaint and misery. She would try hard to be grateful — the disease was destroying her ability to do many things, but it left her imagination intact. She had always told stories to her teammates, or for invented tales for herself about strangers she saw, but what if she were more ambitious? That night, she began constructing an entire world she'd call Aersea in her mind.

Aersea began as a single, floating stone. Rosalind perched on it with her beloved ball-peen hammer — which she knew was not the best tool for the job — to pound and chip the floating boulder into shape. Made of cloudstone, the stone was a white, porous mineral, flecked with mica and lighter than air. When she needed it, another chunk of cloudstone would appear. Rock by rock, stone by stone, boulder by boulder, amid oceans of clouds, the archipelago of Aersea came together. She was a carpenter of worlds.

The construction of Aersea wasn't flawless. Sometimes the wrong stone would appear, a piece of dense granite or quartz or marble, and it would fall, shrinking into the unknowable distance. Sometimes, she would swing the hammer wrong and a piece of cloudstone would shear off and spin away. She'd hew a forest from cloudstone and breathe life into it, imagining it as verdant green, but as life flowed into it, the leaves would resolve to mother-of-pearl, and the bark become noctilucent.

As Aersea grew, she'd gaze out over what she'd created. And it was then she'd notice geographical features she *hadn't* created — a range of low slung hills, an achingly clear lake filled with cloud-white trout, a forest of cloud firs festooned in white needles.

By that time, Muriel had been offered a dream job working for *Destinations*, a travel website with a monthly magazine. She didn't want to accept it, as she knew it would take her away from Rosalind. Their mother and the nurses were good caretakers, but they couldn't be big sisters.

The night before Muriel had to make the decision on the job, she was stretched out in bed with Rosalind and they were staring at the glow-in-the-dark stars on the ceiling. "I don't want to leave you, Rosie." The quiet gasping of the respirator was a constant background noise. Rosalind depended on it more and more of late. Being on the respirator was terrible, like she was constantly drowning. But it was even worse without it — like running the 100m with a pillow strapped to her face.

Rosalind took a deep, raspy breath and said, "I need you to see the world for me, Murzie. Please." The more of Aersea she built, the more Rosalind realized she was going to see none of her own world. Rosalind would miss Muriel terribly, really couldn't imagine what she would do without her, but even worse was the thought of both of them losing their dreams. She buried all the selfish thoughts that would keep Muriel home.

From the pillow next to her, Rosalind took a tattered, pink, stuffed bunny and tucked it into the crook of Muriel's arm. "You can take Energizer with you. It will be like I'm there, too."

Muriel turned away for a moment, blinking back tears. Rosalind offering the bunny was a gut punch — a reminder that her little sister was just a little kid dealing with much more than she should have had to: dying with dignity.

In the end, Rosalind begged for Muriel to take the job, and Muriel relented.

Muriel sent letters and postcards to Rosalind. She texted photo upon photo upon photo of herself and Energizer — from the altiplano of Colombia, with the little stuffed bunny wearing hiking boots and riding on Muriel's shoulders, or of the stuffed bunny perched on the walls of Monsaraz Castle, looking out over the lake-spattered plains of the Portuguese Alentejo. Yet another of Energizer wearing swimming goggles and being held above the Klein-blue waters of Rota in the Mariana Islands. One postcard from the Marianas read:

> *We dove with sea turtles! Okay, Energizer saw them from the dive boat, but still! I'll bring back loads of dive pictures to show you. My love for you is deeper than the Mariana Trench!* ♥ *Murzie*

Many of the landscapes Muriel described would find their way into Aersea.

Time flowed differently there. Rosalind would doze off and a day would go by among the clouds — but when she woke and looked at the clock, only an hour had passed.

But the creating was becoming harder. More and more things she hadn't created herself began appearing. It seemed the worst injustice that she was losing control in both worlds. She did her best to reframe the losses in a positive light. Small towns dotted the landscape. She thought of the movie *Field of Dreams* that her dad had made her watch when she was eleven — the main character kept hearing a voice telling him that if he made it, they'd come, or something like that. There were people living in Aersea. Had she given them a place to live? It had always been her ultimate goal as a carpenter — to provide shelter.

When Muriel wasn't working or traveling, she was home with Rosalind. Muriel was never negative — she didn't want to waste any of her precious time with Rosalind with complaints. They'd talk far into those nights, reminiscing. Muriel told tales of her travels — the Great Wall, the Great Barrier Reef, the Great Ocean Road — and Rosalind about the changes happening in Aersea, where she was spending more and more time. Muriel was fascinated with the depth of detail Rosalind had for her imaginary Aersea.

"Do you remember when we made war clubs that winter?" Rosalind asked. "And then smashed sheets of ice down on the Merrimac?"

Muriel laughed. "You mean those war clubs made out of poison sumac that gave us rashes so bad we missed a week of school? And my left eye actually swelled shut?"

"It was worth it though, wasn't it?"

"Yeah." Muriel smiled, and squeezed Rosalind's shoulder. "Worth every minute of itchy torture. And time with you. Though I remember Dad refused to come near us, afraid we were contagious."

Rosalind asked, "Do you hate Dad?"

"Yeah." Muriel quirked her mouth to the side, thoughtful. "I mean, I don"t want him to die, but I hate him for being such a coward and leaving you. Us. How about you?"

"I did for a little while. Now, thinking of him just makes me sad. But he lent me his dreams of building beautiful things, so I don"t want to waste time hating him anymore."

On the next trip abroad, Murzie met Dylan. He was wanderlust personified, with striking eyes of green sea glass, a disarming smile, and an unfortunate love for the 80s band Styx. By the end of what became a shared trip through Torres del Paine National Park, Murzie knew she was in deep.

Finally, Aersea wriggled free of Rosalind"s creative grasp. She was still able to effect small changes — sweeten a mug of cloudberry wine, darken the feathers of a *jordmow* in flight, change the shape of a distant stratocumulus cloud — but she was no longer the architect of Aersea.

She often felt her life had become an exercise in settling for less — less magic, less running, fewer breaths. *No,* she'd tell herself. *Not settling for less, but embracing what remains.*

The next postcard read:

Hiking the Torres del Paine Circuit. Rained all day. You (Energizer) and I got drenched, but Gray Glacier is amazing. I love you more than the height of Cerro San Valentín! PS: I think I've met someone. ♥ Murzie

And so Rosalind traveled, too, ranging across Aersea, a pilgrim in rough clothing trying to squeeze what she could out of every minute she had left. What she'd loved about running, she poured into hiking and exploring Aersea. She studied the electric-blue icebergs that slid along the surface of *Tarn Screar*, and immersed herself in their blissful silence. Wandering among the massive cloudwoods of *Gruluth Mons*, she wove garlands of their arm length pine needles. She explored the *Gor Sezu* foothills, and passed between the jagged *Hasaped Loam* mountains.

And then, when Rosalind thought she must be somewhere in her late twenties in Aersea years, she also met someone. Heliotrope was a blacksmith with an incongruous, delicate name. Hels, as she preferred to be called, was most certainly not fragile. She was forge-baked and had the low deep laugh of a bellows. When Rosalind was in her strong arms, she nearly forgot about home and her dying body. Rosalind learned Vobidian, the language of the southern *Farth Girchead* peninsula, and the most commonly spoken tongue of Aersea, while Hels picked up a bit of English.

Back at home, a postcard from Portugal read:
Took a wine tour in the Baixa Corgo of the Douro River. Forgot sunscreen. Terribly sunburned. But you (Energizer) and I got buzzed on vinho verde, so the pain is minimal. I love you more than the number of bridges in Porto! Dylan says hello. ♥ Murzie

Muriel found Rosalind more and more detached with every visit, and her health in exponential decline. She began to wonder how Rosalind could possibly still be alive in her wasted body. Muriel hesitated to tell Rosalind about Dylan's proposing atop one of the towers of Kinnity Castle under an Irish sunset.

"I'm super happy...for you," Rosalind said, wishing that she'd be there for the wedding, but knowing she wouldn't be alive that long.

"I love you, Rosie. You're the best little sister I could have possibly asked for." Muriel never missed an opportunity to tell Rosalind she loved her, because she never knew when it might be the last time.

In Aersea, Rosalind poured every last bit of her creation magic into two items: a small cloudstone sculpture of intertwined flowers — a rose and a cluster of heliotrope. And a key that she hoped would do what she asked it to do.

Hels asked, "Where do you disappear to, when you leave me?"

Because when Rosalind woke in the real world, she disappeared from Aersea. How do you tell your lover that you're from another world, and that your body is dying? The tears spilled out of Rosalind. "I want you to know how much your love has meant to me. I never expected such a gift in the short time I had." It felt unfair to Rosalind: she had not one, but two worlds to lose.

"You make it sound like you're dying," Hels said, fear in her voice.

"I had a life before you. And I fear that life will soon take me away." Rosalind handed her a small package wrapped in white linen.

Hels gave a small laugh and handed Rosalind a delicate and intricate pounded copper box in return. Hels said, "Looks like you're not the only one giving gifts." When Rosalind lifted the box's cover, she found a fine silver mirror in the felt-lined interior. In the mirror, she thought she caught a flash of Murzie, Dylan, and Energizer, looking out over a serpentine river edged with small, terracotta roofed houses. The image disappeared quickly enough that Rosalind thought she'd imagined it.

Then Hels unwrapped her present to reveal the cloudstone sculpture of intertwined flowers. Rosalind said, "And I also want you to have this," handing Hels the well-loved and well-used ball-peen hammer that Rosalind's father had given to her. Or at least the version she'd created to design Aersea. Was it only a facsimile? When was the last time she'd seen that hammer in the real world?

The next morning, Hels woke to an empty bed, while Rosalind woke in her gaunt and skeletal body.

Muriel was there and heard Rosalind mutter, "ᔑᓭ ᒲ𝓎 ᓵᔑリ⸃ᓵᒷᔑ."

Muriel asked, "What was that?" Muriel knew words in a dozen languages, and could at least recognize a dozen more languages. And this was nothing she'd heard.

Rosalind drew in a ragged breath and said, "I think... I said... I love you... in Vobidian... language of Aersea." Muriel then knew that Rosalind was probably measuring her life in days, and maybe less. Rosalind's words hadn't sounded like gibberish, but couldn't have been anything else. Muriel was now with her constantly, afraid to leave her bedside.

The next morning, Rosalind managed to force a whisper out: "... love you... Murzie... you're... best... big sister... I could have."

"I love you, too, kiddo. Please don't leave me." But Rosalind didn't respond, lapsing into an unmoving silence — her breath shallow, her heartbeat slowing, slowing, slowing.

Then Rosalind took her last breath on Earth —

Muriel held onto Rosalind's hand until it went cool. She'd cried herself dry — her eyes felt raw and her head ached. Finally, she stood, and then she caught a glint of silver and white in Rosalind's left hand. She was certain it hadn't been there before. How had she missed it? Leaning over, she opened Rosalind's fingers to find a white stone skeleton key with a ball-peen hammer emblazoned on the shank. It was so light it practically floated on her open palm.

— and then Rosalind, just one moment later, took her first true breath in Aersea, opening her eyes to see Hels, a worried expression on her face.

A postcard rested in Hel's hands.

You (Energizer) and I are leaving on the first plane out of Kalispell tomorrow. I'll probably beat this postcard back, but can't wait to see you. Love you to Aersea and back! ♥ *Murzie*

As Muriel approached the bathroom sink, she couldn't imagine how she'd live in a world without Rosalind. She splashed water on her face and looked at herself in the mirror. She looked terrible. But then, for just a moment, Rosalind's face flickered in the reflection. The mirror shimmered like mercury and a small keyhole appeared on its surface. Muriel hesitated, wondering if any of this was real. Could all of those things that Rosalind had told Muriel about Aersea be true? Maybe this was a portal to oblivion — Rosalind had died. Would Murzie be joining her? And if she left, what about Dylan? Pulling Rosalind's cloudstone key from her pocket, Muriel weighed it in her palm. Looking up at the keyhole, she saw that it was smaller. Almost imperceptibly, it was shrinking — there was a diminishing window of time to decide.

Muriel lived a whole life in a few stretched out moments — she married Dylan, they bought a tiny blue bungalow to live in. They got a little pup, a Portuguese podengo pequeno they named Azores. Then they had two daughters, Harper and Isla, born a few years apart. They wrote, they traveled. They loved.

Though Muriel thought she'd cried herself dry, a tear slid down her cheek as a single sob was pulled from her. Then she took two deep breaths, three. Back in Rosalind's bedroom, in one of her desk drawers, Muriel found an envelope and wrote Dylan's name on it. Slipping the engagement ring from her finger, she put it in the envelope and put the envelope on Rosalind's nightstand. She kissed Rosalind on the forehead. "I love you to Aersea and back, Rosie."

Standing before the mirror again, Muriel took out her phone. She stopped herself before she scrolled through pictures she and Dylan shared and instead she opened her messaging app. Tapping on Dylan's name, she typed:

If you truly love me, Dylan, you won't come looking for me. I know it sounds far too crazy to be true, but I've gone to Aersea.
♥ *Murzie*

She hit send.

Setting down her cell phone, she put her hands on the edge of the sink to steady her trembling hands. Closing her eyes, she pictured Rosalind in Aersea.

Then, opening her eyes and reaching forward, Muriel slid the key into the mirror's keyhole.

Travis Burnham's story "Rosalind Dreams of Aersea" was originally published in Metaphorosis on Friday, 17 November 2023. See magazine.metaphorosis.com

About the author

Travis Burnham is a speculative fiction writer and science teacher. Originally from New England, he's lived in Japan, Colombia, Portugal, Malta, and the Mariana Islands, and currently teaches science at an international school in Montenegro. He's a bit of a thrill seeker, having bungee jumped in New Zealand, hiked portions of the Great Wall of China, and gone scuba diving in Bali. He's got some novels looking for homes and can be found online at travisburnham.blogspot.com.

Bas Relief

Joshua Grasso

Sveta twisted and turned in the mirror, lifting her shirt to inspect her stomach, flattering herself that it looked harder, firmer, than it had last week. But no, she could easily pinch the flesh into an unsightly fat roll as usual. She pulled up her sleeves, inspecting every inch of her arm, hoping against hope to find something rough and scaly. Again, nothing but soft, pale skin, or what the upperclassmen liked to call 'soft serve'. All quivering adolescent flesh and nothing substantial.

The only thing remotely tough on her body was the crusty elbow scab she had scraped with a key out of boredom. There were people she knew — well, they weren't friends, of course — who could file down keys and fingernails against their skin. Even one guy whose head was so rock-hard that you could break a board over it. She had watched him once during third-period gym, and he just laughed, saying he didn't feel a thing and asking his pals to do it again and again.

Out of sheer desperation, she peeled off her socks and inspected her toes and heels, hoping the skin had hardened, dried out. But even they were baby-smooth and without blemish. There were a few girls who couldn't even wear shoes anymore, as their toes were granite-hard and could deflate soccer balls with a single kick. But after all, only those who didn't change played sports after high school, since flexibility was the surest obstacle to upward mobility.

She must have been ignoring her texts, because when her phone rang, she saw Malorie's name flash over the screen — and she never called.

"Bitch, do you ever look at your phone?" Malorie said, with a laugh.

"Sorry, I'm getting ready — running late. I'll see you in a few."

"Not today you won't. I'm sick off my ass. I might miss the entire week, who knows?"

"Maly, not again!" Sveta said, throwing herself on the bed. "You can't keep doing this. You've already missed, what, ten or twelve days? You'll get suspended."

"Whatever. We don't belong there anyway, among those privileged, petrified snobs. I'm sick of pretending I give a shit. What's the point of even graduating at this point?"

"Because otherwise you'll spend the rest of your life delivering take-out in this two-bit town. Come on, it's just a few more months. Get your ass in the car."

"Sorry, I really am coughing my brains out. *Cough, cough.* See, you can't fake that."

"Bullshit."

"Just take the bus and stop bitching. Or go pass the driving exam already. I mean, a lot of people fail it twice."

"I've already missed the bus, and if you don't take me...I have to ask her. Please don't make me ask her!"

"You two need some quality time together; you'll thank me later. Say hi to the clones in Calc!"

She wasted five minutes trying to call Malorie back, but she never answered. That only left her enough time to catch her mother before she left for work and ask her — or in this case, beg her — to take Sveta to school, which would add twenty minutes to her commute. The second she walked downstairs and they locked eyes her mother knew. She only shook her head and muttered, "Three minutes, and I'm leaving with or without you."

The drive to school was more strained than usual. Sveta sat in the passenger seat, clutching her backpack against her chest, watching the traffic lights zoom past. Her mother's eyes kept cutting over to her, as if trying to pry through the clothes and see some tell-tale sign of transformation. Even as a child, her mother's hands would sweep over her flesh, poking here, prodding there, looking for resistance. *There's still time, you're still young,* she always told her, but it never sounded encouraging.

"You know, maybe you should see someone? Like a therapist? They say it's often a mental block, and you used to have those nightmares, remember?"

Used to. Still did. Always did. But it was better for her mother not to know what kept her awake at night.

"Maybe it's just not my time yet, okay?" Sveta replied. "You're a late bloomer. And Malorie, she still isn't showing."

"Knowing her parents, I'm not surprised," her mother said, with a snicker. "But you come from a long line of *rockers*. Okay, it started late for me — and like a lot of women, just one arm — but look at your grandparents: they were planted on the hill in their forties. It's inspiring to see them looking down on us, along with the rest of our family...so many generations of Beckers and Burlatskys."

She interrupted her speech to honk at someone who had cut her off, then continued.

"I'm just saying, you're almost eighteen...some kids are already thinking about where they'll be planted. If you already had a stiff arm or leg, we could reserve a spot somewhere on the hill, maybe just behind the house next to Daddy? You want to settle down before all the good places are taken."

"I mean, I guess...I just wish everyone didn't make such a big deal about it. It'll happen eventually, won't it?"

"For most people, yes, but you have to be a little proactive," she said, thoughtfully. "Not to speak ill of your friend, but Malorie lives in a trailer park. Her parents never settled down, and I doubt she will, either. Can you imagine, spending your entire life running around, never knowing your place? I knew early on where I wanted to be, who I was going to marry, even before this," she said, raising her arm. "And your father —"

"Can we not?" Sveta said, burying her face in her bag.

Her father, the famous *rock star* himself, who was in a wheelchair at eighteen. He had even made the local paper; a miracle of science, they called him. By the time she was six he was immobilized in the bedroom, just a living rock that would greet her and kiss her goodnight. A few years later they moved him to the yard, since the doctors said he was still *there*, still with them, though they couldn't say for how long. It only took a year before they felt it was time, and moved him up with his parents on the hill, another Becker to watch over the generations-yet-unborn.

"Sveta, you should be proud of him. I know it's tough not to have him around, but he did this for the family...he wanted the best for all of us."

Honestly, she barely remembered him as a living, functional parent. He had always been that *thing* in the bedroom, and she used to dread going in there at all, which was mostly reserved for bedtimes and birthdays. She hated that look in his eyes, which always seemed distant, like he didn't even know who she was. There were statues that looked kinder, more alive.

"Does it hurt?" she asked, after a pause.

"Does what? This?" her mother asked, holding up her 'good' arm, the one that was cracked and gray. "No, not at all. It's just heavier, that's all. If anything, it gives me comfort. I feel like I've become whole, like nothing can hurt me."

"Really? But what happens when you can't move? When you just have to sit around all day, having people wait on you? Doesn't that scare you?"

"If I didn't have such a loving daughter in my life, yes, it might," her mother said, with a smile. "But I know you'll take care of me. And then I'll watch over you, along with your father, from the top of the hill. You can bring your own kids up to see me, and they can hug me, climb me, whatever they like. We'll still be one big happy family."

"I guess so," Sveta said, seeing her school swing into view through the window.

"So listen, I made an appointment for you next week... the therapist came highly recommended," her mother said. "Just try it, just for a session or two. It might help. Because there's no reason you can't do it...there's nothing wrong with you. Really."

She said that last *really* as if convincing herself, lest she see her daughter as a failed experiment, someone unworthy of the Becker-Burlatsky line. She gave Sveta an affectionate pat on the shoulder as she pulled into the lot and wished her a good day. Sveta gave a miserable smile and ducked out of the car, feeling that she had survived this conversation mostly intact (unlike last time, when they had stopped talking to each other for a week).

Still, the pressure to conform and change seemed more intense than usual; not just from her mother, but from Malorie, too. It had become their only topic of conversation, and the closer they got to graduation, the more she felt she had made a decision, even without making one. It made her examine everyone with new eyes today, seeing those who *were* and those who *weren't*. All the jocks seemed to lumber about, some dragging stone legs across the floor or with faces almost set, so that you couldn't tell if they were happy or pissed off. Most of the popular kids — probably for this very reason — seemed to be well advanced, a few using crutches to get about, but one with a neck so stiff he had to turn his body simply to look at his friends. There were only a handful of girls like her who seemed normal, who moved around efficiently but seemed to hide in the background, with no infirmities to boast of. Had it always been like this? Or were people changing faster, younger, so they could be as safe and watchful as their parents?

At lunch, instead of sampling the cafeteria fare, she ducked into the library and pulled up the yearbook archive on the school's website. She scrolled through the decades, going as far back as the 1950's, watching long hair and t-shirts gradually fade into sideburns and neckties, until finally everyone became indistinguishable from the teachers: frame after frame of well-coiffed girls with giant glasses, and crew-cut boys with funeral-director suits. At first it seemed depressing, as if every one of those 1950's kids was half-chiseled out of marble.

Yet at second glance she wasn't so sure. The further back she went, the more the students seemed to have eyes. Naturally, they all *had eyes*, but these seemed alive, full of mystery and excitement. As she went forward, the stares seemed to dim, to look away, to die out. In recent years, she could sense a kind of dullness creep in, a sense that the kids had nothing to live for. Almost like the transformation had started from the inside-out.

Was that how she felt, watching everyone else turn to stone like clockwork? Was that why she still had nightmares, why she was secretly terrified of seeing a patch of gray or a finger locked in place? Of course she knew it was a good thing; she had seen all the movies and read all the books, all those glorious couples turning to stone together as the sun set behind them. Her mother called it *going back to the earth*, and said there was nothing more natural, more romantic. How strange that people used to die in wrinkled, useless skin that had to be buried out of sight and forgotten. Why settle for tombstones when you could become a living monument for those you loved?

And yet it terrified her. She still woke up most nights in a cold sweat from dreams where she was mounted like a *bas relief* over the fireplace. Her parents and friends would gather to inspect her, offering toasts, saying how wonderfully she completed the room. No matter how hard she screamed they only shook their heads, assuring her that the feeling would pass as soon as she let it go. And then she saw all the other terrified faces on the wall, all of them frozen in screaming stone.

She became so lost in these thoughts that she missed both bells and was late to Biology. By the time she arrived, students were already working in pairs on their next experiment. Her normal partner wasn't there, so she had to sit awkwardly at her desk, waiting for the teacher to notice. She thought about asking to be a third wheel in someone else's group, but she could see the looks on their faces; she was on her own. Mr. Malkin, largely immobile behind his desk, suddenly noticed her and waved imperiously.

"Miss Becker, don't just sit there. Your partner's out sick. You can pick up the lab when he returns. Here, take this to Study Hall," he said, handing her a pass.

"Study Hall? But Mr. Malkin, I can't go there! I mean, I'm not...can't I just work with someone here?" she asked, panicked.

"If you had come earlier, maybe, but I can't stop everyone just for you. Now here, take the pass. I have a lab to conduct."

"Mr. Malkin, please, you don't understand —"

"You've only got yourself to blame," he said, with a look that suggested he wasn't just talking about class.

Horrified, she took the pass and felt the whispers of mockery behind her. Study Hall was reserved for students who were on the fast-track to immobility. It allowed them a chance to take all their normal classes in a single room, since they couldn't possibly make it across the building, much less to lunch, between bells. If she walked in there like this, on both feet, without crutches or an obvious impairment, the jokes would never end. She almost thought about ditching school entirely, but without a ride she wouldn't get far. The only other choice was to hide in the bathroom until the bell rang, but that's where the druggies hung out, and she wasn't stoned enough for them, either. —

She opened the door to Study Hall and the students — a small group of twelve or so — looked up from their desks, students she knew from junior high and grade school. She had watched them grow up, sometimes being friends with them, sometimes not, until they all got lost in a blur of adolescence. Surprisingly, no one laughed or objected to her presence. The teacher gestured for her pass and then went back to his book, similarly indifferent. Sveta scanned the room, trying to think which student she would piss off the least by sitting beside them.

Helen Canevaro. They had been friends for a short space in third or fourth grade, but something had happened, a spat at a birthday party, she didn't remember. She still fondly remembered spending the night at Helen's house once, reading manga and watching old horror movies until three in the morning. Helen looked up at her with a smile and said hello. Gratefully, Sveta slung her backpack over the chair and sat down, smiling back.

"Hey, good to see you," Sveta said, quietly. "Sorry, I know I don't belong here, I'm kind of a loser, but I got kicked out of class. No lab partner."

"No, it's cool, I've only been here for a few weeks," Helen said, gesturing to her foot. "I don't feel like I belong here, either."

Sveta looked down at her right foot, which at first resembled a mud-stained cast. Upon closer inspection, she could see what used to be toes encrusted with a jumble of mottled stone. Otherwise, though, Helen looked completely normal, her bare arms untouched, except for a small bird tattoo near her left elbow. Their eyes met, and Sveta was startled how much Helen looked like that one girl from the crazy Swedish movie where they sacrificed people. Maybe that was the real reason they'd stopped hanging out all those years ago. Sometimes girls could tell when she looked at them a certain way, or for too long, and didn't like it.

"Is it hard...you know, getting around?" Sveta asked.

"Yeah, it's kind of a drag," she said, nodding. "It goes all the way up to my knee. I woke up one morning and it was like that, no warning. My parents were thrilled. They would have bought me a car if they thought I could drive it."

"Shit," Sveta said, with a laugh. "I don't know whether to say *congratulations* or *I'm sorry.*"

"Both, I guess. What about you? Any signs yet?"

"No, nothing. I'm a total failure. The disappointment of my entire clan," she said dramatically.

"I doubt that. You were someone people always looked up to. I remember when...well, never mind, it's silly."

"No, what?" Sveta asked. "Come on, tell me."

"Oh, you probably won't remember...but back in third grade, we went to the county fair together. Your mom took us."

"Oh right, of course," Sveta said, starting to remember.

"Anyway, there was that booth where you had to throw baseballs at bottles. I sucked, couldn't hit even one. But you hit every one, over and over again. There was a crowd of people watching you, cheering you on, and you kept going until the guy kicked you out. Said you were cheating."

"Oh yeah, I forgot all about that! What a dick."

"But you still won that giant rabbit: it was ridiculously big, cotton-candy pink, with these huge floppy ears, remember? And you gave it to me, even though it was yours, even though I begged you to keep it. You even told me — I know, it sounds silly now — that I was your inspiration."

Sveta didn't have a clear vision of winning the rabbit or giving it to Helen, though the general impression rang true. She only remembered a vague, warm sensation in her gut whenever she thought about their brief friendship. It was still one of the happiest times of her life.

"Sorry I made you keep it. Hopefully you got rid of it in the morning."

"No way, I still have her!" Helen said, eyes wide. "She sits right on my bed...sometimes I even use her as a pillow."

"*Her?* Don't tell me you named it?" Sveta said.

"Of course: Anastasia! I think your name inspired me. Whenever I see her, I always remember you, that night we spent together. I hated that we stopped being friends."

"Yeah, I wonder why we did? I guess it doesn't matter anymore, we were just kids. Maybe we can...you know, start over? Especially since we're stuck here together."

"But only here until your lab partner comes back to class, right? Are they really sick?" Helen asked, cautiously.

"I don't know, maybe. I barely even know the guy," she said, with a shrug.

"Good...I don't like competition," Helen replied.

It was only after the bell rang and they went their separate ways that Sveta realized she still had a crush on Helen, and her third-grade game had been smoother than she thought.

As it happened, her lab partner, Sam Dickey, was having unexpected complications from his sudden change. It happened sometimes. They didn't like to talk about it, but a few students were hospitalized when the change was too abrupt, or when it started in the wrong place. She knew at least one kid had died when his heart turned to stone. That was what scared her the most, the Russian roulette of the transformation. It was almost like someone was having a sick joke at their expense, one time choosing something ridiculous, like an ear, and another, an essential organ. She suddenly felt guilty that she didn't even remember what Sam looked like, other than his glasses, which were always slipping off.

However, after a few days of Study Hall, she fell into a comfortable routine with Helen, no longer worried about being witty or stupid or whatever. Mostly she just spent time observing Helen, noticing all the little things hidden in plain view, but which took days and weeks to pick up. Case in point, she realized Helen was filling up page after page with elaborate arabesques, which sometimes coalesced into familiar shapes and faces. Once, without trying to be too sneaky about it, she spied a dreamy portrait emerge on the margins of Helen's homework.

"Damn, did you do that just on the spot?" she asked.

"Oh — yeah, I mean, I'm just scribbling. It helps me think, it always has. It's nothing really."

"If you do that, you must have other stuff, too, like where you're really trying. Can you show me?"

Helen grew a bit red at the suggestion, though it was clear that the scribbles were a subtle invitation to see more. But now she was nervous to go all the way.

"Well, look, don't read too much into this...but I wanted to give you this. I was just worried you would think, *wow, that's weird* or something. But I made it for you."

Helen unzipped her backpack and removed a sketch pad smudged with charcoal on the cover. She opened the cover and flipped past several pages of abstract images, still lives, landscapes, houses. Then she came to one of the last pages, which, after a grin, she nudged over toward Sveta. Sveta could tell what it was even upside-down, even before her eyes really put it together.

It was a portrait of her, a bit idealized, of course, but taken by someone who had paid attention, who caught more than just the shoulder-length hair, the freckles, the little gap in her teeth. She saw her hesitation, her excitement, her awkwardness, her beauty. That was Sveta's first thought when she really took in the portrait: *Jesus, she's gorgeous.* Because she really felt like she was looking at Helen looking at her, and so much of Helen had bled through that it made the portrait feel like a warm embrace that wouldn't let go.

"My God, Helen...this is wonderful. I mean, I wish I looked like that. When did you do this?"

"A few nights ago. I got bored doing my homework...or rather, I couldn't concentrate on my homework. I kept thinking about you."

So there, I said it, her eyes seemed to announce. They were wide-awake eyes, right there, looking to the future. Like those fifties kids in the yearbook, but no longer carved in stone.

"It's wonderful, I love it," Sveta said, stroking it with her hand. "It's perfect."

"Then it was worth doing," Helen said, with a smile. "It's yours, of course. I still have the original."

"Where, in your head?"

Helen gave a little nod that suggested both yes and no. They didn't say another word for the rest of class, allowing Sveta to replay the scene over and over until she knew it by heart.

Sveta waited for Helen after school, saw her coming out of the building on her crutches, her dead leg holding her back, bringing tears of frustration. When she suddenly looked up and saw Sveta, her face went blank, the pain retreating. Then her eyes lit up again. Sveta didn't look at who was watching, what they might think (or what she might think tomorrow). She went right up to Helen and said something, she didn't even remember what, and kissed her. Really quickly, before either of them could think twice. Helen's eyes stayed wide-open in surprise, only closing as she pulled away, drinking it in.

"That's for the drawing," Sveta said, awkwardly.

"I have a few more, if you want to see them. But I keep them at home."

"I want to see everything. I mean, if you'll let me...if I'm not being, you know, too weird or something."

"Whatever...I like weird girls."

A car pulled up just behind them, which Sveta recognized from the general cacophony (shuddering engine, muffled sounds of Black Sabbath) as Malorie's car. She tried to ignore it and steal as much time as she could, but Malorie laid on the horn: a long, impatient blast. Sveta gave a backwards wave in Malorie's direction.

"Shit, I gotta go. My ride. You want to come? We can take you —"

"No, my mom insists on picking me up. But thanks. I'll text you later, okay?"

Another honk. Sveta gave Helen a quick squeeze of the hand and darted into the passenger seat of the 'Gremlin' as they called it, though she had no idea what brand or model it was. Malorie zoomed off and even went between the parked buses with their STOP signs extended. A few kids flipped her off.

"I'd be doing them a favor," she muttered. "So what, are you hanging out with her now?"

"Yeah, I mean, we're friends," Sveta said, cautiously. "I met her in Study Hall. She's funny, you'd like her."

"I heard she was a stuck-up bitch. But, I mean, if *you* like her."

"I do. She's cool. So, you actually came to school today. What's the occasion?"

"Girl, I guess I'm celebrating," she said, accelerating dramatically out of the parking lot. "I tried to text you, but you were too busy with what's-her-face."

"Celebrating? Why, did Steve send you a dick-pic or something?"

"Honestly, they look the same as his selfies, so who knows? But for real, check this shit out," she said, revealing her left hand, which she had kept hidden at her side.

Flashing it in Sveta's face, she revealed four fingers that were completely stone, with only one, the pinky, unscathed. Sveta shrieked and immediately grabbed it, running her fingers over each one, amazed and terrified by the transformation. Only a few days ago Malorie had made fun of all the *stoners*, as she jokingly called them, comparing the stratification of torsos and biceps. But now she seemed almost giddy over her change, having already posted it across social media, where, she explained, it already had hundreds of likes.

"My parents are flipping out," Malorie said, trying unsuccessfully to wiggle her fingers. "You know how they said I was on my own for college? Well, guess who just put up five thousand bucks?"

"You're joking! Really? Just because of this?"

"Hell yeah, because of this. A lot of people say if you get fingers first, that's a good sign. It means you're as good as gold by your twenties. So if I can get into State, or even one of the liberal arts schools, I might jumpstart fingers into an arm and a leg — or hell, even a torso!"

"But weren't you going to take a gap year or something? So you could travel the country, hike all over the Southwest? Remember the postcard I sent you of the giant saguaro? You were even going to get a tattoo."

Malorie frowned at the reminder, clearly from a different time, a different life. The world before she knew she had a future, or a body worth investing in.

"I mean...that would be cool, but I can't just waste an entire year when I could, you know, be getting ahead. And why go to Arizona or wherever when there are so many good colleges here?"

"And that's what you really want?" Sveta said, hesitantly. "You just seemed so happy, like you had everything figured out. This shouldn't change things completely."

"But it does, like a million percent! I never thought I would have a chance to settle down, find a place on the hill where everyone can see me. And who knows, after college I might be solid rock. Think what that would mean to my parents!"

"To be a statue before you're thirty?" she said, unable to hide her disappointment. "You saw what happened to my father; I barely knew him, Maly. What if you have kids? Is that how you want them to remember you? Because they won't remember you at all. You'll just be that thing in the garden, or up on the hill, reminding them to study hard and eat their vegetables."

Malorie abruptly switched lanes and pulled into an abandoned gas station where they used to hang out, where Malorie allegedly made out with some guy who just graduated. The car slammed to a halt and Malorie just glared at her, her soft hand gripping the wheel.

"I thought you would be happy for me," she said, her deep voice cracking. "You're the only person I really wanted to tell, Sveta. Because I knew you would give a shit. Or at least understand. I wasn't supposed to change and you know it. My parents are soft-skinned, trailer-trash rednecks. And I'm trailer-trash, too."

"No, Maly, I do — I get it. I *am* happy for you. I just don't think you should be in such a hurry to be like everyone else. You're different than them, you always said so. That's why we're friends. And we'll still be friends, no matter what."

"What the fuck do you know about me?" Malorie said, giving her a shove. "Maybe I've wanted this my whole life but was too scared to ask? Maybe I didn't want to be disappointed like I always am? People don't give two shits about me around here, Sveta. I don't have parents, a reputation like yours. I'll always be *that girl* to them."

"Who cares? I like *that girl*, don't you? And since when do you need them to like you? It's us against the world, remember?"

Malorie gave a world-weary laugh, as if she had heard this before, many times, in fact, and still didn't buy it. Sveta tried to backtrack, but Malorie cut her off, rolling down the window and yelling "bullshit!" at the top of her lungs. Sveta waited for the moment to pass, for Malorie to realize she was overacting and apologize, but it seemed she was just warming up.

"We were never on the same side," Malorie said, eyes flashing. "You're still the same old Sveta, slumming it with me until you find something better. But you don't know the first thing about me...like the reason I hate your guts."

"Do tell," Sveta muttered.

"You're everything I want to be, everything I tried to believe in. You made me feel that it was okay to be who I was. But then I started to see that you didn't even believe in yourself. People used to look up to you, you know? You were the girl *most likely to succeed* and shit. But now...they talk a lot of shit behind your back. They think you've given up; we all do."

"Why, because I'm not practicing to become a lawn ornament? Is that what little kids really dream of doing when they grow up? Why can't we look around, get lost, not try to be exactly like our parents? Why is everyone in such a rush to do nothing for the rest of their lives?"

"Actually, I'm trying *not* to be like my parents," Malorie said, sucking her teeth. "But I'd like to see how far you get with what's-her-name. You think she really cares about you? Today, maybe, but tomorrow she's going to want something real, something lasting. I know I do."

"Then lucky for me she's not like you," Sveta snapped. "No, she's the person I thought you were, the one I felt safe with, who I trusted more than anyone on earth. But I guess friendship's only skin deep…so you'll need a new friend to go with your fucked-up hand."

They drove home in silence, and when they pulled up to Sveta's house, Malorie just sat there, idling. Sveta just sat there, too, trying to think of whether to salvage their relationship or blow it to hell. Malorie beat her to it.

"I love how no one's supposed to change but you," she said, looking away. "I have to remain the fuck-up, the loser, while you figure it out. And once you do, you sure as hell won't wait for me. You'll leave me in the dust."

"Maly, that's not true. I've always had your back."

"You mean you've *held me* back. When I talked about college, or having kids, or anything you don't agree with, it's always *don't do it, it's not you, you'll regret it*. But what if I don't have the same regrets as you?"

"So your answer is to do what everyone else does, to follow them off the same fucking cliff? That's your idea of finding yourself? No, you're smarter than that."

"Everyone goes there for a reason," Malorie said, coldly. "It's what we all secretly want. Like falling in love, having a family. No one stays in the valley unless they have to, even if they lie to themselves and say they prefer it. Life looks better up on the hill, and you know it. At least, your father did."

"Fuck off, Malorie," she said, and opened the door.

"You first," Malorie returned.

As soon as Sveta got out, Malorie sped away, music blasting. Sveta knew she wouldn't see her again for months, maybe not ever. Now she had no one to talk to, no one to console her for being different, no one to confide in about her feelings for Helen. Of course, that's what choosing your own path was all about: being alone, choosing the road less traveled by. She had to have faith in the destination, in ending up far away in some happily-ever-after, even if it never was. All the same, the conversation hit its mark, and she replayed Malorie's words and her responses far more than she cared to. Even when Helen started texting her after dinner, she was only half-listening, thinking about *who* Helen was talking to: the now-her or the one-to-come? The one who had rock legs like Helen did, or the loser who never would?

After a few days, Sveta had made her decision: she and Helen had to break up. Partly it was everything Malorie had told her; partly it was her own fear of commitment. But what really clinched it was the meme making the rounds of the school, a picture of two people playing Paper-Scissors-Rock, the hands of one opponent forming scissors, the other forming rock. On the 'rock' someone had Photoshopped a picture of Helen's head, and on the 'scissors', Sveta's. Though the words of the meme had a few variations, the most consistent one said *Happy Valentine's Day*, with a copy even making its way to her locker at school. The message was clear: rock always beats scissors, and not even love can change the rules of the game. She shuddered to think how often Helen had seen it, and what she must have thought the first, second, and fiftieth time it swam through her feed.

Sveta had to tell her face-to-face, and it had to be at school, so she wouldn't waver and change her mind at the last minute. Of course, it was harder now that Sveta's bio partner had returned and she was back in class doing make-up. Worse still, without Malorie, her mother had to pick her up from school, and she was always there at 3:15 on the dot. So Sveta had about five minutes to waylay Helen, find somewhere semi-private, and tell her the truth. She spent the entire day planning her route, worried about the distance between their rooms and the congestion in the hallway. When the release bell finally rang, she was the first one out the door, pushing and prodding her way across the building to Study Hall, which was precariously close to the exit. A few minutes late, and Helen would slip through the doors and make it into her mom's car before Sveta could say a word.

She made it in record time, just as people were starting to trickle out of other rooms, though Study Hall seemed comfortably full (it took them much longer to leave, obviously). Sveta flattened herself against the wall, eyes picking out every jock and bonehead who left the room, excited — yet crushed — when it wasn't Helen. Seven or eight people came out, then a few more, then one more... then the teacher himself, who flicked off the lights.

Holy shit, where was she?

She knew Helen was here today, because she had said she had a Calc test and couldn't chat over breakfast. Frantic, Sveta began sweeping up and down the hallways, looking for any sign of her presence. She checked both of their lockers (nope), circled back to her last-hour class (no one), and even checked the bathrooms, trying to match the shoes beneath each of the stalls (Nikes; Helen only wore Converse). After five or six minutes she knew it was too late, that somehow she had missed Helen, even though she had covered all the bases and left nothing to chance.

As her heart stopped racing, she became aware of a steady, pulsating hum just around or behind her. Shit, her phone! In her anxiety she had missed an entire stream of texts from Helen. Pulling them up, they all basically said, *Where are you? Really need to talk! Meet me in the locker room. Are you coming? Sveta? Hello???*

It took her another three or four minutes to make her way to the locker room (the hallways were packed now), but it was a well-chosen spot, completely dead. She found Helen sitting in a dark corner of the room on a bench, hugging her knees while she stared down at her phone, waiting for a reply. Sveta swept in and started apologizing, saying she was sorry but they really had to talk, it wouldn't take a minute...but that's as far as she got.

Even as she was explaining, her mind was processing Helen's face and expression. She had been crying. Her eyes were red and there were tissues all over the floor, so she had obviously been here awhile. She must have skipped out early to come here, which explained why Sveta hadn't seen her in Study Hall. But wait, had Helen figured it out? No way, she had been way too careful — and hell, she hadn't even known it herself until just this morning. Sveta walked over and took her hand, squeezing it.

"My God, Helen. What happened?"

Helen gave a little laugh, her expression more happy-sad than distraught, her eyes burning with some hidden passion she couldn't betray. Helen stood up and pulled her close. They embraced, and Helen whispered something in her ear, which sounded like, *Well, I guess I'm all yours now.* What did that mean? As they embraced, Sveta instinctively reached out to support her, since without her crutches there's no way Helen wouldn't —

"Holy shit, your crutches! Helen, where…?"

She was standing straight on both legs, her eyes brimming with tears.

"Sveta, it's gone. Just like that. I woke up this morning…and it was gone. I was too scared to tell you. I made up the Calc test. I've been working towards it all day."

Open-mouthed, Sveta looked down at Helen's bare feet (she had taken off both shoes and socks) and saw two beautiful feet, painted nails and all. She didn't know what to say or think, so she sputtered with a kind of choking laugh, which made Helen laugh even harder.

"I wanted so badly for it to go away. Every night I begged God or whoever was listening to get rid of it. I didn't want anything to take me away from you. And now…well, I don't know what to think. But I'm happy…I *think*!"

"I don't understand, it's gone, like, really gone?" Sveta said, shaking her head. "So you're not…you're not going to be one of them? You can do that?"

"I mean, it's happened before, you hear stories, but I didn't believe them. I guess it helps if you're really in love," she said, looking up at her. "Sorry if that freaks you out, but that's where we are right now. I'm in love with you, and I want you to know that I gave this up, all of it, for you."

Sveta started crying, and she just stood there, pressing her head against Helen's, feeling happier than she knew what to do with. Sveta realized how stupid she had been to come here, to say what she thought was kindness. It would have been kinder to simply tell her the truth: that she was scared. Scared to fall in love, scared that Helen had made a mistake, scared that she would have to watch Helen figure it out in slow motion.

"But what about your parents? They were so happy… what are you going to tell them?" Sveta asked.

"I don't know; I don't care. They'll just have to deal with it. Because honestly, I was only worried about you."

"You really think I give a shit about what your leg looked like? That I liked you for that?"

"No...but when everyone else does, or would, it's hard to make exceptions. I still can't believe you see me, the real me, rather than...someone else."

"I see you...I look at you every day, and never stop looking," Sveta replied, kissing her. "That's why I'm in love with you, too."

"What if that's not enough? I mean, for now it is, but what if you feel differently later on? That's what I'm scared of. I might never grow it back, Sveta. This might be it. And I'm cool with that...I don't want to be that girl anymore. I want you to love me like this."

"Then good, let's both be over it! Whatever happens, we won't regret what we lost. We're just freaks of nature. The losers left behind to love each other."

Helen laughed, and they kissed each other again and again. She could almost believe they would be happy now, even without the future she once planned, that everyone else in the world expected. She nuzzled against Sveta's cheek, kissed her neck, brushing the hair away so she could nibble her ear.

"Oh God! Sveta!" Helen exclaimed, almost leaping back.

"What? What?" Sveta said, catching her. "What's wrong?"

Helen's eyes were large, alive, frightened. Her hand flew to her mouth as she backed away. Sveta began feeling all over her face, trying to wipe away invisible bugs, when a finger grazed her ear. Or what used to be her ear. Its once-smooth surface was now furrowed and sharp. She felt it again and again, hoping it was just some trick of the moment, excitement and fear running rampant.

But no, it was there, and it had changed. She had changed. Part of her was horrified, wanting to rip off the offending ear. Another part was secretly relieved that she could still do it, after all. That she wasn't a lost cause like everyone (well, her mother) feared. Strangely, she had slept soundly for the past few nights without a single nightmare, as if she had finally made peace with her fear. Of course, she didn't want it for herself, her mother, or because of anything Malorie said; she wanted it for Helen, to prove to her that they could still be together. Maybe that's why her father had been able to do it so young, with so much of his life still ahead of him. Because he had a 'Helen' too.

"But I thought...you couldn't," Helen whispered.

"I can't! I mean, I couldn't! I have no idea how this happened. I guess...I don't know, I was scared to lose you, too."

"So you gave me the one thing I can't return," Helen said, with a laugh. "Well, Merry Christmas, Sveta! I got you the same thing."

"Thanks, it's just what I wanted," Sveta said.

She stumbled forward and fell into Helen's embrace, enveloped in tears and silence. Sveta's phone began vibrating again, a stream of texts from her mom, wondering where the hell she was and if she wanted to start walking home from now on? She returned it to her pocket, didn't care whether she walked home or stayed in this room for the rest of the night. She could only stare at Helen and remember that Keats poem about a lover chasing a nymph for all eternity, never catching her, always in the heat of pursuit. That's where she felt she was with Helen right now, and where they always would be; their fingers almost touching, their happiness real, but not of this earth.

"What do we do now?" Helen asked.

"Just hold me," Sveta said, closing her eyes. "Maybe if we stay here long enough, we'll fossilize into a *bas relief* so some modern-day Keats can write a poem about us. You know that poem...*beauty is truth, truth beauty, — that is all ye know on earth, and all ye need to know.*"

"You're such a show-off," Helen said, smiling. "Yeah, we read it in AP-English. But I think it's about an urn, and not a bas-whatever."

"Same difference. It's old, it's beautiful, it tells the truth."

"What truth?"

"Like Keats, we're going to live forever. And that's all I need to know."

Joshua Grasso's story "Bas Relief" was originally published in Metaphorosis on Friday, 11 November 2022. See magazine.metaphorosis.com

About the author

Joshua Grasso is a professor of English at a small university in Oklahoma, where he teaches classes in British and World Literature, writing, and comics. He holds a PhD from Miami University where he specialized in 18th c. British Literature. When not teaching or writing, he enjoys hanging out with his two boys (one of whom is college bound!), reading everything he can get his hands on, and hunting for old vinyl and cds of classical music.

@JoshuaGrasso

Her Spirit Animal

L.A.W. Butler

Atynleigh leaned into the wind as she pulled her wool shawl closer around her face. The freezing wind was part of her daily trek along the shores of the great lake, yet someone had to check on the well-being of the creature that lived on the high point above the cove. In Atynleigh's small, damaged family, that someone meant her. The creature must be attended to, and Atynleigh was a dutiful child. So, she shrugged the pack on her back into a more comfortable position and trudged on.

Far above the cove the dull sun added a meager warmth to the dark slate that formed a grassless apron in front of the hut where the creature lived. This morning he had painfully made his way to a high stump of stone that separated the path from the lake cliff and was resting in the sun. His eyes wandered to the restless, gray waters of the great lake below him. Sometimes he looked, and with some regard, to the low mountains and thick forest that lay to the east and south, and to the steeper valley with its swift, narrow river that formed the western lands. But the lake, stretched across the northern horizon, was his home, and it was this that he longed for.

Knowing that the girl would surely come that day, the man — if man he was — had clumsily stoked a fire for tea. He knew the child would be cold and he knew the burden he placed on the family in the valley.

The sun was the width of an outstretched hand above the horizon when Atynleigh approached the hut. She called to the creature as she approached the cabin.

"I am here," she heard in response.

She knew it was difficult for Creature to speak aloud. His voice came in a wet, soft whisper. Yet, she had heard the words of his greeting clearly, with its strange, precise accent. At such times she knew he had been thinking the words. When Creature used his mind instead of his throat, his words came easily. She also knew that he could hear her thoughts. But just as it was easier for him to speak with his mind, it was easier for her to speak with her throat, and this was how they communicated.

Atynleigh remembered when she and her mother had found — rescued, saved — the creature from death on the stone beach some distance from their home. He had been injured and in pain from a fearsome wound on his side.

She and Mother had been fishing far down the cove. Fish had been sparse for weeks and they had followed signs of schooling fish past the safety of the harbor. Mother was a skilled fisherman, from a long line of men and women who had made their living on the lake's water. Atynleigh's mother and father had enjoyed fishing together, but Father had died months ago and now Atynleigh was Mother's fishing companion.

They had entered a shallow cove where a rippling surface spoke of an abundance of fish. They were about to toss their net when Atynleigh stayed her mother's strong arm and nodded noiselessly toward the near shore. A man appeared to be crawling across the beach, not even crawling so much as moving his limbs in response to unremitting pain. All of this, as well as something undefinable about his dark, rough appearance, made mother and daughter hesitate as they scanned the shoreline for danger. These were unsettled times. Even aiding the obviously sick or wounded required a serious decision.

"We need to get closer," Atynleigh whispered.

Mother nodded. They were both thinking the same thing. If someone had been on this shore to help Father, he might have lived instead of bleeding out in frigid water, alone and without hope. On that fateful day, rising waves from a sudden storm had thrown Father, as skilled a man as there was in a small boat, into the shallows. He would have survived with only bruises, but he had crashed down on a broken iron hoop from a submerged and rotten barrel. The metal drove deep into his thigh, cutting the femoral artery. Without help, he had never stood a chance.

That loss gave both mother and daughter courage to offer this stranger the lifeline which had been denied Atynleigh's father. Still, they approached cautiously. Mother slid from the boat as it hissed against the pebbles and grounded itself on the shore. Atynleigh, with her sharp eyes, would watch the tree line for possible danger. They did not need to discuss these arrangements, they simply knew.

The man had rolled on his back and looked in their direction. He had clearly been aware of their approach. Now, he neither moved nor made a sound. He lay a short ten yards from shore, his head toward them with golden eyes watching their every move.

"Do good."

"What?" her mother asked.

"I said nothing," Atynleigh replied, looking at her mother for the first time since the boat came to its stop. "I thought you told me..."

They both looked toward the man with his pleading eyes. They were sure he had made no sound, but they knew what they had heard. Atynleigh impulsively joined her mother in the water as they ran together — to do good.

They needed the strength of their desire to do the right thing, for as they approached the injured man, they saw that it was, in fact, no man at all.

"A Spirit Animal," Mother whispered, stopping short some distance from the creature. She had hesitated as she said this and both Mother and Atynleigh looked at each other and then back to the creature. Spirit animals were known to exist in this lake, sometimes seen, sometimes feared, sometimes revered in a way just short of worship. The Spirit Animals were creatures of legend and song. They were neither man nor beast, but part of both worlds and it is said that they could talk to both the fish and the fishermen. Many a person who had disappeared was said to have been called to the lake by a Spirit Animal, never to be seen again. There were others who said they would have been lost except for a Spirit Animal that guided (or carried) them to a safe shore after a storm or accident.

Atynleigh shook with fear and awe; this was certainly the creature of the legends. What lay before them had the configuration of a man, but the scales and gills of a fish. He had a muscular tail and spiked dorsal fins down his back like a lizard. His face was reptilian. The eyes were golden, large, and bulging, with pupils constricted in pain. Down the creature's side, from armpit to hip, a bloody slice had been opened by some sharp object.

The creature looked at them again and they heard more thoughts, but of garbled and uncertain meaning. The creature was able to capture feelings more than specific words, though sometimes one emerged as the other.

"Spirit Animal," was suddenly repeated back to them, and then, softer, the repeated plea, "...do good."

Atynleigh had looked to her mother, fearful, wondering what they should do. Mother's worried eyes moved from her daughter to the creature and then her shivering lips closed in a look of decision and determination. Mother hurried back to the boat, caught up the net and ran back to her daughter.

"We will spread this beside the creature, lift him on to it as best we can and ferry him back to the cabin. I can care for the wound there."

They went to work but heard no more from the creature save a feeling of intense pain when they moved him.

He was still alive when they brought him to their cabin.

●

From the early days of Creature's recovery, even those perilous first days lying on a pallet by the fire in their cabin, Atynleigh had noticed his golden eyes following everything she and Mother did. He tried to understand their thoughts and share his with them, but communication was halting and incomplete. Creature had watched as they spent the long, cold nights working, working, working, until the brief hour before exhaustion sent them to bed. Once they called the day's work enough, she and Mother would pull out the chess board and play a fast, deadly game.

Their game of chess was not the slow, studied game of deep thinkers. Theirs was like their lives, a series of quick decisions.

Mother and Father had played chess. They had taught Atynleigh while she was still sitting on their knees and as she grew older, that any one of that trio might win on any given night. Their board was simply functional, but the pieces — ah, those chessmen. Father had carved them from walrus tusks. They were tiny because tusk was a precious commodity. But the carving was fine and animated, with carefully detailed faces.

The creature had quickly become fascinated with the nightly chess match.

Two days after Creature came to the cabin he was starting to move painfully and slowly. Each time he reopened his wound, but the bleeding was less each time. He ate hungrily. That would have been a problem, except that fish had started coming to the cove. The first day a mass of mussels had apparently thrown themselves onto the shore by the cabin, enough to fill a bucket. It had turned into a feast for all of them.

By the fourth day Creature had been lucid enough to ask what this 'chess' was. A full week later Creature hobbled toward the chess board and began observing the game. He watched, trying simple questions using his soft, bubbling voice, or speaking directly into their minds. Five days later, absorbed in the game, his webbed hand moved hesitantly toward a piece on the board, a bishop, carved to look both haughty and bored.

"Yes" Atynleigh said, "that is the man I was going to move." She looked at him with astonishment. "Do you know where I wanted him to go?"

"A line." His claw hovered above the board in a diagonal. "Capturing a rook." The claw stopped above Mother's ward man, shaped like a Berserker, shown biting down on the top of his shield.

"Can you move it?"

Creature's golden eyes locked on Atynleigh's brown ones. She moved her head to encourage him. In response, his claws curled inward, moving them out of the way. He used the knuckles of the hand, just above the webbing, to grasp the bishop and deftly move it across the board, pushing the rook out of the way. He then carefully plucked up the rook and set it aside.

The room filled with Atynleigh's laughter. She and Mother both laughed — perhaps for the first time in months. This movement of a clawed hand from a healing stranger had made them feel a lightness that had been rare in their cabin.

●

It was at the end of his third week of recovery, during such a chess match, that the full danger of their situation closed around them. The match had barely started when Creature straightened his back, his eyes closed into slits, and focused on the door.

"They come."

Mother did not hesitate or question the creature. There was danger close and closing.

"Move. Make yourself as small as you can in the dark corner of Atynleigh's bed, back, under the slant of the roof."

"I can fight."

"You will lose. Do as I say."

When Mother used that tone, no one could withstand her. Atynleigh watched Creature roll back onto the small bed where it was wedged between the hang of the roof and the slant of the steps going to the loft where Mother slept.

Mother and daughter then pulled the rough blankets of Creature's pallet off the floor and threw them over the huddled figure of the lake-man, making a mess of unmade bed in the dark corner. They moved the low table with its chess board intact over the clean and flattened space where the pallet had been, roughing the dirt floor with their feet as well as they could. Mother scattered the wood fire enough to lower the light of the cabin just as they heard the men approach.

A fist pounded on the door.

"Who is there?" Mother called.

"The Reeve of the shire, Widow. Open."

Mother opened the door and let the firelight fill the entryway. There were three men dressed in rough tunics and wool capes. Two were men from the village. All were on foot. She glanced from the faces of the men she knew to the one she did not.

"Reeve Tomasil, it is late. Is there trouble?" She looked past them as if the trouble were waiting in the clearing.

"We come to warn of trouble. The fisherman here is certain there is sign of a Spirit Animal, wounded and ashore, in this area." Reeve Tomasil pushed the stranger forward as he spoke. It was as close to an introduction as was possible in this primitive community.

The stranger then spoke with a surly voice, trying to assert authority where he had none, "We need to inspect the houses. Make sure he isn't hiding."

Mother laughed and pushed the door wide open. "Look all you want, Reeve. But I think if I had seen a lake monster in my house, I would be seeking you instead of the other way around."

The stranger stepped forward and wrenched the door from Mother's hand.

"I'll have my own look around."

"No, sir. The Reeve may, but you shall not."

The stranger was shocked by this barrier to his wishes. He started to push past Mother but that proved to be a problem as the woman stood her ground.

"The Reeve is known to me and is welcome in this house. I do not allow that familiarity to every person. Certainly not a stranger who does not know a proper welcome." As Mother said this, she fixed the stranger with her eyes and seemed to grow both taller and straighter. For the first time all of them noticed that she had come to the door with a fish skinning knife in her strong right arm.

As the stranger took a short step back, Mother addressed the men she knew.

"Tomasil," Mother said trying to sound genuinely concerned, "has anyone been injured by this Spirit Animal? I could bring my medicines. You know I stand ready to help."

"No, Widow." The Reeve was weary of the long searches this stranger had insisted upon over the last weeks and he was not used to being offered help by the families he interrupted. It showed in his eyes and Mother now used that to seal a quick end to this visit. She spoke softly.

"You must be very tired. My daughter and I have a little left of our supper, but the rest is yours if you wish."

She stepped back from the doorway she had blocked to the stranger, and her act of generosity and openness had the effect she had counted on.

"No. No, we won't be staying, Widow. What little you have belongs to you and the child. We have warned you and checked the house. It is all we need."

"But it could be lurking..." the stranger tried to protest, but he was stopped by the tired Reeve.

"Our work is done here. We wish you a quiet evening, Widow."

"And a bright morning to you," Mother said.

Atynleigh joined her mother as they stood at the open door and watched the three men retreat down the path toward the village far out of sight. They stood in the lighted door just long enough to appear completely fearless and innocent, then closed the door, both shaking uncontrollably.

They stoked the fire to a bright blaze and slowly uncovered Creature. He too was shaking, but not from fear or cold.

It was a long time until his anger subsided. He spoke only with his mind that night.

"I must leave your house."

"You are not ready. We did not bring you this far to lose you out of fear — or anger."

"I put you in danger."

Mother hesitated, then stated a simple fact. "There is danger. True. And we do need to get you out of here. We were as lucky as we were smart tonight."

"Mother," said Atynleigh, her voice soft but earnest, "I have an answer, but it is a hard answer. We need to get Creature to the cliff hut. Even if the Reeve returned with men, Creature would see them and escape to the lake, down the cliff ropes long before anyone could walk the path."

Mother sat silently. The idea had occurred to her as well. The cliff hut was a small, barely functional shelter built on the top of the hill just to the west of their cabin. It had been built by Atynleigh's great-grandfather as part of a coastal warning system. An open fire on its heights could be seen far down the lake shore as well as inland. Such fires, passed from hilltop to hilltop, were a way to warn of marauders, though such times were now long past. The cliff ropes had been added years later so that careless people, caught on the small beach below during high tide, could climb to safety.

But how to get Creature to the hut? He had not been able to take more than a step or two across the dirt floor of the cabin. He fed himself, but only with food which had been presented to him. Yet, tonight's near miss had thrust the decision upon them all.

Somehow, Creature used the information in their minds to glean an accurate picture of the place and path.

"I can do this cliff path. But now, in the dark, before anyone sees us." Then he added with fierce resolve. "Or I must return to the lake, healed or not."

It was decided. It was done.

Slowly, with exhaustive effort, ever more frequent rests and moans of excruciating pain, the trio made their way from cabin to hut. Mother had gone ahead to lay a fire, prepare a pallet and bring up a sack of provisions, then returned to help Atynleigh guide and support Creature up, ever up.

"Child..." he had started once.

"Not now, Creature. We will talk when you are at the top."

But they had not talked then. Upon entering the hut Creature had collapsed half on and half off the pallet without word or sound of any kind.

Mother had insisted that both she and Atynleigh return to the cabin. After carefully tending the low fire and setting some dried fish within the reach of the lake man when — and if — he awoke, they returned to their home. They were in their beds just before daybreak, and still asleep at noon. During that entire time, a fog so thick it took one's breath away covered the entire cove, hiding both cabin and cliff.

That had been weeks ago, and now in the cold sunlight, Atynleigh ran toward the hut and the creature, who had become her friend.

Creature had risen clumsily from the rock upon which he had been sitting. The purplish scales of his face were gray at the tips and his jagged wound was a raw line that glowed white in the pale sun.

"I have rare medicine," Atynleigh said. "Mother trapped a beaver, and the musk glands have miraculous oils. She said you will feel the difference."

Atynleigh paused to look closely at the wound. It was raw, pink under pearl and as jagged as the thrust of the spear that he said had caused the near-fatal cut. Her hand moved close along its line but did not touch the fragile tissue. She sniffed at it.

"It doesn't smell. It is closing without infection."

"There is less pain. But the flesh is...stiff."

"That is how these things heal. We need to get you inside. Mother's salve will help."

Creature followed her into the hut and settled himself with a groan on a low stool.

"Let us see if this salve is the miracle Mother says it is."

She removed a pot of oily, amber-colored salve from her pack. It smelled strongly of musk and camphor. Her fingers took a dot of the thick gel from the pot and lightly moved it across the wound. Creature never moved, though she felt a long intake of breath through the gills on either side of his neck.

"Mother says you should feel a numbing tingle at first, but then relief. Do you understand?"

Creature nodded.

"She says it will speed the healing."

"That is good, child." He spoke these words in his whisper.

He always found Atynleigh's name to be too much a jumble of sound to attempt. She was just 'child' to him.

She put the pot of salve on the table. She had something she wanted to ask him.

"When my father was alive, he told me stories of the spirits that live in the great lake. He thought he saw you, or someone like you, once near the island at the west end of the lake. Father described a creature much like you."

"I seldom go to that island, but others like me find it comforting."

"Are there many of you?"

"Few. Fewer all the time."

"Are you the Spirit Animal that the tales talk of?"

"Spirit is too big a word. I am an animal, like you."

"I think you are the Spirit Animal of the fables." Atynleigh said this solemnly. She and Mother had talked about this. They were sure they knew who he was and much of what he was capable. "Do you bring the fish to our cove?"

"I can call them."

"We are grateful for that."

The creature did not smile, for his mouth was not capable of that, but Atynleigh felt a smile in what he said next, "Child, do you want to play the game? Or are we going to carve our own today?"

"Both. First we play."

In the days that had followed the difficult move to the cliff hut, while fall had inched toward early winter in the mountain community, Atynleigh and her Creature had started carving a new chess set, just for them.

The pieces were small, each one the length of one of Atynleigh's fingers. She fashioned the pieces as her father had, with curious little postures and attitudes. Her queen seemed worried and held her hand to her cheek. Atynleigh's king was vigilant, with a sword held across his knees. The bishops were looking for sin and sorrow with scowls on their faces.

Atynleigh had started not with any of these pieces, but with the knights. She knew they would be the hardest piece to capture, sitting on small, Nordic horses. They needed the extra width of the base of the precious walrus tusk, the last two her family had, so she began with her knights, and it was then that she made a stylistic decision that would affect every piece on the board.

She attacked the delicate ivory with purpose and precision. When she had finished the first knight, she held it out to Creature for inspection.

A bubbling sound much like a chortle came from Creature's throat.

He was looking at a chessman with the features of a man, riding a stout horse. But the eyes were remarkable. They were not the eyes of a man, but the round, bulging eyes of a fish, staring with a challenging intensity out of a human face. They were, unmistakably, the eyes of Creature, yet just human enough to make one assume that the carver either lacked skill or was making a joke.

Atynleigh and Creature's free time had passed in much this way — playing and carving. They were ready to start the last three pawns that stormy winter day. They would begin after they played their game of chess.

Perhaps it was the intervening slate of the hillside that interrupted Creature's sense of surrounding. Perhaps it was the soothing balm or strong camphor of the salve. Perhaps it was just his increasing contentment in Atynleigh's presence, or his intense efforts to expand the language between them, but Creature did not intuit the danger until it was too late.

The persistent stranger that had almost found them out in Mother's cabin had not forgotten his ill-treatment that night. When he received word of the abundance of fish on Mother's drying rack, he was certain that she knew more of the lake monster than she had shared. He had observed both the cabin and the hut from a distance. Smoke from the lofty cliff hut could not be explained save by the presence of an unknown. He had followed the daily trek of the child to the hut. And today he had chosen to make his secretive climb up the brushy, western side of the cliff. He would come upon them from the back side of the hill. If they ran down the eastern path, he could catch them easily — a young girl and lake man more used to water than land. The south side was an impenetrable tangle of brambles and berry bushes. North lay only the sheer drop to the lake, surely too great a fall with too shallow a bottom for even the creature to make that a viable choice. There would be no escape.

The stranger moved with cunning. As he raised his head above the slate rocks at the top of the cliff his presence became known in an instant but too late.

With a throaty hiss Creature rose with a speed that turned the inside of the hut into a shamble. The table, board and chessmen were overturned. Atynleigh's safety and escape became his only focus. Creature threw the door open and held it wide.

"Run, child."

Atynleigh understood a tone so forceful. She charged through the door and almost ran into the stranger as he appeared around the corner of the hut. He had a long knife in his hand and his instinct was to grab for the girl as she flew past him. His hand caught her sleeve and spun her to the ground.

That was his mistake.

"Monster," was the only word Atynleigh heard from the creature.

In the instant the stranger's attention had been turned to Atynleigh, Creature moved toward the assailant. He was slow but his bulk and returning strength were all he needed to grab the man's arm with one clawed hand, twisting it around his back and pushing him away from Atynleigh and toward the cliff.

At first the stranger tried to free himself, slashing backwards with the long knife. If any of the blows met flesh, they had no effect. Atynleigh was scrambling to her feet when she saw Creature straighten and twist hard on the man's arm. The bones of the stranger's arm cracked apart, followed by an anguished scream.

"Don't. Don't!" the man screamed, but Creature was pushing the evil presence steadily toward the cliff. At the edge of the precipice Creature lifted the stranger entirely off the ground.

With a mighty heave the stranger sailed off the cliff. A wailing cry followed his body down.

But there was still danger. Creature's efforts had brought him tottering too close to the edge. He reached out his right hand to steady himself on the single rocky protrusion near him. It should have been easy, but Atynleigh also saw the paroxysm of pain along the raw line of his wound. His arm reached out to steady himself on a rock, but the muscles contracted in pain, missing the rock. Gravity took Creature's body over the edge.

Atynleigh reached out to him in futile desperation. "No," she screamed.

She watched as Creature fell, haphazardly at first, then he straightened himself, arched his back, and rolled over. There was a shallow bottom to the cove here and he needed to enter at as horizontal a plane as possible while still cutting into the water. The impact was intense. She listened hard for one last thought, but if it was there, it trailed off before fully formed.

In the weeks that followed Atynleigh finished the chess set that she and Creature had made together. She and Mother played a single game with it, so that each piece knew its place and purpose. Then Atynleigh made a stone container of soft pumice and placed each piece carefully inside the hollow of it. She sealed the lid with wax and then made her way to the beach at the base of the cliff. On a thin strip of land well beyond the high tide line she buried the stone container deep in the soft sand.

"It is here," she said, "for us; a bridge across two lands."

For years, even after she grew to adulthood, with children and then grandchildren of her own, Atynleigh would come to this spot. She would sit near the chess set and talk to Creature, as though he were alive and lying in the shallows just off the cliff. Sometimes she was sure she could hear his soft words drift across the water to her. Always the same.

"Do good."

It is of note that for many years fish were a regular presence off the cabin by the great lake. It is also of note that the chess set was discovered hundreds of years after even Atynleigh's grandchildren had grown old and died. The Lewis Chessmen, as they are called, were found in 1831 on the shores of Lake Uig on the Isle of Lewis. They can now be seen in the British Royal Museum. They are beautifully carved, quite small, and have bulging, fish-like eyes.

L.A.W. Butler's story "Her Spirit Animal" was originally published in Metaphorosis on Friday, 17 June 2022. See magazine.metaphorosis.com

About the author

Ms. Butler began writing speculative fiction in 7th grade after bingeing on a stack of Superman comics. Her academic background in ɔoth science and economics allows her to find many strange and wonderful plɛces to put spunky girls and enlightened creatures of all kinds.

Visions for the Independent City of New York

Cidney Mayes

Addie Bell was six years old when she first held colored drawing pencils between her uncoordinated fingers and made marks on a crumbling map of the old, flooded tunnels beneath the city. It was a typical pastime for a child of her age, but looked different depending on what district of the Independent City of New York the child found themself living in. If Addie had resided in the Cloud District, she would have colored with a stylus on a tablet, swiping in a palette of pixels to drop red into the waiting outline of an apple on her device. Her street would have been clean, her clothes pristine, and the top of her house would have reached like a golden chapel into the sky. If she had lived in the Mids, Addie would have sat in a clump of other children her age, sharing supplies, and fighting over who would get to use their orange pencil to color in the sweet fruit on their alphabet worksheet. Her father would have had a blue-collar job and kept things in the Cloud District running smoothly. He would have been compensated well for his services. Instead, Addie Bell was one of the few children in the Deep, the level of the city that sat closest to the polluted water, to own such a nicety as colored pencils and thought herself very lucky to have such a treasure.

Addie's father, Charlie, was a weathered man with gnarled, arthritic hands who walked the dank streets collecting all manner of items. An accident on an oil rig had robbed him of good posture, unable to perform the necessary heavy lifting out at sea, so he walked the streets and shores looking for things to sell, objects dropped by those who lived above or washed up on the street banks with the tide. Items that would fetch a good price with the junkman were quickly sold, but occasionally he would bring home a gift to his daughter. It was just the two of them who lived in a city-appointed, wooden shack that could not keep out the damp. When he saw the pencils on a grimy street corner, fallen through a grate in the scaffolding above that held the rest of the city aloft, he pocketed them.

His daughter's rise to fame, and subsequent tragic fall, was not something he anticipated when he handed her the mildewed, tattered box of half-used drawing pencils.

Addie was fascinated with her new colors. Boxes, scraps of paper, and even the walls of their shack became her canvas, filled with faintly drawn shapes and lines. She knew that it would be very hard for her father to find more of the magic pencils, so she used them lightly, delicately, leaving whispers of luminous color one might miss unless they looked carefully.

The day after her father had given her the pencils, Addie went with her neighbor, Mrs. Martinez, while her father went off to pick through flotsam. Together, Addie and Mrs. Martinez walked for half an hour up the winding, unsteady steps to the lower Mids to take their usual spot. While Mrs. Martinez, a short woman with ink-black hair and a kind face, thrust her wooden cup into the path of passersby, pleading for alms, Addie entertained herself by drawing on the cracked concrete, relishing the soft scratch of her pencil against the pebbly surface. Mrs. Martinez's benefactors were quick to give Addie a bit of their change, too, amused and maybe a little wistful that she knew nothing yet of life's hardships and cruelty. Addie accepted the coins shyly, placing them with a muted *clink* into her dress pocket.

She dutifully gave the coins to her father that night. She didn't need them. She had her magic pencils. Besides, her father used the money to buy them something good to eat. Slices of not-too moldy bread and pale cheese, which they toasted over their stove. Addie drew a picture of herself and her father, eating their cheesy toasts together, which he accepted with wet eyes and pinned to the wall of their shack.

●

Everything changed the day a city official, clothed in white and carrying a tablet that glowed blue, meandered down the street. He stopped occasionally, making notes on his screen, and commiserating with his assistant about the poor conditions of the Lower Mids. Addie watched out of the corner of her eye and noted that the hem of his pristine robe was smeared with dirt. He mumbled to his assistant, something about 'real change this term'. He stopped in front of Addie's spot and cocked his head, staring at her with the curiosity of a cat watching a fish floundering in the shallows.

Addie kept her eyes fixed on her work. She drew faces of people on the street with surety, tiny birds who rummaged through the trash bin with realistic detail, and the market streets of the Mids with captivating perspective. Her drawings had a strange, bright quality due to her odd color choices. Addie felt the hair on the back of her neck prickle as the man watched her. Finally, he cleared his throat, and asked, "Child, what is your name?"

"Addie Bell," she replied, not looking up from her work. People around them grew quiet. Mrs. Martinez clutched her wooden cup and took a few steps closer to her charge.

The city official, more astute than his peers who had never left their borough in the skies, sensed the uneasiness at his presence. The citizens were wary of his pointed interaction. "Well, Addie Bell, might I commission you to draw something for me?" He held a silver coin between two fingers. It caught the light, and the small crowd grew larger.

Addie looked up from her work then, sensing the shift in the air. Her face pinched in confusion. She had seen men in pristine, pale clothing walking in the streets every once in a great while, but never had any of them spoken to her. Nor had she ever seen a silver coin before. "I only trade for 3 coppers," she said nervously.

The crowd tittered as the city official flashed a toothy smile. Addie's cheeks flushed; her stomach flipped. She felt suddenly self-conscious. Everyone was looking at her.

"I see. This is worth two hundred coppers. If you draw what I ask for, you are welcome to keep the extra." He kept the smile plastered on his face as his assistant withdrew a smaller tablet and held it in front of her, capturing the interaction on video.

Addie looked to Mrs. Martinez for confirmation of this sum, who gave her a tight nod. "Okay. What would you like me to draw?"

"Have you ever seen the city from a distance away, where all the buildings can be seen together, reaching into the sky?"

Addie shook her head as her eyes pricked with tears. She didn't understand what the man wanted, and everyone was still staring. All she knew how to draw was what she saw, and she had no idea how to draw what he wanted.

"Let me show you." The city official swiped his fingers around his tablet and flipped it around for her to see the photo of the city's skyline.

Addie stared at the picture for thirty seconds, taking in the shapes and details of the buildings that stacked on top of one another, clawing for purchase, trying to escape the rising sea beneath them. "Okay," she said, once she had memorized all she needed to. She spread a clean sheet of paper on the concrete and began to draw, now oblivious to the swell of people around her. Addie grabbed colored pencils, seemingly at random, as the buzz from the crowd fell into the background. She used her whole arm to draw wide swaths of color, painting the sky in a frenzied rainbow, then placed the buildings against it, exactly as she had seen in the photo.

When she was done, she stood and placed her hands on her hips, scrutinizing her work. Satisfied, she handed the drawing to the city official as his assistant took a photo of the exchange. Everyone clapped politely. The city official handed the silver coin to Addie, who thought it felt very heavy, and left with his drawing. The crowd dispersed, and Addie and Mrs. Martinez bought a hearty dinner to bring home, as well as a sealed box of brand-new colored pencils which Addie clutched tightly to her chest.

The video, artfully edited by the official's press team, went viral the next day. The drawing was posted to the city official's website with the tagline *a vision of what the Independent City of New York could be.* Cloud District citizens, as well as Upper Mids, loved it. The comments poured into all social channels, hashtags trended, and approval ratings went up, up, up.

Addie was unaware that anything had changed. The next day, she and Mrs. Martinez returned to their street corner and went about their business as usual. They did not know that the city official was very astute and knew just how to keep the buzz going. He made some calls and secured for Addie Bell a scholarship to a prestigious STEAM Academy where science, technology, engineering, art, and mathematics students studied to become the next generation of city leaders.

More men wearing cloud-white uniforms appeared that afternoon, stepping out of a black car. Addie felt her stomach twist into knots as they approached. Mrs. Martinez stepped in front of her, blocking her from their view. It took some convincing for Mrs. Martinez to move aside and let them talk to the young girl. They asked where her father was, and when she told him, one of the men scrunched up his nose like he'd gotten too close to the Deep's standing water. With Addie leading them, they descended rickety stairs to the banks of the Deep.

Her father stood, arms crossed and shabby clothes hanging from his thin frame, as the official's men showed him a piece of paper with a shiny seal. They spoke of moving, of government allowances, of giving Addie *opportunity.* Addie's father stood as still as stone, distrustful. He believed it was all a sham until they showed him the viral video, and asked Addie herself. "Wouldn't you like to go to school? To take some art classes?"

Addie's eyes grew wide. She nodded, unable to speak. Mrs. Martinez often spoke of school. It sounded like a wonderful place.

Seeing Addie's face, her father finally set down his collection bucket, grabbed his daughter's hand, and followed the men. Mrs. Martinez and their neighbors watched them go, with smiles that did not quite reach their eyes.

Another video aired on the city broadcast. It was a compilation of quick cuts set against an uplifting song, showing Addie accepting her scholarship, moving into a house on the outskirts of the Cloud District with her father, and walking past the gates of the STEAM Academy. Her life, compressed into a forty-second press piece, could not convey the unbridled joy she felt as she stepped into her first art class, how her heart fluttered against her ribs, how her fingers itched to draw.

In the Academy, students sat in a ring, their heads bowed like acolytes before their easels. Each flicked their eyes towards the center of their circle, observing a bowl of fresh fruit set before them. A white-robed instructor sat Addie before an easel and told her to draw. The next two hours flew by in a blur of color and shape. Addie had never known such peace, to sit and draw undisturbed, listening to gentle music.

At the end of the class, the work was critiqued. Addie listened as students commented on one another's shading techniques, use of color, or perspective. Addie's drawing was last. It left the class speechless. She did not simply draw the fruit and the table on which it sat like everyone else. She drew her view of the whole room, including the instructor as he paced between easels, the students at worship before their own art, the sweeping pillars that held the ceiling aloft, in her signature display of churning color.

Addie twisted her hands, nervous at their silence. Tears stung the corners of her eyes as her fear and shame grew. Her art did not look like everyone else's.

"It is extraordinary," the instructor finally declared, and students began hounding Addie with questions. They clapped her on the back, praised her composition, and marveled at her color palette. Addie smiled so wide that her cheeks began to hurt and felt as if her chest could burst from happiness.

After that, people began to call Addie Bell *singularly talented, visionary,* and *genius.* A month went by, then two, and Addie settled into her new life. She and her father took to spending their weekends in the park, taking picnics of fresh fruit and bread. Addie like to draw her father sitting in the grass, running his hands through it, marveling at its softness, head tipped to welcome the sun on his skin. In the Deep he'd always been hunched, plagued with coughing spasms. A visit to the doctor had finally cleared the ailment in his chest, and he now breathed much more easily. While Addie went to school, he got a job in the Mids sorting scrap metal in a factory. It wasn't glamorous work, but he made a decent wage and was home in the early evening to share supper with his daughter and listen to her talk excitedly about her day.

As she grew up, Addie became the most celebrated artist in her school. Requests for her artwork poured into the Academy from Cloud District citizens, for everyone with taste wanted a Bell original for their homes. Her instructors encouraged her to examine the world around her, noting the line, shape, and shadow of her environment. Addie drew and painted, observing her subjects closely. And the more she saw, the angrier she became.

It started with small things, trivial points of friction with her classmates. The other students who grew up in the sun and sky knew nothing of the damp that swallowed those who lived below them in the Deep. They teased her for being an outsider, then grew jealous when she stole all the attention of her art teachers. She did find friends, and enjoyed spending time with them, but they could never understand where she had come from. When she tried to tell them what it was like growing up in the Deep, she was met with uncomfortable silence. Such things were not talked about. The news did not even mention any happening south of the Mids. "Well, you live here now," they would say, and the conversation quickly moved on to shopping and crushes.

Her father did not like to linger on the past, either. Addie could not bear the pain in his eyes when she tried to bring it up. So, the picture in her mind of the Deep grew faded and fuzzy, time softening the harshness of her memory. But she always thought fondly of Mrs. Martinez and wondered how she was doing. It did not seem right to bury the past so easily, so she kept the dulled shards of her memories, the jabs from her classmates, their lack of understanding, pressed tight against her ribs where they pricked her heart when she lay in bed, trying to find sleep.

On the day of her sixteenth birthday, the dulled shards of her pain were sharpened to razor points when she saw the news. The broadcast played on the screen in her room as she dressed for school. There was no way to change the channel. The broadcasts came at scheduled intervals, morning and night, regardless of if they were wanted or not. The reports reminded them all how lucky they were, and the dangers of what happened when one strayed too far from the confines of the Cloud District. This morning, the broadcast was a tale of the latter. A report on a crackdown of panhandling in the lower Mids, an effort for city-wide improvement.

Addie watched in disbelief, hairbrush halfway through her tresses, as Mrs. Martinez flashed across the screen. She, and a few other faces she recognized, were moved off their street corner by Cloud guards. The old woman's hair was streaked with silver, the lines of her face deep with dismay, her back hunched, but there was no mistaking her. Time had not been as kind to her as it had to Addie.

With trembling hands, Addie tied her hair into its neat twist. She hugged her father goodbye, slung her bag over her shoulder, and marched to school. Her thoughts were in tangles. At the beautiful gates where she had nearly wept with joy upon first seeing them, she felt her cheeks flush and acid creep up her throat. Her feet were cemented to the sidewalk. The sight of Mrs. Martinez's face had rattled something deep within her, and Addie could not make herself go inside. Instead, she turned on her heel and began the very long walk out of the Clouds.

Addie strode past the towering, gilded homes to the first flight of stairs made of cement and iron. Down she went, minutes turning to hours, descending to the Mids. The smell of standing water filtered up from the Deep even here. It stung her nose and sharpened those memories that had gone as soft and blurry as blended pastels. Her shoes were dirty and stained by the time she reached the corner where she'd spent her days drawing on the rough concrete. Mrs. Martinez was nowhere to be found. There were very few people around and the street was oddly quiet, given that it was midday. Addie hadn't really expected her to be here. She took a long breath through her nose, adjusted her school bag, and took the rickety stairs back down to the Deep, ignoring the strange looks from passersby.

The shack was smaller than she remembered. Addie rapped on the rough wooden door with her knuckles, and a faint voice called through it. "Who's there?"

Addie spoke past the lump in her throat. "It's Addie, Mrs. Martinez. Addie Bell."

The door opened a crack. Only Mrs. Martinez's wide eyes were visible. "Oh, mija, it's really you. Come in, quick."

Addie stepped inside the shack and took the offered seat on a three-legged stool. Mrs. Martinez sat on her bed with a groan. "Mija, what are you doing here? Don't you have school? A smart girl like you shouldn't be missing your classes."

"I came to see how you were doing." Addie decided not to tell her that the reason for her visit was because she had seen her on the broadcast, and that she wanted to relieve herself of the invisible guilt that she carried with her. She had thought that seeing Mrs. Martinez would make her feel better. It only made her chest ache.

Mrs. Martinez's eyes darted to the door. "That's very sweet, but I think you should go back home." She inhaled a wet, raspy breath and coughed, her body shaking under the attack.

Addie stood, alarmed. She sounded worse than her father ever had. "You should see a doctor," she said, once the coughing had subsided.

"No doctor will see me," Mrs. Martinez croaked.

"Why not?"

"I don't have insurance."

Addie narrowed her eyes. "What's insurance? You're sick. Papa saw a doctor and ..." Addie stopped at the sad look that passed across her former caretaker's face. Her cheeks burned, mortified. Of course, her father had only seen a doctor when they moved into their Cloud house. "I'm sorry," she said softly.

"It's okay. I'm glad you came to see me. I've missed you, but you really should be in school."

Addie stood and gathered her bag. "You're right. I'm happy I got to see you. Bye, Mrs. Martinez." She gave the old woman a careful hug and left. Instead of heading towards the shaky stairway, she walked along the damp, grimy streets of the Deep, stopping when she reached the sickly lapping of the water's edge. Had it always been this far up the street?

She stood, gazing out past the gloom of the rusty beams that held the city aloft. The water sloshed in and out, reeking of sewage and decay. A dead seagull, wings akimbo, floated nearby.

Whispers of dissent had been bubbling up from the Deep for some time. She had overheard her classmates, the children of government officials, share stories in hushed voices. They spoke of strikes, protests, retaliation. The ember of anger that had ignited in her chest this morning turned into a roaring flame. The sea was eroding homes, eating away at their crumbling foundations, yet the Mids did not welcome the people who lived in the Deep into their level of the city. Addie could not imagine the Clouds ever doing anything to help.

She looked at her shoes, stained from her trek. Shame made her eyes prick with tears. She'd been so blind; dazzled by the sparkling life she'd been given. Why had she been chosen, out of all the people here, to move up to the Clouds? Addie felt, suddenly, that she did not deserve it.

That night at home as she lay in bed, unable to sleep, she searched for her own name on her tablet. She found a video that had aired after her first art class. A reporter had taken a short clip of Addie with her still-life drawing, the one she'd been so proud of on her first day. When asked about the nature of her composition, she replied that she'd drawn what she saw. She scrolled and found the video from the city official, the one with the tagline, *a vision of what New York could be.*

Addie pushed herself out of bed and hastily cleared her worktable. She grabbed her colored pencils and began to draw a copy of her own artwork. She drew it nearly identical to the original, with swirling colors and the city skyline. Only this time, she added a slashing line of blue: the ocean rising to swallow the city, bodies floating in the water. She scrawled *a vision of what New York WILL be* across it in jarring red.

By the time she was done, the sun was just beginning to rise. Addie readied herself for school, ignoring the broadcast that played yet another cautionary tale. She placed her newest piece into her portfolio, tucking it safely between other drawings. Addie hugged her father a little tighter than usual as she said goodbye.

While everyone else was in their classes, Addie stole away to the workroom. She made dozens of copies of her newest piece, printing bundles of flyers which she shoved into her bag. Lastly, she made a large banner, wider than her arms and half as tall as she was. Perspiration beaded on her brow as the laser printer did its work, rolling out her print one inch at a time. It finished just as morning classes were dismissed. Her heart pounded in her ears as she rolled up the giant banner and marched back out the school gates.

She walked, head held high, straight to the heart of the Cloud District. At every corner, she tossed a few flyers from her bag, marring the pristine streets. She moved quickly, not stopping to hear the shocked murmurs at her behavior, or the fearful whispers of rebellion. A little drone began to follow her once she was three blocks away from her destination. She broke into a run, anxiety making her swift.

On the steps of the capital, Addie dropped her school bag and rolled out her banner. The drone had caught up with her and was now beeping shrill commands. Heavy footsteps sounded on the marble steps, but Addie did not look up from her work. She pushed the paper until it unfurled across the stairs. She stood, hands on her hips, studying her work. She could not hear the shouts above the sound of her own pounding heart, but she felt hands grab her roughly at the elbows. She was steered into a car that hovered off the street by Cloud guards, their faces obscured by helmets.

Addie did not feel scared until they escorted her to a windowless, white room that smelled of antiseptic. Her stomach clenched in fear as they pinched her arm with a needle that put her to sleep, and set about dissecting what had given this girl from the Deep the audacity and to paint the world in such colors.

Addie Bell's fall from grace was a brief news headline on the evening broadcast. Too many people had seen the flyers for the incident to not be addressed. It made for a wonderful cautionary tale. Clouds sneered at their screens and removed their Bell originals from their walls in shame, for the little girl from the Deep had no real talent at all. It was, in fact, a horrible anomaly of her vision that distorted her way of viewing the world. For Addie Bell was colorblind and did not perceive the world as those with all their proper eye cones did. She had been picking colors blindly, scribbling nonsense onto her canvases. There was no real *vision* there at all. And her vulgar art did not paint the whole picture, the effort the city was making to stem the rising seas, to help clean up the streets of the lower districts. The Clouds washed their hands of her and went about their lives.

Addie was questioned. The government wanted to know whom she was working with, who had given her orders to destroy her own art. Her answers were simple, and honest. After a few hours of questioning, when they had given up trying to extract names of other dissenters from her, they left her alone in a cell.

Her father watched the nighttime broadcast in stunned disbelief. He couldn't believe that his sweet, gentle daughter had done something so rash. He pressed his gnarled fingers to his mouth as images of her face flashed across the screen. He had no idea the rage she had carried inside her. His own anger had burned down to ashes long ago. He shrugged back into his jacket and walked under the golden glow of streetlamps to city hall.

No one could tell him where his daughter was. There was no record of her or where she had gone. He was turned away politely the first three times. On the fourth day, armed guards escorted him down the pristine marble steps where Addie had unfurled her banner, forbidding him from asking again.

In a last effort, he traipsed back down to the Deep, as Addie had done a week prior. He knocked on Mrs. Martinez's splintered door, and was welcomed in. She gasped wetly for breath. Her skin had the telltale gray tinge of lung sickness. When he told her of what had happened to Addie, fat tears slid down her cheeks.

"But you should be proud," she said as she dried her face. "She's a very brave girl."

He wanted to feel pride. Instead, he felt hollow. He thanked Mrs. Martinez for her time and began his long trek home, heart aching. Addie had given him something he could not give her in return: safety, and a place among the Clouds.

After the first few weeks, Addie lost track of how long she'd spent in the prison. She wondered if it had done any good, spreading her message through the streets. She hoped her father could forgive her, even if he never understood why she'd done it. Over time, her face paled, regaining the ghostly pallor of her girlhood. Her days dragged on in monotony, devoid of sun, art, and companionship. Sometimes, Addie found her fingers curling delicately, as if embracing one of her pencils, the habit hard to shake. At night, she fell asleep with a soft smile upon her lips and dreamed of a sky stained with a kaleidoscope of color.

Cidney Mayes's story "Visions for the Independent City of New York" was originally published in Metaphorosis on Friday, 1 December 2023. See magazine.metaphorosis.com

About the author

Cidney Mayes is a middle school librarian from Portland, Maine with a passion for anything magical. She is a book reviewer of children's and young adult novels, and has been an educator since 2015. Her recent published works include short fiction in West Avenue Publishing's *A Coven of Witches* anthology, *Metaphorosis* magazine, and *Carmina* magazine. When not writing, you can find her giving tarot readings, walking in the woods, or playing board games with her husband and friends.

Copyright

Title information

The Speculative Teachers' Lounge

ISBN: 978-1-64076-298-5 (e-book)
ISBN: 978-1-64076-299-2 (paperback)
ISBN: 978-1-64076-300-5 (hardcover)

Copyright

Publisher

Metaphorosis
a magazine of speculative fiction

Metaphorosis Magazine is an imprint of
Metaphorosis Publishing
Neskowin, OR, USA

www.metaphorosis.com

"Metaphorosis" is a registered trademark.

Discounts available

Substantial discounts are available for educational institutions, including writing workshops. Discounts are also available for quantity purchases. For details, contact Metaphorosis at metaphorosis.com/about

Metaphorosis Publishing

Metaphorosis offers beautifully written science fiction and fantasy. Our imprints include:

Metaphorosis Magazine

Plant Based Press

Verdage

Vestige

Joyful Heave

You can also find us:
@metaphorosis.bsky.social (Bluesky)
@Metaphorosis@writing.exchange (Mastodon)
www.facebook.com/metaphorosis

Help keep Metaphorosis running at
Patreon.com/metaphorosis

See more about some of our books on the following pages.

Metaphorosis
a magazine of speculative fiction

Metaphorosis is an online speculative fiction magazine dedicated to quality writing. We publish an original story every week (2016-2023) or month (2024), along with author bios, interviews, and notes on story origins.

We also publish monthly print and e-book issues, as well as yearly Best of and Complete anthologies.

Come and see us online at magazine.Metaphorosis.com.

The Metaphorosis Library Collection

Plant Based Press

plant
based
press

Vegan-friendly science fiction and fantasy, including anthologies of the year's best SFF stories, from 2016-2020.

Chambers of the Heart
speculative stories
by
B. Morris Allen

A heart that's a building, a dog that's a program, a woman sinking irretrievably — stories about love, loss, and movement.

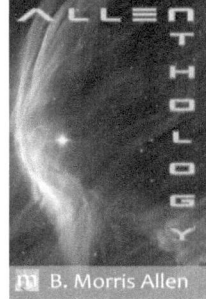

Susurrus

A darkly romantic story of magic, love, and suffering.

Allenthology: Volume I

Including three full collections of SFF stories.

Science fiction and fantasy books for writers — full of great stories, often with an additional focus on the craft of speculative fiction writing.

Reading 5X5 x3

Changes

How do stories move from 'maybe' to published?

Here are 15 case studies of stories published in *Metaphorosis* magazine.

Reading 5X5 x2

Duets

How do authors' voices change when they collaborate?

A round-robin of five talented science fiction and fantasy authors collaborating with each other and writing solo.

Including stories by Evan Marcroft, David Gallay, J. Tynan Burke, L'Erin Ogle, and Douglas Anstruther.

Score

an SFF symphony

An anthology with an emotional score from the heights of joy to the depths of despair — but always with a little hope shining through.

Reading 5X5

Five stories, five times

See how different writers take on the same material.

Reading 5X5

Writers' Edition

Two extra stories, the story seed, and authors' notes on writing.

Vestige

Novelettes, novellas, and novels by Metaphorosis authors.

The Nocturnals
Mariah Montoya

Night is Dangerous. Day is deadly.
Where day and night last thirty years, humans move constantly stay ahead of the night and cruel Nocturnals that call it home. But a boy is lost out there.

Science fiction and fantasy anthologies with innovative and unusual themes.

Museum Piece
an unusual collection

A gallery of the strange and outrageous

Step right up and enter a world of wonder and oddities! These museums are not your typical tourist traps. From the Museum of Lost Dreams to the Museum of Fine Regrets, each exhibit will take you on a journey you won't soon forget.